I dumped the garbage into the pit and shoveled dirt over it. I wondered where Helen was. I'd figured she'd come on home after three-thirty, but she wasn't home yet. I didn't know what that meant. I didn't think she'd go to visit those two girls who liked her, because she'd have to tell them what she was crying about. Where else would she go? If it had been me, I'd have gone off into the woods someplace to take my mind off it, but Helen wasn't much for going into the woods. Where could she be?

<hr>

With his brother Christopher Collier, JAMES LINCOLN COLLIER is the author of several books for young readers, including the Arabus family saga—*War Comes to Willy Freeman, Jump Ship to Freedom,* and *Who Is Carrie?*, all available in Dell Yearling editions, as well as the Newbery Honor Book, *My Brother Sam Is Dead.* Mr. Collier lives in New York City.

When the Stars Begin to Fall

JAMES LINCOLN COLLIER

Published by
Dell Publishing
a division of
Bantam Doubleday Dell Publishing Group, Inc.
666 Fifth Avenue
New York, New York 10103

ISBN: 0-440-20411-9

RL: 4.6

Reprinted by arrangement with Delacorte Press

Printed in the United States of America

July 1989

10   9   8   7   6   5   4

RAD

For Asa

When the Stars Begin to Fall

ONE

I was up in my room trying to fix my stereo when I heard the car drive in. I looked out the window. An old Buick was coming up the dirt driveway, going slow so as not to splash water up out of the puddles in the drive left over from last night's rain. I couldn't see who was in the car, but I knew it was Charlie Fritz and some friend of his. I knew what they were coming for too. They were going to get my sister, Helen, up in the barn with them. That's all they ever came around for. I hated it when they came. It made me feel rotten, and usually when it happened I would go out for a walk.

I decided to concentrate on getting my stereo to work right. It wasn't much of a record player. Dad had found it in the town dump and brought it home for me. It had a bad hum. I'd figured I could fix it, but I never had been able to get the hum out, so it wasn't much use to me. Still, I kept trying.

I heard the doors to the Buick slam, and then I

heard them knock on the kitchen door. The front door was nailed shut because it was so warped that if you opened it you'd never get it shut again. I heard Helen let them in, and then I could hear them talking and laughing. I figured they'd brought some beer. They usually did when they came to see Helen.

I wished Mom were home. When Mom was home, they took Helen off for a drive in the Buick, and I didn't have to know anything about it. But Mom had walked down the road to Mrs. O'Brien's to watch one of her shows there, because our TV didn't get that channel too clearly. I didn't know where Dad was. He never told us where he was going. He just got up in the morning, hardly said anything to anyone, ate his breakfast, and got into the truck and went. Sometimes Mom would say, "Frank, where will you be in case anybody wants to know?" He wouldn't even answer. He'd just grunt and go out and drive away, and not come back until supper time.

So my sister was safe for a while. She was sixteen, I was fourteen. I didn't want to think about it, so I made myself concentrate on the stereo. After a little while I heard the kitchen door open and shut, and their voices outside. They were going up to the barn. I decided to get out of the house. I couldn't get that stereo to work anyway.

I waited until they had got into the barn and were out of sight, and then I went downstairs and out through the kitchen door. It was almost the end of April but still cool, and the grass didn't need to be cut yet. Dad said he didn't care if it was ever cut—that was too tidy and middle-class for him; he didn't care if it grew up into a hay field. But I kept it cut—as much as I could anyway—with our old mower. It helped the looks of the old place some, but there wasn't much you could do about dressing it up. The paint was mostly peeled off, and some of the window-panes were missing and Dad had filled them in with cardboard. The old gardens that had once been there were full of weeds, and big rocks sat on top of the garbage cans out back so the raccoons wouldn't knock the tops off and spread the garbage all over the yard. Dad always said he didn't care if the place fell down; it wasn't his, why should he put time and money into somebody else's place? That made sense, but still I wished we had a place like most of the kids around there had, with nice lawns and curtains in the windows and rugs and things. We didn't have much furniture, and it all came from secondhand stores. The sofa had a hole that Mom kept a towel over, and there was nothing on the living room floor but a little old beat-up hooked rug. Dad always said he couldn't afford any better, and besides, he didn't want all that middle-class nonsense anyway.

Besides, there was always a couple of junkers sitting next to the driveway that Dad had bought for a few bucks and towed home with the idea of repairing and selling them for a few hundred. He would do it, too—he was kind of a junk expert and could generally figure out a way to get some value out of things somebody else had thrown away. But usually it took him months to get around to it, and meanwhile the junkers would sit there with their tires flat and the bodies rusting and weeds growing up around them.

There wasn't much hope of dressing the place up, but I cut the lawn anyway. It helped some. Mom liked it when I did it. She always said I was the only one who ever did anything around there.

I went across the lawn feeling sad and low about everything—the weeds in the garden and the paint peeling off the house, and Helen up there in the barn with Charlie Fritz and that other guy. I crossed the lawn, and jumped over the stone wall that divided the old pasture from the lawn. Sumac and small cedars were beginning to grow in the pasture. In a few years it would be filled with brush, and after that the woods would come down the hillside and take over. I trotted up the sloping pasture to the woods beyond the next stone wall. I liked going into the woods. They were clean and natural, and there wasn't anything junky there. I climbed over the stone wall and stood there looking around. Being so far upstate New York, the trees were just beginning to bud, and when you looked off through the woods, it was like a thin yellow light was coming out of them. I looked down. There was a patch of moss right where I was standing. I knelt and ran my hand over it to feel the softness, carefully, so as not to tear any of it up.

Then I sat down on the stone wall, and began looking through the woods for birds. I knew about birds. I'd been studying them for years. I loved seeing them swoop and dart. They moved so fast, you could hardly believe it. You'd see one take off, and the next thing it'd be all the way over to the other side of the pasture. That time of year there was always plenty of birds around—dark-eyed juncos, tufted titmice, nuthatches, and lots more. The nuthatches made me laugh, because they walked up tree trunks upside down.

I was interested in fish too. Sometimes I would go down to some creeks and streams I knew about, and lie by the bank watching the fish down in the water. You couldn't do that on the Timber River, which was the big one around there, because it was polluted, but you could on the little streams that fed into it. It was terrible the way the Timber River had got polluted, but nobody seemed to be able to do anything about it.

So I sat there on the stone wall watching the birds. I wished I had a pair of binoculars. Old Man Greenberg sold them in the Sports Center. The ones I wanted cost forty dollars, and I never could get forty dollars together. Every time I got fifteen or twenty dollars saved, something would come along that I had to pay for—new tires for my bike, or a school trip or something. It was no use asking Dad for stuff like that. He always said he was broke, and besides, he wasn't about to spend a lot of money on stuff like that.

After a while I heard voices, and I knew they were coming down out of the barn. I went back across the pasture. I could see the three of them come out of the barn and head for the car. I climbed over the stone wall into the yard. Charlie Fritz and the other guy got into the car. Helen stood there near the car. She was frowning and looking sad. "Where are you guys going?" she said.

"No place special," they said.

Her shoulders sagged, but she didn't dare ask if she

could go with them, because she was afraid they would say no. So she stood there watching until they had driven away. She looked sad and frowned. Then she saw me come across the lawn. "What are you looking at?" she said crossly.

"Are you in love with Charlie Fritz?" I said.

"What makes you think that?" she said.

"It seemed like it," I said. "You shouldn't go up to the barn with those guys. If Dad ever catches you, he'll kill you."

"I don't care," she said. "It's none of his business."

Then she went into the house and up to her room. I knew she felt lousy because those guys hadn't asked her to come with them. They never did. And the reason why they never did was because we were trash. Some people said we were no-goods. Some said we were low. But mostly they said we were trash. Mom was trash, and Dad was trash, and my sister and I were trash. Nobody in town would have anything to do with us if they could help it. It took me quite a while to learn this. But things slowly happened, and I learned it.

The first thing that happened was when I was little, five or six. Maybe even littler than that. Helen and I were playing somewhere. All I can remember is that it was a grassy place and we were playing with a bunch of kids. Some woman came along in a station wagon and said for everybody to get in, she would take the kids for a Carvel. But when Helen and I started to get in, she said we couldn't come with the other kids. She said she couldn't have us in her car. When we got home later, we told Mom. She put her head down on the kitchen table and cried. Helen and I didn't understand it, and we forgot about it. Years later I remembered it, and I realized why the woman wouldn't let us get in her car. It was because we had cooties in our hair.

By the time I was in the second grade, I was beginning to see that the other kids didn't like us. When we tried to go over and play with them in school, they would usually say, "You stink." I never thought much of it. I figured it was just the kind of thing kids would say to each other.

But then one day when I was in the third grade, I walked into the classroom and somebody had written on the blackboard "Harry White stinks." Suddenly I knew they meant it.

I got red and felt uncomfortable and sat in my seat looking down at my desk. Then I began to lose my temper, the way I always do. I stood up and shouted out, "I'll punch the one who did that." They all started to shout back, "You stink, Harry, you stink." Just then Mrs. McGarvey came in and they shut up. She erased the words from the blackboard and said that she would keep everybody after if it happened again. Then, when three o'clock came, she kept me after and talked to me.

"Harry, do you have a bathtub in your house?" she said.

"Sure," I said, trying to figure out why she was asking that.

"And a washing machine for clothes?"

"No," I said. "We don't have a washing machine."

"How does your mom wash your clothes?" she said.

I stood there thinking, and after a minute my head got hot and I scratched my scalp. I couldn't remember how she washed our clothes. "I guess she does it some way," I said.

"Harry," Mrs. McGarvey said, "I think the other children would be nicer to you if you took a bath every day. And ask your mom to be more frequent about washing your clothes."

I couldn't wait to get out of there, I was blushing so hot. It was true. We stank. We weren't clean. I stank and my sister, Helen, stank too.

I felt red and sweaty, and I didn't dare take the school bus home but walked the whole four miles up to Mountain Pass Road, where we lived. I didn't say anything to Mom or Dad but went right into Helen's room to tell her about it.

Our rooms were pretty small, but it didn't matter because we didn't have much furniture anyway—just our beds and a table for doing our homework on, and hooks that we'd put up for our clothes. We kept some of our clothes in the cardboard boxes under our beds.

Helen was lying on her bed when I came in; she was wearing her old blue jeans and an old sweater. I looked at her and I saw that Mrs. McGarvey was right. There was a big cocoa stain on the front of her sweater, the knees of her blue jeans were dirty, and one of them had a hole as big as a quarter. There was dirt in her fingernails, dirt on her hands, dirt around her ankles where they came out of her socks. "Helen, we stink," I said. And I told her what had happened at school.

She jumped off the bed and started for me. "It isn't true," she shouted. "It's a lie." She started to swing at me.

I jumped out of the way. "Don't hit me," I said. "I didn't say it."

"I'll get them," she shouted. "I'll get the ones who said it."

But after that she was in the bathroom a lot more. So was I. It took us a long while to learn how to be clean. We had to learn that you couldn't just wash the parts you could see, but had to wash your ears and your hair once in a while, too, and clean your finger-nails with a knife or a bent paper clip or something. We helped each other. If I saw that Helen's ears were dirty or something, I'd tell her. She would make me comb my hair in the morning before we went to school. We weren't just being nice to each other either. We wanted to make sure that the other one didn't disgrace us. But I figured it was worth the trouble, because once we got clean, the other kids would finally like us.

It was harder to keep Mom and Dad from disgracing us. We didn't dare tell Mom to start washing our clothes more often. We just started doing them ourselves, washing our jeans and things out in the bathtub and hanging them on chairs and things to dry. It took us awhile to learn about that, too: that you couldn't just wash things out once every couple of weeks but had to do it all the time. We never knew what Mom thought about it. She must have known we were washing our own clothes, because they were hanging all over the place. But she never said anything, and I figured that she never felt guilty about it or anything—she just figured that kids ought to be responsible for washing out their own clothes. But I knew that the other kids in the third grade didn't wash their own clothes.

We couldn't get mad at Mom, because she had something wrong with her. I never knew what it was. I guess nobody ever knew what it was. She just seemed to be tired all the time. Dad was always taking her over to the county hospital for tests and checkups. They never could cure her. She had to sit around a lot in her bathrobe and watch TV. Sometimes Helen had to make supper, because Mom was too tired. So we didn't blame Mom for not washing our clothes—she couldn't help it.

So anyway, after a while we started being clean, but it didn't help us very much. The other kids still weren't too interested in doing anything with us. We didn't have any friends. For one thing, they said that the Whites stole. Once when I was in sixth grade I came into the cafeteria with my lunch bag. There was an empty seat near where a bunch of kids were sitting at a table eating. I went over and sat down. There was a watch lying on the table, and when I sat down, some kid said, "Don't touch that watch, White," and snatched it up.

"I wasn't going to touch your watch," I said. "What do I want to touch your watch for?"

"Everybody knows your family steals."

"What?" I said.

"Your sister steals stuff out of the drugstore. My sister said so."

"That's a lie," I said. I was beginning to lose my temper.

They all turned toward me, getting ready to gang up on me. "Oh, yeah? What about the chain saw your dad stole from the Otto brothers?" The Otto brothers owned the biggest gas station in town.

"Jim Otto was wrong," I shouted. "Dad bought that chain saw from somebody."

"Oh, yeah?" the kid said. "The cops told my dad it was Jim Otto's chain saw all right, but they couldn't prove it."

"That's a lie," I said. I jumped up and started to go for the kid, but Mr. Creasy came over and broke it up. "Take your lunch into the janitor's room, White," Mr. Creasy said.

"He started it," I said. I was sore and breathing hard.

"Don't give me that," Mr. Creasy said. "Go eat in the janitor's office."

But the truth was, I wondered. I sat there in the janitor's office with the mops and buckets all around, smelling the soap and the disinfectant and such, mixed in with the smell of my peanut butter sandwiches, and thinking about the time Jim Otto had come out to the house with the cops. That afternoon Dad had brought home an almost new chain saw. He said he'd bought it from a guy who'd got a bigger one and sold this one to Dad cheap. I was pretty excited about it, and I got Dad to promise he'd teach me how to use it. While we ate supper I kept looking over at it sitting on the kitchen floor. It was bright red, clean, and solid. It excited me. And we were just getting finished with supper when there was a knock on the back door. Dad went to answer it and found Jim Otto standing there with a cop.

Otto pointed at the chain saw. "There it is," he said. "That's it." He started to push past my dad to get the saw.

My dad grabbed Jim Otto by the arm. "Oh, no you don't," he said, as calm as could be. "You don't walk into a man's house without his permission. Out you go."

Jim Otto looked my dad in the face. He was pretty red and sore. "That's my saw, White. I got witnesses who saw you out back of my store this afternoon."

It amazed me how calm Dad was staying. "That doesn't alter the fact that you need a search warrant before you come into a man's house. Now get out before I have you arrested for trespassing."

"That's my saw, White," Jim Otto shouted.

"I'm going to count to three," my father said. "If you're not out then, I'm going to have this officer arrest you."

"White—"

The cop took Jim Otto's arm. "Better come on outside, Jim," the cop said.

"I don't just mean outside," my dad said. "I mean off my property."

"Come on, Jim," the cop said. And they left.

They came back two days later with a search warrant, but the chain saw wasn't there anymore. "Somebody swiped it off the back of my truck," Dad told Jim Otto. "It wasn't your saw anyway."

Jim Otto was pretty sore, and he cursed Dad out

until Dad told him to shut his mouth or he'd shut it for him, and the cop made Jim Otto leave. The truth was, though, that nobody had stolen the chain saw from the truck. Dad had taken it over to Watertown and sold it for fifty dollars. I was disappointed that it was gone, because it was so pretty, not like Dad's old beat-up chain saw. I said, "Dad, if it was your saw, why did you have to sell it?"

"They were going to make trouble about it. Jim Otto's been out to get me for a long time. I don't need that kind of aggravation."

"Why is Jim Otto out to get you?"

"He thinks I cheated him on a load of cordwood. Which I didn't do."

Sitting there in the janitor's room, smelling the disinfectant and the peanut butter, I wondered: Would Dad really steal anything? I just didn't see how he could—my dad wouldn't steal things. I remembered how calm he was when Jim Otto and the cop came. If he'd really stolen that chain saw, he wouldn't be calm, would he?

But it was true about Helen shoplifting out of the drugstore, because every time she swiped something she called me into her room and showed me what she'd got. It made her feel good to shoplift stuff. I couldn't understand it. A couple of times I'd been with her in the drugstore when she was swiping stuff, and it made me feel nervous. But Helen got a kick out of it.

So people thought we were dirty and stole and were just in general no good because of the junkers rusting by the driveway and the paint peeling off the house. I finally learned that nothing we did to get the other kids to like us would do any good. I was in the sixth grade when I learned that. The science teacher had a bird-watching club that met after school on Wednesdays. They'd go someplace in his station wagon to watch birds. I figured if I joined it, maybe I could make friends with some of the other kids. So I signed up, and I went a couple of times. I really liked it. I got a bird book out of the library and began studying the birds. Then, on the third Wednesday, while we were waiting around after school for the science teacher to get his station wagon, I started to go into the boys' room. I opened the door and I heard one of the kids say to another one, "Let's get the front seat. I don't want to sit next to Stinky White."

It made me go red, and mad and sick inside all at once. I ducked out of there and out the side door and hid in the areaway. Around the side of the building I could hear the science teacher say, "Where's White? Has anyone seen White?" I heard the horn honk, and after a minute the station wagon drove away. I never went back to the club. I just studied birds on my own.

After that I realized that the other kids would never like us, and I decided to forget about it. At school I didn't try to belong to any gang. Helen and I were by ourselves. Oh, there were a couple of girls who would let Helen eat lunch with them—girls that she sat next to in class and had got to know a little. And if the guys were getting up a softball game at lunchtime, they couldn't stop me from playing if I decided to. But we didn't have any real friends. Nobody ever said to us, "Hey, what are you doing after school?" We generally went home after school every day because we didn't have anything else to do. It was like we'd got a black spot on us, and couldn't rub it off, no matter what we tried.

I stood there in the backyard looking at the house with the paint peeling off, knowing that Helen was upstairs in her room feeling lousy with herself and wishing now that she hadn't let those guys come over, and suddenly I got sore. It wasn't fair; it wasn't right. What had we ever done to anybody? I was mad at Charlie Fritz, and mad at Dad for not having a regular job, and mad at everybody. I smacked my fist on my leg so hard, it hurt, and gritted my teeth and said out loud, "I'm going to do something. I'm not going to be trash anymore."

TWO

Timber Falls was a poor kind of a place. It was way upstate New York in the Adirondack Mountains, and there were always stories in the *Timber Falls Journal* saying how American prosperity had passed the region by, and giving figures on unemployment that showed that the towns around there were a lot worse off than towns in other parts of the state.

Timber Falls wasn't much of a place anyway. Main Street had a railroad track running down one side of it and a row of buildings along the other side, mostly old brick buildings. There was the drugstore, the hardware store, a bank, Old Man Greenberg's Sports Center, a couple of supermarkets, and down at the end of Main Street the town hall. That was about it. The train station across from the row of stores by the railroad track was closed because hardly any trains went through there anymore. You couldn't buy a ticket to anywhere there. About the only trains that came through were freight cars going up to the carpet factory.

The carpet factory was the big thing. A lot of people in Timber Falls worked there. Dad always said that if the factory ever closed, the town would just dry up and blow away. Mom was always trying to get Dad to go to work there so as to have a regular job, but Dad wouldn't. He would say that he wasn't ready to be anybody's slave yet.

The other thing was the mountains. They were everywhere you looked. You could stand in the middle of town and look all around, and everywhere you saw mountains. All year long they changed colors: brown in the spring, then going yellow as the trees budded and then light green as the buds came out, and dark green as summer came on; and in the fall going red and yellow and then brown once more when the leaves fell; and then white when the snow fell. They were always changing.

Rich people came up to hunt in the mountains in the fall. Leastwise, they seemed rich to me. Most of them had two or three expensive guns and fancy tents and cookstoves. Dad said, "I wish they'd stay where they belong, and keep away from here." But most people said they brought in money—buying shells at the hardware store, and steaks at the supermarket, and whiskey at the Liquor Mart.

It was beautiful up in the mountains. Sometimes, when Dad was in a cheerful mood, he'd take me up there. He'd fill a thermos bottle with coffee and pour in a slug of whiskey. We'd drive into town and get two big roast beef sandwiches and a Coke for me at

Red's Deli. Then we'd drive up into the mountains on the winding tar road, park the car on a dirt tote road, and hike on up to this place Dad knew about, where there was a rock cliff that jutted out of the side of a mountain. Up there you could see for miles and miles out over the Adirondacks. There was nothing out there but mountains and woods, and nothing in the woods but birds, deer, bear, and fish in the streams and lakes. We'd sit there and eat our roast beef sandwiches, and Dad would drink his coffee and whiskey, and we'd talk. "It's a satisfying view," Dad said one time. "No people."

"Why don't you like people, Dad?"

"Wait'll you know them better. I've been knowing people for forty years, and the less I have to do with them the better. Look at 'em all, robbing and cheating and stealing, so a man can hardly make a living. And then if you have anything left, they tax it away from you."

It didn't seem to me that it was everybody else's fault that Dad didn't have a regular job, but I didn't say that. "I thought you said you didn't have to pay any taxes," I said.

He gave me a look. "When did I say that?"

"A while ago," I said.

"Well, you just forget about that, Harry. Just forget I ever said it."

So I changed the subject and we talked about the hunters and deer, and Dad said maybe he'd get a couple of shotguns and we'd go after deer ourselves. But I knew he never would. Mom never knew how much he had. If she needed money for food, she would ask for it, and he would grumble and give it to her.

Actually I didn't go hiking with Dad in the mountains all that much. When you got down to it, I don't think it happened more than two or three times. Mostly Dad was quiet and kept to himself and didn't do much with the rest of us. He left in the morning without saying much. Mostly what he did was odd jobs. He'd truck stuff for people—pick up their trash when they had a big housecleaning, or move their furniture for them when they moved. Sometimes he did a little tree work, sometimes he'd do house painting, sometimes he'd do carpentry. He'd do anything so long as it wasn't regular and didn't last more than a week. Every time Mom got on him about going to work in the carpet factory, he would say that he couldn't stand being regimented like that. It was all right for the middle class with their fancy sofas and washing machines, but he had more spirit than that.

Mom was thirty-four and Dad was forty-two. Dad had been married once before, but we didn't know anything about that. Being as Mom and Dad had been married for seventeen years, you would have thought Mom would have known better than to get on Dad about a job, but she never gave up. She started in on him that night after Helen let those guys come over. She was opening some cans of Heinz beans. We were going to have franks and beans again. We ate a lot of stuff like that—franks and beans, canned hash and eggs, cold cuts, spaghetti and meat sauce out of a can—because, as Mom always said, it was cheap and nourishing. But Helen said it was because she would rather watch TV than cook. It was because of her being tired so much, I figured. Helen got her looks from Mom. She said Mom could be pretty if she took some trouble over herself.

Anyway, that night Dad came in through the kitchen door at supper time and said, "The clutch is going on the truck. The whole truck is going. They're going to make me buy at least two new tires to pass inspection this year. That's a hundred bucks even if I can find some used ones. I'll have to put four, five hundred dollars into it just to get through the rest of the year."

"That's good money after bad," Mom said. She was standing at the stove in her bathrobe and furry slippers, stirring the beans. It was an old gas stove, and the pilot lights didn't work anymore. You had to be careful about lighting it, because sometimes it would light down inside somewhere instead of on the burner.

Dad sat down at the kitchen table. It was an old pine table Mom had bought for ten dollars once and painted blue. It had been pretty when it was just painted, but it had got all scratched up since. "When's supper?" Dad said. "I'm hungry." He started to take off his boots.

"Soon," she said. "Frank, maybe you should give up the truck."

He looked at her. "Doris, how am I going to make a living without the truck?"

"You could take a job at the carpet factory."

"I figured that was coming," he said. "No way. I'm not about to make myself somebody's slave yet."

"It's good money, Frank."

"I don't care about the money. Besides, why should I add to the world's pollution?"

"I don't see why that's your worry, Frank."

"It ought to be everybody's worry," Dad said. He took off his socks and rubbed his foot. "These boots never did fit right."

I said, "I wondered where that stuff in the river was coming from. It's from the carpet factory."

"It sure is," Dad said. "Of course, they won't admit it."

"I thought it was against the law to pollute."

"It is," Dad said. "But people like them don't pay any attention to the laws. They're arrogant, those biggies with their Cadillacs and fancy houses. They run the factory anyway they want, regardless of the law. They do *anything* they want regardless of the law. They cheat the workingman, they cheat the public with lousy goods, they pollute, then they get some fancy accountants to figure out a way to get out of paying taxes on their money. No way I'm going to go out there and work for guys like that."

"Harry," Mom said, "where's Helen?"

"She's up in her room," I said.

"Tell her supper's ready," Mom said.

I went upstairs and into Helen's room. She was still lying on her bed. "You're supposed to knock before you come in," she said. She was in a pretty bad mood.

"Why do you let those guys come over if it always makes you feel bad?"

"It's none of your business," she said.

"Someday Dad's going to catch you and he'll kill those guys."

"I said it was none of your business," she said.

"Supper's ready," I said.

She went on lying on her bed. "Two more years," she said. "Two more years and I'll graduate and then I'm going to get out of here so fast, nobody'll believe it."

"Where would you go?"

"I don't know," she said. "Anyplace, so long as it isn't Timber Falls."

I didn't want her to go. I knew I would miss her. She was about the only person I had to talk to. "Don't you think you'd get homesick?"

"For this dump?"

"Well— But I mean for Mom and Dad." I really meant for me.

"Them?" She spit when she said it. "What have they ever done for us?"

"Well, still," I said. I was hoping she would say she would miss me.

But she didn't. "I hate them," she said.

That made me feel kind of funny. "You don't really hate them," I said.

"Yes, I do," she said. "Yes, I do."

"Still," I said. "Anyway, supper's ready."

After dinner Mom turned on one of her shows and sat there watching it with Helen. But it wasn't interesting to me, so I went out and sat on the back steps and watched it grow dark; I saw the sky go deep blue, and finally the stars came out. The peepers were going like mad, too, and the air had that damp spring smell to it.

I liked watching the stars come out. I would pick out a part of the sky that had no stars yet, a place where there was nothing but that deep blue. I would stare at it and stare at it, and all of a sudden there'd be a star there. It was like magic.

I did that a few times, until I got tired of it, and then I started to think about Helen going away. She had two more years of high school, and I had three. She talked a lot about what she was going to do after she graduated. Sometimes she said she wanted to go to school to become a dental technician. They made good money, she said, and she could have a nice apartment or condo or something, with wall-to-wall carpets and a big color TV and nice furniture, the way it was in some of the other kids' houses. Sometimes she said she was going to go to Hollywood and try to make it in the movies. That idea worried her, though, because she didn't think she was pretty enough. I would tell her she was pretty, but she had a hard time believing it. She would say, "No, I'm not pretty. My nose is wrong and my mouth is too big and my hair is always funny." When she was in that mood, she would decide to be a dental technician.

When I graduated, I was going to go into the air force. There was a reason for that: If you were in the air force, nobody could say you were trash. It wouldn't matter that I stunk in the third grade, or that the paint was peeling off our house and my dad didn't have a regular job. If you were in the air force, nobody could say you were trash. The thing was, you needed a high school degree to get into the air force.

I never told Mom and Dad about my plan. I knew what Dad would say about it. He would say that going in the air force was a sucker's game. I would just be cannon fodder for the biggies who ran the country.

I wondered: Did Helen really hate Dad and Mom? Or did she just say that because she was in a bad mood? I didn't hate them. Sometimes I got mad at them for things they did, but I didn't hate them. Mom was okay, really. She tried her best to do things right. It was only that she was tired so much. Dad was okay, too, sometimes. I just wished he wouldn't talk about the biggies all the time. I never knew whether to believe him when he talked about them cheating everybody and polluting the Timber River and such. I wished I knew if he was right.

He was right that there was pollution in the Timber River, though. I knew because times when I'd be lying by the river looking at the fish, just watching them flash around, changing direction all in an instant, I'd see on the top of the water flashes of red and green and yellow. It was some kind of chemicals, or oil or something.

But how did Dad know that it was coming from the carpet factory? Wouldn't the police or somebody have made them stop if they were really polluting the river? I knew it was against the law, because we'd studied it in social studies. It probably wouldn't be too hard to find out, I figured. The stuff would be coming out of a pipe or something. The carpet factory was right next to the river, so it would be easy to run a pipe from the factory to the riverbank. Of course, I didn't *know* that was the way they would do it, but it made sense. It wouldn't be hard to find out either. You could just go out there and walk along the riverbank until you saw the pipe or whatever it was. Something like that would be easy enough to spot.

Suddenly it came to me that I could go out there and look for the pipe myself. I could find out if Dad was right—that the carpet factory really was polluting the river. If they were, I could report it to the police, and they'd make the factory stop it. There'd be a big story in the *Timber Falls Journal* about me. I'd be a hero. The other kids at school would want to be friends with me, and nobody would say I was trash anymore.

I began to get really excited. The more I thought about it, the better an idea it seemed. All I had to do was find that pipe. What would be so hard about that? I was so excited, I couldn't sit there anymore but started walking around on the lawn.

Would I really have the guts to do something like that? Or would it be one of those things that you just *think* you're going to do and never get around to actually doing? It was exciting thinking about it, though, and I walked around going over it all in my mind: how I would go out to the river, walk up and down the bank until I found the pipe, and then go and get the police and the reporters and stuff. They'd take pictures of me and write a story about it in the papers. It was exciting thinking about it. But after awhile a little spring breeze came up, and it got chilly and I went in.

In the morning I had to finish my geometry homework while I was eating my breakfast, and I didn't have a chance to think about tracking down the river pollution. I had only got my geometry half done when Dad said, "Harry, I want you to bury the garbage this morning." The town garbage trucks didn't come out that far, so we took it out into the woods and buried it.

"The bus is coming soon," I said.

"You can skip school for once," he said.

"I can't, Dad," I said.

"It's a waste of time anyway. If it was me, I'd close the schools down and put all those lazy so-and-sos to work. What do you learn down there anyway? What's the use of that stuff?" He pointed to my geometry homework.

I knew that I would need to pass geometry if I wanted to go into the air force, but I didn't say that. "I have to pass it," I said.

"Frank," Mom said. "He has to go to school. It's the law."

"Forget about the law," Dad said. Then he got up, put on his jacket, and went out. In a moment we heard the truck start and go down the driveway.

Mom said, "You better come right home from school and do the garbage, Harry."

"Okay," I said. So, between everything, I didn't remember about the carpet factory and all that until I was on the school bus. There's a place where the Timber River runs alongside the road into town. The sun was bright and glinting on the water, and when I looked out at it, I remembered.

The whole idea of finding where the pollution was coming from was more scary in the daylight than it had been at night. It wasn't just something to have a daydream about, but real. The river was real and the carpet factory was real and the people who worked there were real. Maybe I ought to forget about the whole thing. Maybe it wouldn't make me into a hero anyway. Maybe I'd go on being trash.

Then I told myself I was just being chicken. I was just afraid of standing up to the grown-ups. What difference did it make that I was just a kid? What mattered was who was right, didn't it? But still, I felt nervous about it, and I wondered if I would really do anything about it.

I hadn't finished my geometry because of Dad interrupting me at breakfast, so I forgot about the pollution and worked on the geometry as best as I could with the school bus bouncing every which way. I didn't think about it again until lunch.

Our school was old because Timber Falls was poor. The cafeteria was in the basement. There were steam pipes overhead, and the fluorescent lights were on all the time because hardly any light came in from outside. The folding tables were all carved with initials, and there was always a sort of tomatoey smell down there.

Helen and I were supposed to bring our lunches instead of buying cafeteria food. Dad said there wasn't anything wrong with sandwiches, we needn't expect to be raised in the lap of luxury. Mostly I tried to remember to make my lunch the night before. There was usually enough stuff in the icebox to make good sandwiches out of—some leftover cold cuts or hot dogs, or baked beans. I liked cold baked bean sandwiches with a lot of mayonnaise. Cold hot dog sandwiches with catsup were good too. But if I forgot to make my lunch the night before, I would only have time enough to make peanut butter and jelly sandwiches. They were good, too, but you got tired of them after a while.

Helen never bothered to make a lunch. If she had some money, she bought a hot lunch in the cafeteria, and if she didn't, she'd beg something from somebody, mostly me.

When I came down to the cafeteria, I saw her sitting by herself at the end of a table, reading a romance. There were these two girls who would sit with Helen, but sometimes they were with other people, and Helen would be afraid to go over and sit with them in case somebody started making remarks. I never sat with anybody except Helen. If they didn't want me around, I wasn't going to make them. So I went and sat with Helen, and opened my lunch bag. "You still in a bad mood?" I said.

"I just felt like reading," she said.

"Don't you have any lunch?"

"No," she said. She went back to reading.

"You want half a sandwich?" I said.

"No," she said. "Can't you see I'm reading?"

"Don't you have any money?"

"Stop bothering me," she said. Then I saw her face get red. I looked around. Charlie Fritz was coming

slowly through the crowd carrying his tray and looking around for a place to sit.

"Charlie Fritz is coming," I said. She looked back
down at her book, but her face stayed red. "He's
coming right toward us," I said in a low voice.

Helen flicked up her eyes to look, and then looked
back at her book again. A little bit of sweat came out
on her upper lip, and she nervously licked it away.
She was still red. Charlie kept on coming closer. He
was looking around here and there, and I figured he
didn't see us. Helen flicked her eyes up to look at him
again, then flicked them back to her book. He was by
the next table now, standing there, still looking
around. Then he saw a place he wanted to sit, and
started to come right by us.

Helen looked up, and licked at the sweat on her
lips. Finally Charlie saw her. "Oh, hello, Helen," he
said.

"Do you want to sit here, Charlie?" she said.

"I guess not, Helen," he said.

She blinked. "Oh," she said. Her face went redder
than ever, and she looked back down to her book.
Charlie went on by and sat down with some guys a
couple of tables away from us. Helen kept her eyes
on her book, but she was hot and sweaty anyway. I
looked over to where Charlie was sitting with the
other guys. He was leaning forward, talking in a low
voice, and the other guys were leaning forward toward him. Every once in a while one of them would
take a quick look over at Helen. I wanted to go over

there and slug them. I wanted to start heaving dishes at them. I just hoped Helen wouldn't look up.

But she did. I guess she couldn't help herself. She looked up and she saw them, all leaning their heads together across the table, listening to Charlie; and two of them were staring right at her.

When they saw her looking, they snapped their heads away. Helen's face stopped being red and went pale white. She blinked and bit her lip. Then she closed her eyes, and the tears began rolling out of them.

"Helen," I whispered, "don't pay any attention to those guys."

She jumped up, threw her hands over her face so that nobody could see the tears, and ran out of the cafeteria as fast as she could go. I watched her run. Charlie Fritz and those guys stopped talking and watched her, and then everybody in the cafeteria was silent and watched her run through the tables with her hands over her face, bumping into chairs and things. Suddenly she was gone. For a moment the cafeteria was dead quiet, and I could hear the *tap-tap* of Helen's shoes as she ran up the cement cafeteria stairs. Then the cafeteria noise started up again. I picked up Helen's book and began pretending to read it, because I knew a lot of them would be staring at me. I didn't feel like finishing my lunch. I just wanted to get out of there, but I wasn't going to walk out in front of them all. So I sat until the bell rang and the place emptied out. I got up, darted up the cafeteria steps, and trotted away from school through the sunshine, feeling just terrible. There was one thing I didn't have any question about anymore: I was going to do something to show everybody in Timber Falls that we weren't trash.

THREE

I didn't really know where I was going. I just wanted to get away from school. I took the school road and then swung onto a side road where there wouldn't be much traffic. I was feeling sort of numb, and trying not to think about Helen. Instead, I thought about the pollution in the Timber River.

If they were dumping stuff in the river, it had to be coming out of a pipe somewhere along the riverbank. All I had to do was walk along the riverbank until I found it, then get a camera from somewhere and take some pictures of the pollution coming out. I wasn't exactly sure what I would do with the pictures. I figured there had to be some sort of state agency in Albany that was responsible for pollution. Or maybe the police. Or maybe I would just give the pictures to the *Timber Falls Journal* and let them run a big story about it. Then I could send the story to the agency in Albany or whatever it was.

In fact, that seemed like the best idea. They were

bound to take the whole thing more seriously if they saw a story about it in the paper than if some kid just sent in some pictures. That was the way to do it: Get the story in the paper first. Of course, I didn't have a camera, and neither did Mom and Dad. We'd never had one, as far as I could remember. In the ads on television families always have cameras and take pictures of their trips and vacations and kids' birthday parties and all that. We didn't go on any trips to take pictures of. Sometimes Dad went off for a few days or a week. He always said it was for a job out of state, but he never said where it was, or what it was, and we never knew for sure. But the rest of us never went on trips, so we couldn't have had pictures of them even if we'd had a camera.

We had birthdays, though. I mean, we didn't have real birthday parties with other kids coming over and balloons and hats and stuff. On our birthdays Mom would buy us a present—a toy or a doll or something when we were little, a sweater or a jacket when we were bigger. She would make something special for dinner that we liked—hamburgers and french fries or something—and she'd buy a cake and ice cream, and we'd blow out the candles and all that. But we never took any pictures of our birthdays, or Christmas or anything else. About the only pictures of myself I'd ever seen were one of Mom holding me when I was a baby, and another one that Helen and I took in a photograph machine once when we all went over to Watertown to see Mom when she was in a hospital for tests.

So getting hold of a camera was going to be a problem, but I figured I could solve it some way. I'd think about it for a while and see what came to me.

No matter how I tried to change the subject in my head, I couldn't help thinking about Helen. I didn't think she had gone home. If she came home early, Mom would want to know why, and Helen sure wouldn't want to tell her. I figured she would hang out someplace until three-thirty when we usually got home. I felt sorry for her. Going back to school the next day and facing everybody was going to be hard for her.

The truth was that it was Helen's own fault. I knew that. If she hadn't let those guys come around, none of it would have happened. But I guess she wanted so much to have some guys come to see her, she couldn't stop herself.

Still, I felt bad for her. What had happened to her wasn't right and it wasn't fair, and if Dad had only got a real job and a real house, maybe things would have been different. But there wasn't any use thinking about that. It wasn't Dad's way. He was his own man, he always said. He wasn't going to spend his life taking orders from the middle class. The whole thing confused me a lot. It wasn't fair for Helen; but why should Dad have to get a real job just for Helen?

I wondered what time it was. I couldn't go home either, not until three. But I had to go someplace where no cop was likely to come along and ask me why I wasn't in school. I would have to get away from town. And suddenly, just like that, I decided I would go out to the carpet factory just to have a look around.

I didn't know much about the place. I'd gone out there two or three times with Dad when he had something to deliver and needed help unloading. It was a big one-story cement block building with a corrugated iron roof. It had been there a long time— forty years maybe. Behind it there was a blacktop parking lot, which ran down to the Timber River. That was about all I knew about it.

I could get from the school road to the carpet factory without going through town. So I headed on out, going as quick as I could. In a little while I came to the road that ran along the Timber River out to the carpet factory. It was pretty out there. The river was boiling along with the spring rush, and the mountains stood all around me. Sometimes the road swung in close to the river so that it was not more than fifty feet from the bank; other times it swung away from it, so there was maybe a quarter of a mile of woods between the river and the road, and I couldn't see the river at all, or hear it boiling along either. It was only a couple of miles out to the factory, and after a while I began to get close.

Here the road was a good way from the river, with the woods in between. I kept on going, and pretty soon I came to an eight-foot-high steel mesh fence running along beside the road. I stopped and in a minute I realized that the fence turned the corner there and ran off down through the woods toward the river. I knelt down pretending to tie my shoe and took a look to see if anybody was around. A car was coming up the road. It slowed down when it came to me, but then it went by. I waited until it was out of sight, and then I slipped into the woods and worked my way along the steel mesh fence down to the river. I stopped on the riverbank and looked through the fence. It turned the corner again here and ran along the riverbank upstream in the direction of the carpet factory. It was pretty clear that the mesh fence must go all around the factory. I looked up at the top of the fence. There was barbed wire along the top. I could come back here with a pair of Dad's wire cutters and get through that easily enough, but I had a hunch that it would set off an alarm if you cut the barbed wire.

I turned back and looked at the river. Here, this close to the factory, the water had a kind of greenish tint to it, and the little spots of foam on the surface didn't look to me like ordinary whitecaps. I decided to take a look at the factory itself. I went back to the road and began walking along again. In a couple of minutes the woods ended, and there was the factory, about fifty yards back from the road, with a little lawn and some bushes out front, and behind it, as much as I could see from my angle, the parking lot and the loading docks. There were maybe a hundred cars in the parking lot.

The steel mesh fence went right along the whole thing and disappeared into more woods on the other side. It would go all the way around, I figured. There was a big steel mesh gate in the middle of the fence, where the factory road went in. The whole place was pretty well guarded, and I wondered why. I figured there was always the risk of thieves.

Anyway, it was going to be pretty impossible to get

in there and prowl around looking for the pollution pipe. How was I going to find it? Then it came to me that if I crossed the river, and went along on the opposite bank, I would see it. I didn't know how big a pipe you needed for something like that, but, I figured, from the amount of pollution that was in the water, it couldn't be some little piece of one-inch pipe. It would be a twelve-inch pipe or something. It wouldn't be hard to spot something that big sticking out of the riverbank.

I looked up at the sun, and judged that it must be getting on toward three, so I started for home, feeling a whole lot better. It felt good to be working on something interesting like this. It was sort of scary, too: but what was the danger? It wasn't going to be much of a problem going along the opposite riverbank trying to spot that pipe, I figured.

Mom was sitting at the kitchen table drinking a cup of coffee. She had a dress on, like she was going somewhere. "Where have you been, Harry? I've been so scared. My heart's been pounding so, I thought I'd have an attack."

I began to feel scared myself. "What's the matter? I've been at school."

"No, you haven't," she said. "They called from school. They said that you and Helen ran off after lunch. I've been so worried."

"Ran off?" I didn't know what to say.

"That's what they said. Where's Helen?"

"I don't know," I said. I wasn't worried about Mom so much as Dad. Mom wasn't much for punishing us. Dad always told her that she had to bear down on us harder. But Dad would hit you if he got mad enough. Suddenly I saw a way out. "I don't know where Helen went. I was looking for her."

"Harry, they said Helen was upset."

I didn't know what to say, but I had to tell her something. "She was crying in school," I said.

"Crying? What was she crying for?"

"I don't know," I said. "She was just crying."

"She didn't say where she was going?"

"She didn't say anything. I went looking for her, but I couldn't find her. I figured she came home."

"Where did you look?"

"Just around town," I said.

She took a sip of her coffee. "I'm so worried," she said.

"I have to bury the garbage before Dad gets home," I said.

I went outside, picked up the garbage can from behind the house, and toted it past the barn up into the woods. About a hundred feet in, there was a pit I'd dug for the garbage. We would dump the garbage in and cover it over with some dirt so that the animals wouldn't get into it. About every three months I would have to cover over the garbage pit with the dirt that was left, and dig a new one. The pit was pretty full. I was going to have to dig a new one pretty soon. I hate that: it was hard work and took a morning.

I dumped the garbage into the pit and shoveled dirt over it. I wondered where Helen was. I'd figured she'd come on home after three-thirty, but she wasn't home yet. I didn't know what that meant. I didn't think she'd go to visit those two girls who liked her, because she'd have to tell them what she was crying about. Where else would she go? If it had been me, I'd have gone off into the woods someplace to take my mind off it, but Helen wasn't much for going into the woods. Where could she be?

I wished Dad would come home with the truck so we could go out looking for her. Mom ought to be doing something. She didn't have a car, but she could be trying to find out where Dad was, to tell him. Or she could be phoning around to people to see if anyone had seen her. Or she could call the police. Do something, instead of just sitting there drinking coffee and worrying. That was the trouble with Mom: There didn't seem to be much to her.

I finished up the garbage and carried the can back to the house. Helen still wasn't home. I hosed the garbage can out so it wouldn't stink. Then I went up to my room so as to be where Mom couldn't start asking me questions. All my schoolbooks were still in my locker at school where I'd put them at lunchtime, but I was supposed to be writing a report on the ecology of the Adirondacks, which I knew a lot about anyway. So I started on it.

But I couldn't concentrate. The longer the day went on, the more I worried about Helen. Why wasn't she coming home? It began to grow dark, and still she didn't come. She always came home by supper time. There wasn't much else for her to do. I told myself that she was just messing around somewhere, and tried to concentrate on my report. Then I heard Dad's truck drive in and stop. The door slammed.

Maybe Helen had got a ride home with Dad. I jumped up and ran to the window. It was just Dad. He took his toolbox out of the back of the truck and carried it up to the barn. Then he came back down to the house and went in. I jumped up and went downstairs. Mom was still sitting at the beat-up blue kitchen table drinking coffee. Dad was standing in the middle of the kitchen. He said, "What do you mean she's run off?"

"They called from the school. She was crying and ran out of school. Harry went looking for her, but he couldn't find her."

"Crying?" Dad said. "What was she crying about?"

"I don't know," Mom said. She looked like she was about to cry herself.

Dad looked at me. "What's this all about, Harry?" he said.

"I don't know," I said. "I think she was pretty upset about something."

Mom started crying. "I don't know what we're going to do, Frank."

Dad sat there for a minute, frowning and thinking. Then he said, "It probably wasn't anything. Nerves or something. Let's eat."

Mom tried to stop crying, and wiped her eyes with a tissue.

"No, Frank, something's wrong. It isn't like her. I just know something's wrong."

"You're making a big thing out of nothing. She probably had some trouble with her boyfriend. It'll all blow over. Let's eat." He sat down at the table.

Mom stood up and faced him. "Frank—"

"Stop worrying. She's probably made it up with the guy already, and she's fooling around with him and forgot the time. She's sixteen. She isn't a baby. So what if she's ten minutes late."

"Please, Frank, please."

He sighed. "All right," he said. "All right. Come on, Harry, let's go find her."

We weren't going to find her. By now I knew that she'd run away. Where, I didn't know. But I knew that she wasn't around Timber Falls anymore. I didn't say anything; I just got my jacket, and we went out into the truck. Dad started the engine. "Where does she usually hang out?"

"Mostly everybody goes to Teddy's Pizza Parlor," I said. Helen went there sometimes, I knew, but she usually didn't have enough money, not unless she could borrow some. We drove into town and stopped at Teddy's, which was between the hardware store and the liquor store. "See if she's in there," Dad said.

I didn't want to because everybody in there would know who I was looking for. But I couldn't argue with Dad, so I got out of the truck and went into Teddy's. Charlie Fritz was there, sitting at a booth fooling around with a couple of guys. He looked at me, but he didn't say anything. I turned around, went out, and got back into the truck. "She isn't there," I said.

"Where else is she likely to be?" he said. "Who's her boyfriend? Maybe she's over at his house."

"She doesn't have— She isn't going with anyone right now," I said.

"She doesn't have a boyfriend?" he said. "A girl

that pretty doesn't have a boyfriend? What about her girlfriends?"

"I don't know, Dad," I said. "She doesn't have too many friends."

"That can't be right, Harry," he said. "She must have friends. She's pretty and smart, she ought to have lots of friends."

"She doesn't have too many friends," I said.

"I don't understand that," he said. "I just don't understand it."

He didn't know anything about Helen. He didn't know anything about who she was, or what she did, or what her life was like. What could I say to him? How could I explain to him that the whole time Helen was in elementary school she stank? How could I explain to him that everybody we knew thought we were trash?

We drove around town for a while, looking into the stores that were still open, and then we drove home. Dad didn't say very much but just looked straight ahead all the way home.

FOUR

After Helen had been missing for two days, Dad went down to the cops and told them about it. They put in a missing person report and told him not to worry, teenagers were always running off and usually came back by themselves. When Dad came home, he told Mom, "It's just a phase or something. She'll come back. Give her a few days of missing her meals and she'll come back." Then after that he seemed to forget all about her.

But Mom didn't. She moped around the house worse than ever. She could hardly get herself to cook —all she'd do was open some cans of stew or something and heat it up on the stove. I could tell that Dad didn't like it, but he didn't say anything. She even stopped watching TV. Mostly she sat at the kitchen table in her bathrobe drinking coffee. At night she just picked at her food.

"I can't stand watching you pick at your food like

that," Dad said. "Stop worrying, she'll come home soon."

To tell the truth, seeing Mom so low all the time got on my nerves too. Once I went into Helen's room looking for a pencil, and I caught Mom sitting on Helen's bed, holding Helen's sweater in her hands and smelling it. "My poor baby," she said when I came in. "I'm so worried about her."

I was worried about her too. I knew that she didn't have any money, because she hadn't had enough for lunch the day she ran away. She hadn't taken any clothes either. They were all still in her room where she'd left them. How was she going to live with no money and no clothes?

I wondered where she'd gone. Farther downstate, I figured—Rochester, or Albany, or maybe even New York City. I'd been down to Rochester on a school trip to see a science exhibit that one of the photograph companies there put on, but I'd never been to New York. Helen had been to New York once on a school trip; they saw some Shakespeare play and spent the night in a big hotel. When she came back, she was all excited about New York—how big it was and how many people there were there, and the wonderful things that the stores were packed full of. She couldn't get over the stuff in the shop windows—books and records and cameras and clothes and hi-fis and silverware, anything you could think of. So she might have gone to New York. You could hitch there in a couple of days. But what would she eat while she was hitching?

I really missed her. We used to fight a lot, but when

you got down to it, she was the only person I had to talk to. We talked about Mom and Dad a lot—about Mom being sick all the time, and Dad not having a regular job, and us being poorer than everybody else. We talked about why we never saw our relatives. Dad's brother lived out in California, and he had children that were our cousins. We knew what they looked like, because we'd usually get a Christmas card from them with a photograph on it. There were two girls and a boy, and they were eight, eleven, and thirteen. We wondered what they were like, and what their life was like in California. Mom said that Dad's brother did real well—he was a foreman in a printing plant out there and made a lot of money. Dad said that was okay if you didn't mind being regimented, but it wasn't for him.

Mom's parents lived in Binghamton. They were our grandparents, but we never saw them, even though it wasn't more than a couple hundred miles down there. We never got a Christmas card from them, and Mom didn't talk about them very much, and not at all when Dad was around, so we didn't know much about them. But once I heard Mom talking to them on the telephone—I don't know how I knew it was them, but I knew. Afterward Mom cried and cried. Mom would talk to Helen about them more than she did to me. Helen said that our grandfather was sixty years old and was a carpenter. The whole thing was, they didn't like Dad, Helen said.

So we didn't know much about Mom's parents, but we didn't know anything at all about our other grandparents, Dad's folks. He hardly ever said anything about them at all. Once when we drove out into the mountains and he was in a good mood, I asked him where they lived.

"Out in Oklahoma," he said. "They were mean and I never got along with them. My old man put me to work in the fields when I was fourteen, and I ran away after that as soon as I could." But that's all he would ever say about them.

Helen and I talked about things like that a lot, but one subject we didn't talk about was being trash. We just didn't say anything about it to each other. I wouldn't have minded talking about it, but Helen didn't want to. Every time I started to get into it, she would say that I was exaggerating or something. She would admit that we were poorer than most people in Timber Falls, and that our house was junky, but she wouldn't admit that everybody in town thought we were trash. The reason why she didn't have any boyfriends, she said, was that she wasn't pretty enough, or didn't have the right personality, or didn't have nice clothes. Each time it was something different. After a while I stopped trying to talk to her about it.

Even so, we talked about most things, and we did a lot of things together. When Helen was in the third grade, and I couldn't read yet, she would read me stories in bed when we were supposed to be asleep. She'd come into my room with a library book and get into bed with me, and read to me in a low voice so Mom and Dad wouldn't know we were awake. I really liked that, having somebody to snuggle up to; and I'd listen and get sleepy, and finally I'd doze off

and Helen would say, "You fell asleep again, Harry."
And I would say, "No, I didn't, I just closed my eyes."
Then she would make me tell what had happened in
the story, and of course I couldn't, and she would say
that she wasn't going to read to me anymore. But she
always did.

When we got older, we used to play cards in the
afternoon when there wasn't anything else to do. We
played go fish and old maid mostly. For a while we
had a Monopoly set. I don't know where it came
from. It wasn't whole: we had to use buttons for the
pieces, and there wasn't the right amount of money,
but we played it anyway. Sometimes the game would
go on for days, and of course, we always ended up
fighting. I don't know what happened to the Monopoly set. After a while it was gone.

Sometimes on the weekends, if Dad wasn't around
giving us jobs, we went bike riding. Helen got her
bike first, when she was around eight. Dad said bikes
were a middle-class luxury he couldn't afford, but
Helen begged and pleaded with Mom, and finally
Mom got Dad to get Helen a bike. It was a beat-up
old Schwinn that he'd got used somewhere. Helen
found some paint out in the barn and painted it. She
painted the fenders blue and the frame red and the
seat yellow. I sat in the barn watching her. By the
time she was finished she had blue and red and yellow all over her—her hands, her face, her ears, her
hair. She thought the bicycle was beautiful, and so
did I at the time. I was only about six then, and it
seemed to me just the smartest idea to paint the bike
different colors. A couple of years after that Helen

got a better bike. It was a bike somebody's kids had got too big for, and they gave it to Helen. I guess they felt sorry for her. So Helen gave me her bike, and now it was my turn to paint it, and I made it all green, which was the kind of paint there was most of in the barn.

After that we took bike trips. I was maybe nine or ten, and she was twelve. We would make peanut butter and jelly sandwiches. If we had any money, we would buy Cokes and Devil Dogs or boxes of cookies. Then we would ride out to this place we knew of, where there was a stream coming down from the mountain. The road crossed over the stream on a little bridge, and down from the bridge in the woods a little way was a grassy place by the side of the stream. You couldn't see it from the road. We would go in there and be secret and tell each other what we were going to do when we were grown-up; and we would eat our lunch, and swim if it was really hot, for that mountain stream was pretty cold even in the middle of summer.

Then after a couple of years Helen began going to high school and got interested in guys, and we didn't do stuff together so much. But I remembered all the things we did. It made me sad to think of them, and I wished Helen would come back.

Having Helen run off like that just made the talk about us worse. The kids at school were curious, and they kept coming around and asking me where she had gone and what she was doing. Even the seniors and juniors kept asking me, guys that I hardly knew and that had never paid any attention to me before.

They'd come up to me and say, "Hey, White, I heard your sister ran off to California." Or they'd say, "Hey, White, I heard somebody saw your sister down in New York hanging around Times Square." Or they'd say, "Hey, White, I heard your sister got busted for drugs." They were hoping to find out something really bad about her. It didn't matter what it was, just as long as it was something bad.

I would answer, "It's none of your business." If it was some guy older than me, he'd tell me to watch my mouth, but he'd go away because he knew he shouldn't be asking private stuff like that. If it had been somebody else's sister, everyone would have been shocked and afraid to bring it up in public. But with us it didn't matter: it was just what you would expect.

So I stayed away from people as much as I could. But the whole thing made me more determined than ever to show everybody in Timber Falls that we were as good as they were.

I planned that I would go over to the other side of the river and look for the pollution pipe on the next Saturday. Dad would have work for me. He always did on Saturday. But he usually went off somewhere himself, so I'd be able to get away.

That was the way it worked out. He told me to get started on another garbage pit, which would be four feet deep in the middle, and ten feet across. So I went out right after breakfast with a shovel and a pick and began digging. It was going to be a pretty day—a warm spring day with a fresh, new smell in the air, and with birds swooping across the fields and through the woods, gathering twigs and grass for their nests. It would be a nice day to go exploring along the river. I dug away for a while, working up a pretty good sweat. Then I heard the truck start, and I tossed down the shovel and went back to the house, just in time to see the truck pull out of the driveway. I went into the house and made myself some lunch, for I figured I'd be gone until the afternoon. There was some sliced American cheese in the icebox, and a dish of cold string beans, which were pretty good in a sandwich if you put a lot of mayonnaise on them. Mom was watching TV, but she came out to the kitchen to see what I was doing.

"Where are you going?" she said.

"Out to look for birds," I said.

"Be sure to work on the garbage pit," she said, "or you'll get in trouble with Dad."

"I will," I said. "When I come back."

She looked at me, mighty sad. "You're a good boy, Harry. I hope you'll always be a good boy." I knew she was thinking about Helen.

"I'm not so good, Mom," I said. I put the sandwiches into a paper bag.

"My poor baby," she said. She was still thinking of Helen. "I can't understand what made her do it."

"I don't know, Mom," I said.

"Did she ever say we were treating her badly?"

"I don't think so," I said. "She never said anything like that." How was I supposed to tell the truth?

"It makes me feel so bad to think of her out there someplace all alone."

"I've got to go," I said.

"Be a good boy, Harry," she said.

I didn't usually bother to hitchhike into town, because people who knew who I was wouldn't pick me up in case I had cooties. But this time I tried it so as not to waste time, and a stranger came along and took me into the town.

The Timber River ran alongside the town about a quarter mile from the main street. Back in the old days, when there was a lot of logging in the Adirondacks, the river had been used for floating logs out to the sawmills. Timber Falls had grown up around the sawmills as a lumbering town. Actually there weren't any real falls there—just some rapids where the river ran down a steep slope below town. A road ran up each side of the river—a pretty good concrete road going out to the carpet factory on our side, and a beat-up old blacktop road running along the other side, where there were some dairy farms. To get to the old blacktop road, you went over the railroad tracks and then crossed the river on an old steel bridge painted silver.

So I did that; and when I got to the middle of the steel bridge, I stopped. I stood there, looking down at the river through the steel supports, feeling the sun on my back. There was stuff in the river all right—streaks of green, and patches of oil filled with wavering rainbow colors. The colors were pretty, but not if you knew what was causing them. If you knew, they were ugly.

I walked across the bridge and came to the blacktop that ran along this side of the river. The blacktop was all busted up because the farmers who lived farther out ran their tractors and harvesting machines along it. They weren't supposed to, but they did, and they broke up the blacktop pretty quickly.

I began to walk out along the blacktop. Along the riverside there were some trees, and along the other side, open fields, some of them filled with last year's corn stubble, some of them black dirt where the farmer had already plowed for this year's corn. After a bit the road veered away from the river, so that there was maybe a hundred yards of woods between the road and the river. You couldn't see the river at that distance, and you couldn't hear it either.

I went on for a while until I figured I was getting to a point opposite the carpet factory on the far bank. I took a look around, and when I didn't see anybody, or any cars coming, I slipped into the woods, moving as quick as I could to get to where I wouldn't be seen from the road. When I was far enough in, I slowed down and walked to the river. About ten feet from the riverbank I crouched down and looked out across the river. About fifty yards upstream on the other side I could see the steel mesh fence where it came down through the woods, turned, and then went along the riverbank.

I backed off into the woods a little bit, so anybody who happened to be on the opposite bank wouldn't see me, and began moving slowly along upstream. Every couple of minutes I'd stop and push back toward the riverbank to see what I could spot. I didn't see anything that looked like a pipe.

After a bit the woods on the opposite bank ended,

and there was the factory, sitting in the middle of the
blacktop parking lot. Being as it was Saturday, there
weren't many cars there—just a dozen or so. Some
trucks were parked at the loading platforms. I didn't
see any people.

I figured if there was a pipe, it would come out
around there. I worked my way a little upstream
until I was directly opposite the middle of the factory. Then I stopped and began looking along the
opposite bank. It was hard to make out anything. The
river was a couple of hundred feet across, and a lot of
brush and weeds grew on the opposite bank.

I looked up at the factory to see if there was any
sign of a pipe coming out of it. From where I was
standing I could look into the factory and see the
shapes of some machines. Still no people.

Then I noticed a security guard walking across the
blacktop parking lot toward the river. I stood watching. He came all the way down to the steel mesh
fence that ran along the river at the edge of the
parking lot, and stood there, looking across the river.

Suddenly I realized that he was looking at me. I'd
gotten too close to the riverbank. I froze. I was about
five feet back into the woods, partly in the shadows
and partly in the sunlight. There was no way I could
tell whether he could actually make me out, or had
seen movement and was just suspicious. I didn't
move, and after a minute he turned and trotted off
across the parking lot and disappeared around behind the factory.

Now what? Had he seen me? Was he going to call
the police? Would he get into a car and come after

me? That was a pretty scary idea. My view of the factory gate was blocked, and I wouldn't be able to see a security car driving out.

Still, I wanted to find that pipe. I took another good look along the riverbank opposite to where I was standing. Then I moved back into the woods a little, and continued on upstream the way I'd been going. Every fifty feet or so I dropped to my knees and crawled out to the riverbank as close as I dared, and scanned the bank opposite. I went on doing this until I was a half mile above the factory, and then I gave it up. If there was a pipe coming out of the riverbank, I missed it.

But I knew that the pipe had to be there, because when I looked down into the Timber River at the place where I was, which was a good bit upstream from the factory, the water was clear. There wasn't any green tinge to it, or any rainbowy patches of oil, the way there was farther down. They had to be dumping stuff into the river somewhere, and I couldn't see how they could do it except from a pipe. Probably they'd camouflaged it. What I needed was binoculars. I wondered if Dad knew anybody who had a pair of binoculars I could borrow. Anyway, the best thing was to give up for the day and see if I could get hold of some binoculars somehow. For one thing, I had to go home and finish the garbage pit.

I was worried about going home, though. I was afraid that the security guard might be out there on the beat-up blacktop road waiting for me to come out. Or maybe he'd called the cops, and they would come patrolling as I was walking along. I decided I'd better wait a little, so I pulled back into the woods out of sight of the river, sat down with my back against a big maple, and ate my sandwiches. They tasted pretty good after all that running around in the woods. Then I went carefully through the woods until I came to the road. I had a look around. There was nobody there, and so I started for home.

It was around three o'clock when I got back. Dad was already home. He was up in the barn working on something. I went on up and saw it was a sickle bar, for mowing fields. He'd got the parts carefully laid out on the old plank floor and was washing them off with kerosene from a coffee can.

The barn was pretty beat-up. The paint had been gone off it for years. The sides were gray, and the wood was so soft, you could scratch it with your fingernail. There were cracks where the boards had shrunk and warped, and a couple of the windowpanes were broken. Dad said he wasn't going to pay good money to fix up somebody else's barn.

Inside, along one wall, there was a long workbench with Dad's tools scattered on it. Most of the rest of the space in the barn was filled with Dad's junk. There was an old V-8 engine Dad had got somewhere, a couple of power mowers, some worn truck tires—oh, just a mess of stuff. And more was hanging from the beams above—coils of rope, pieces of chain, old fan belts, loops of wire. Dad liked junk.

Upstairs was the loft. There was some old furniture there that belonged to the people we rented it from: an old sofa, a couple of bureaus, some busted chairs—

things like that. The loft was where Helen would go with Charlie Fritz and those guys.

"Where'd you get the sickle bar, Dad?" I said.

"I bought it from some guy for fifty bucks. He couldn't get it to work." He didn't look up but went on cleaning the sickle bar parts.

"What are you going to do with it?"

"There's work around cutting fields," he said. "You can get twenty-five bucks an hour for that kind of work." Then he looked up at me. "Where've you been? I thought I told you to dig a garbage pit."

"I started it," I said. "I'm going to finish it up now. Listen, Dad, you don't have any binoculars, do you?"

He looked back at the sickle bar and began unbolting the engine from the carriage. "What do you need binoculars for?"

"For birds," I said.

He grunted. "If you need binoculars, Old Man Greenberg's got plenty of them in the Sports Center."

"I haven't got enough money to buy any. I keep trying to save, but I always have to spend it."

He didn't look up but went on twisting the nut with the end wrench. "I didn't say anything about buying them," he said.

For a moment I didn't get what he meant. Then I got it. I felt weird, like I'd suddenly been shifted into another place. "What?" I said. I couldn't think of anything else to say.

He went on swinging the end wrench round and round. "You heard me," he said.

"I couldn't do that," I said. I still felt weird.

"What do you think, you're better than everybody else?"

I began to grow hot, and to blush. "I just couldn't," I said.

He took the end wrench off the nut and unscrewed it with his fingers. But this time he looked at me. "Now you listen to me, Harry. Do you think those guys don't steal, those biggies with their Cadillacs and fancy houses? How do you think Old Man Greenberg got that Mercedes of his? How do you think that Herbst over at the carpet factory got that big house?"

I hated the idea that my father stole. I just wanted to get away from him. "I don't know," I said.

"They lie, cheat, and steal. That's how."

"But I don't see—"

"You don't see." He wasn't working on the sickle bar anymore. He was just kneeling there, looking up at me. "Well, I'll tell you how. They make deals with each other to underpay their workers, to fix prices and overcharge for the garbage they make, and when they pile up the dough, they get some smart accountant to get them out of paying taxes. Oh, you better believe it, Harry, these biggies are the real crooks. If the stuff they do ever came out, they'd all go to jail just like that. But it won't come out because they're in with the government, and the cops don't dare lay a finger on them. But let some poor working-man take a can of paint off a truck so he can support his family, they bang him in jail and throw away the key. That's what cops are for—to keep the working people in line. Did you know that, Harry? Did you know they invented the police to keep the poor from taking back what the rich stole from them?"

I felt like I was being smothered. I wanted to get away from him. "I didn't know that," I said.

"You think about it, Harry," he said. He started to work on the next nut. "Think about it."

I didn't say anything for a minute. Then I said, "Well, I better go dig the garbage pit."

I went out into the woods and began to dig, and while I dug, I thought about it. So Dad *had* stolen the chain saw from Jim Otto. I began to remember other things. Once Dad came in with a brand-new set of socket wrenches that was worth fifty or a hundred bucks. Once he came home with a little black-and-white TV because Mom had been complaining she couldn't see her shows on our old one. Once he came home with a pair of brand-new snow tires for the truck, still in their yellow paper wrappings. I remembered asking him why he hadn't had the tire store guy put them on the wheels, the way they usually do. He told me that the guy had been too busy. But now I knew.

It made me feel sick. Maybe we were trash after all. Maybe everybody in Timber Falls was right: The Whites were just plain no-good. Oh, we were clean now, and didn't stink. But what difference did that make if we stole? The thing that made me sickest about it was that everybody *knew* we stole. They hadn't caught Dad yet, but they knew. Jim Otto knew that Dad had stolen his chain saw, because he'd seen it sitting on our kitchen floor. Jim Otto had told it all over town, so everybody knew. And I was sure that there were other things. I was sure that when stuff was missing, people remembered that Dad had been around. So they knew, and it wouldn't do me any good to deny it, because it was true. We stole.

What about all that stuff Dad always talked about the biggies stealing from the working people? Was Dad right? Was it true? It sounded just like an excuse to me, but I didn't know.

Then I had another thought: Would I grow up to be like Dad? Would I become a crook too? Thinking that made me feel even worse. Look what happened to Helen: She had started to do wrong herself. Could it happen to me too? Would I start having temptations to steal that I couldn't control, the way Helen couldn't control herself when those guys came around? Maybe I would. The idea made me feel empty inside, and I decided to keep a close watch on myself, just to make sure I didn't take anything at all that didn't belong to me, even something as small as a paper clip.

FIVE

Two days later Dad came in at supper time and handed me a brand-new pair of binoculars. "Here," he said.

I took them and stared at him.

"Don't worry," he said. "I paid for them."

I knew I had to say thanks, but it was an awful struggle. "Gee, Dad, they're great."

"Don't lose them," he said. "They cost forty bucks."

"Gee, Dad," I said. "I won't lose them."

I took the binoculars up to my room, laid them on the bed, and sat next to them, staring at them. They were beauties all right. Seven by thirty-five, just right for bird-watching. For birds you don't want them too powerful because powerful glasses have a small field and you can't cover enough area. It thrilled me to look at them, so new, and sleek. I loved just looking at them. After a minute I picked them up. I loved holding them too. They felt heavy and firm.

I set them back down on the bed, and stared at them some more. For I hated them too. They scared me. Dad had stolen them, there wasn't any question about that. If he'd bought them, they would have come in a box with instructions and all that, not just plain like they were.

I took them outside to try them out while there was still some light. I slung them around my neck, climbed over the stone wall, went into the old pasture with the sumac and little cedars growing in it, and began looking at things. The binoculars were terrific all right. A couple of robins were building a nest, and I could bring them in so close it seemed like I could touch them. They were great binoculars, just what I needed for finding the pollution pipe.

But why should I bother with that anymore? I let the binoculars hang down from the strap. If everybody in Timber Falls knew we stole, would it make any difference what I did to stop being trash? And suppose I went out there to the factory and the cops came along and caught me with the binoculars?

I wondered who he'd stolen them from. Probably Old Man Greenberg. Although, when I thought about it, it wouldn't be easy to steal anything from the Sports Center. It was a pretty small store. Old Man Greenberg sold guns and tennis rackets and badminton sets and shotgun shells. From behind his counter he could see pretty much everywhere in the store. It wouldn't be easy to steal from there.

Maybe he had stolen them from some store over in Watertown. Or maybe he'd just happened to see them lying on the seat of somebody's car, and reached in and grabbed them. In Timber Falls people didn't usually lock their cars when they went into a store. It wouldn't be hard to steal from a car.

The more I thought about it, the more it seemed that he must have known where they were, and just gone and took them. He might have seen them in somebody's house when he was delivering cordwood or hauling away somebody's junk. Maybe he'd seen them hanging on a nail behind a bar somewhere. I just didn't know.

The problem was that I couldn't return them even if I decided to, because I didn't know who to return them to. And I couldn't walk around with them hanging around my neck, because at any moment I might run into the guy he'd stolen them from. And if I just hid them away and never used them, Dad would ask me why I wasn't using them, and I wouldn't have any good answer to that.

Anyway, I was afraid that Old Man Greenberg would suddenly turn up with a cop, the way Jim Otto had, so that night I hid the binoculars in the cardboard box where I kept my clothes. But no cops came that night, or the next night, and in a few days I stopped worrying about it. I hammered a nail into the window frame and hung the binoculars on it where I could see them when I was in bed. Whenever I got a chance, I practiced with them, focusing on birds, squirrels, and chipmunks out the window. And on the next Saturday I took them back out to the woods by the carpet factory.

I kept them buttoned under my jacket all the way. Even so, going through town, I was pretty scared that somebody might spot the strap around my neck, and the bulge under my jacket, and guess what it was. But nobody did, and I got out there okay. It was a cloudy, raw day, the kind where it looks like it might rain. I was glad of the weather, though, because it darkened the woods, and made it harder for anybody to see into them. I slid cautiously in among the trees, and then started along through them. In a few minutes I began to make out through the branches and tree limbs the shape of the factory across the river and the empty parking lot around it. I dropped flat and crawled forward over the dead leaves on the ground. When I was three feet from the riverbank, I stopped. I didn't dare go any farther, because I would be pretty easy to spot from the factory if anybody was looking.

I propped myself up on my elbows and raised up the binoculars. When I got them adjusted, I began to scan the whole factory, going from one side of the parking lot all the way across to the other—the blacktop, the cars, the cement block factory building, more blacktop. And I'd got just about that far when I saw the security guard. He was sitting on top of one of the loading platforms, smoking a cigarette. I could make him out pretty well through the binoculars. He was maybe in his fifties or something, and getting bald. A flashlight and nightstick hung from one side of his belt, and a pistol from the other. I wondered if he was allowed to shoot people who were trespassing. Anyway, he was a good long way from me, and I didn't think he would be able to see me in the woods, dark as they were, unless I started moving around in clear view. Just then he flung down his cigarette, jumped off the loading platform, and went off quickly around the building, out of sight.

I scanned the rest of the plant, moving the binoculars around until I'd covered every inch of the factory. I didn't see anything suspicious—no pipe running out of the side of the factory, no big valves and dials. That didn't surprise me very much. If they were dumping stuff in the river on the sly, they were sure to bury the pipe, or hide it some other way.

Now I began to work the binoculars slowly along the riverbank opposite, starting as far upriver as the first bend. It was pretty hard to make anything out, even with the binoculars, for there was brush growing out of the bank, rocks sticking out here and there, tree branches hanging down, and dead sticks that had fallen out of the trees. I went slowly, covering every inch of the bank as carefully as I could.

I didn't find anything—nothing that looked like a pipe jutting out of the riverbank. I was disappointed: I was sure that a pipe was there, somewhere. How else would that stuff get into the river?

So I started moving the binoculars along the bank again, going in the other direction this time, and suddenly, when I was searching pretty far upriver, I saw something. I held steady and readjusted the focus to make it as sharp as could be. There was something there all right, something that looked like a black shadow running down the riverbank. What interested me was that it had a straight edge. You don't see anything straight in the woods: everything is crooked, or curved, or wiggly.

I had to get a better look at it, so I crawled back into the woods, and then ran a little ways in a crouch upstream toward where I'd seen the straight-edged shadowy thing. When I was getting close, I dropped flat again and crawled out toward the riverbank, stopping a little way back in the shadow of the woods.

But when I raised the binoculars, I realized that I didn't have a very good angle on the shadowy thing. I crawled forward a little farther, then rose up to my knees, and focused the binoculars on the opposite bank. And just when I did that, I realized that the security guard was standing across the river by the steel mesh fence that ran along the riverbank. He'd spotted me all right. Worse than that, he could easily see that I was using binoculars.

"Hey you," he shouted across the water. "What're you doing there?" He put his hand on the butt of his pistol, but he didn't draw it.

I slid back into the woods, mighty scared. "Hey," he shouted again. "Come out of there. I want to know what you're doing."

I was out of his sight now, and I stopped to think. If I was going to get a good look at that shadowy thing, I'd have to go farther upstream. What if the security guard jumped into his car and came after me? What if he called the cops? I didn't want to be caught with these binoculars around my neck, that was for sure.

I stood there feeling worried and nervous. I couldn't decide what to do. It would take the security guard a good ten minutes to drive from the carpet factory into town, cross the steel bridge, and then come on up the beat-up blacktop road to where I was. If he phoned the police, they might get to me quicker, but not much quicker, unless they happened to be on patrol out there. Either way I had a little time, if I moved quickly.

So I told myself not to be chicken and began to jog through the trees upstream to get a better angle. I was pretty nervous, though, and every couple of minutes I'd stop to listen for the sound of cars, or somebody coming through the brush. But I didn't hear anything, and in a few minutes I figured I was far enough along to get a look at that straight-edged shadow.

I dropped into a crouch and slipped along toward the river until I could just begin to see it again through the trees. Then I fell flat and squirmed ahead on my belly, keeping a good eye out for anybody moving around across the river. When I got within four or five feet of the bank, I could see the opposite side well enough, and I slowly raised myself up and had a look back downstream to the place where I'd seen the security guard before. He was gone, and I knew that he was either calling the police or coming after me himself.

Now I raised up the binoculars and adjusted the focus. And right away I saw it—a black iron pipe about twelve inches in diameter sticking out of the riverbank at an angle that slanted down. There was brush all around it, which explained why I'd had such a hard time spotting it, and I figured they'd planted the brush there themselves for camouflage. But below the pipe there was a deep furrow in the bank where nothing grew. They'd been pouring some kind of chemicals out of that pipe, that was clear enough.

For a few minutes I knelt there looking at the pipe through the binoculars, hoping I'd see something come out. I was feeling pretty nervous, and I kept my ears open for sounds of somebody moving in the woods. Still, I was pretty happy, for I'd found it at last. Now I *knew* that the carpet factory was polluting the Timber River: that dead furrow beneath the pipe proved it as much as anything could.

What I needed to do now was to take some pictures of the pipe that I could show to the editor of the *Timber Falls Journal*. It would be best if I could get a picture when stuff was flowing out of the pipe. That might be pretty hard. I had a hunch that they dumped the stuff at night, when people were less likely to notice it. But maybe it would be enough to take a picture of the pipe with that furrow beneath it. It seemed pretty convincing to me. There was only one problem: I didn't have a camera, and I sure wasn't going to ask Dad to get one for me.

Suddenly I heard voices. I jumped. They were somewhere in the woods behind me. I couldn't make out the words. I leapt up and strained to listen. Someone was searching for me. It sounded like they were out by the road, a little downstream from me. My heart was racing and I began to sweat. Moving as quiet as I could, I slipped back into the middle of the woods, halfway between the river and the road, and headed farther upstream, to put whoever it was behind me. Every little bit and I'd stop to listen, and after a while I realized that the voices were gone.

What did that mean? Had they stopped talking, or had they gone away? I decided to slip carefully back to the road and see if anybody was out there. I went along with my body bent as low as I could, and after a bit I could see the road and the fields beyond it through the trees. I dropped to my knees, and crawled, swiveling my head left and right so as to catch a glimpse of anyone coming from either direction. Then I came to the edge of the woods, and stopped. There was nobody there. I stood up, and just at that moment the police car came sliding slowly by. The cop looked at me and I looked at the cop. There wasn't any hope of running or flinging the binoculars off into the woods. The car stopped instantly, and the cop at the wheel was out of it before I could move. The security guard got out the other side of the car.

SIX

"What're you doing here, son?" the cop said.

I knew him. He was the same guy who had come out to the house with Jim Otto that time that Dad stole the chain saw.

"I told you he had glasses," the security guard said. "He was spying."

The cop ignored him. "What's your name?"

It's a terrible thing to know that the minute somebody knows your name they'll think you're a thief. It made me feel hurt and sore and confused. I thought about giving the cop a false name, but I didn't dare. It would be worse if he caught me lying. I decided that at least I wouldn't be ashamed of it, and I looked the cop in the face and said, "My name's Harry White."

The cop squinted at me. "You one of the Whites out on Mountain Pass Road?"

"That's where I live," I said.

"Where'd you get the glasses?"

There was nothing to do but tell the truth. "My dad gave them to me."

"White," the security guard said. "I know who those people are. Stole the glasses, you can count on it."

The cop waved his hand at the security guard to shut him up. "You can't go accusing people of stealing without proof," he said. Then he turned back to me. "Sure your dad gave them to you?"

I was beginning to lose my temper, which I knew I shouldn't do. "He gave them to me," I said.

The cop looked at me some more. "What are you doing out here?"

"Looking for birds," I said. "Somebody said there was a pileated woodpecker down by the carpet factory. I was looking for it."

"The carpet factory's across the river," the security guard said.

"I didn't want to get too close and scare it. I figured I'd try to spot it from this side of the river." I didn't know if they believed me, but it was a good story.

The cop went on staring at me. Then he said, "Get in the car."

"I didn't—"

"Get in the car."

I got in the back and sat there, feeling scared and sore and confused all at once. I just sat there with my feelings going every which way, wondering what they were going to do with me when they got me down to the police station.

But the cop didn't start the car. Instead he began talking into the radio. "Eddie," he said, "have we got anything on a pair of binoculars?" He turned around to me. "Let me see 'em." I unslung the binoculars and gave them to him. "Pair of seven by thirty-fives. Look new."

The radio crackled and sputtered, and I sat there waiting and sweating under my jacket as if it was July and not April. Then the voice came back on: "Nothing. Nothing recent anyways."

I was so relieved, I almost grinned. But I kept my face still. "See, I told you," I said.

The cop swiveled around in the seat and stared me in the face. "Okay," he said. "But stay away from here. This is private property. Next time I'll take you in and book you for trespass. Understand?" He handed the binoculars back.

I jumped out of there as fast as I could, and started walking for home. So maybe Dad hadn't stolen the binoculars after all. He hadn't stolen them from the Sports Center, anyway, because Old Man Greenberg would have reported them missing. You had to do that to collect the insurance. And, too, most other people around Timber Falls would have reported it to the police if they were stolen.

Still, why had they come without a box and the instructions and all? That was hard to explain. Dad wouldn't have taken them out of the box and then thrown the box away. He would have brought them home in the box.

Then something else came to me. Maybe they weren't new. Maybe he had bought them second-hand. That would explain why they hadn't come in a box. So maybe he hadn't stole them after all.

Thinking that made me feel a whole lot better—not just about the binoculars but about everything. Suddenly I began to feel pretty cheerful. I had a terrific pair of binoculars, and I'd found that pipe. That was the great thing. I'd found the pipe, and now I knew for sure that the carpet factory was polluting the Timber River. There wasn't any doubt about that. For one thing, there was that furrow: weeds grow up awful quick, especially in the spring, and if they weren't spilling stuff into the river from that pipe down the bank, there'd be something growing there even in April. For another thing, it was plain as could be that upstream from the factory the water was clear, and downstream from it, it was tinged green, with oil slicks on the surface. The proof was all there.

But would people believe it? Would the newspaper people believe it if some kid, especially one everybody thought was trash, came in and said that the carpet factory was polluting the river? I wasn't sure. I needed more proof, and the obvious thing was to take some photographs. It wouldn't be hard to take pictures of the pipe during the day, if I was willing to chance going out there again. But the best thing would be to go out there some night and get some pictures when there was stuff actually pouring into the river. That would be proof nobody could deny. But I had no camera, and how was I going to get one?

That night, after supper, I went outside and sat on the back step to think about it. There weren't any stars out, or any moon, because it was so overcast. I remembered a song we had at school that went, "My

Lord, what a morning, when the stars begin to fall."
It was about Judgment Day, when the sinners would
be judged. I wondered if that was right, did the people who did wrong ever get punished, or did they go
on getting away with stuff forever?

I sat there thinking about things like that, listening
to the peepers and smelling the cool damp of the
spring night. The only light came from the kitchen
window. It fell on the lawn in a yellow square. There
was a little breeze, and I knew I would have to put on
a sweater if I was going to sit out there very long.

I couldn't ask Dad about a camera, that was for
sure. I didn't know how much it would cost to get a
camera with a flash attachment, but I'd seen some
advertised on TV for around thirty bucks or something. It was the same story as raising money for
binoculars. I'd have been glad enough to work to
earn the money, but there wasn't much work around
for kids. Work was so short around Timber Falls that
grown men got the odd jobs. If somebody needed the
snow shoveled out of his driveway, or his lawn cut, he
would hire a grown man. People felt they ought to
give the work to a man with a family to support. They
even had grown-ups packing bags at the checkout
counters at the supermarkets, where in other towns
they had kids. I knew because there was a story about
it in the paper.

So I couldn't buy a camera; and I wasn't about to
steal one, even if I had the nerve to try it. The only
thing left was to borrow one, and there was nobody I
could borrow anything from.

I was sitting there worrying about that when I heard a voice, just a quick whisper, say "Harry."

At least I thought I heard it. I've had that happen before, where you distinctly hear somebody call your name, and you look around and there's nobody there, and you realize you've been hearing things. So I figured that's what it was this time, because who could be around?

But then it came again: "Harry."

"Who's out there?" I said.

"Shss, shss" came out of the dark.

"Who's there?" I whispered.

"It's me," the whisper came back. "I'm up by the barn."

It was Helen. I jumped up, ran quickly up toward the barn, and stood by the barn door looking around. It was pretty dark, and I couldn't see her.

"I'm in here," she said. "Don't turn on the lights." Then I saw her, just a black shape edged up against the barn door. I slipped inside where nobody could see me from the house, and she threw her arms around my neck and kissed me.

"Where've you been?" I whispered.

"Shsss," she said. "Let's go up in the loft. We can turn on a light up there. You can't see it from the house."

She started to climb up the loft ladder, in the dark, and I started up behind her. She was carrying something. "What's that?" I said.

"New suitcase," she said.

We got into the loft and, feeling our way through the furniture and junk, moved down to the other end. She turned on a little light she had rigged up with an extension cord that ran through a crack in the floor down to a plug below. She'd made a kind of little room at this end of the loft, sort of a private room where she could have guys over. I looked at Helen. She'd changed. She was wearing her old jeans, but she had on a fancy new pink blouse with a lot of frills down the front, and she had a new black purse hanging from her shoulder. She'd changed her hair, too: Instead of just hanging down the way she usually had it, it was piled up on top of her head. She had on a lot of makeup, too—lipstick, and stuff on her eyelashes and cheeks. She was different all right.

"Where've you been?" I said in a low voice, although I didn't think they could hear us in the house anyway.

"New York City," she said. "I've been down in New York City."

"I thought you might go there," I said. "Where are you staying?"

"I've got a place to stay with some people," she said. "Some other girls. Women, I guess."

"You mean they just let you live there?" I said.

"I pay rent." She seemed proud of that. "I'm earning money."

"You got a job?" I said.

"Yes," she said. She unslung her purse, snapped it open, and held up a wad of bills. "Look," she said.

"Wow," I said. "What kind of job?"

"Just some kind of a job," she said.

"I mean in a store or something?"

"Here," she said. She took a hundred-dollar bill out of the stack and handed it to me. "Keep it," she said.

"A hundred dollars?" I said. "A hundred dollars?" I'd never had that much money in my life.

"Sure," she said. "Keep it. I've got plenty of money."

I wondered where she was getting all that money from. "Somebody at school heard you were dealing drugs."

"Oh, them," she said. "Those kids don't know anything. They don't know anything about New York. Why do I care what they think, Charlie Fritz and those guys. They're just a bunch of hicks."

"Are you sure you're not dealing drugs?" I said.

"Why should I deal drugs? I don't need to deal drugs. I've got plenty of money."

"You must have a pretty good job."

"Yeah," she said. Then she said, "Harry, you ought to see what it's like down there. There's anything you want there. You can go to the movies all the time and eat anything you want to eat. We're always going to the movies, these women I'm living with, and we don't bother to cook but eat out most of the time, or send out for stuff. If I want some beer or wine or something, they get it for me."

I decided I wouldn't ask her where she was getting the money from anymore. "How old are these women? Do they drink a lot?"

"They're in their twenties, I guess. They drink some, but mostly they get high. They get high all the time. I can, too, if I want. They don't mind giving me joints if I want to get high."

"Aren't you worried about the cops?"

"No," she said. "Down in New York the cops don't care what you do. Sometimes I can't believe it, being down there."

"Don't you miss home any? Don't you ever get homesick?"

She frowned. "Well, sometimes," she said. "The first couple of nights I was pretty homesick."

"Did you hitch down?"

"Yes," she said. "A guy picked me up and took me down to the thruway, and then I got a couple of rides to Albany and after that somebody took me to New York City."

"Weren't you scared riding with strange guys?"

"Yeah, sort of. The first guy kept reaching over to pat me on the leg or on my shoulder or something, and the guy that took me down to New York wanted me to go out to dinner with him and go to a nightclub and stuff, but I jumped out at a red light. I said, 'Thanks for the ride, I have to get off here,' and I jumped out. But I tell you, Harry, it didn't matter if I was scared, it didn't matter what those guys did to me, anything was worth it to get away from here." Suddenly she looked hard and angry. "I'm never coming back here as long as I live."

I didn't like to hear her say that. I would miss her a lot. "It isn't so bad here," I said.

"Yeah, sure," she said. "Yeah, sure. You know what they think about us in Timber Falls. They think we're nothing. They think we're the scum of the earth."

It was the first time she'd ever admitted it. "I used to tell you that," I said. "You would never believe it."

"Who would want to believe something like that?" She was still looking hard and sore. "Who would want to believe that your family is the scum of the earth? It's because of Mom and Dad. It's because Dad won't get a regular job and Mom wouldn't keep us clean and all that."

I decided I wouldn't say anything about Dad stealing. It would make her hate Timber Falls even more. "And having a junky house," I said, "with the paint peeling off and old cars in the yard."

"I'm never coming back," she said. "After this I'm never coming back."

"It's making Mom sad," I said.

"I don't care," she said. "I don't care if she dies of sadness. I don't care if they both die."

That kind of talk scared me a little. "You don't really want them to die, do you?"

"Yes, I do. Yes, I do." She put her hands over her face and started to cry, but then she stopped herself. "Listen, Harry, I came up to get my clothes and stuff. You have to help me get it. I'll pay you."

"You don't have to pay me. You already gave me a hundred dollars." I wondered why she came all the way home for those old clothes when she had all that money.

"That wasn't for anything," she said. "That was for nothing."

"How am I going to get your stuff out of there? I mean Mom will go up there and see everything gone."

"I'll be out of here by that time. The minute you get the stuff out, I'll pack it in the suitcase and go."

"Dad might not be around tomorrow," I said. "Sometimes he takes off on Sundays."

"We have to do it tonight," she said. "We have to wait until they're asleep. Then you can go into my room and throw the stuff out the window. I'll pack it up and hitch over to Watertown. I can get a bus there."

"I don't know if I can stay awake until they go to bed," I said.

"They don't stay up too late," she said. "You can have some coffee."

It worked out just the way she figured. I went back into the house, and upstairs, and opened Helen's window. Then I went downstairs and sat watching TV with Mom and Dad for a while. They stayed up for the news and then they went to bed. I went up and lay there on my bed for a while. After a little I shut off my light like I was going to sleep, and went on lying there in the dark with my clothes on. When I figured they were asleep, I tiptoed into Helen's room and looked out the open window. I could hardly see anything, but I could just make her out waiting out there. I threw her stuff down. There wasn't much of it: a pair of jeans, a couple of blouses, a sweater, some underwear, a pair of beat-up running shoes, and a pair of regular shoes. It wouldn't anyway near fill the suitcase she'd brought.

When I'd flung everything down, I decided to take a chance and go down to say good-bye. If Mom and Dad woke up, I'd say I thought I heard a raccoon trying to open the garbage cans. So I crept out of Helen's room, down the stairs, and out the kitchen door. Helen was around the side of the house jamming her stuff into the suitcase. She wasn't folding it or anything—just jamming it in. I knelt down and helped her, and then without saying anything, we went down the dirt driveway and out onto the road. We could hardly see each other. The peepers were still going and it was pretty chilly.

"You ought to put on your sweater," I said.

Suddenly she put her arms around me and squeezed me. "Sometimes I get so homesick. I keep on missing you, Harry."

"Maybe you ought to come back," I said.

"No," she said. "I'm never coming back. I get homesick sometimes, but I'm never coming back."

"There's nobody for me to talk to now," I said.

"I know," she said. She took her arms off me. "I didn't really come up to get those clothes," she said. "I just missed you. I came up to see if you were all right."

"I'm okay," I said.

"In three more years you'll graduate and you can leave too."

I didn't say anything. So she squeezed me again. "Well, I better get going." She turned and started walking off fast down the road. In a moment I couldn't see her anymore. I wondered when I would ever see her again.

SEVEN

It took Mom three or four days to realize that Helen's stuff was missing. I guess she was trying to stay away from Helen's room and forget about her, but one day, just as I was coming in through the kitchen door after school, she was coming down the stairs with a funny look on her face. "Harry, Helen's clothes are gone."

I tried to look surprised. "Gone?" I said.

"Yes, they're gone," she said. "You don't know what happened to them, do you?"

"I didn't do anything with them," I said.

"I know you didn't," she said. "You're a good boy, Harry." She stopped to think. "Maybe your dad packed them away."

But when he came home for supper, he was just as surprised as she was. He went upstairs and stood in the middle of Helen's room, looking around. There wasn't much to see—a few of her books under her bed, and some makeup on one of the windowsills.

"Nobody would have stolen the stuff," he said. "It wasn't worth stealing." He stood in the middle of the room scratching his head. "I'll bet she took her clothes herself. I'll bet she came up here some time when nobody was home and took them herself." He gave me a quick look. "You haven't seen her, have you, Harry?"

"No," I said.

He cocked his head and stared at me, but I managed to give him a straight look. "It had to be her," he said. "If anyone wanted to steal something from around here, they wouldn't have taken a few old clothes. They'd have taken the TV or some of the tools out of the barn. It had to be her."

"You mean she was here?" Mom said. "And she didn't want to see us?" She put her hands over her face and began to cry. It made me feel awful to see her cry like that, when I knew where Helen was.

"At least we know she's all right, Doris," Dad said.

Mom went on crying. "I don't care," she said. "I want my baby back. I miss her so much. I want her back."

"She's sixteen, Doris," Dad said. "She'd have left home in a couple of years anyway."

"Maybe she wouldn't have," Mom said. She tried to stop crying and it made her gasp. "Maybe she would have gone on living at home."

The whole thing seemed weird to me. How could Mom think Helen would want to go on living in some junky place like ours with a tough father who paid hardly any attention to anybody and a mom who spent all her time in a bathrobe watching TV? Didn't they know anything about us? But I didn't say anything.

"Doris, that's wishful thinking," Dad said. "Helen's pretty, she's bound to get married soon anyway. Maybe that's what happened. Maybe she and her boyfriend ran off to get married." He looked at me. "Who's her boyfriend, Harry?"

He'd already forgotten that I'd told him she didn't have a boyfriend. "I don't think she had a boyfriend," I said.

Mom shook her head. "Helen wasn't interested in boys," she said. She stopped crying and wiped her eyes on her bathrobe. "She told me so. Once I asked her if she had a boyfriend, and she said no, she wasn't interested in boys. Helen's young for her age. She's still my baby." She looked like she was going to start crying again, but she didn't.

Of course Helen had to tell Mom she wasn't interested in boys. How else could she explain why she didn't have a boyfriend? Could she tell Mom that she didn't have a boyfriend because all the boys thought she was trash? I couldn't stand thinking about it anymore, and I went out to the barn to see if I could get the lawnmower started. The grass was getting long and it was about time I started cutting it. It was always a problem getting the mower started the first time each spring.

The main thing was, now I had the hundred bucks that Helen had given me. That meant that I could buy some kind of camera to take photographs of that pipe with. For I was determined to go back there again, regardless of the risk. I would just be more careful this time.

The big problem was the hundred-dollar bill. If I tried to pay for the camera with a hundred-dollar bill, they were bound to think I'd stolen it. Any other kid could say he'd got it from his father, or his grandfather had given it to him for his birthday, or something, and they'd believe him.

Could I say that my sister had sneaked up from New York and had given it to me? No, I couldn't just spend the hundred-dollar bill the way anyone else could. I'd have to get it changed into fives and tens first, which wouldn't look so suspicious.

I wished I'd thought of it and asked Helen to give me tens instead of a hundred. But it was too late for that. The big question was, where to cash it?

In the end I had to ask Dad to change it. I hated to do it, because I knew what he would think. But I didn't have any choice. So one night at supper I said, "Dad, I found a hundred-dollar bill."

"What?" he said. "You found a hundred dollars?" He gave me a look. "Where?"

"On the street," I said. "In front of the bank. Somebody must have dropped it when they came out."

He squinted at me. "In front of the bank?"

"I want to change it, but I figure if I asked them to change it at the bank, they'd think I stole it or something."

"Found it?" he said. He gave me a grin. "Sure, you found it."

I expected that, but it made me mad anyway. "I didn't steal it," I said.

"Did I say you stole it?" he said.

I was feeling plenty hot. "You can't say I stole it."

"Frank, Harry wouldn't steal," Mom said. Then she looked at me. "You didn't steal it, did you, Harry?"

"I didn't steal it, everybody," I said.

"You see, Frank," Mom said. "He didn't steal it."

"Okay, he didn't steal it," Dad said. "Give it to me, and I'll cash it for you."

The truth was, I didn't want to give it to him. I didn't really trust him. I thought he might have a hundred dollars in his wallet and could change it right then. But I realized that he probably didn't have a hundred dollars on him very often. So I handed over the bill. He tucked it into his wallet, and the next day he brought me back the change in tens. He counted off ten ten-dollar bills, and then he took one off the top and put it into his pocket. "I figure anybody who is that rich can make a contribution to the household expenses," he said.

It made me good and mad, but I didn't dare say anything, for I knew that if I argued with him, he'd just take another ten to show me who was boss.

The next day after school I went to the drugstore and bought a camera. It was an Olympus with a built-in flash and timer so you could take pictures of yourself. I bought a lot of color film, and extra batteries, and a case for it. The whole thing cost fifty-five dollars. It was a lot of money, but at least I was getting something for it.

It felt really good to have my own camera. I took it home, put it down on the kitchen table, and sat there staring at it. I really loved looking at it. I loved looking at the dials and the various buttons and knobs for switching on the flash or the timer, so you could take a picture of yourself. I figured I'd do that; I figured if nobody else would take the pictures of me when something interesting was happening, I'd take them myself. I just wished Helen was back. I could have taken a lot of pictures of her. She would have liked that.

Mom came out into the kitchen and saw the camera. "Oh, my," she said. "What a fancy camera. How much did it cost?"

I told her.

"My goodness," she said. Then she looked at me. "Harry, you didn't steal that money, did you?"

"Mom, I didn't steal it."

"Honestly?"

"I swear it, Mom."

"You've always been a good boy," she said.

"I wouldn't steal anything," I said. I hoped that was true. It still worried me that maybe someday I would.

She sighed. "I wonder if you should have returned the money."

"Returned it? Who would I return it to?"

"Why, the bank."

She was right, of course. If I'd really found it the way I'd said, I probably would have taken it into the bank and asked if they knew who'd lost it. But, of course, I hadn't found it—Helen had given it to me. "How would they know who lost it?"

She sighed again. "Yes, I suppose that's right. You deserve it, Harry."

I didn't know if I did. But I was going to keep it. To

change the subject, I told Mom I would take some pictures of her, to try out the camera. She made me wait until she put on a dress instead of her bathrobe and combed her hair. She kept fussing and fidgeting like she'd never had her picture taken before. To tell the truth, I guess it had been a long time since she'd had her picture taken. The only pictures of her that I'd ever seen were the one of her holding me when I was a baby, and a couple that she and Dad had taken on their wedding day, which were in a double frame on the dresser in their bedroom. They were just pictures of Mom and Dad, looking young, standing with their arms around each other in front of an old brick building in Watertown—the courthouse, or the justice of the peace's office, or something. So I took some pictures of her, and when she discovered about the self-timer, she had me take some pictures of the two of us standing there together.

After I'd taken a bunch of pictures of Mom, I went outside and took some more, some with the flash and some without. And that night, after it was good and dark, I walked down the dirt driveway until I was a good way from the barn—about as far as I figured I'd be from the pipe when I was photographing it—and took some flash pictures. I shot up the whole two rolls on these various tests, and the next day I took them into the drugstore to get them developed. They came back the next Monday. They were pretty good, and I was satisfied that I'd be able to get good pictures.

Mom was tickled over the shots I'd made of her. When she dressed up and combed her hair, and smiled the way she did for the camera, she really looked pretty. At supper she showed them to Dad. He said it was a lot of middle-class baloney, but a couple of days later I noticed that he'd got one of them taped up in the cab of the truck. And later, when I got to meet my grandparents for the first time, I saw sitting on their mantelpiece in a little frame a picture of me and Mom standing side by side. Mom had sent it to them that Christmas. But that was later.

Now I was all set, and I was pretty nervous. If they caught me out there again, they were sure to know that I wasn't watching any birds, I was up to something. I was bound to get into serious trouble with the police. It wouldn't be just trespassing; they'd figure out something worse to charge me with.

But going out there at night would be an advantage. For one thing, the security guard wouldn't be able to see me—at least not until I fired off the flash. For another, if anyone did come after me, they'd have an awful hard time finding me in the dark woods. Somehow, I could manage to lose them and escape. There was an awful lot of woods in the Adirondacks to hide in.

It rained the whole next weekend. I hadn't been able to get the lawnmower started before, so I spent most of the weekend working on it. Because of the rain Dad was around a lot, and I knew he could get it started easy. He liked fooling around with engines, and he could usually get them to work. But I didn't want to be around him anymore. I didn't like the feeling of having him near me, his old work shirt and jeans, and the stubble on his face from not shaving. Once during the weekend he came out and stood there watching me strip the engine down. "Want some help?" he said.

"No," I said, not looking up. "I can do it myself." And I did. Once I got the jets cleaned out, and the air filter washed, and cleaned off the spark plug and put in fresh gas, it started. I was proud of myself, even if it had taken most of the weekend to do it.

All the next week I kept watching the weather report on TV, and by Thursday I knew it was going to be a good weekend—sunny and seasonable weather, the way they say. I didn't care how warm it was, so long as it wasn't raining and the woods were dry. I knew I might have to sit out there with the camera for a while, and I didn't want to get soaked and start sneezing, or something.

It turned out to be a perfect day for cutting wood too. Dad had an order for a couple of cords, which would pay a hundred dollars. Whenever we got an order for cordwood, we went up into the woods that sloped up toward the mountains behind the house. It wasn't our land—we just rented the house—and we weren't supposed to cut wood there, but we always did. Dad was careful just to cut here and there so we wouldn't make a big clearing that would be obvious. He cut low to the ground, so that the stumps were practically flat, and if you kicked a little dirt over them, you wouldn't notice them unless you were looking for them. We mostly cut dead stuff, anyway, which burned easier. The people we rented from didn't come around much. Dad said they were afraid to because he might demand they fix up the house. I knew that wasn't it, though, because once Helen, after she got interested in guys, asked Mom why the people wouldn't fix up the house a little. Mom said it was because we paid such a low rent, Dad couldn't ask them to do anything to the house.

So we took Dad's old chain saw up into the woods and cut. Dad ran the chain saw, and I trimmed the branches off the logs and scattered the brush around the woods so it wouldn't be in a noticeable pile. In a couple of years it would begin to rot away. We worked all morning and into the afternoon, and then we drove the truck up into the woods as far as it would go, loaded it up, and drove around to the people who had ordered the wood.

It was a big house, one of these old farmhouses that somebody had spent a lot of money fixing up. It was white clapboard with big maple trees and a lot of lawn around it. A bluestone driveway circled around to the back. There was a new-painted red barn here, and some nicely pruned apple trees beside the barn. A Mercedes was parked on the bluestone. It was some place all right. I wondered what it would be like to have all that money and be able to have everything you wanted. Would I ever have that much money? I didn't think so; I didn't think you got paid a whole lot in the air force—just a good salary. It kind of hurt to know that I'd never be rich. Dad always said that money corrupted people, and he wished he was corrupted. I didn't know if it did or it didn't, but I sure wished I had money.

We crunched over the bluestone and stopped be-

hind the house. A man came out of the kitchen door
and started walking toward the truck. He was wearing blue jeans with a crease in them and a bright red
flannel shirt and shiny loafers.

"That's Herbst," Dad said in a low voice. "He's one
of the biggies at the carpet factory. House cost a half
million dollars to do over. They practically had to
rebuild it. You don't get that kind of money running a
chain saw. You squeeze it out of the working people."

Mr. Herbst came up to the truck, and Dad and I
got out. Dad spit on the bluestone. It was his way of
showing Mr. Herbst that he was as good as Mr.
Herbst was, and wasn't going to take anything from
him.

Mr. Herbst looked at the wood. "Is it good and
dry?"

I knew it wasn't, but Dad didn't lie about it.
"Mixed," he said. "Some dry and some green. You
want a mix. Green burns hotter and slower." He spit
again.

Mr. Herbst didn't say anything but turned and
started to walk back to the house. "I want it in the
basement," he said. "I'll show you where."

We followed him into the house through the
kitchen door. I'd never seen such a kitchen in my life.
It was gleaming and bright and spotless, and it had
everything you could want—a fancy stove, a wall
oven, a dishwasher, a garbage compactor, a micro-
wave oven, and other stuff I couldn't figure out. It
was some kitchen.

The cellar door was across the kitchen from the
back door. They'd laid newspapers on the floor tiles

so we wouldn't mess the floor when we carried the wood in. "This your boy, Frank?" Herbst said.

"He's my boy," Dad said.

Mr. Herbst looked at me. "You go to school, son?"

"Yes," I said. "I'm in ninth grade." It felt pretty funny to me to be talking to one of the biggies from the carpet factory, knowing that pretty soon I was going to go out there and catch them polluting the river. It didn't scare me exactly; it just felt funny.

He stared at me. "The police picked up a kid with a pair of binoculars out at the plant a couple of weeks ago," he said. "That wasn't you, was it?"

I was shocked that he knew about it, and I flashed hot. There wasn't any use in lying about it, though. "I was looking for birds," I said.

"What's this?" Dad said. "You didn't tell me you got picked up by the cops."

He didn't really care if I got picked up by the cops. He was just acting that way so he would look like a good father.

"It wasn't anything," I said. "I was looking for a pileated woodpecker that somebody said was in there, and the cops wanted to know what I was doing. They thought I stole the binoculars." The minute I said that I wished I hadn't.

"Who said you stole them?" Dad said. "Nobody's going to make accusations like that to me. I'm not going to put up with it."

"It wasn't anything, Dad," I said. "They checked and found out they weren't stolen."

Dad's jaw was jutting out. "They better have," he said.

Mr. Herbst didn't say anything; he just stood there listening, and I was embarrassed to have this conversation in front of him. Finally he said, "You'll see where the wood is stacked. There's beer in the refrigerator when you're finished." Then he went out of the kitchen through a swinging door.

EIGHT

That night I sat on the back steps, watched the stars come out—and I thought about it. It seemed strange to me that Mr. Herbst had known about me getting picked up by the cops out by the carpet factory. He was one of the biggies there: why would they have bothered him about finding some kid in the woods looking for birds? They wouldn't have, unless they believed there was more to it—unless they were suspicious and had guessed that I wasn't really looking for birds. That worried me a good deal because it gave me the idea that they didn't really believe my story. What were they thinking? Who actually knew about the pollution pipe?

I didn't think that most of the people who worked at the carpet factory would know about it. If they did, somebody would have been bound to report it to the police, or tell the editors of the *Journal*. But a few of them had to know about it. Whoever it was who turned the valve had to know about it, and probably several people were in on that. Then the security guards had to know about it. I didn't know how many security guards they had, but if they only had one on duty at a time, each guard working an eight-hour shift, that made three; and it seemed likely to me that there would be more than one on duty during the daytime, when they had to have somebody on the gate. And, of course, at least some of the biggies knew about it. When you added it up, it seemed like at least a dozen people must have known about that pollution pipe. So it wasn't any big secret, and why would they worry about me finding out?

But maybe I was wrong about it. Maybe the security guard was the one who turned the valve to let the chemicals run into the river. Maybe the only people who knew about it were the guard himself and one of the biggies like Mr. Herbst. *He* knew about it, that was plain, because the security guard had told him about me being out there with binoculars, and they wouldn't have told him if they hadn't been worried about me spotting that pipe.

The only thing that was clear about it was, they didn't want anybody spotting that pipe. It was chancy for them, I figured, because they could never tell when a hunter might be out there; or somebody looking for birds; or some people just having a walk in the woods after Sunday dinner. Anybody could spot that pipe by chance, and they had to be worried about that. And I guessed that was why the security guard told Mr. Herbst that he had caught me out there. Even if it had been true that I was only a kid looking for birds, they had to be worried that I had seen that pipe and might report it.

Did they believe my story? I figured they probably did: why would they suspect some ninth-grade kid of going out there to look for that pipe? But if they caught me out there again, especially at night with a camera, I could lie until I was blue in the face, and they wouldn't believe me. Then what would they do? They would want to keep me quiet, that was sure, and how would they go about that? They'd be sure to press some kind of charges against me so as to get me sent away to a place for juvenile offenders.

I was beginning to feel like maybe I ought to forget about the whole thing. If something went wrong, I was going to be in an awful lot of trouble. Once I'd been convicted of a crime, I'd never get into the air force. There wouldn't be a chance of that. There wouldn't be any chance of getting respected around Timber Falls after that either. Having Helen run off hadn't helped improve our reputation. It didn't matter that she had good reason to run off, and it didn't matter where she was, and what she was doing. They all believed that she had run off to do something bad, and *was* doing something bad.

So there were a lot of good reasons for giving the whole thing up. But I didn't want to do it. There was something stubborn in me that wouldn't let me quit. I wanted to do it, and I was going to take the chance.

The real danger would be in shooting off the flash camera. I'd be safe enough going out there at night. There was never much traffic on that beat-up blacktop road. Anyway, I could spot the headlights of a car coming along, long before they would see me, and I could duck into the woods until it went past. So I'd be safe enough getting out there; and once I got into the woods, I'd be safe enough there.

But the minute I shot off the flashgun they'd know it. Well, there would always be the hope that the security guard would be around the other side of the factory when I shot the camera off, and wouldn't see the flash, but I couldn't take a chance on that. The minute I shot the flash off I would have to run for it. It would take ten minutes for the security guard or the cops or anybody to get out there, and in ten minutes I could run a mile on up the road and hide in the woods. There wasn't any way you could find somebody in the woods, especially at night, unless you tracked them with dogs, and I didn't think the Timber Falls cops had dogs. There was another bridge across the river two or three miles farther upstream. I could make my way up there, and be home in half an hour. If worst came to worst, I could swim across the river and go home cross-country through the woods. It wouldn't be much fun hiking home through the woods wet, but it would be safe. There were an awful lot of woods around there for them to search through.

So that was the plan. I waited a couple of days to give myself time to see if there were any flaws in it. I couldn't find any, so on Wednesday, after supper, I sneaked the camera and the binoculars out into the yard and hid them under a bush. Then I swiped Dad's flashlight out of the truck. It was a big one, the kind that takes four batteries, and had a powerful beam. I wondered if he had stolen it. Suppose they found out that the binoculars were stolen after all, and the flashlight, too—they'd put me down for a thief in a minute, and send me away. It was the chance I'd have to take.

I hid the flashlight under the bush, with the camera and binoculars. The stars were bright; it was going to be another clear night. I went into the house and watched TV with Mom and Dad to stay awake. They went to bed after the ten o'clock news. I went upstairs, too, got under the blankets with my clothes on and my shoes off, and waited until I figured they were asleep. Then I picked up my shoes, slipped down the stairs in my stocking feet and out the kitchen door. I sat down on the back step, put my shoes on, and then collected the stuff I'd hidden under the bush. I stuck the flashlight through my belt, slung the binoculars around my neck, and buttoned them and the camera under my jacket. Then I took off, jogging for a hundred yards, then walking for a while, and then jogging again. The moon was just beginning to come up through the trees.

There weren't many cars out. I didn't need to hide yet, so when I saw one coming, I would stop jogging and just walk casually along like some kid on the way home. Finally I got to town. I went through as quickly as I could without looking suspicious. If a cop who knew who I was spotted me, he was bound to ask me where I was going, and I'd have to lie and go home.

But nobody bothered me, and in a couple of minutes I was out of the town and across the steel bridge.

I went along the beat-up blacktop road that led out to where the pollution pipe was. Now I would have to be more careful; but no cars came along, and in a little while I turned off the road, into the woods.

The moon was up, and it was about as bright a night as it could be. In the open you could easily see a person fifty yards away. If anybody was watching, they'd have seen me slip into the woods, for sure. In the woods it was darker, and I couldn't see the brush underfoot very well. But the tree trunks were clear enough, and I was able to move along at a pretty good pace. It would have helped to use the flashlight, but of course I didn't dare. You could spot a light moving through the woods a long way off.

In a bit I began to hear the river rustling along through its banks. I slowed down and went forward easy and quiet as I could, and soon I could see the long white shine of moonlight glinting on the water I dropped flat, crawled forward until I was right at the edge of the riverbank, and lay there staring out across the river.

The carpet factory was about fifty yards farther upstream from where I was. I didn't have any trouble seeing it: spotlights on the corners of the building were shining down into the parking lot, and there were more lights on posts at various places in the parking lot. Only a couple of cars were in the lot, and some trucks had been pulled up to the loading docks. I didn't see any people—no security guard or anyone else.

I pulled back into the woods and made my way upstream past the factory building, until I was opposite the point where I figured the pipe stuck out of the riverbank. I dropped down, crawled forward to the edge of the bank, and lay there looking out. The moon on the river was almost as bright as day, and I could see it flash and shine as the water rippled along. But the opposite bank was a different story. The moonlight fell on the bank at an angle, and it was hard to make out anything on it. It looked like patches and scraps of light and dark. I could hardly make out the shape of anything.

I saw right away the mistake in my plan. Unless I managed to spot the pipe, I would have to use my flashlight, and that would give me away. I wished I'd had sense enough to make some kind of mark on a tree or something, to show where the pipe was. Or maybe memorized something on the opposite bank just above the pipe, like a tree with a crooked branch or a fork. But it was too late for that.

I lay there staring across, tipping my head this way and that way, hoping to catch a glimpse of that straight black edge that would tell me where the pipe was. But I didn't see anything.

Maybe I was in the wrong place. Maybe the pipe was a little farther upstream or farther down. I slid back from the riverbank, went along a little bit, and took another look. I moved my eyes carefully along the bank, turning my head slowly. Still nothing. So I moved back down in the other direction, hoping that if I got a different angle on it I'd spot it. But I didn't.

Now what? I pulled the flashlight out of my belt and held it in my hand. It was a powerful light, so I was sure I'd be able to find the pipe pretty easily if I used it. But it would be pointing directly at the carpet factory, and there was no way that the security guard could miss it. Suppose it took a little while to find the pipe. Every minute it took would cut into my escape time.

I thought for a minute. One thing I could do would be to go home, come back again in the daylight, and mark the spot where the pipe was. Then I'd have to come back again another night to take the picture. The whole idea of that made me feel sick, for it meant coming out here twice more, and the risk of getting caught was a lot more. No, I'd better get the whole thing done now.

Then another idea came to me. I was bound to hear the noise when the pollution came splashing out. At least it seemed to me that I would, even over the rustling of the river. That would tell me where the pipe was, and I could take a couple of quick shots with the camera and make a run for it. It would be better that way because it would give me positive proof that they were dumping chemicals into the river.

So I sat there near the riverbank, listening to the noises of the night—the river sound and the peepers, and once a car going along the road. After a while I realized that I had dozed off. I rubbed my eyes and yawned, and shook my head to get the sleepiness out of it, and for a moment I felt wide awake. Then I started to doze again. I shook myself awake once more, but I knew that sooner or later I would fall asleep.

That was no good because I might be sound asleep

when the stuff poured out into the river. Now what? Either I had to forget about the whole thing and go home, or I had to take a chance. If I found the pipe right away, I'd be all right. I sat there thinking, and trying to get my nerve up. Finally I got up on my knees, set the flash on the camera, and laid it on the ground right in front of me where I'd be able to grab it in a hurry. Then I raised up the flashlight to point it out to about where I thought the pipe might be, took a deep breath, and turned it on.

The beam hit the opposite bank. No pipe. I moved it quickly left and right. Still no pipe. I swung it farther upstream, darting it back and forth along the bank, but now it was at a sharp angle and making a lot of shadows dance and leap around as I moved it. I'd never see the pipe among those shadows even if it was there. I stood up, and just then I heard the sound of a car starting by the carpet factory, and in ten seconds a Jeep came racing across the empty parking lot toward the riverbank. I grabbed up the camera and began to work my way through the trees as fast as I could move, tripping on the underbrush and bumping into things. When I'd made fifty feet, I snapped the flashlight on again and beamed it across the river. Still no pipe. I snapped the flashlight off, and then a spotlight from the Jeep hit the trees over my head. I was making a mess of the whole thing, and I knew I ought to forget about the pipe and make a run for it. There was bound to be a radio in the Jeep, and for sure the security guard had already called the police.

I ducked back into the woods. "Hey you," a voice

shouted. I looked across. The security guard was standing beside the Jeep, working the spotlight through the woods a little upstream from me. His other hand was on the butt of the pistol in his holster. As the light came around to point directly at me, everything disappeared into a great shining haze. I put my head down to get the light out of my eyes and prayed that he wouldn't see me.

Now what? Should I run for it? Where was that pipe? Was it back down the river in the other direction? What should I do? Across the river the man was shouting again. "Come on out of there, you. Come on out onto the bank where I can see you."

Cold sweat was dripping down my face. Keeping low, I began to work my way through the woods back downstream, until I was below the place where I had first turned on the flashlight. I wondered if the security guard would take a shot at me when I turned on the flashlight. I snapped on the light, and the beam hit the opposite bank. There was the pipe, and flowing out of it was a steady stream of liquid that shone green in the light. I hadn't been able to hear it after all. The guard shouted again, and the spotlight from the Jeep began to swing along toward me. I dropped flat, to be low in case he took a shot at me. Then I raised up the flash camera, sighted at where I'd seen the pipe, and fired it. The spotlight fell on me, and if the guard wanted to shoot me, he had a pretty good target. I shone the flashlight across the river again to make sure the pipe was there, rewound the camera, and fired it again. Then I grabbed up the flashlight and ran through the woods as fast as I could, banging into things, stumbling, and falling. In a minute I burst out onto the road, and here came the police cars, two of them, their spotlights shining into the woods as they came.

NINE

They told me to get in, and they took me down to the police station. The police station wasn't much. It was just a couple of rooms in the back of the old redbrick town hall. There were two cells behind the rooms. I knew because our class had gone there once when we'd had a tour of the town for social studies. I wondered if they were going to lock me in one of the cells.

They took me inside the station. There wasn't much to see. A fat cop who usually directed traffic at the school in the mornings was sitting behind a desk covered with papers. A radio sat on a table near to him. On one wall was a long bench, and on the opposite wall, a small table with a coffeepot on it, cups, a container of milk, and a box of doughnuts. Those doughnuts looked mighty good to me.

The cops who brought me in made me sit down on the bench, and then they went outside again. The fat cop at the desk didn't even look at me. I just sat there alone, feeling lousy—not scared so much as just low as could be. Everything was finished and done with. They would call my dad, that was for sure, and he was bound to belt me a few times for getting him into trouble with the cops.

Oh, how I wished I'd never started the whole thing. Oh, how I wished I'd minded my own business and put up with being trash and gone along until I graduated and could get into the air force. Why had I started this crazy thing? Why hadn't I had more sense?

But what had I really done wrong? Was there anything wrong with trying to catch the factory polluting the Timber River? That was against the law. Was there anything wrong with trying to stop people from breaking the law? Sure, I'd trespassed. That was true. But around Timber Falls everybody trespassed all the time. Outside of town there was nothing but woods and fields and mountains, and nobody knew who most of it belonged to, and nobody cared. They fished and hunted and went on picnics and walks wherever they wanted to go, and nobody paid any attention. Around there trespassing was hardly a crime. So what had I done wrong? Nothing, really. I was going to end up being convicted of stealing mainly because my name was White.

I began to get mad. It wasn't right and it wasn't fair. I thought about standing up and telling the fat cop at the desk that I hadn't done anything and they couldn't keep me there. But I decided I'd better not make things worse, so I just sat there and waited to see what would happen.

Ten minutes went by and then twenty. I was surprised. It wouldn't have taken Dad that long to come down there. But he didn't come; I was trying to figure out why, when the door opened and Mr. Herbst came in. That was a shock all right. He was wearing his creased jeans and loafers and a fancy heavy sweater that buttoned up the front. The cops who had picked me up came in behind him. He looked like he'd got out of bed and dressed in a hurry. He stood in the middle of the room looking at me for a minute. Then he turned to one of the cops. "Where'd you actually find him?" Mr. Herbst said.

"We picked him up just as he was coming out of the woods."

"The same place?"

"No," the cop said. "Maybe a mile further back downstream toward town."

Mr. Herbst put his thumbs in his belt and looked at me for a while. The cops didn't say anything but waited for him to talk. It was clear enough that he was the boss there, not the cops, and he'd decide what was to be done with me. "Okay, Harry," he said finally. "What's this all about?"

"I was looking for birds," I said.

"In the middle of the night?"

"Owls," I said. "I was trying to photograph owls."

He stared at me for a minute more, trying to decide what to believe. Then he said, "What gave you the idea that there are owls in there?"

"I know they're there," I said. "When I was there before, I saw owl pellets."

Mr. Herbst looked at one of the cops. "I don't know anything about birds," he said. "Is that reasonable?"

The cop shrugged. "Could be. They have a bird club at school. Sometimes you see them along the roads with their field glasses."

Mr. Herbst looked back at me. "You belong to the bird club, Harry?"

It made me blush to think about that, I don't know why. "No," I said. "I just study birds on my own."

He stared me right in the face in that way he had, thinking. Finally he said, "Did you see any owls?"

"I think so," I said.

"You can see in the dark?"

"On a bright night like this you can. They're light-colored. That's why I came out tonight, because it's so bright."

"And you took a picture of it?"

"I hope so," I said. "I tried, anyway."

He reached out his hand. "Mind if I have a look at the camera?"

I didn't want to give it to him. I was suspicious of him. "I—"

But the cop shook a finger at me. "Give it to him, White." I handed it over.

He looked it over for a minute. "Brand-new," he said.

"The kid's got a lot of new stuff," the cop said. "Binoculars, big flashlight."

I was beginning to lose my temper. "I bought that camera," I said. "It's mine."

"Don't get smart, White," the cop said. "Where'd you get it?"

"It's mine," I said. "I bought it at the drugstore. I have a receipt."

"Where'd you get the money?"

I knew I ought to be polite and not make everything worse, but I couldn't help myself. "I don't have to tell you that," I said. "It's none of your business."

"Don't worry, White," the cop said. "We can find out."

Mr. Herbst hadn't been paying any attention but had been turning the camera over in his hands, examining it. Then he put the camera into the pocket of his jacket and said, "Let him go." That was all; nothing more. But I knew what he was going to do. He was going to develop the film to see what I had been taking pictures of.

"Hey," I said. "That's my camera. You can't take that."

"Don't worry, Harry. You'll get it back. I'm just going to borrow it for a few days."

"Hey, wait a minute," I said. But he turned and walked out of the police station. "Hey," I said to the cop. "That's my camera. He can't take it like that."

"He's just borrowing it, White," the cop said. "Now you better get out of here before you get into real trouble. You're lucky you got let off. We could have booked you for a dozen things. Now scram on home."

There wasn't anything I could do about it, and so I left, feeling sore and scared and pretty mixed-up. It wasn't right for them to take my camera, and it wasn't right for them to treat me the way they did. They were the ones who were breaking the law, not me; but still, somehow I felt that everything was all my fault, that I was some kind of a criminal. The only luck I had was that Mom and Dad didn't hear me come home.

I woke up late the next morning. I realized right away that I'd missed the school bus. Dad was already gone, and Mom had forgotten I was there. When I came down, she said, "Oh, dear, I didn't realize you were still here. I thought you'd gone."

I didn't want to go to school. Everything from last night was still bothering me too much. "I don't feel good," I said.

She put her hand on my forehead. "You aren't hot," she said.

"I feel like I'm getting a cold," I said. "I think I'll stay home." I ate two peanut butter sandwiches on toast, which was all there was for breakfast, and then I went upstairs and lay on my bed and thought.

The whole thing had come to nothing. Mr. Herbst had the film and my camera. I figured he'd give the camera back, but he sure wouldn't give the film back. He would burn it, and there would go my proof. I couldn't possibly dare to go back out to the carpet factory to take more pictures. If I got caught out there one more time, they were bound to do something to me. I didn't know what, but something.

Why hadn't they arrested me last night? Why hadn't they charged me? The answer was pretty clear. If they took me to court, it was bound to come out about the way the factory was polluting the river. So Mr. Herbst didn't want to make a fuss over it. He just wanted to keep the whole thing quiet. He would destroy the film, and give me my camera back so I wouldn't make a fuss about that either. And that would be the end of the whole thing.

I didn't see how I could stand three more years of high school—three more years of no friends, and nobody talking to me except to say something snotty about Helen; three more years of knowing that everybody was looking down on me, of knowing that when I went into a store the owners were particularly keeping an eye on me all the time I was in there. And now Helen was gone, and I didn't even have her to talk to. I missed her all right.

I wondered where she was and what she was doing. I hoped she wasn't getting into some kind of trouble. All that money she had, had made me pretty suspicious. I just hoped she wasn't dealing drugs. She could get into bad trouble for that.

I went along for three or four days to make myself forget it, and then one day when I was coming out of school and heading across the parking lot to get on the bus, a big Mercedes pulled up beside me. Mr. Herbst was driving. He opened the door on the passenger side. "Get in," he said. He was used to giving orders, I could tell. The way he did it you just automatically did what he told you. So I got in and slammed the door. When I looked out the side window, there was a bunch of kids staring at me. They were pretty surprised to see trash like me getting into a car like that. I didn't want to smile, because I wanted them to think it was a normal thing for me, but I couldn't help it.

Mr. Herbst pulled out of the parking lot. "I think we need to have a talk, Harry," he said. "Let's go

down to my office where we won't be interrupted."
He drove through town and out along the road to the
carpet factory. All the way he asked me questions
about myself—how I was doing in school, what my
hobbies were—and about our family and so forth. I
didn't trust him and I didn't tell him any more than I
had to, and finally we got to the carpet factory. He
pulled into a parking space by the front door that had
a little sign on it saying MR. HERBST. We got out, and I
followed him into the front corridor past a desk
where a receptionist sat answering the phone. Down
at the end of the corridor there was a door with a
glass panel in it. On the door was lettered FREDERICK
J. HERBST, PRESIDENT. He was a biggie all right, and I
was going to talk to him in his office. The whole thing
puzzled me.

We went into the office. There was a big desk, a
sofa, a big glass table with fancy magazines lying on
it, a bookcase full of books, a thick blue carpet on the
floor, and a couple of easy chairs. It was more like a
living room than an office. I wondered if presidents
of companies always had offices like that.

Mr. Herbst sat down behind the desk and told me
to sit in one of the chairs. Then he leaned back in his
chair with his hands behind his head and stared at me
for a while. He did a lot of staring at people. I figured
he did it to worry you. Finally he said, "I got that film
developed, Harry. You weren't taking pictures of
owls."

I didn't say anything. There wasn't anything I
could say.

"Who put you up to this?" he said.

"Nobody," I said. "I did it on my own."

He shook his head. "No, you didn't, Harry. No high school kid is going to start an investigation like this on his own."

"Nobody put me up to it," I said. I didn't like being called a liar, and I was starting to get sore. "It was my own idea."

He sat there with his hands behind his head staring at me for a while. Then he said, "Harry, you'd better tell me the truth. I can make life pretty tough for you. I have a lot of power in this town. If I tell those cops I want you booked, they'll book you. We'll get you for something. Trespassing, malicious mischief— something. We'll put you down as incorrigible and send you off to a juvenile home for a couple of years. That'll be on your record for the rest of your life."

I didn't know if he really could do it, or was just bluffing, but it scared me plenty anyway. "I told you the truth," I said. "I can't help it if you won't believe me."

He took his hands from behind his head, put them on the desk, and leaned forward, watching my face. "Did your dad put you up to it? Was it that?"

"Dad doesn't know anything about it," I said.

"Is he trying to blackmail me? Is that his game?"

"I told you, I did it on my own. Dad doesn't know anything about it."

"Harry, I've tried to be easy with you, but if you go on lying to me, I'm going to have to get tough."

"I'm not lying," I said.

"Yes, you are," he said.

I jumped up. "Don't call me a liar," I shouted. "I

never did anything wrong. You're the one who's doing wrong. You're dumping stuff into the Timber River. I saw that stuff coming out of that pipe. You're the one who's doing wrong, not me."

He leaned back in his chair again. "Okay," he said. "Calm down. Let's try to keep it on a friendly basis." He reached into a drawer and took out my camera. "Here's your camera." He slid it across the desk, and I picked it up and stuck it in my jacket pocket. He took his wallet out. "I owe you for a roll of film," he said. "Is ten bucks enough?"

"It was only three-fifty."

He handed me the ten across the desk. "Keep it," he said. "Call it even for the loan of the camera."

I didn't want to take the extra money, but I didn't have any change, so I put the ten in my pocket. Then he picked up his phone, pressed a button, and said, "Get a driver to take Harry White home." He got up, came around from behind his desk, and shook my hand. I didn't want to do that, either, but there wasn't any way out of it. "No hard feelings," he said. "We'll talk about it some other time. I sympathize with your viewpoint, but you've got to understand ours too." He let go of my hand. "Go out to the receptionist. Somebody will take you home. And when you see your dad tonight, ask him to give me a call."

TEN

I hated being pushed around that way. I hated being called a liar. I hated having him threaten to put me in jail and all the rest of it. He was the one who was breaking the law, not me. I'd seen that green stuff coming out of that pipe, even if I didn't have the pictures to prove it. I was a witness. And I knew where the pipe was—I wouldn't have any trouble finding it now. Suppose I went down to the newspaper and told them what I knew. They were bound to run a story about it, and then people in Albany would hear about it and send somebody out to investigate. I could show them where the pipe was, and in the end the people from Albany would make them stop the pollution. It might work after all. But should I do it? Maybe it would just get me in more trouble. Maybe I ought to forget the whole thing and just sweat out three more years of being trash. The more trouble I got into, the more I was likely to ruin my chances of getting into the air force.

That night, when Dad came in, I told him that Mr. Herbst wanted him to call. I didn't say anything about going to his office or any of that. I just said that I'd bumped into him on the street after school.

Dad said, "I don't like working for that rich slicker. He's too smooth for me, with those two-hundred-dollar shoes and those hundred-dollar shirts. What did he want?"

"I don't know," I said. "Do his shoes really cost two hundred dollars?"

"What difference does it make to him what they cost?" Dad said. "He's taking the money out of the hides of working people anyway."

"Do you work for Mr. Herbst a lot?" I said.

Dad shrugged. "I got to make a living," he said. He sat down and began taking off his shoes.

"I didn't mean that," he said. "I just wondered if you knew him."

"Yeah, I know him," Dad said. "I wouldn't trust him as far as I could throw him. He's slick."

For the first time I began to think that maybe there was something to what Dad always said about the biggies taking it out of the hides of the workingman. Herbst was doing something wrong, and he was going to a lot of trouble to cover it up. That didn't exactly mean that he was taking it out of anybody's hide, except the ones who wanted to fish in the Timber River. But it did seem like he didn't mind breaking the law and lying about it. Would he ever get caught? When the stars began to fall would the sinners really be judged?

For a couple of days I thought about it. Was there

any way Herbst could get me into trouble if I went to the editors of the *Timber Falls Journal* and told them what I'd seen? Could he go back now and get me for trespassing or something, or was it too late? He had a lot of power in town, he said, and I knew he was right, from the way the cops had let him decide what to do about me—letting him take my camera, which he had no right to, and all that. But what could he actually do to me?

I couldn't figure it out, but it worried me, and I kept wondering if I ought to drop the whole thing. For a while I thought about sending the newspaper an anonymous letter. There wouldn't be much use in that, though. In the first place, they wouldn't know who it was who could show them where the pipe was. In the second place, I wouldn't get any credit. Besides, Herbst was bound to know who had sent in the letter anyway.

The sensible thing, I knew, would be to drop the whole idea. But I didn't want to; I was tired of being pushed around and called a liar. So in the end I decided I would do it. I would write a letter to the paper and sign my own name to it. It might be risky, but it was better than being pushed around.

The next day I bought some letter paper and envelopes at the drugstore, and went home and sat up in my room writing the letter. It took me a long time to get it right. I didn't want to tell any lies about it, because if they caught me lying about part of it, they wouldn't believe any of it. But I didn't want to tell the whole truth, either—about how I'd started the whole thing to get people to respect me, or about being caught by the cops, and all of that. In the end I wrote:

> To the Editor:
> The carpet factory is deliberately polluting the Timber River. I know because I saw a green liquid coming out of a pipe in the riverbank near the factory. This is illegal, and somebody should tell the people at Albany about it.
>
> > Yours truly,
> > Harry White.

I wondered if the newspaper editors knew who I was. I wondered if they knew how everybody in town looked down on us because we stole, and Helen had run off, and Dad didn't have a regular job. Would the editors decide that being as I was a White I was a liar, and they shouldn't trust what I told them? I thought about putting on some kind of a PS saying that I wasn't a liar and they could trust me, but I couldn't think of any way of saying it that wouldn't sound silly, so I let it go. And the next day, after school, I went to the post office and mailed the letter.

The *Timber Falls Journal* came out on Thursdays. I mailed my letter on Monday, which meant that I had to wait a few days before the letter came out. I was pretty excited. When the letter came out, there was bound to be a lot of talk about it around town. I wondered what the kids at school would think. They would be pretty surprised all right, and a lot of them would wish that they'd thought up the idea first.

But I was nervous, too, for there was no telling

what Herbst might do. He would want to get me if he could. The question was whether he could or not.

Finally Thursday came. It drizzled all day, and after school I walked through the drizzle to the drugstore and bought a copy of the paper. I didn't want anybody to see me reading it—I didn't know why, I just didn't. So I went across Main Street and around in front of the railroad station. There was a bench on the station platform, with a roof over it, where people used to wait when they had passenger trains. I went and sat on the bench to keep out of the drizzle, and opened the paper. My hands were shaking and I felt weak. I flipped through the paper until I came to the "Letters to the Editor" column and raced down it.

My letter wasn't there. Maybe they had decided it was so important, they would put it in another part of the paper, I thought. I went back to the first page and went through the whole newspaper from beginning to end. The letter wasn't anywhere. I started from the back and went through the whole paper again, looking as carefully as I could, just to be sure I didn't miss anything. But my letter wasn't in.

I sat there watching the drizzle fall onto the shiny steel tops of the railroad tracks, and I wondered. I didn't want to think they had decided not to run my letter because I was trash and couldn't be trusted. Maybe it took them longer than a few days to get a letter in. Maybe they had others ahead of it. Or maybe you had to get your letter in a week in advance or something. There could be a lot of reasons why my letter wasn't in the paper. There was only one thing to do, and that was wait until next week's paper. So I balled the paper up, threw it into an oil drum they had for a trash can at the station, and went on home through the drizzle.

That night, when Dad came home from work, he said less than usual. He just walked into the house, poured himself a drink of whiskey, and didn't say anything to anybody. For a while he sat there at that scratched kitchen table drinking his whiskey. Then he said, "Harry, come out to the barn. I want to talk to you."

He'd found out something, that was for sure. He went out the door, and I went out behind him in the drizzling rain. When we got out to the barn, he leaned up against the workbench, which was all cluttered with tools and rags and bits of wood. I went over and leaned against the workbench, but a little way from him, so as not to be too close. I didn't look at him but stared out into the dark drizzle at the end of the day.

"I saw your pal Herbst today," he said. "He had me come over to his office."

"Oh," I said.

"He told me the cops caught you out there by the carpet factory taking pictures."

"I wasn't doing anything wrong, Dad—"

"Shut up," he said. "I didn't say you were. He said it wasn't likely anybody would get back in there again. They're going to put a chain fence around that whole area and put a couple of dogs in there. So stay away from there from now on. You might get hurt."

"I wasn't planning on—"

"Shut up. I haven't finished." He was being mighty tough, and I didn't understand why. "Now you listen to me close, Harry." He stopped and gave me a hard look to make sure I was taking him seriously. "I want you to forget all about anything you saw in there. I don't want you to say a word about it to anybody. Hear?"

"But, Dad," I said. "They're pollut——"

He hit me. He smacked me hard across the face. It spun my head around, and I staggered away from the workbench and almost fell. I was dazed and shook my head to try to clear it. His words seemed to be coming from a distance. "I told you," he said. "Just forget about it. Just forget it for good. You hear me?"

My head was clearing. I licked my lips. I could taste salt and I knew I was bleeding. I stared at him.

"You hear me, Harry?"

I knew he would hit me again if I didn't answer. "Yes," I said in a low voice. He turned and walked out of the barn and I sat down on the rough plank floor and began to cry. My face hurt, but that wasn't it. Why was Dad siding with Herbst, after all the terrible things he'd said about Herbst? He never liked Herbst. And he'd always said he himself was against pollution.

For a long time I sat there on the barn floor. I knew that Mom and Dad were in the kitchen eating supper. I was hungry, but I didn't want to see either of them. So I went on sitting there, getting hungrier and hungrier. Finally I got up and went down to the house. Mom was washing the dishes, and Dad was in the other room watching a baseball game.

"There's some hash on the stove, Harry," Mom said in a low voice. "I kept it warm for you."

It wasn't Mom's fault that Dad had hit me, but I didn't feel like saying thank you to anybody. So I just got a plate and helped myself to some hash out of the frying pan.

"Don't be too upset with Dad," she said. "He's only doing what he thinks is right for the family."

I didn't understand that. Why was hitting me right for the family? "He didn't have to hit me," I said. I sat down at the table with my plate of hash.

She sighed. "I know," she said. "But he said you gave him an argument."

Dad came into the kitchen. I wouldn't look at him, but bent my head down and started eating. He didn't say anything but put on his jacket and went out the kitchen door. In a moment we heard the truck start and drive away. And that was when I remembered that the next Thursday my letter about the pollution would come out in the paper. I sat there frozen, a forkful of hash stopped in midair. If that letter was published, he'd give me a real beating. I didn't understand why he was so strong on me keeping my mouth shut about the pollution pipe, but he was, and he would near beat me to death when that letter came out.

ELEVEN

"What's the matter, Harry?" Mom said.

"Nothing," I said. "I just thought of something." I shoved the forkful of hash into my mouth, but I didn't feel like eating any more. If that letter was published, I'd be finished. I just had to get it back.

The next afternoon I went over to the newspaper office after school. It was just outside of town, in the downstairs of an ordinary house. There was a regular front door with a wooden sign screwed onto it saying TIMBER FALLS JOURNAL. I was feeling pretty nervous. I didn't know if I was supposed to knock, or just walk in, or what. Finally I opened the door and went in. A little fence divided the room in half. Behind the fence were a slim young man and a woman with gray hair. They sat at desks heaped with papers, and beside each desk was a typewriter on a little green metal table. Behind them an open door led to another room. I could see a part of a desk through the open door.

The woman looked up at me. "Yes?" she said.

"I sent a letter to the editor last week," I said. "I changed my mind about getting it printed. I'd like to get it back if it isn't too late," I said, trying to be polite.

She smiled. "You changed your mind?"

"I decided I didn't want to get it printed," I said.

"We don't always print the letters we get," she said. "We might not have planned to print yours."

That was a relief, but I had to be sure. "It was about pollution at the carpet factory."

She gave me a funny look. "Oh, that letter," she said.

"Yes," I said. "I hope you won't print it."

She got up and walked through the open door into the room behind her. In a minute she came back and sat down at her desk again. An older man appeared at the open door. He had a gray mustache and was wearing an unbuttoned vest. He was smoking a pipe. For a minute he stood in the doorway looking at me. It made me feel like I'd done something wrong. "You wrote that letter?" he said finally.

"Yes," I said. I figured he was the editor. "I hope I can get it back, if it isn't a lot of trouble," I said, still trying to be polite.

He sort of nibbled on the mouthpiece of the pipe. "You're one of the Whites from Mountain Pass Road?"

I hated that. "Yes," I said.

But at least he didn't tell me to go away. "Come on in for a minute."

I opened the gate in the fence, went between the

two desks and into the back room. He had a big desk, which was also covered with papers, and a typewriter on a green metal table. There was a faded rug on the floor, bookshelves filled with books on one wall, a huge map of the Adirondacks on another, and a big, worn overstuffed chair in one corner. He pointed to the armchair. "Have a seat." I sat down, and he went behind the desk and sat down.

He nibbled at the pipe a little and then took a puff on it. "You actually saw a pipe out there by the carpet factory? Actually spilling something into the river?"

For a minute I thought about telling him it was all a lie, that I'd made the whole thing up. But I didn't want to make my reputation any worse than I had to. "Yes, I saw it. But I want to forget about it."

"Tell me exactly what you saw," he said.

That worried me. It sounded like he was trying to get information for a story. "I'd just as soon—"

"Don't worry," he said. "I'm not going to get you in trouble. Just tell me what it was."

There wasn't much of a way around it. "Well, it looked like a twelve-inch iron pipe sticking out of the bank and angling down toward the water. It's pretty hard to spot because there's a lot of foliage around it, and if you weren't looking for it, you probably wouldn't notice. But there's a furrow below the pipe running down to the water. You can tell there's been chemicals coming out of the pipe, because nothing is growing there."

"So you didn't actually see anything come out of it?"

"Yes, I did," I said. "I went up there one night with

a flashlight, and I saw chemicals or something coming out." I decided not to mention the pictures I'd taken.

He squinted at me and took another puff on the pipe. "You actually saw something pouring into the river."

"Yes."

"What did it look like?"

"Like greenish water," I said.

"You're positive."

"Yes." He didn't say anything for a minute. Then he said, "What were you doing out there?"

I was afraid he would ask that. I didn't want to tell the truth. I didn't want to say anything about not wanting to be trash anymore. I didn't want to talk to him about being trash at all. So I told my old story. "I was looking for birds. Somebody said they saw a pileated woodpecker up there. They're rare."

He nodded. "Yes, I know they're rare. A couple of times we've done stories when somebody's spotted one." I could tell that he believed my story. "Why did you go back at night?"

Suddenly I began to wonder how much he knew about what I'd been doing. Had the cops told him that they'd picked me up out there with a flash camera? Maybe they had. I decided I'd better stick as close to the truth as I could. "I saw that pipe the first time I was out there, and I figured that was where the pollution was coming from. I figured that if they were dumping stuff, they would do it at night. I just went back to see if they were."

"That's when you saw liquid running from the pipe?"

"Yes, but then somebody spotted me from the factory and called the cops. They said I was trespassing and took me down to the station house."

"I'll bet they did," he said. His pipe had gone out, and he lit it with a lighter. "Did they charge you with anything?"

I decided it was best to keep Mr. Herbst and all that out of it. "No, they just let me go and told me not to hang around there anymore. But please," I said. "I don't want anybody to know about it now."

He puffed on his pipe, blowing smoke around the place. "I'm curious," he said. "How come you changed your mind?"

I couldn't think of anything to say. I hadn't figured anybody was going to ask me a lot of questions, and I hadn't worked out a story. I felt myself go red, and then I looked down at my hands. Finally I said, "I don't want to discuss it. I just changed my mind."

"Cops say anything about keeping your mouth shut?"

I shook my head. "They just said to stay away from there."

"Somebody offer you some money to withdraw the letter?"

When he said that, something came to me: Had Herbst bribed Dad to keep me quiet? Would he have done something like that? Would Dad have taken a bribe from somebody he hated? When I thought about it, I knew he would. He'd say that if they were stupid enough to offer him some money, he'd be glad to take it. "No," I said. "Nobody offered me any money."

"You sure?"

"I'm positive. I wouldn't take a bribe."

He knocked his pipe out on a big ashtray on his desk. "And you won't tell me why you changed your mind about it."

I couldn't tell him the real reason. He'd want to know why Dad had hit me, why Dad was so serious about keeping the whole thing quiet. I knew there wouldn't be very good answers to that. I wondered: If Dad *had* taken a bribe, could they send him to jail for that? To be honest, I wouldn't have minded him going to jail, but who would pay the rent? I said, "Nobody offered me any money. I just don't want to discuss it."

He started to fill his pipe again from a leather pouch. "Well," he said. "You don't have to worry about it. There was no way we were going to run that letter. As a matter of fact, I burned it."

What a relief that was. I was safe from Dad. But I was pretty surprised too. "You burned my letter?"

"Harry— You said your name is Harry?"

"Yes."

"Harry, you're not the only person in town who knows what's going on up there. I've known for years that they've been polluting the Timber River. Some of the guys who work up there know. The union shop steward knows, because I've talked to him about it. Some of the town officials know, because I've talked to them too. And the fishermen all know because you can't eat the trout out of there anymore. It's got a taste to it."

Well, that was about the biggest surprise I'd ever had. I just sat there with my mouth open, feeling sort of silly. "If they all know, why hasn't anybody done something about it?"

"It's simple. Fred Herbst has said the main office will close down the factory if they force him to put in pollution controls. The carpet factory is just part of a larger company. They say that the factory isn't profitable as it is, that they're only keeping it open for the good of the town, and so forth."

"Is that true?" I said. "Isn't it profitable?"

He shrugged. "You'll never know and I'll never know. There's no way the town can force them to open their books, and even if we did, they probably have the accounting worked out to make it look unprofitable whether it is or not."

"Is it legal to do that?"

"Sure, if the tax people accept it. But it doesn't really matter. Herbst says that if the factory is forced to put in pollution controls, they'll have to close, and people around here aren't willing to take the chance. This area has been depressed for a long, long time. That carpet factory provides a lot of jobs to people around here, and those people cash their checks in the local stores. You walk into one of the supermarkets some Friday night when they're in there with their families, and watch those cash registers ringing up eighty, ninety, a hundred dollars at a clip. Close the carpet factory and you'd close half the stores in town."

"Doesn't anyone care about the river being polluted?"

The editor puffed out a mouthful of smoke. "Sure they do," he said. "Given their choice, people would rather see the Timber River cleaned up. But to most people being out of work is an awful lot worse than a little pollution."

There was something about it I didn't understand. "You mean that people like the town officials and the union shop steward and whoever knew about it got together and decided to keep quiet about it?"

He frowned, puffed on his pipe, and thought for a minute. "Well, not exactly. I don't doubt that the town councilmen have discussed the whole thing quietly among themselves. I know for a fact that about five years back the Sportsmen's Club invited Herbst to their monthly meeting. That's a matter of record. I covered the meeting for the paper. That's when Herbst made it clear that the factory would be closed if they were forced to put in pollution controls. I front-paged the story. After that people just decided to shut up about it. It wasn't a question of getting together on it. They just quietly shut up."

I just sat there. I didn't know what to say. My whole idea had been wrong from the beginning. It had all been a waste of effort. I felt plain stupid. "So it wouldn't have mattered even if I'd brought you in pictures of the pollution or something."

He shook his head. "I'm not going to run that story. Not until there's popular support for it." He puffed and then gazed at the smoke slowly curling and twisting upward. "I was considering it. At the time that Herbst told the Sportsmen's Club that he'd close the factory if they tried to do anything about pollution controls, I considered really going to town on it. I'd just got started checking into it when I got a phone call from the president of the Merchants' Association. He told me flat out that if I started a crusade against the factory, all the stores in town would pull their advertising out of the paper. I figure Herbst had leaned on him, but he wouldn't admit it. You can't run a newspaper without advertising—no advertising, no paper."

"You mean the store owners can tell you what stories to run?"

"Harry, no newspaper can afford to offend its advertisers. You can do it occasionally, up to a point. But you can't do it very often. And you certainly can't take a stand directly opposite to what they think are their best interests. That's just the way it is."

"Isn't polluting against the law? Aren't the councilmen supposed to stop it if they know somebody's doing it?"

He thought about that for a minute. "Of course, there are state and federal laws of various kinds, pretty strict ones too. But it wouldn't be up to the councilmen to do anything unless there were antipollution laws on the town books. It wouldn't be their jurisdiction." He thought some more. "I don't know whether Timber Falls has an antipollution ordinance or not."

"But if it did, the councilmen would have to enforce it, right?"

He thought about it. Then he said, "Harry, if you

want to make a crusade of this, that's up to you. But I'm warning you, if you do, your dad will never get another day's work in Timber Falls, and nobody around here will ever speak to you again. I'm serious. And it might be a lot worse than that. A fellow who thinks he'll be out of work, and likely to lose a home that he's spent twenty years working for, will do almost anything to stop it."

TWELVE

Three days later Dad drove into the yard at supper time with a brand-new Ford ton-and-a-half truck. Mom saw it through the window and said, "Here comes Dad with the new truck."

"New truck?" I said. "Dad bought a new truck?"

"He worked out a deal with the man."

We ran out into the backyard. Dad was standing next to it with his hand on the door panel, kind of patting it. It was a beauty—maroon, and it had a winch on the front. Everything on it shone like jewels. Dad just stood next to it patting it and grinning. I couldn't remember when I'd seen him smile that much. "How do you like it?" he said.

"It's a beauty, Dad," I said.

"Look inside, Harry," he said, smiling some more. "It's got everything—AM and FM, CB, the works." I looked inside. It had that new-car smell, the seats were shiny and clean, and there wasn't a speck of dust on anything. It was something all right. "Now, I want you to keep it clean, Harry," he said. "That's your job. And if you do it right, I'll teach you how to drive it."

It was the binoculars all over again—beautiful as could be but with a kind of rotten odor to it, so that I was drawn to it and driven away from it at the same time. For, of course, he'd bought it with his bribe money from Herbst. I didn't know whether Herbst had given him enough money to buy the whole thing. Probably not; probably he'd given him part of it, and Dad would pay the rest on time. It didn't matter. To get that beautiful new truck he'd ruined my plan for getting something done about the pollution in the Timber River. He'd sold me out. And I resolved right then and there that I wasn't going to keep the truck clean. I wasn't going to lay a finger on it. He could do it himself.

Of course, he wanted to take us for a drive. I didn't want to go, but there wasn't any way I could say no. We got in. There was plenty of room for the three of us in the cab. "It's a lot better than the old truck, Harry," Dad said. "You won't have to ride in the back when we go someplace." He'd already forgotten about Helen. Then he began telling me about clutching and shifting and the rest of that. I knew a lot about that already anyway.

I thought about it later when I was sitting on the back steps watching the stars wink on one by one. I didn't want to be any part of the truck, or Dad, or anything. I didn't want to learn to drive on it, and I didn't want Dad to teach me to drive. I didn't want him to do anything for me. Not that he'd ever done very much. He'd taken me up into the mountains a couple of times and stolen me a pair of binoculars. But now I didn't want him to do anything for me at all. If he was to offer me a hundred bucks out of his bribe money, I wouldn't take it. I didn't want any part of it.

What made me the maddest about it was his interfering in the whole carpet factory thing. It wasn't any of his business. He had no right to do it. He had no right to interfere. Sitting there on the back steps, I stopped watching the stars come out, and began to get mad. I wished there was something I could do about it. So what if everybody in Timber Falls was sore at me. Nobody there liked me anyway. So what if Dad wouldn't be able to get any more jobs around there. Why did I care about that? It could all go to pieces as far as I was concerned. I'd just as soon see everything go to pieces anyway.

I wondered if there was anything I could do about it. I wondered if there was any way to get the town councilmen to do something. The newspaper editor had said that if there was some law on the books of the town, they might have to do something. At least that's what I thought he said. I sat there trying to remember. It seemed right to me. If there was a law, they'd have to do something about it.

Suppose there was a law—would I really be able to do anything about it? Would I really *want* to do anything about it? If I made a lot of trouble over it, would everybody in town stop giving Dad work? They might, I figured. What would happen then? Dad would give me a real beating, that was for sure. What else? I didn't know.

But at least I could find out about it. I could find out whether there were any laws on the books about polluting. So the next day after school I went to the old redbrick town hall, with a pen and my assignment notebook. The town hall had been built in 1890 when there had been a lot of logging in the area and the town was richer. You could tell when it had been built, because the date was carved into a slab of stone over the door. I hadn't been in the town hall very often. I'd gone in there that time our social studies class had studied the town, and I'd been there a couple of times when Dad had business there. I couldn't remember what. The place had a musty smell. The floors had got dirt ground into them that you'd never get out, and the radiators were old and banged and whistled.

I went in and stood in the hall looking around. I saw doors with little signs above them which stuck out into the hall: ASSESSOR, ZONING COMMISSION, TOWN COUNCILMEN. Finally I saw the town clerk's office. The door was open and I went in. There wasn't much to it: just a room with a couple of women sitting behind desks, a table with a few books lying on it, some filing cabinets, a picture of George Washington and a big map of the town hanging on the wall. One of the women was young and had blond hair. The other was older and fat; she had a big dish of candy on her desk. "Yes?" the blond one said.

"I'm doing a school project," I said. "I have to find out what laws the town has on pollution."

"Pollution?"

"Air pollution and so forth," I said, to throw them off.

"Pollution," the fat woman said. "Are they going to start up again?" She took a candy out of the bowl and unwrapped it. "Want one, Jeanette?" she said to the blonde.

"I better start watching my weight," the blonde said. "I won't be able to get into my new dress." She looked back at me. "What do you want to know, exactly?"

"The pollution laws," I said. "What the pollution laws are."

"It's a school report?" she said.

The fat woman put the candy into her mouth. "Some of these teachers ought to learn to keep their noses out of things."

"Who's your teacher?" the blond woman said.

I was getting myself into trouble, because if they checked up they'd find out I was lying. I began to feel a little sweaty. "Mrs. Heinz."

"It isn't a very popular subject in Timber Falls," the younger woman said.

"Well, I don't know about that," I said. "I just have to find out if the town has any laws about it."

The blond woman sighed, got up, and went over to one of the filing cabinets. She opened a drawer and took out a big loose-leaf notebook filled with photocopies. "Here's the town code," she said. "Be careful with it. Sit over at that table and see if you can find what you want."

So I did. The town code was pretty confusing.

There was a table of contents in the front, but it didn't say anything about pollution or the environment. I tried a couple of other topics that seemed like they might be right, like water, rivers, and air; but they weren't. Finally I just gave up and began going through it one page at a time, scanning each page in hopes of hitting what I was looking for. It was pretty boring, and when I'd spent an hour and had only got a quarter of the way through the loose-leaf pages, I got discouraged and was ready to give up.

But I made myself keep going by telling myself that if I didn't find anything in another half an hour, I could quit, and about fifteen minutes later I found something. It said: "Town Ordinance #3762 Enacted February 17, 1969, in Respect to the Quality of the Environment." The ordinance was about a page long, and I read it all the way through. It was pretty hard for me to understand. Some of it I couldn't figure out at all—I just didn't know what some of the words meant. But the basic idea was clear enough: Nobody was supposed to dump *anything* in any of the rivers or creeks around town. You weren't supposed to throw in even a cigarette butt or pieces of bread for the geese when they came through in spring and fall. You could fish, you could swim, and you could have a boat on the rivers, although most of them were too small or had too many rapids for boats. But you couldn't dump anything in.

So the laws were there all right. And the next question in my mind was whether the town councilmen *had* to enforce the laws. Could they ignore laws if they chose? That was the next thing I had to find out.

I copied out of the town code book the parts about throwing stuff in the rivers, then I gave the book back to the blond woman. "Did you find what you were looking for?" she said.

"I think so," I said.

"People ought to watch where they put their noses," the fat woman said.

I blushed a little, and went outside to think about it. Who would know if the town councilmen had to enforce the pollution laws? The newspaper editor would know. I figured he was probably busy and wouldn't want to be bothered by me, but it was worth trying anyway. So I went down Main Street and out the side road to the newspaper office. When I walked in, the editor was standing in the front room. His pipe was in his mouth, and he was putting on his jacket. "You're back again," he said.

"Yes, sir," I said, to be polite. "I wanted to ask you something."

He frowned and looked at his wristwatch. "I've only got a minute," he said.

"It won't take long," I said.

He nodded toward the open door to his back office. "Okay, come on in."

I followed him in. He sat down at his desk with his jacket on, and I stood in front of the desk. "I looked up the town code," I said.

"Oh?" he said.

"There's a law all right," I said. I showed him what I'd written in my notebook.

He took the notebook, read it over, and handed it

back to me. "So you're going to do something about it after all?"

"I don't know," I said. "I'm thinking about it."

"I'll say this," he said. "You've got a lot of guts."

When he said that, the funniest feeling swept over me. I didn't understand it. I felt sort of warm and dazed. For a minute I forgot what I was going to say, what I was doing there, why I had come. I stood there feeling that feeling.

"So what did you want to ask me?" he said.

I remembered where I was. "Well, the thing is, do the town councilmen have to enforce the law, or can they decide which laws they want to enforce?"

"Oh, no, they have to enforce the laws," he said.

"Why haven't they, then?"

"Well, for one thing, that law was passed a long time ago. They probably don't even know it's on the books. But more important, they know the people of this town would run them out of office if they tried to enforce it." He took the pipe out of his mouth and pointed it at me. "Harry, I admire your attitude," he said. Once again that funny feeling rolled over me. "But you're going to get yourself into an awful lot of trouble if you go on with this. And you're not going to do the town any good."

"Maybe Herbst is just bluffing," I said. "Maybe he won't really close the factory if they have to put in pollution controls."

He stood up. "You might be right," he said. "But nobody around here wants to take the chance." He looked at his watch again. "I've got to go," he said, and gestured toward the door. I went out, and he came along behind me. When we were outside on the street, he stopped and put his hand on my shoulder. "I didn't want to say this inside in front of the others. Do you realize that Herbst gave your Dad five thousand dollars to make you keep quiet?"

Five thousand. The truck probably cost around fifteen thousand. I was surprised he knew about it. "I know," I said. "Dad bought a new truck."

"Your dad wanted Herbst to give him a truck. They settled on five thousand dollars. What's he going to say when he finds out you're not shutting up?"

He certainly knew a lot about everything. It was beginning to sound like a bunch of them were getting together on it. "He'd give me an awful beating if he found out," I said.

He looked at me. "Don't you think that's a pretty good reason to drop it? Your dad has his faults, but he's always kept a roof over your head and food on your plate. He won't be able to do that anymore if you go on with this."

I knew I shouldn't ask, but I couldn't help myself: "How come you know so much about it?"

"Harry, I've been editing this paper for over twenty years. I know things about Timber Falls you wouldn't believe. That's the business I'm in. After you'd been into the office the last time, I called Herbst. I wanted to find out what he was doing. I wanted to know what was going on just in case there was a story in it after all. I don't want to be scooped by some other newspaper in my own town. I try to keep on top of things. That's my job after all." He looked at his watch again. "I really have to go. I'll just say once again, you don't know what kind of mess this could blow up into. I think you ought to drop it."

I looked at him. "I don't know," I said.

He shook his head. "You're a gutsy kid all right." Then he turned and walked away, and I stood there with that feeling running over me again. It was a feeling I'd never had before. Then suddenly I got what it was: It was the first time in my whole life that I remembered anybody saying anything nice to me, outside of the family. I'd never had anybody admire me before.

I started to walk on home feeling kind of funny and surprised. My thoughts flashed here and there without much sense to them. The funny thing was, with the editor saying all those good things about me— that I was gutsy and he admired my attitude and all that—I wasn't so sore about the whole thing anymore. Maybe I was doing wrong to keep on with it. Maybe it wasn't right; maybe it was the wrong thing to do. Maybe I ought to just drop the whole thing.

Suddenly I realized that it was getting on toward supper time. I started to walk faster. But just then Dad came along in the new truck and picked me up. My good mood went away. I just didn't like being with him.

He was monitoring the CB. Some guy was talking about an accident over on the state highway. "Harry, I took the truck up the old tote road this afternoon. It just waltzed up that steep hill in third, just waltzed up it. Maybe over the weekend I'll start teaching you how to drive it."

He was pretty cheerful about that truck all right,

but I didn't want to talk about it. I didn't want to talk about anything to him. So I sat there quiet.

"Cat got your tongue?"

"No," I said. "I'm just tired is all."

"You getting enough sleep?"

"Sure," I said. "I'm just tired." Luckily we got to the house just then, and I could stop talking to him. We pulled into the driveway, and we hadn't even gotten out of the truck when Mom came running out of the house. It startled me because Mom didn't usually come running anyplace like that. "Frank," she cried. "Frank. The police called. They arrested Helen."

We jumped out of the truck. "Arrested?" Dad said. "Where is she?"

"In New York. They found her in New York. She's in jail. My poor baby." She began to cry.

"Stop wailing, Doris," Dad said. "What did they get her for?"

Tears were running down Mom's cheeks. "Drugs," she said. "They say she was selling drugs. And prostitution."

THIRTEEN

Dad got back into the truck and drove into town to talk to the police, and I sat there with Mom, saying things like maybe it wasn't true, maybe they'd got her mixed up with somebody else. It didn't make her feel any better. Of course, I knew it was all true. But I couldn't say that to Mom.

Finally Dad got back with the story. Helen had got picked up for prostitution, along with the women she was living with. When they searched her purse, they found a lot of cocaine in it. At first she wouldn't tell them where she came from or anything, but then they said they would send her away for a couple of years, so she told them who she was. She was over sixteen and they could charge her, but they were willing to send her home in the custody of her parents if she'd go. The New York cops called our cops, and they worked it out so that Dad could drive down to New York and get her. So he fixed himself a thermos of coffee and set off to drive to New York. It would take him maybe six hours to get there and six hours to get back.

It was terrible. Now it was going to go all over town that Helen was a prostitute. Nobody in Timber Falls would ever talk to her again. Not even Charlie Fritz. And nobody would talk to me either. As far as us ever getting over being trash around there, that was finished. I could become a general in the air force and I'd still be trash so far as Timber Falls was concerned. Before we'd been no-good; now we would be nothing at all. I wondered if the storekeepers would even let us in their stores anymore. I wondered if they would serve us.

The funny thing was, I didn't feel sore at Helen. I just felt so sorry for her. It was going to be terrible for her to ride for six hours in the truck with Dad. He'd hit her. He was bound to do that. He wouldn't feel sorry for her at all. He'd bawl her out the whole way and belt her if she answered him back. But that wouldn't be the worst of it. The terrible part would be going to school and having all the kids stare at her and talk about her. Nobody would want to eat with her at lunch. They would get up and move if she sat down near them. I didn't know how she would be able to stand that. I felt so sorry for her.

That night, sitting on the back steps, I thought about it. And what it seemed to me was this: Here was poor Helen who'd never done anything wrong to anybody, who only wanted to get some boy to like her; and who had had to wash her own clothes since she was eight years old; and who had never got much of anything from anybody; here she was, a disgrace and an outcast. And Herbst who was polluting the Timber River, lying about it, and bribing people was rich and respected and could do anything he wanted. And the newspaper editor who had known all about the pollution for years and was covering up for it was respected and admired around Timber Falls. And the merchants around town who had pressured the newspaper editor to shut up about it—they were making good money and were respected in the town. And all the other people in Timber Falls who knew about it and had kept their mouths shut. And Dad who had taken a bribe to force me to shut up was going to belt Helen good for what she had done. Was it right? Was it fair? Maybe the stars would never begin to fall.

Suddenly I didn't care what people thought of me anymore. I didn't give a damn, not a single damn. I grit my teeth. I knew what I was going to do: I was going to get revenge on all of them for Helen. I was going to make the biggest stink about the pollution that I could, and close the carpet factory down.

What was the best way to do it? I wasn't sure. I could start with the town council. They were supposed to be enforcing the law, weren't they? I couldn't remember exactly what the town ordinance said, so I got up and went inside to look for the assignment notebook I'd written it down in.

The notebook wasn't anywhere in the kitchen or the living room. I didn't remember going up to my room since I'd been home. I'd been too busy trying to cheer Mom up. But I went upstairs and looked anyway. It wasn't in my room. There wasn't that much stuff in my room that you could lose anything there.

So I went back downstairs and looked in the kitchen again, and all of a sudden I realized where it was. I stood still, frozen, in the middle of the kitchen, my hand in midair like I was catching something. I'd left the notebook in the truck. It had been lying on the seat beside me, and when Mom had come running out of the house shouting that Helen was in jail, I'd forgotten all about the notebook and just jumped out of the truck. It must still be there, lying on the seat, opened to the page with the pollution ordinance written on it. Dad would just have to take one look, and after that he'd kill me.

But maybe it had fallen out of the truck when I'd jumped out. Sometimes that happened. I got a flashlight and went out to the dirt driveway and looked all around where the truck had been when I'd jumped out. It wasn't there.

There was still a chance that Dad wouldn't notice it lying on the seat, especially if his mind was on Helen and all. Or that it fell off the seat onto the floor where he wouldn't notice it. Or that it slid into the crack between the seat and the door and would fall onto the street when Helen opened the passenger door to get in. All I could do was hope.

But losing the notebook wasn't going to stop me from getting revenge for Helen. I don't know why I thought of it that way—as getting revenge. She didn't have anything to do with it really. She wasn't much interested in whether anyone was polluting the Timber River. But still, it seemed like revenge to me. And I was bound and determined to do it.

Was there any way I could do it without Dad finding out? There might be. I wouldn't go to a town council meeting. I'd just go to see one of the councilmen privately and hear what he had to say. After that I'd figure out what to do next.

So I had decided that. I turned off the flashlight and went back to the house. Mom was sitting in the living room watching TV. I figured she was planning on staying up until Helen got home. I figured she would have trouble going to sleep anyway until they were back. But I didn't see how they would get home until morning, so I went to bed.

When I got up in the morning, the TV was still going and Mom was asleep in her chair in front of it. I quietly shut it off, fixed myself some peanut butter on toast for breakfast, and went to school. I wasn't looking forward to it very much because of everybody knowing what had happened to Helen. But nobody said anything, and I figured word hadn't got around yet. And after school I went back to the old redbrick town hall and went inside.

For a minute I stood there smelling the musty smell and listening to the radiators bang. A couple of doors down the hall I could see a sign saying TOWN COUNCIL. I went down there and listened by the door. No noise came from inside. I took a deep breath and opened the door. The room was empty except for a couple of desks, some wooden chairs against a wall, some filing cabinets, and an American flag.

I shut the door again and went back to the town

clerk's office. The same two women were sitting there. The fat one was unwrapping a candy from her bowl. "I'm being naughty today," she said. "I've already eaten four of these." Then she saw me. "You're back? What is it this time?"

"Nothing," I said. "I was just wondering if any of the town councilmen were around."

"What's this about?" she said. She looked suspicious.

"Mr. Novick might be in around four," the blond one said. I had a half hour to wait. So I went outside and sat on the steps. I leaned up against the redbrick wall and worked on my English homework. After a while a Volkswagen Rabbit pulled up, and a youngish man wearing chinos and a blue flannel shirt got out. He came up the steps and passed me to go into the town hall. I figured it might be Mr. Novick, so I followed him in. He stopped at the town clerk's office and asked for his mail. The blond woman handed him some letters. "This kid wants to talk to you," she said.

He looked around at me. "Sure, what is it, son?" He seemed like a pretty cheerful guy.

"It's sort of private," I said.

He smiled. "Okay, let's go down to the office." Smiling like that, he was making me feel hopeful. He went down to the town council's office, and I followed him in. He sat down behind one of the desks, and I stood there until he told me to sit down in one of the wooden chairs. He looked through his mail for a couple of minutes, frowning and dropping the envelopes onto the desk, and then he looked up at me and smiled again and said, "Okay, what is it?"

I took a deep breath and said, "I've got proof that the carpet factory is polluting the Timber River."

His smile went away like something you wipe off a blackboard. He looked at me and then he said, "What's your name?"

Here it came again. "Harry White."

"From Mountain Pass Road."

"Yes," I said.

He put his hands together in front of his face like he was praying into them, and sat there thinking and looking out over his hands at me. All the while I kept getting more and more nervous until I wanted to jump out of the chair. Finally he took his hands away from his face and said, "I figured that's who you were. I've been hearing about you."

I wondered who he had heard it from. Herbst? The newspaper editor? The cops? Who else was in on it? I figured it was most likely the cops who had told him. "I saw it myself," I said.

"Look, Harry, I think you ought to forget all about this."

"It's against the law," I said.

"That's no news," he said. "We all know that. But that isn't the point." He looked at me some more. Then he said, "I thought your dad told you to drop it."

He knew about that too. He couldn't have got that from the cops. He must have got it from the newspaper editor or Herbst. "He did. He belted me good and told me to forget about it. I decided not to."

"Harry, what got you into this thing in the first place?"

"I did it on my own," I said. I was tired of lying about it, and I decided to tell the truth, all except the part about being trash. I would never discuss that with anybody. "I knew they were dumping stuff in the river, because when I went out to the river to watch the fish, I could see it. I decided to investigate, so I went out there and found that pipe." I figured if he knew as much about it as he did, he'd know about the pipe too.

He drummed his fingers on the desktop. "Are you telling me that nobody put you up to this—some environmental group or something?"

I shook my head. "Nobody did," I said. "I figured it out for myself."

"And you saw the pipe. But you didn't actually see anything coming out of it, did you?"

"Yes, I did. I went out there with a flashlight one night and I saw it."

"How do you know it was chemicals? Maybe it was ordinary waste water."

"It wasn't," I said. "It was greenish. Besides, nothing was growing underneath the pipe."

"Okay," he said. "Let's say I believe that you did this yourself. And let's say I believe that you really saw the stuff. If you make an issue out of it, you're going to stir up a lot of trouble around town. There are a lot of angles to it you don't understand. This is something for us adults to worry about. You worry about your schoolwork, and let us worry about this."

"Maybe they really wouldn't close the carpet factory," I said. "Maybe they're just bluffing."

He gave me a funny look. "You know about that, huh?"

"Yes," I said.

"Well, then maybe you can understand that around here jobs matter a lot more than a little bit of pollution."

"It isn't a little bit," I said. I was beginning to get stubborn, and I knew I was going to lose my temper soon.

"Okay, a lot. It still doesn't matter stacked up against people's jobs."

"But maybe they're bluffing," I said. "Why can't you—"

He slammed his hand down on the desk. "You're meddling in something you don't know anything about. You're going to end up causing a lot of trouble for the people in this town. Stop giving me that baloney that you're doing this on your own. Who put you up to it?"

He was angry, and I was scared, but I wasn't going to give in. "Nobody put me up to it. Don't call me a liar."

He slammed his hand on the desk again. "I'll call you whatever I want to call you, son. You're just out to make trouble because that's the kind you are. You and your whole family."

I jumped up. "You can't say that to me," I shouted.

He jumped up, too, and his chair crashed over behind him. "Oh, yes, I can," he shouted. "If you go any further with this, we're going to run you and your lousy family out of Timber Falls. You're nothing but trash anyway, lying and stealing and now your sister—"

I grabbed up the chair behind me and swung it over my head. "You say anything more about my sister and I'll kill you," I shouted.

He jumped around the desk. I started to swing it around, but he was a lot bigger than me, and he grabbed it before I could get in a good swing. He started to jerk it away from me. I let go and turned and ran out of the office, and down the corridor and out of the building. Once I was outside, I looked back. He was standing at the door of the town hall, but he wasn't coming after me. I turned and walked on toward home, so mad and hurt I couldn't stop crying. The tears kept running down my face until I was almost home.

FOURTEEN

Helen was sitting in the living room next to Mom, watching a soap opera. "Hi, Helen," I said. I was glad to see her. I was feeling pretty awful about everything, and I was glad to have somebody I could tell it to.

She gave me a scared look.

"I'm not sore at you," I said. "I figured it wasn't your fault."

She looked relieved and got up and gave me a hug.

"My poor baby," Mom said.

"Let's go out back," I said. So we went outside and sat on the back steps. "I'm glad you came back," I said. "I didn't have anybody to talk to."

She got a tough look on her face. "I'm going to run away again as soon as I can. I've got six months probation, after that I can leave. I'll be seventeen anyway."

"Are you supposed to go to school?"

"Yes, but I'm not going to," she said. "I'm not going to have all those dumb kids staring at me all day long.

I'm not going anyplace where I have to see Charlie Fritz. I'm going to get a job over in Watertown. As a waitress in a luncheonette. Dad says he can fix it up. Dad says he'll take me to the Watertown bus every morning."

I didn't say anything. I knew I shouldn't ask whether she was really a prostitute, but I was pretty curious. "What was it like, Helen?"—which was a way of asking so she didn't have to answer.

"It wasn't so bad," she said. "I didn't mind it so much."

"You didn't?" I said.

Then she bent over, covered her face with her hands, and began to cry. "I hated it," she said. "It was awful. But the other girls teased me for being proud." She started sobbing so hard, she couldn't speak for a minute, and I put my arm around her shoulder. Her sobbing eased up a little. "Then I found out that if I got high and drank some wine, it wasn't so bad. That's why I got all that coke. I was going to try to make money that way." She stopped sobbing, wiped her eyes on her shirt, and sat there looking calm. "It was a dumb idea. If they'd caught me just for prostitution, it wouldn't have been such a big deal. They wouldn't have called up Dad."

"Well," I said. "I'm glad you're back."

"I was homesick," she said. "I didn't think I would be. How could anyone be homesick for this dump?"

"Mom missed you," I said. "She kept saying 'My poor baby' and stuff like that. She cried sometimes."

Helen frowned. "I don't care," she said. "I'm going to leave again as soon as I can."

"Even if it makes you homesick?"

"You get over being homesick," she said. "The other women told me that. They said they were homesick, too, when they first came to New York, but they got over it in a few weeks."

"Are you going back to New York?"

"No," she said. "Not there. Someplace else. Someplace where nobody knows me and I can start over again from the beginning. Where nobody knows about our family and going to school dirty and Dad stealing, and—" Suddenly she stopped and looked at me. "I didn't mean to say that," she said.

"I already knew he stole," I said. "I didn't know you knew."

"I found out years ago," she said. "I didn't want you to know."

That surprised me. "How did you find out?"

"Remember that bike I had, the first one?" she said.

"The one you gave me?"

"Yes," she said. "I knew the kid he stole it from. That's why I had to paint it—so nobody would recognize it."

"You knew it was stolen all along?"

"Yes," she said. "But I couldn't give it back. Dad would have thought I lost it."

"He hit me—" I began, but then we heard the sound of the truck, and in a moment it came up the driveway. I stood up, feeling scared and nervous, not knowing what to expect. The truck pulled to a stop. For a moment Dad sat in the cab looking over to where we were sitting on the back steps. Then he got out of the truck. He was carrying my assignment notebook. He came slowly across the backyard toward me. When he got up to me, he said, "Come to the barn," in a quiet voice.

"No," I said.

"What?" he said. He came up so close to me that I could hear him breathing. "I said come up to the barn."

"I'm not going to," I said.

He stared at me, his face close to mine. "I thought I told you to forget about that carpet factory business."

"I'm not going to do what you say anymore," I said. "You're a thief and a liar. You're nothing but—"

He grabbed me by my shirtfront. I tried to twist away, but his grip was too tight. He slammed me across the face with his open hand. My head rang, and I heard Helen shriek. I felt dizzy, and I swung out, not knowing what I was aiming for, and caught him in the gut. He grunted and slammed me across the face again. I shook my head, trying to clear it, and swung at him again. This time I caught him in the chest. He swung back his arm. Helen shrieked again. Then she jumped on his back and began clawing his face with her fingernails. He gave me a sort of push, and I staggered backward, but I didn't fall. He reached around behind him, grabbed hold of Helen by the arm, and jerked her loose from him. She fell down. I started toward him, but he didn't move. Long red lines down his face were oozing blood. His mouth was twisted, and he was breathing hard. I stood there waiting to see what he would do. If he went for Helen, I was going to tackle him. I figured if I got him down, the two of us could do a pretty good job on him.

He touched his cheek and looked at his fingers to see the blood. "Get out of here," he said. "The two of you pack and git. Now."

Mom came out onto the back steps. "My God," she said. "Oh, my God." She put her hands over her face. "What have you done to them, Frank?"

"You shut up," he said. Then he went in the house.

I stood there feeling dizzy. My head hurt, and my nose and mouth were bleeding. "Someday I'm going to kill him," I said. "Someday."

Mom came down the steps and took me by the arm. "Are you all right, Harry? What did he do to you?"

"I'm going to kill him," I said. I spit out blood.

"Don't say things like that," Mom said.

"I got him good," Helen said. "Next time I'll use a knife."

"Helen, don't say things like that," Mom cried.

We heard water running in the kitchen sink, and I knew Dad was washing his face where Helen had scratched him. Then he came out of the house. For a minute he stood there looking at us. Then he said, "I told the two of you to git. I don't want to find you here when I get back." Then he walked past us, got into the truck, and drove away.

"Don't pay any attention to him," Mom said. "He'll get over it. He's just mad. He'll get over it."

She was right, I figured. If I stayed clear of him for

a couple of days, and let him see that I wasn't doing anything more about the carpet factory, he'd get over it. But I knew *I* wouldn't get over it. I would never get over it. And I was going to get out of there as soon as I could—in a few days, a week, a month. As soon as I could work something out I was going to leave. I had an idea about where I might go too. I figured my grandpa and grandma might want to have me. They might let me live with them until I graduated. Maybe they would want to have Helen too. I would see.

And there was another thing. I was never going to worry about being trash again. That was for sure. I'd learned something. I hadn't been able to do anything about the carpet factory polluting the Timber River, and I saw now that I would never be able to do anything about it. Even if I got somebody from Albany to come up, they wouldn't find anything. The whole town would cover it up. The town council and the newspaper editor and Herbst and everybody would cover it up, and anyway, who was going to believe one fourteen-year-old kid whose whole family was trash?

There was one other thing I'd learned: It wasn't me who was trash—they were. They lied and covered up and gave bribes and polluted the river so you couldn't swim in it or eat the fish out of it. I wasn't trash—they were. I would never forget that lesson.

"Harry," Helen said. "Do you feel all right?"

"I'm all right," I said.

"Do you feel like eating?" she said. "I'm going to make spaghetti and meat sauce."

"It's nice to have Helen around again, isn't it, Harry?" Mom said.

You'll find a friend in these bestsellers by

Judy Blume

___ARE YOU THERE GOD? IT'S ME, MARGARET....	90419-6	$2.95
___BLUBBER	90707-1	$2.95
___DEENIE	93259-9	$3.25
___IT'S NOT THE END OF THE WORLD	94140-7	$3.25
___STARRING SALLY J. FREEDMAN	98239-1	$3.25
___THEN AGAIN MAYBE I WON'T	98659-1	$2.95
___TIGER EYES	98469-6	$3.25

Dear Readers,

Before becoming an author I had the good fortune of spending over twenty years working with animals all over the world. When asked what my favorite animal is, I answer without hesitation: "Elephants!" The next question is usually "Why?" which is not as easily answered as the first question. I have been bumped, smashed, picked up, stepped on, and caressed by these wonderful beasts. I once had an elephant run away . . . with me on her back! I have seen five elephants born. An 8,000-pound mother giving birth to a 225-pound calf is not a sight easily forgotten. I've watched as the mother and "auntie" locked trunks together gently lifting the struggling calf to its feet for the first time.

Twenty years of experiences and memories with elephants are difficult to reduce to a simple answer. Perhaps this is why *Elephant Run* is the fourth book I've written about these magnificent animals . . . and I think my last on the subject.

The first novel I got published was called *Thunder Cave*. It's an adventure story about a boy who goes to Kenya to find his research biologist father who is studying African elephants. But what about Asian elephants?

I spent weeks deep in the jungles of Burma (Myanmar) living in elephant villages doing research for *Elephant Run*. I set the novel in the Pacific theater of World War II because this is a place and time seldom written about for young people.

Elephant Run is my tenth novel and it took me ten years to complete. I hope you enjoy the adventure as much as I enjoyed writing it.

Roland Smith

Other Novels by Roland Smith

Thunder Cave

Jaguar

Sasquatch

The Last Lobo

Zach's Lie

Cryptid Hunters

Jack's Run

elephant
run

elephant
run

roland smith

SCHOLASTIC INC.
New York Toronto London Auckland Sydney
Mexico City New Delhi Hong Kong Buenos Aires

ISBN-13: 978-0-545-09787-1
ISBN-10: 0-545-09787-8

Text copyright © 2007 by Roland Smith.
All rights reserved. Published by Scholastic Inc., 557 Broadway, New York, NY 10012,
by arrangement with Hyperion Books for Children, an imprint of Disney Children's Book Group.
SCHOLASTIC and associated logos are trademarks and/or registered trademarks of Scholastic Inc.

12 11 10 9 8 7 6 5 4 3 2   8 9 10 11 12 13/0

Printed in the U.S.A.   40

First Scholastic printing, September 2008

For my precious Burmese ruby, Marie

Part One

The Plantation

When Nick Freestone was young, he and his mother lived on a farm in Kansas.

They weren't there long, but what Nick remembered most about that time were the violent thunderstorms that washed over the cornfields during the night. The noise and lightning were terrifying. But it was nothing like the bombs that dropped from the night skies of London, where he and his mother were living in 1941. The Nazis called the bombing raids blitzkrieg, or lightning war. The British simply called it "the blitz."

Every night, the German Luftwaffe droned across the channel—the noise distant at first, then closer, followed by the *whomp . . . whomp . . .* of bombs hitting buildings. It was dark in the subway tunnels, where they took shelter, which was just as well—this way no one saw the others' fear. They sat on benches, shoulder to shoulder, thigh to thigh, with their heads down and eyes squeezed shut against the dust shaken from the ceiling. Some prayed, some crossed their fingers, some did both, hoping the bombs would fall on someone else.

When the all-clear siren sounded, they walked calmly upstairs to the street. Some of the people made jokes, others chatted about the weather or food rationing. No one talked about the blitz, or the smoke in the air, or the red glow of burning buildings in the distance.

Until November 30.

The siren sounded a little after midnight. Groggily, Nick got out of bed and joined their housekeeper, Mrs. Knolls, in the underground station down the street. His mother was at work at the American Embassy. His stepfather, Bernard, an Army intelligence officer, was on a secret mission somewhere in France.

When the all clear sounded, they walked up the stairs. As soon as they stepped outside, Mrs. Knolls screamed, joined by several others. At first Nick didn't know what all the fuss was about. Then he saw the fire.

A thermite incendiary bomb had hit his apartment building. These were small bombs, eighteen inches long, weighing only a couple pounds, but the Luftwaffe dropped them in something called a bread-basket that carried seventy-two bombs at a time.

The fire brigade was already there, but it was too late. His mother arrived in an embassy car an hour later and took him back to her office. He slept on her sofa.

The next morning Nick and his mother went back to the apartment. There wasn't much left.

"Were you able to contact Bernard?" Nick asked.

She shook her head. Bernard had been gone for nearly a month behind enemy lines. She was worried about him. So was Nick.

"What are we going to do now?"

His mother looked at him with her beautiful green

eyes. She pointed at the charred remains of their apartment.

"Before this happened I talked to your father," she said.

Nick was surprised. There were few phones in Burma and none on the teak plantation his father owned.

"The situation in Burma is unstable," she continued. "But things here are worse. He thinks you would be safer with him."

Nick held his breath.

After a long pause she said, "I agree with him. I'm sending you to Burma."

Burma 1

"You were born on a hot Burmese day without a breath of wind!" Nang shouted above the engine noise as he steered the old truck along the narrow dirt road. "When you came into the world you screamed so loud we heard you in the elephant village."

He paused to stick a cheroot into his mouth, but didn't take both hands off the steering wheel to light it—to Nick's relief.

"I was in the village because my wife was expecting Mya, who came along three weeks after you were born." He glanced at his daughter, who was sitting between them, then dodged a rather large boulder in the middle of the road, narrowly missing it. "I rode my elephant deep into the forest to find your father and his catching crew. We returned to Hawk's Nest two days later, leading a beautiful young elephant. You were a week early, and your father was two days late." He shook his head. "That was when the big trouble began between your mother and father. After that, she did not like him anymore."

"She likes him," Nick said, which wasn't exactly true.

"That is why you were named Nicholas Gillis Freestone," Nang continued, "instead of Jackson Theodore Freestone the Fourth. This was your father's punishment for being late."

"Gillis is my mother's maiden name," Nick said.

"Yes, but if it had been up to your father, you would have been named after him, your grandfather, and your great-grandfather."

Nick gripped the dash as Nang maneuvered the truck around a hairpin curve with a drop-off of at least five hundred feet.

Smiling with relief as they made it safely around the curve, Nang added, "But your father did get to name the elephant he captured that day. He called him Hannibal."

After a week on boats, trains, and airplanes, Nick was finally back home, and already he felt more comfortable than he had ever felt in London, or America, for that matter.

Nang and his daughter, Mya, had picked him up at the Rangoon airport in a flatbed truck with a very large elephant named *Ma Chew*, or Miss Pretty. His father had bought her from another plantation. She was certainly pretty, with long legs and a regal bearing. As they drove away from the airport, her massive head cast a shadow on the hood of the truck, which made it look like there was an elephant flying above them.

Nick thought the truck would tip over around every

curve, but Nang said that Miss Pretty had been on many trucks. "She knows when to lean," he explained.

Miss Pretty did a lot of leaning on the three-day trip to the plantation. They traveled on roads that didn't look like roads, past flooded rice paddies, by fields being plowed by oxen, through small towns and villages, up mountainsides, beneath dark bamboo forests, across streams and shallow rivers.

Nang steered the truck around three more sharp curves. When they reached a rare straightaway, Nick asked him if his mother was ever happy on the plantation.

Nang considered this for a moment. "Yes, there were times she seemed very happy, but these were overshadowed by her fears."

"What was she afraid of?"

"Everything," Nang answered. "Snakes . . . your father's house, Hawk's Nest, which she thought was haunted; but her biggest fear was that you would be carried away by a tiger and be devoured."

"You're kidding." Nick knew about her fear of snakes and the haunted plantation house, but she had never said anything about tigers eating him.

"I am not," Nang answered. "This is why she kept you inside Hawk's Nest most of the time. But you did manage to escape one day. Do you remember?"

"Christmas day," Nick said with a smile. "Father smuggled me out of the nursery. I was five."

Nang laughed. "Yes. He took you out while your mother was still asleep."

Nick remembered it like it was yesterday. One of the Freestone traditions was to tour the plantation on elephant back on Christmas day. His mother didn't like the tours and insisted that Nick was too young to participate. But early that morning his father picked him up out of his bed, and, tiptoeing down the servant hall past his sleeping nanny, he carried Nick out the back door. Waiting for them, flapping his ears, his trunk investigating the unfamiliar smells coming from the garden, was Hannibal. His huge ivory tusks gleamed pink in the early morning light. A wooden bell hung from a rope around his neck. Hannibal was fifteen years old at the time, and his father was convinced he would become the plantation's greatest *koongyi* elephant.

"We use the koongyi to catch wild elephants and for the most difficult tasks," his father had explained. "They're a special breed with a rare combination of strength, intelligence, and courage. Hannibal has all these elements." He ruffled Nick's unruly black hair. "And so do you, Nicholas."

He tapped Hannibal behind the front knee with his elephant stick, or *choon*, then used the raised leg as a step to climb up onto his neck. Nang lifted Nick up to him. And sitting between his father's legs, Nick went for his first trip on elephant back.

When they returned to Hawk's Nest, much later than expected, his parents argued. A few days later, Nick and his mother were on a ship bound for the United States. Nick had developed a mild case of pneumonia, which she insisted on having treated in the United States.

After the pneumonia had run its course, his mother's excuse for not returning was that Nick was still too frail for the tropical climate. After this, it was his schooling. Then Bernard, an old school friend of hers from New York, came back into her life. She divorced Nick's father, married Bernard, and they moved to London, where Bernard was posted with the U.S. Army.

When they left Burma in 1933, she had known it was a one-way voyage.

Nick was unhappy in London. Despite being British on his father's side, he had a hard time fitting in. He sounded and thought differently from the boys and girls at his school. He was "a Yank adrift in a sea of Brits," as Bernard put it.

Even though his mother had remarried, she didn't interfere with Nick's correspondence with his father, who wrote to Nick several times a year. When a letter arrived from Burma, she placed it unopened on a silver tray in the foyer, where Nick was sure to see it.

At first the letters were short and simple, but as

Nick got older they became longer and more involved. His father wanted him to know everything about the teak plantation—past, present, and his plans for the future.

He told Nick how his great-grandfather, Sergeant Major Jackson Theodore Freestone, had mustered out of the British army after serving in India, bought three elephants with the last of his money, and traveled deep into the Burmese jungle with two elephant drivers, or *mahouts*, as they are called in India.

Standing on a broad plateau above a wide river, the Sergeant Major told the mahouts, "We'll build the elephant village down by the river and the plantation house right where we are standing. I will call the house *Hawk's Nest.*" The Sergeant Major was a great admirer of birds of prey.

The plantation was nothing more than raw jungle back then, filled with venomous snakes, leeches, tigers, leopards, flying squirrels, and sun bears. There were pangolin, macaque, gaur, hog deer, sambhur deer, muntjac, civet, swarms of biting insects, and of course, the wild elephants they planned to capture and train to harvest the valuable timber.

In addition to the letters, his father sent him books about forestry, elephant husbandry, Burmese culture, tropical medicine, and the religion of the country: Buddhism. Some of these books were difficult to understand, but Nick dutifully studied them anyway, gleaning what information he could.

It was a foregone conclusion, at least in Nick's mind, that he would one day return to Burma and eventually take over the family forestry business.

"But not until you graduate from the university," his mother had insisted, hoping that by that time, Nick's desire for elephants, timber, and the tropics would have diminished. Nick had thought about Burma every day for the past eight years. All he had ever wanted was to return to the plantation.

At first Nick was disappointed that his father hadn't been in Rangoon to meet him, but his disappointment passed quickly under Nang's cheerful banter. Nang's English was excellent, and his knowledge about the places they drove through was nothing short of astounding. He knew every tree, plant, and animal they came across. He also seemed to know someone in every village along the route. Wherever they stopped, people appeared with food, pots of green tea, and gossip, which was how information was passed from place to place in the jungle.

"Very few telephones in Burma," Nang said. "Or radios. Just people with busy mouths."

Nang was his father's *singoung*, or foreman, in charge of all the timber elephants and mahouts on the plantation.

"In Burma, mahouts are called *oozies*," Nang

explained as they drove, "which means, the man who sits on the neck. And my family has been sitting upon elephants since my grandfather, Taung Baw, came here with the Sergeant Major."

Nick's father had written to him about Taung Baw, which meant "Hilltop" in Burmese. He was a legend, and not just on the plantation, but throughout Burma. He was given the name Hilltop because he was discovered on a hill in India when he was just a few hours old. A group of mahouts working in the forest found him beneath a banyan tree and took him back to their village. His mother and father never stepped forward to claim him.

By the time he was a teenager, he was the greatest mahout in all of India. It was said that he knew the secret language of elephants—that he could talk to them as one human speaks to another human.

But Hilltop did not like all of the attention his fame brought to him, so when the Sergeant Major asked him to come to Burma, he was eager to go.

"My son, Indaw, who you will meet at the plantation," Nang continued, "is an excellent mahout. And Mya here is also very excellent with elephants, but in Burma, women cannot become mahouts. A pity, but it is the tradition."

Mya was not nearly as talkative as her father. In fact, she had barely said a word to Nick since they'd picked him up in Rangoon. She spent most of the long trip looking out the rear window at Miss Pretty. When they stopped for the night, the cow was off-loaded and tethered to a tree. Mya went into the forest with her machete, or *dah*, and cut piles of fodder, while Nang prepared their meal, which consisted of rice and whatever meat or fish they had picked up along the way. After dinner they unrolled their woven mats and bedded down for the night, serenaded by frogs, crickets, the grunt of a sambhur deer, and the occasional raspy roar of tigers.

Late on the third night they arrived at the plantation. Nick expected his father to be waiting for him at Hawk's Nest, but once again he was disappointed. His father wasn't there.

"Plantation business," the head houseman, Bukong, explained apologetically. "Very busy. I will show you to your room." He limped up the stairs, helped by a bamboo cane.

The Campfire 2

After Mya and her father dropped Nick at Hawk's Nest, they tied Miss Pretty to a tree in the jungle and cut enough bamboo to last her through the night.

"It's late," Mya's father said. "We'll leave the truck here and walk. I don't want to wake the village."

When they got there, they were surprised to see a campfire burning and several mahouts sitting around it arguing. Mya's father put his hand on her shoulder and held his finger to his lips. They stood in the shadows and listened.

"Rangoon was bombed today," one of the mahouts said.

"We don't know that for certain."

"I tell you it's true. The city will fall soon."

"What if it is true? Rangoon is a long way from here."

"He's right. Why would the Japanese bother us?"

"My cousin said that he saw a patrol not far from here just a week ago."

"It could have been a British patrol."

"No, they were Japanese. There is no doubt. He

14

was able to get a very good look at them."

"Your cousin is lucky the Japanese didn't see him."

"The Japanese are not our enemies. Their war is with the British. It's not our war."

"It's our country."

"It used to be our country until the British came and took it away," Magwe said.

Magwe's family had been on the plantation as long as Mya's family. His grandfather was the second mahout the Sergeant Major had brought from India with Hilltop.

"The Japanese are here to liberate us," Magwe said. "If you had any sense you would know this."

"How do you know they're here to liberate us?"

"I have my sources."

A thorn in Nang's side, Magwe was always second-guessing the singoung's decisions and causing dissension among the other mahouts. He was lazy, unkind to his elephant, and bitter that Mr. Freestone had made Mya's father singoung and not him. In Mya's opinion, Mr. Freestone should have kicked him and his family off the plantation long ago. But her father told her that Mr. Freestone would never do that. *To do so would be bad luck*, he had said. *This plantation started with the two mahouts, and their descendents will always be here. Tradition is important to Mr. Freestone, as it should be.*

"I wouldn't be surprised if Nang and his daughter do not return," Magwe said.

Mya nearly said something, but her father anticipated her outburst, and shook his head.

"They'll be back."

"Nang will never leave the plantation."

"You overestimate him," Magwe said. "I suspect
that Mr. Freestone sent him away to prepare things.
Mr. Freestone's son is not coming to Rangoon. Only a
fool would have his son come to Burma now."

"What about Indaw? Nang would not leave his
son behind."

"Of course not," Magwe said. "Indaw is in this
with them."

"But what will they do? Where will they go?"

"Now, those are interesting questions," Magwe
answered. "It's possible they won't go far. They might
stay right here in Burma and fight the Japanese. Hiding
in the forest, making sneak attacks on our liberators.
And who will be punished for these attacks?" He
paused. "*We* will be punished. Our wives and children
will suffer. Some will die. And Mr. Freestone will not
care. His only concern is for his precious plantation
and for the profits he makes on the trees harvested
with our sweat and blood."

"Go home," Nang whispered to Mya, then stepped
into the dim light of the campfire.

Mya did not go home.

Nang squatted down across from Magwe without
a word. He took a cheroot from his shirt pocket and lit

it with an ember from the fire. The other men stared at him like a spirit, or *nat*, had appeared out of the trees and joined them. Nats are forest spirits, and almost everything that goes wrong on the plantation is blamed on them. The mahouts built little houses, or shrines, outside their homes called *natshins* and offered the spirits food and other gifts, hoping to keep the nats happy so they stayed inside the shrines. If the nats didn't like the offering, they came out and tormented the mahouts and their families.

Nang looked each man in the eye one at a time. Some looked away; others, like Magwe, met his gaze with defiance.

"Miss Pretty is a beautiful elephant," Nang said. "She'll make a fine addition to the herd. And Mr. Freestone's son is a fine boy. He's up at Hawk's Nest. You'll all get a chance to meet him tomorrow."

He looked at one of the mahouts. "Tin, how are the two calves doing?"

"The training is going well," Tin answered. "We should be able to let them out of the crush sometime this week."

Nang turned to another mahout. "Won Lin, how is Kawlum's leg?"

"Nearly healed. She will be ready for work in a few days."

"Good. Because we have a lot of work to do." Nang puffed on his cheroot and waited.

"What were they talking about in Rangoon?" someone finally asked.

"The Japanese," Nang said.

"We heard that Rangoon was bombed today."

"It's possible," Nang said. "But there were no bombs when we were there. I wouldn't worry about it. The British and our soldiers have set up defenses all around the city. They're ready for whatever comes."

"And if the defenses fail?" Magwe asked. "What then?

Nang ignored the question. "You all know me. And you know that I believe we should have our independence. What you may not know is that Mr. Freestone also believes Burma should be an independent country, governed by its own people. He has been quietly working on this for many years. Regardless of what the Japanese have been saying, if they take this country they will not give us our freedom. They will enslave us."

"We're slaves now," Magwe said.

"You are free to come and go as you please under the British. You can leave this plantation any time you like and get a job at another plantation. I agree that our situation here under the British is not ideal, but it will be far worse under the Japanese."

"We've decided to meet at the pagoda tomorrow morning to discuss this," Magwe said. "Everyone is invited."

"Including Mr. Freestone?" Nang asked.

"No," Magwe answered. "He's been gone for three days. He's out with Captain Josephs. Indaw is with them. I don't suppose you know where they went or what they are doing?"

"Plantation business, I suppose," Nang said, standing up. "If we are to meet tomorrow morning, I suggest you all get some sleep."

Hawk's Nest 3

A warm breeze blew through the screened window of the bedroom, ruffling the mosquito netting around Nick's bed.

He opened his eyes. It was still dark out, but by the sounds coming from outside, dawn wasn't far off. He heard people talking and laughing in the distance. A generator motor rumbled somewhere near the house. He got up and switched on the overhead light. As he pulled on his pants, a quick movement on the ceiling caught his eye.

Lizards.

At least a half dozen of them scurrying toward the light to hunt for insects.

The larger lizards took up positions closer to the bulb, where the hunting was better. One of the smaller lizards made a desperate lunge for a juicy moth, missed, and fell onto the mosquito netting. Nick tried to free it, but the more he tried, the more tangled it became.

"It's a nuisance when they get balled up like that."

Nick jumped. "Father!"

He stood in the doorway, grinning, with an old rucksack slung over one shoulder, a rifle over the other. It was all Nick could do to stop himself from throwing his arms around him. But he was fourteen now—too old for that.

His father stepped into the room. "Sorry I couldn't make it to Rangoon to meet you."

"That's all right," Nick stammered. "Nang and Mya took good care of me."

"And how was Miss Pretty?"

"She was no trouble at all."

Nick hadn't seen his father since he had visited London two years before. He had aged. His black hair had a little gray in it now. His tea-color eyes had sunk deeper into the sockets, as if he had lost weight. He hadn't shaved. His clothes were soiled and sweat-stained. During his visits to London he was always immaculately groomed. In all the photographs Nick had seen of him on the plantation, even on elephant back supervising mahouts, he was crisply attired. Nick wondered if he had been ill recently. Malaria was common in Burma, and his father had suffered many bouts of it over the years.

"How's your mother?" he asked.

"Good, considering the blitz and the apartment burning. She's been very busy at the embassy."

"I imagine so. And Bernard?"

Nick shook his head. "He's been out of the country

for a while. We haven't heard from him."

"Bernard is resourceful. I'm sure he's fine."

His father and Bernard had gotten along very well. "You've grown."

"A bit," Nick said self-consciously. He had gained some weight since the war started. School sports had been all but canceled, and with the air raids and curfews, it was difficult to get outside to exercise. He changed the subject. "Have you been out all night?"

His father nodded. "And I'm afraid I'm going to have to leave again, but I should be back late this evening or early tomorrow morning."

Nick tried to hide his disappointment.

"I know this is not the kind of homecoming you imagined, but it can't be helped," he said. "When I get back we'll go out for a Christmas ride."

Nick had almost forgotten about Christmas. During the long journey from England to Burma he had lost track of time. "What day is it?"

"December twenty-fourth," his father answered. "Someone will be up later this morning to show you around the village." He walked closer to the netting. "Now, let's see what we can do about that lizard." He set his rucksack and rifle down. "The lizards moved into the house before the Sergeant Major finished building it. I suppose they have more right to be here than I do, in some respects. They certainly keep the insects under control."

The mesh had wrapped around the lizard so many times it looked as if it were encased in a cocoon. "Not this one," Nick pointed out.

His father smiled. "When they get this tangled it's easier to cut them out and have the net mended." He handed Nick his pocketknife. The handle was made of ivory. Carved into the ivory was an intricate scene of timber elephants harvesting logs.

Nick opened the worn but sharp blade and cut around the writhing lizard, leaving a hole in the netting big enough for a flying fox to pass through. The mummified lizard squirmed in his palm. "Now what?"

"I'll show you." His father took the lizard and picked at the netting until he loosened an edge, which he pinched between his thumb and index finger. "It's the lizard's tiny claws that cause the trouble with the nets." He squatted down and began gently shaking the cocoon just above the floor. With each shake, another layer of netting came loose. "You just let gravity sort it out."

The lizard dropped to the floor, hissed at them, then skittered under the bed. Nick held out the pocketknife.

His father shook his head. "I want you to keep it."

"I couldn't." Nick knew how much the knife meant to his father. The handle had been carved by the Sergeant Major himself.

"My father gave it to me, and his father gave it to him," he said. "It's your turn to have it now. We'll call it an early Christmas present."

Nick looked at the knife's yellowed, ivory handle. "I'll be careful with it."

"No, you'll use it like all the Freestones have used it. It's not a priceless heirloom to be taken out on special occasions and shown off. It's a knife . . . a tool."

Nick put it in his pocket. "Thank you."

His father reached for his rucksack and rifle.

"You're going right now?"

"Yes, Indaw is meeting me out front. I just came by to—"

"I'll go with you." Nick started digging through his trunk to find a shirt.

"Not today, Nicholas," his father said gently.

Nick looked up at him. "I go by Nick now."

His father nodded, then continued. "I need to check out some things. Too many people tagging along could make it a little dicey. You understand."

Nick did not understand, but he didn't want to get into an argument with his father the first day on the plantation.

At the bottom of his trunk was a small box. He took it out and gave it to his father.

"What's this?"

Nick smiled. "An early Christmas present for *you*. Open it."

Inside the box was a small diary with pale blue paper and a leather cover. Embossed on the cover in gold letters was his father's name. Nick had found it in a shop down the road from their apartment. It was one of the few things that had survived the fire.

His father fanned through the blank sheets. "It's very nice indeed."

"I didn't know if you kept a diary or not."

"I'll put it to good use." He slipped it into his rucksack. "Thank you. I'm sorry for this confusion, Nichol . . . Nick. Believe me, I wish circumstances were different." He started for the door, then stopped and looked back. "You may hear some rumors when you get to the village. Don't be alarmed."

"What kind of rumors?"

He stared at Nick for a moment. "About the Japanese," he said.

"When we passed through Rangoon, we saw the fortifications and a lot of British soldiers," Nick said. "Do you think the Japanese are going to invade?"

"They started bombing the city yesterday."

"Will it affect us here?"

"At some point, yes." His father looked at his watch. "I really have to go. We'll talk more about it when I get back. When you're ready, go down to the dining room and they'll serve you breakfast. Again, I'm sorry about this."

"I'll be fine," Nick said, although he wasn't entirely

certain if this were true or not.

"I'll see you later, then." His father turned and walked out of the bedroom.

It looks like the war has followed me halfway around the world, Nick thought. Is this why Father was out all night?

He stepped out onto the veranda. A red sun was rising above the river, and he got his first glimpse of the elephant village two hundred yards below Hawk's Nest. The villagers were awake and busy. Smoke drifted toward the house from the cooking fires. He breathed in the spicy smell and watched the children feeding the chickens and pigs wandering among the houses. His father had written to him about the village and the people who lived there.

The Burmese, both men and women, wear long colorful skirts called longyis—*a simple tube of cotton cloth knotted at the waist to keep it up.*

The villagers' simple one-room houses are made of bamboo and teak and are built on stilts to keep the water out during the monsoon season from mid-May to mid-November. The stilts also discourage snakes from taking up residence inside (and there are many snakes here). The mahouts and their families sleep on the floor on woven mats, which are rolled up when not in use.

His father had offered to run electricity down to

the village from the generator that supplied Hawk's Nest, but the mahouts declined the offer, preferring to light their homes with the kerosene lanterns and candles they had always used.

The mahouts do not embrace change easily. There is a special place they go to discuss such things. It's called the pagoda—an ancient ruin the Sergeant Major discovered soon after he arrived here. It's located half a mile from Hawk's Nest. In the old days, before Hawk's Nest was built, the Sergeant Major met the mahouts there every morning before they went out into the forest to work.

Nick looked downriver. A group of women were making charcoal by burying smoking black embers in the sand along the bank. There were few men in the village. Nick guessed that most of them had already gone into the forest to retrieve their elephants.

Timber elephants work five or six hours a day during the morning. In the afternoon it becomes too hot. The mahouts set the elephants free to wander where they will during their off hours. Each elephant wears a wooden bell around its neck so the mahout can find it in the forest. Some elephants wander as many as six miles during the night. If the behavior persists, we put fetters on their front ankles to slow them down. Each bell sounds a little different, and each mahout knows the sound of his elephant's bell. Dangerous

elephants are given iron bells so people know to stay away
from them. Hannibal wears one now.

A dusty car pulled up in front of the house. A man
with red hair and a bushy mustache, wearing a military uniform, got out. From the veranda, Nick
watched his father approach the car and shake the
man's hand. They were joined by a Burmese boy not
much older than Nick, wearing a purple longyi. His
father gave the boy a broad grin.

That must be Indaw, Nick thought. Nang's son.
Why is *he* going with them and not me?

Nick waved, but they didn't see him. They got into
the car and drove away.

Before going down for breakfast, Nick decided to look
around upstairs.

When he was young, he hadn't been allowed on
the second floor. His mother was afraid he would fall
down the stairs, and his father was afraid he would
disturb the houseguests, of which there were many
back then. The nearest town of any size was over sixty
miles away—a two-day trip during the dry season,
and nearly impossible during the monsoons, except on
elephantback. When visitors came, they usually spent
several nights.

There were seven bedrooms upstairs: three large
bedrooms at the front of the house and four smaller

ones at the back, each with a private bath. The rooms were nearly identical, with dark hardwood paneling and small fireplaces. Above each fireplace was a magnificently carved elephant—a theme carried throughout the house. Even at five, Nick had thought the fireplaces were an odd touch in the tropics. His mother had told him that the Sergeant Major was a little "quirky" and had designed the house with a fireplace in nearly every room to remind him of the chilly nights in England.

Each bedroom was furnished with a large bed draped with mosquito netting, a writing desk, a vanity, a dresser, and a wardrobe. The teak floors were covered with thick oriental carpets.

The back bedrooms had a view of the garden, which was just as Nick remembered it. When he was little he was allowed to play out there, but only after the gardeners checked all the bushes for snakes. The reflecting pools were clear enough to see the koi feeding on the bottom, the hedges were neatly trimmed, and the paths looked as if they had been raked that morning. Nick was happy to see his father was still maintaining it. He had wondered if he would after his mother left. She'd loved the garden.

Between the back bedrooms was a flight of stairs leading down to the servants' quarters and Nick's old nursery, which was near the kitchen. This is where he'd spent most of his time. He could still close his eyes and recall the quarters—every nook and cranny. The servants' rooms were not nearly as grand as the upstairs bedrooms, but it was a happy place. His parents had been good to the servants, and the servants had been very kind to him.

The three front bedrooms overlooked the river and the elephant village. Nick's bedroom was on the left, the room in the middle was unoccupied, and the third room was his father's.

He stood in his father's doorway. The bed was still made, verifying he had not slept in it the previous night. Next to the bed was a reading chair and a table with two photographs in a small hinged frame. He stepped inside for a closer look. The first was a photo of Nick sitting between his father's legs on top of Hannibal. The second was a photo of his grandfather holding him when he was baby. His grandfather had died when Nick was six months old.

Sitting next to the table lamp was a stack of books. He scanned the titles. *Bushido and the Samurai; The Rising Sun: Japan's Rise to Power; Matsuo Basho: Japan's Master Poet; English/Japanese Dictionary*. And many others. It looked like his father had been preparing for the Japanese for some time.

Nick left the bedroom and walked down the staircase to the ground floor. The entry hall was checkered with black-and-white tiles, which had always reminded him of a giant chessboard.

The front door was big enough to let a small elephant through. He pulled it open, then closed it with a satisfied smile. When he was little, no matter how hard he tried, he could not budge that door.

To the right of the entry was his father's office and library, the largest room in the house and, by far, Nick's favorite place when he was young. Along the walls were floor-to-ceiling shelves filled with books. In the center of the room was a huge desk carved out of a single piece of teak by the Sergeant Major. The desk was called "the Helm," because this is where most of the plantation decisions were made. Nick used to play under the desk nearly every day while his father worked on plantation business above. His favorite game was to protect the Helm from invading enemies with his lead soldiers.

He got down on his knees and felt under the desk for the old cigar box he used to store the soldiers in, and was surprised to find it exactly where he had left it. His toy army had not deserted the Helm.

On the wall behind the desk was yet another fireplace, but this fireplace was much bigger than the ones in the bedrooms. And there was another difference. It was filled with ashes. Nick set the cigar box on the desk and walked over to it. The ashes were still warm. Someone—his father, he presumed—had started a fire that morning. Why? It was at least eighty degrees in the house. He wandered over to the walk-in vault to the left of the fireplace. The heavy steel door was closed and locked. The inside, he remembered, was lined with file cabinets, where all the plantation papers, correspondence, and other valuables were kept. Had his father been burning files? he wondered.

He walked back to the fireplace. Above the mantel were three large portraits. The one on the left was the Sergeant Major in his military uniform riding a tusker in the forest. The portrait in the middle was his grand-father, Jackson Theodore Freestone the Second, sitting at the Helm taking care of plantation business. Nick's father was in the portrait on the right. Like the Sergeant Major, he was astride a huge tusker, but crouched in front of the bull was a tiger ready to pounce. The bull's ears were flared, his trunk curled under, ready to strike. An iron bell hung around his neck. Hannibal.

His father had written him many letters about the famous bull, and Nick wasn't surprised to see him in the portrait. Five years earlier, during the course of a single night, Hannibal had been transformed from a trusted koongyi into the most feared and dangerous animal on the plantation. A tiger had attacked him. The wounds healed, but Hannibal was never the same after that.

Nick stared at the portraits for a long time. He saw himself in the men—the black hair, the prominent hawklike nose. His physique was different, though.

He wasn't nearly as lean and hard as the men in the portraits. Another difference was in the eyes. Theirs were dark and piercing. Nick's were green, like his mother's. But he had inherited another trait from the men, one that could not be seen in the portraits. Something his mother called "Freestone Blood." The Freestones were brash, stubborn, and had bad tempers.

At one time or another, she had warned, *all of the Freestone men have gotten into trouble because of their Freestone blood. It will be your undoing if you don't learn to control it.*

As Nick looked around the library he began to feel uneasy. One day he would be sitting behind the Helm, in charge of the mahouts, the servants, the elephants, the trees, the village, Hawk's Nest . . . all of it. How was he going to learn everything he needed to know? He hadn't been raised here like the men in the portraits. He felt a sudden urge to get out from under the Freestones' piercing stares.

Nick returned the box of soldiers to its hiding place. As he stepped back into the entry hall he had another realization: aside from his father, he hadn't seen anyone in the house.

When he was young, the house had been filled with activity, especially in the morning. A parade of people streaming in and out the front door, cleaning, setting flowers in every room, making beds, dusting, polishing, sweeping . . .

He rushed into the servants' quarters. They were empty. The only movement came from the whirring ceiling fans. The house was immaculately clean, but where were the servants?

He stepped into his old nursery, expecting to see it totally changed—after all, it had been nine years since he'd been there—but to his surprise it was exactly the same. His crib was still in the corner. Next to it was a small bed, which he had graduated to not long before he left Burma. On the nightstand was his reading lamp with the cowboy-and-Indian shade. Opposite the bed was the small fireplace, where he'd once believed the boogeyman hid. The window was covered with an iron grate—the only window in the house that was—something his mother had insisted on.

He opened the toy box and found his six-shooters, stuffed animals, books, puzzles, balls, airplanes, trucks, blocks. . . . Strange his father would leave everything as it was. He wasn't the sentimental type. Had he thought we were coming back?

He left the nursery and walked down the hallway to the kitchen. Surely there would be people there. Every pot and pan hung in its place, the sinks were gleaming, the counters wiped down, the floor swept, the griddle warm to the touch, but there were no cooks or servants. What's going on here? he wondered. He pushed open the swinging door to the dining room. The long table was set for one person. He took the silver cover off the plate. Scrambled eggs, bacon, toast. Next to the plate was a pot of tea. All of it warm, but not hot. Clearly it had been sitting there a while.

Desperate to talk to someone, he grabbed a slice of toast and left the house.

The Elephant Village 4

In his hurry to get down to the village, Nick nearly ran over a Buddhist monk walking up the trail.

"I beg your pardon," Nick stammered, out of breath, embarrassed.

The monk smiled but said nothing. He was old. Most of his teeth were missing, and those that remained were stained orange from chewing betel nut, a mild narcotic that grew wild in the forest. His head was shaved. He wore a faded saffron-colored robe, tattered and muddy at the hem, where it dragged on the ground. He was carrying a black, enameled alms bowl.

Nick put his hands together in front of his face and bowed—the traditional Buddhist greeting. The monk returned the bow.

On the trip from Rangoon, Nick had seen dozens of Buddhist monks. Sometimes they walked alone, sometimes in groups, carrying their bowls. Because they were not allowed to kill anything, including plants, they had to rely on the kindness of strangers to eat. When people put food in their bowls, they received a blessing in return. The monks were not allowed to refuse an offering, they could not take more food than the bowl held, and the food had to be eaten before midday—their only meal of the day.

Nick was still holding the toast he had taken from the table. He held it out, and the monk opened the bowl's lid with a trembling hand. As Nick put the toast inside, he saw that it was the only offering the monk had received that day. He wondered if the monk's trembling hands were caused by his age, or by hunger.

"I'm Nick Freestone."

The monk smiled but did not respond.

"Jackson Freestone's son," Nick added.

The monk remained silent.

Nick pointed up the trail. "There's no one at the house. I just came from there. Do you know where everyone is?"

The monk's expression did not change.

Nick figured he didn't understand English, or else he had taken a vow of silence. Whatever the reason, it was clear he wasn't going to answer his question. Nick was about to say good-bye and continue down to the village when he remembered the food he'd left on the dining room table.

"Wait here." Nick motioned for the monk to stay where he was. "I'll be right back."

He ran back up the trail to the house, took two quick bites of scrambled egg, ate a piece of bacon, scraped the rest into the napkin, then ran back down the trail. The monk hadn't moved.

"It's not much," Nick explained, "but it's good." He stuffed the food into the bowl, filling it almost to the top.

The monk bowed his head and mumbled some words Nick didn't understand, then continued up the trail toward Hawk's Nest.

"There's no one up there," Nick told him again, but the monk didn't turn around. Nick stared after him for a moment, then turned and walked the rest of the way down the trail to the elephant village.

Except for a few chickens pecking in the dirt, pigs wallowing in the mud, and a couple of dogs lounging in the shade, the village was deserted. This explained the monk's empty bowl. But where were all the people he'd seen from the balcony not an hour before?

Nick climbed the steps of the nearest house. "Hello? Is anyone here?"

He stuck his head inside. There was no front door. No glass or screens on the windows. No mosquito netting. No furniture. Along one wall was a shelf with a few bowls and cooking utensils. An old calendar with a photo of a snow-covered mountain hung on another wall. In one corner was a metal bucket filled with charcoal. The sleeping mats were rolled up in another corner. The only color came from the longyis hanging on nails.

Nick began to think he should have waited at Hawk's Nest for the mahout who was going to show him around. Maybe the guide is up there right now, wondering where I am, he thought.

Nick hurried down the rickety stairs and started back through the village, but something stopped him. A sound. Metal on metal, faint but growing louder. He waited, listening.

A shadow appeared behind a house thirty feet in front of him. He glanced at the animals. All of them—the pigs, the goat, the dogs, even the chickens—were also staring at the shadow. Something yellowish, dense, as big around as a lamppost appeared from behind the house, followed by a massive gray trunk, then a head, ears, and legs the size of small trees. The biggest animal he had ever seen stepped out into the open. Nick forgot to breathe. Metal on metal. The iron bell. Hannibal.

The bull raised his trunk, scenting the air as he drew closer. Paralyzed with fear and awe, Nick could not seem to make his legs move.

Hannibal's right ear was torn. The left tusk was two feet shorter than the right. Scars ran from the top of his head to the base of his trunk. The tiger's claws had plowed deep. Nick couldn't see them, but he knew from his father's letters, there were more scars on his flanks and back.

The iron bell fell silent. Hannibal stood in front of

Nick with his tusks inches from his chest. Nick told himself to run, but his legs remained rooted in place as the terrible ways elephants kill echoed through his head.

. . . impale you with a tusk, stomp on you with their feet, throw you, bash you against a tree, crush your head in their mouths, do a headstand on your chest . . . The cows are generally passive, but the bulls are an entirely different story. You can rely on a bull, but you can never give him your complete trust. With little warning he will turn on you as quick and deadly as a cobra. . . .

Nick never saw the hit coming. One moment he was looking at Hannibal's ragged scars, the next he was flying backward, the last ounce of air knocked from his lungs. He hit the ground on his back. His chest felt as if it were on fire.

Hannibal walked over and stood above him, one yellow tusk nearly scraping the ground. *Impale . . . stomp . . . bash . . . crush . . .*

Nick had never felt terror like this. Numbness. Acceptance of the inevitable. He was going to die in a dusty Burmese elephant village.

Hannibal ran the wet tip of his trunk all over Nick's body, then did something totally unexpected. He walked away.

Metal on metal, the sound of the iron bell . . . faded.

Drenched in sweat, Nick took in several painful gulps of air, got shakily to his feet, and looked in the direction the bull had taken.

Hannibal wasn't there.

The Guide 5

Mya knocked on the front door of Hawk's Nest, but there was no answer.

The boy must still be asleep, she thought. She didn't blame him. Mya was tired too. If her father hadn't woken her for the meeting at the pagoda, she would still be on her sleeping mat dreaming of Miss Pretty. She knocked on the front door again, and when there was still no answer, she sat down on the steps to wait.

The meeting that morning was more of the same, with her father and Magwe arguing about what to do if the war came to the plantation. The other villagers seemed evenly divided, some siding with the British, and others thinking a Japanese occupation would be good.

Mya had no opinion one way or another. Regardless of who occupied the country, she would never become a mahout, which was all she had ever really cared about.

When she was a little girl she trained village dogs to let her ride them. When she outgrew the dogs she rode the pigs, and after that, the oxen. Her father and the other villagers were amazed at her ability with animals.

"She's fearless."

"There isn't an animal alive Mya can't train."

"She must have been a great mahout in her former life."

"She is as good with animals as her brother, Indaw."

"It's a shame she was reincarnated as a girl instead of a boy."

Her father and Aunt Kin-Kin thought she would give up on becoming a mahout as she got older.

"Elephants are dangerous, Mya," her father had lectured her on more than one occasion. "It's one thing to ride a village pig or dog. Those are domestic animals. Elephants are wild and cooperate with us out of kindness when their mood is right. I have personally known seven mahouts who have been killed by elephants."

"If working with elephants is so dangerous, why have you encouraged Indaw to become a mahout?" Mya would ask. "Certainly you love him as much as you love me."

"Indaw is a man, and all the men in our family have been mahouts. It's tradition. And as a man he is much stronger than you."

"Stronger than his elephant?"

"Of course not."

"Have you ever met a mahout stronger than his elephant?"

"No."

"So strength has little to do with controlling an elephant."

"I'm not talking about physical strength."

"Then what kind of strength are you talking about?"

Her father would throw his hands up in the air whenever they argued. "It's tradition! Women are not allowed to become mahouts. It's bad luck to even think about it!"

Aunt Kin-Kin, who had raised Mya after her mother had died, was no less strident in her objections to Mya's wish, but she used a completely different argument. "There is no place in the deep forest for a young woman, or an old woman, for that matter. When mahouts get off by themselves they become as wild as nats. They are completely different than they are here in the village under the influence of women. You're too young to understand, but you wouldn't want to be out in the deep forest with them. Every time something went wrong you would be blamed for it because you're a woman. You need to let go of this notion, Mya."

Mya had tried to do as they asked, but when her father invited her to pick up Miss Pretty, her desire to become a mahout returned stronger than ever. She could not seem to take her eyes off the elegant koongyi. It was as if she had known Miss Pretty since she was a calf—impossible, because Miss Pretty was nearly three times as old as Mya, but still there was something between them, something she had stayed up pondering most of the night.

Mya left the pagoda long before the meeting was over. Her father had asked her to check on Miss Pretty, then go up to Hawk's Nest to meet Nick Freestone and show him around the village. She was surprised her father had asked. Normally, when a new elephant was brought to the plantation, a mahout was assigned and he immediately took over the responsibilities for the elephant's needs. And being asked to show Nick around was even more unusual. In Mr. Freestone's absence, her father or a senior mahout should have been picked to do this. Mya was eager to do both tasks. In fact, she had stayed well out of her father's way all morning in case he changed his mind.

Mya had checked on Miss Pretty before going up to Hawk's Nest, and found she'd eaten all of the bamboo they had cut the night before and had stripped every branch in reach. When Miss Pretty saw Mya, she started flapping her ears and thumping her trunk on the ground.

"Thirsty?" Mya asked. "Hungry, too, I suppose. I can get you some water, but I didn't bring my dah, so food will be more difficult. But I'll see what I can do."

She found the water bucket, which had a few extra dents from Miss Pretty kicking it around during the night. "I see you have a little temper when things aren't going your way." She filled the bucket in the stream and brought it back.

Mya steadied the bucket, careful to stay just out of Miss Pretty's reach while she eagerly sucked the water up and blew it into her mouth. The first and second buckets were emptied quickly, but with the third, Miss Pretty took her time, which allowed Mya to think a little more about why her father had given her this honor.

Perhaps he's changed his mind about me becoming a mahout. Why else would he ask me to help him pick up Miss Pretty? she wondered. Was the trip a test to see if I am still interested in elephants?

Mya had been very good the past month. She had sneaked over to the elephant training camp only once in that entire time. She couldn't resist. Two five-year-old calves had been taken from their mothers to start their training. Mya had sat hidden in a tree hour after hour, ignoring the biting insects, and even the green tree snake until it slithered a little too close, forcing her to climb higher to get out of its way. The only trouble with sneaking was that she could not tell anyone about it afterward. Back at the house she had to listen in frustrating silence as Indaw and her father discussed how the training was going. She didn't dare offer her opinions because that would give her away.

But today will be different, she thought. Today I can ask any question I want, go wherever I please, including the training camp, because I'll be with Nick Freestone. Father did not put any restrictions on me, and there are certainly no restrictions on where Nick Freestone can go.

"Enough?" she asked Miss Pretty. "If you quit pulling on your rope and stop fretting so much, you'll be more comfortable. I'll get you a little bit of food, then I have to go."

She went back to the stream and gathered an armful of bamboo, wishing she had remembered her dah. A real mahout always had a dah strapped around his waist and his choon in his hand. Indaw had made her a choon when she was eight years old. It wasn't a very good one. The iron tip was dull, and the handle was made of bamboo instead of teak, but it had worked well enough on pigs and oxen. She would have to ask him to make her a proper choon. One that Miss Pretty would respect.

"Listen to me!" she said aloud. "Father's not going to give me Miss Pretty."

She lay the bamboo in front of Miss Pretty. The pile looked pitifully small in front of the big elephant, but that was all she could do for the moment. "I'll be right back with Nick Freestone and give you some more."

* * *

Mya had left Miss Pretty two hours ago and was still sitting on the porch, waiting impatiently for Nick to wake up. How long can someone sleep? Perhaps I should go back down and check on Miss Pretty again.

She stood and was about to do just that, when Nick came stumbling up the path from the village. His clothes were smeared with dirt and sweat, and his face was as red as a betel nut. He raised his arm in greeting, then grimaced in obvious pain.

"I thought you were still inside," Mya said. "What happened to you?"

"I walked down to the village."

Mya stared at his clothes. He looked like he had *rolled* down to the village.

"Oh," Nick said, brushing away some dirt. "I slipped coming up the path." He wasn't about to tell her that Hannibal had knocked him down. "Where is everyone? You're the first person I've talked to except for my father and an old monk."

"Your father is here?" Mya asked in surprise. Mr. Freestone and Indaw weren't expected back until the following day.

"Not anymore," Nick said. "He stopped in for a moment early this morning, but he had to leave again."

"Was Indaw with him?"

"Yes. At least I think it was him. They were with a British officer with red hair."

"Captain Josephs." Why hadn't Indaw stopped by to see her? she wondered. He usually did when he was near the village. "The village had a meeting this morning," she said.

"At the pagoda?"

"Yes." Mya was surprised he knew about the pagoda.

"That explains where everyone was," Nick said. "Well, I guess I better go in and get cleaned up. Someone is supposed to come by to show me around."

"I'm that someone."

"You?"

Mya nodded. He looked a little disappointed. "If you're not feeling up to it I could—"

"No, no . . . I'm fine. I just need to get into some clean clothes. It'll only take a few minutes. Do you want to wait inside? It's cooler." He opened the front door.

"I'll wait here," Mya said, staying put on the porch. It was a well-known fact that Hawk's Nest was haunted.

The Training Camp 6

The pain in Nick's chest and ribs was bad—he was barely able to take in a full breath without screaming. But this was nothing compared to the embarrassment he felt.

Every book he'd read about elephants warned against getting near one without a mahout present. He had not only violated this cardinal rule, he'd done it with a bull elephant wearing an iron bell. He should have slipped into one of the houses until Hannibal had passed through the village. He couldn't believe how stupid he'd been. He was lucky to be alive.

Each step up the stairs sent a hot stab of pain throughout his rib cage. When he reached his bathroom, he filled the tub with hot water. Before the war he had been on his school's rugby team and knew a little something about treating injuries. He took off his shirt, looked in the mirror, and gingerly felt his chest and ribs, wincing in pain. Two or three broken or cracked ribs, maybe four. He looked at the tub. Taking a scalding hot bath in the middle of an already blistering morning was not his idea of fun, but he knew it was the only thing he could do to stop the muscles from stiffening.

After the bath he felt a little better, but it still took him a long time to get his clothes on, especially his socks and shirt. He was halfway hoping that Mya had gotten tired of waiting and left, so he could go back upstairs and lie down. But when he opened the front door, she was still sitting on the porch.

"I'm sorry I took so long."

Mya gave him a curt nod, then started down the trail a lot faster than Nick would have liked. When she reached the bottom, instead of going left toward the village, she took a trail to the right.

"Where are you going?" Nick whined, struggling to keep up with her.

"I have to check on Miss Pretty," she called back, and if anything, she started to walk even faster.

Nick caught up to her in a small clearing with a stream running through it. He could see the torn-up ground and the barked tree Miss Pretty had been tied to, but she wasn't there now. "Where is she?"

"Someone took her away."

"Who?"

"My father," Mya snapped. "Or another mahout."

"Is everything all right?"

"Yes."

It was obvious by her look and tone that she was upset about something. She turned away from him, looking like she was on the verge of tears. Nick wanted to do something, but he had no idea what that might be. He took a step toward her. "Is there anything I—"

Mya turned around. "Are there mahouts in Britain?"

Nick stopped. "Uh . . . no. Why?"

"In America?"

"No . . . I mean, they have elephants in zoos in both countries, but—"

"Are woman allowed to take care of them?"

"I don't know. I guess so . . . if they wanted to."

"Not here," Mya said sharply. "Only men can become mahouts."

Nick didn't know why she was snapping at him. He wasn't responsible for Burmese customs.

She crossed a small stream and started to walk away.

"Where are you going now?" he asked.

"To the elephant training camp," she said, without looking back. "Are you coming?"

"I guess so. How far away is it?"

"Not far."

Nick learned that "not far" to Mya was about six miles. His father had written to him about the terrible heat, but the letters had not prepared him for this. Each breath of hot humid air seared his lungs as if they were being parboiled, and the cracked ribs were not helping matters. He began to seriously doubt he would have the strength to make it back to Hawk's Nest after they got to wherever they were going.

As they approached the camp they heard men's voices, but the talk ended abruptly when Mya and Nick stepped into view. There were a dozen mahouts sitting around a small fire, smoking cheroots and drinking tea. The men glared at the intruders in suspicious silence. Nick glanced at Mya. She seemed as surprised at their icy reception as he was.

One of the men got up from the circle, threw his cheroot in the dust, crushed it with his bare foot, and started shouting at Mya in Burmese. Nick didn't understand what he was saying, but his message was reflected perfectly in Mya's stunned and embarrassed expression. They weren't welcome here.

"What's he saying?" Nick demanded, his Freestone blood boiling to the surface.

Mya started to answer but was cut off by the man before she got a single word out.

"I was telling Mya that women are not allowed in the training camp," he said in nearly perfect English. "A fact that she well knows."

Mya's cheeks flushed, and she bowed her head.

"That's no reason to shout at her," Nick said. "And our presence here is actually my fault."

Mya looked up.

"I asked her to bring me here. I apologize if I've violated one of your customs, but I just arrived last

53

night, and I could not have possibly found this camp on my own."

The man walked up to Nick and stopped an inch from his chest. "What are *you* doing here, then?"

Nick straightened up as best as he could with his sore ribs. "My name is Nick Freestone, and I assume I'm free to go wherever I please on the plantation with whomever I please. And you are?"

"Magwe," the man said.

The name sounded familiar. "Am I wrong about going where I please?" Nick asked.

Magwe didn't answer. His attention had been drawn away by something just beyond Nick's right shoulder. Nick turned and saw the monk from that morning standing at the edge of the clearing. The other mahouts quickly got to their feet and bowed their heads.

The monk returned their bow, then approached. Magwe lowered his head and started speaking quietly in Burmese.

"Use English, Magwe," the monk said. "The boy does not speak our language."

Nick looked at the monk in surprise. Why hadn't he used English when they'd met on the trail?

Magwe explained that Nick and Mya's sudden appearance had startled the men, and that was why he had been upset. Nick began to protest, but remembered his mother's warning about the Freestone blood, and stopped himself.

"Mr. Freestone himself," Magwe continued, "usually gives us some warning before he pays a visit. This way there's time to prepare the camp. And Mr. Freestone would never bring a female here. It's well known that their presence will upset the nats and bring bad luck."

The monk regarded Magwe with mild distaste as he listened to his explanation. When Magwe finished, the monk turned to Mya and smiled with obvious affection. Mya returned the smile, then bowed.

"There have been women in the training camp before," the monk said. "And I don't recall the nats causing any mischief because of it."

"What women have been here?" Magwe asked.

"Mrs. Freestone, for one," the monk answered. "She used to come here often. She liked watching the elephants being trained."

This was news to Nick. He was under the impression that his mother didn't even like elephants. She had certainly never mentioned visiting the training camp.

"That was a long time ago," Magwe said.

A far-off look came into the monk's eyes. "For me it seems like yesterday. I don't think the nats will mind Mya being here, but I am wondering why you're here today, Magwe."

Magwe shifted uneasily. "We were just passing by," he said. "With Nang busy and Indaw gone, I thought I should check on the calves."

"I saw Nang not an hour ago," the monk said calmly. "He was wondering where you were. He said that you and your mahouts were supposed to be up on Swe Hill working. In two hours it will be too hot for your elephants. Perhaps you should go to your assigned area."

"We were on our way there when Mya and the boy arrived," Magwe said.

Nick bit his tongue. They weren't on their way anywhere when he and Mya got there.

"Let's get back to work!" Magwe said and walked over to a line of elephants tied to a picket at the edge of the clearing. Several of the men joined him. They untied the elephants, clambered up on their necks, and rode off into the forest without another word.

As Nick watched them leave he wondered who this monk was.

"My mother used to come to the training camp?"

The monk smiled. "It was your grandmother who enjoyed watching the elephants," he answered. "Her name was Mrs. Freestone, too."

"This morning on the path," Nick said, "you didn't speak."

"I was practicing walking meditation," the monk said.

Nick nodded, although he had no idea what walking meditation was.

* * *

After Magwe left, most of the remaining mahouts dropped their surly attitudes. The monk followed along silently as the head elephant trainer, Tin, showed Mya and Nick around the camp.

The two five-year-old elephant calves were being held in the center of camp in small enclosures made of logs.

"The enclosure is called an elephant crush," Tin explained, "which is very much like the cattle chutes you use in America. It doesn't crush them, of course; it confines the calf so we can get around it safely until it learns to accept our presence."

"How do you restrain larger elephants?" Nick was thinking of Hannibal, who had been much bigger than these calves when he was captured.

"We put them in bigger crushes," Tin answered happily.

"Where are their mothers?"

"We fettered them on the far side of the plantation so they wouldn't come here to rescue their calves."

"Does that happen?"

"Oh, yes," Tin said. "Mothers are fond of their babies."

The calves were both about five feet tall and seemed to have adjusted to the separation. The mahouts constantly talked to them as they demonstrated what the elephants had learned.

"Pick up your pretty feet. . . ."

"*Hmit, hmit* . . . Lie down, lie down . . . The ground is soft. . . ."

"*La, la* . . . Come, come . . ."

"I have a treat for you of tamarind and salt. . . ."

"A timber elephant is trained its entire life," Tin explained. "When it goes into the forest with its mother, the calf learns by watching her move logs. We call this period C.A.H., or Calf at Heels. At age five, they begin their formal training. The calves will be here for three or four months. We will teach them to lie down, to come, pick up objects with their trunks. We introduce them to the saddle, or the *ohndone*, and the padding that goes beneath it."

There was a pile of padding lying next to the crush. Nick bent down and touched it. "It feels like bark," he said.

"The padding is called *thay-ay*," Tin explained. "It comes from the *bambwe* tree. It protects the elephant's back from chafing and sores."

Nick stood up. "What happens after they accept the saddle?"

"We get them used to having a mahout on their neck and teach them the meaning of the feet and toe commands we use to guide them. When they leave here they will become baggage elephants for twelve or thirteen years until they are strong enough to work in the forest as timber elephants."

All together there were eight elephants in the camp. The oldest was a twenty-two-year-old bull named Ba Shin.

"Why is he here?" Nick asked.

"The rage is upon him," Tin answered. "He's in *musth*, or as we call it in Burmese, *mone*."

Nick had read all about musth. Once a year, bull elephants went into a period of temporary madness and became very aggressive, attacking mahouts, other elephants, and anything else that got in their way. The only remedy for the condition was to tie the elephant to a stout tree until the musth passed, which usually took about a month.

All four of Ba Shin's legs were roped. The area in which he was tied looked as if a cyclone had passed through it. The bull had uprooted every bush and plant within reach and had plowed the ground around him into soft loam with his heavy tusks. As they approached, he started straining against his ropes in an effort to get at them.

Tin stopped twenty feet from the farthest reach of his trunk. "In another two weeks he should be back to his former self."

Nick found it difficult to believe that Ba Shin would ever be back to normal. His eyes bulged with murderous fury. Both temples were swollen, oozing a thick yellowish discharge that stained the side of his head. Nick shuddered, realizing that he wouldn't be alive now had Hannibal been in musth.

"Perhaps we should leave him alone," Mya suggested.

Nick couldn't have agreed more. The tree Ba Shin was roped to did not look substantial enough to hold him. He followed Mya back to the calves and sat beside her on a log. She stared at the calves in much the same way she had stared at Miss Pretty through the rear window of the truck. It was almost as if she were committing to memory every movement they made.

"Magwe is a bully," Nick said.

Mya turned to him. "You didn't have to defend me like you did."

Nick wasn't sure if she was thanking him or criticizing him. "Who is he?"

"A mahout."

"He seemed to have a lot of influence over the other mahouts."

Mya shrugged. "His family has been here a long time. His grandfather was one of the two mahouts who came with the Sergeant Major."

Of course! Nick thought. That's why the name sounded familiar. His father had mentioned Magwe in a few of his letters.

"And the monk?"

"Taung Baw," Mya said. "Hilltop."

Nick gawked at her, then looked back to the monk,

who was still standing with Tin near Ba Shin. "Are you saying that the monk is actually *the* Hilltop?"

Mya nodded.

"Your great-grandfather?"

Mya nodded again.

"He'd have to be close to a hundred years old."

"Some say older."

"I was told he left the plantation when the Sergeant Major was still here."

"Sixty years ago," Mya said. "But he came back."

"When?"

"When I was a little girl."

"You're kidding me."

Mya shook her head.

"Surely there was no one in the village who could recognize him after sixty years," he said. "How do you know it's really him?"

The monk stepped closer to the mad Ba Shin. He put his hand on one of his tusks and leaned his old shaved head toward the bull's ear, as if he were saying something to him.

"Because Hilltop can speak to elephants," Mya answered. "And the elephants understand."

Indaw 7

Nang did not come home all night, so Mya couldn't ask him about his intentions for Miss Pretty. But she did find out that it was he who had taken the elephant the day before to do his plantation rounds. This meant he had not yet picked a mahout for Miss Pretty. There was still hope.

As soon as she rolled up her sleeping mat she went next door and told Kin-Kin that she was going out to find her father.

"I want you to stay in the village," her aunt said. "Hannibal was here yesterday, you know."

It would be hard not to know. When Mya returned from the training camp, the entire village was in an uproar over Hannibal. No one had actually seen him, but his footprints were easy to spot because of their size and the missing toenail on his right front foot. Magwe ranted for nearly an hour about how Mr. Freestone should have destroyed Hannibal long ago.

"He promised that he would keep track of Hannibal," Magwe reminded everyone loudly.

In addition to having Hannibal wear the iron bell, Mr. Freestone had promised to send Nang or Indaw into the forest to check on Hannibal every few days. If Hannibal was getting too close to the village, they would drive him away—or use a koongyi to drag him away if necessary.

With her father busy and Indaw away with Mr. Freestone, no one had checked Hannibal's whereabouts in the past week. Mya didn't know what all the fuss was about. All he had done was walk through the village. Other timber elephants did this every day. And it had been at least three years since Hannibal had caused any trouble.

Magwe was so worried about Hannibal returning that he had posted children in trees at the outskirts of the village to watch for him. He announced that when the Japanese came he would take care of Hannibal once and for all.

"We're going to clean your father's house," Kin-Kin said. "You can begin by sweeping the porch. I will start inside."

Kin-Kin, a normally calm and cheerful woman, seemed unusually tense to Mya this morning. Hannibal lurking near the village was a worry, but it didn't fully explain her aunt's mood.

Mya finished sweeping the porch and had just started on the stairs when she heard a familiar laugh a few houses down from theirs.

"Indaw's back!" she shouted, throwing her broom down and running toward the sound.

As always, a large group of people were gathered around her brother.

"So," Indaw was telling the group with a bright smile, "Hannibal came through yesterday, and he didn't push a house over or kill anyone?"

Several people nodded.

"Then it seems to me that our rogue is showing signs of getting better. Perhaps the tiger nat has left him."

Magwe joined the group. "And perhaps," he said, "Hannibal didn't kill anyone because there was no one here for him to kill. We were all at the pagoda yesterday when he came through."

Indaw's smile didn't falter, but his eyes lost some of their merriment at the sight of Magwe. "Yes, I heard. I'm very sorry I wasn't there."

"Where were you?" Magwe asked with undisguised suspicion.

"Plantation business," Indaw answered without pause. "Which reminds me . . . Mr. Freestone wants to see you up at Hawk's Nest."

"Why?"

"You'll have to ask him," Indaw answered. "And I wouldn't keep him waiting."

Magwe gave Indaw a casual shrug as if this were not an unusual request, but everyone there knew it was. With the exception of Nang and Indaw, mahouts were rarely summoned to Hawk's Nest. Magwe left the group and started up the path.

Indaw watched him go, then turned to Mya. "I heard you were at the training camp yesterday."

There were no secrets on the plantation. "I had every right to be there," Mya said defensively. "Father asked me to show Nick Freestone around, and the training camp is—"

Indaw held his hand up with an affectionate grin. "You were lucky Hilltop showed up when he did. But, of course, he has a knack for that." He turned back to the group. "Don't worry about Hannibal. I'm sure he's a long way from here by now. But just to make sure, I'll track him down and find out what he's up to." He took Mya's hand and started walking toward the house. When they were far enough away, he asked her what Nick Freestone was like.

"He sweats a lot," Mya answered. "And he's fat. I was afraid he was going to collapse on the way back from the camp."

Indaw laughed. "He'll lose weight here. And as to his sweating, it was probably snowing in London when he left. He'll get used to the weather."

Mya wasn't so sure. "He said he fell on the trail and injured himself."

"How?"

"I didn't see it. But he was very stiff afterward. On the way back from the training camp he was moving very slow and could barely walk."

"Must have been more serious than he let on."

"He said that you were at Hawk's Nest yesterday."

"Briefly."

"Why didn't you come down to the village to see me?" Mya scolded.

"There wasn't time."

"What's going on, Indaw?"

"What do you mean?"

"Everyone is acting strangely. Kin-Kin, Father, you . . ."

"What do you think of Miss Pretty?" Indaw asked with a grin.

"You're changing the subject," Mya said, smiling. "But she's beautiful!"

"She ought to be. Mr. Freestone went to a lot of expense to get her here."

"Why?" Mya asked hopefully.

"Shh, not now," Indaw said with devilment in his eyes.

They had reached their father's house, and Kin-Kin was standing on the porch with her back to them, hanging up the wash. Indaw ran up the stairs and hugged her from behind. She screamed like a young girl and started slapping and pushing him away, trying not to laugh, and failing.

"Is there any food in my father's house?" Indaw asked.

"The only thing my disrespectful nephew thinks about is his stomach."

Mya followed him inside. There was a bag filled with clothes sitting in the middle of the bamboo floor. Rolled up next to it was Mya's sleeping mat.

"What's this?" she asked.

"We're going on a trip, little sister," Indaw answered. "With Miss Pretty."

Mya would have jumped for joy if Kin-Kin hadn't started weeping.

The Christmas Ride 8

Nick sat up and groaned. With difficulty, he got out of bed and made his way to the bathroom—slowly. It was hard to tell where one ache ended and another began.

He and Mya had left the training camp soon after Hilltop had worked his miracle on Ba Shin. Nick still wasn't convinced that the monk was one of the two original mahouts, but there was no denying the remarkable change in the bull after the monk spoke to him. Tin and the other mahouts were hand-feeding Ba Shin by the time Nick had left the camp.

When he stumbled into Hawk's Nest after the tour, dinner was waiting for him. He ate by himself at the long dining table, but he wasn't alone. Bukong, the head houseman, stood close by, watching every forkful of food he put into his mouth, which made Nick a little uncomfortable. When he finished, he asked Bukong about Hilltop.

"A very holy man," Bukong said.

"Where did he go when he left the plantation?"

"Some say he returned to India. Some say he went up into the high mountains to stay in a monastery.

And still others insist that he never left at all—that he stayed right here in the form of an elephant until that elephant passed away and gave him back to us."

Nick seriously doubted that, but didn't say so.

"Does Hilltop live in the village?"

"Oh no, he lives in the forest."

"Where?"

Bukong shrugged his shoulders. "No one really knows."

Nick found this a little hard to believe as well. "Why did he leave the plantation all those years ago?"

"His wife and youngest daughter were attacked by a tiger."

"Like Hannibal," Nick said.

"Yes, but far worse. They were killed. After that, Hilltop shaved his head and devoted his life to the Buddha."

Perhaps Mother's fear of tigers was warranted, Nick thought. He asked Bukong about the Japanese invading Burma.

"They will be here soon, I think."

"How soon?"

"I can't say."

"What do you think about the Japanese?"

"Some want to see the British out of our country, some want them to stay."

"I hardly think the Japanese would be better than the British," Nick said.

Bukong smiled. "Yes, but the Japanese have promised to give us our independence." He started to clear the table. "If you'll excuse me, I have things to attend to." He limped off into the kitchen.

Nick thought about all this as he soaked in the tub. His father wanted Burmese independence, too. During his last trip to London he had lobbied Parliament on behalf of several plantation owners for Burmese independence, but the politicians turned a deaf ear to his pleas, and the newspapers attacked him, stopping just short of calling him a traitor.

Nick came down the stairs a little easier than he'd gone up the night before, but he was still very sore.

When he got to the entry hall he heard voices coming from the library. The door was open, and two servants were lingering outside, pretending to clean, though it looked to Nick like they were eavesdropping. When they saw him, they gave embarrassed bows and scurried away. Nick walked into the library without knocking.

His father was sitting at the Helm. He had shaved, and his clothes were clean and crisp. He still looked tired, but much improved from the day before. He was glaring at the man sitting across from him with such intensity that he didn't notice Nick come in. The man said something in Burmese.

His father responded in Burmese, and although

Nick could not understand the meaning of the words, the harshness with which they were spoken was clear. His Freestone blood was up.

Nick started to back out of the library, but his father saw him. "Nick?"

"Good morning," Nick stammered. "I'm sorry I—"

"No, please come in." His father stood. "Merry Christmas."

"Merry Christmas," Nick said. But it didn't seem anything like Christmas.

"I'd like you to meet—"

The man stood and turned around.

"Magwe," Nick said. "We met yesterday at the elephant training camp."

Magwe smiled, then bowed as if he and Nick were the best of friends. Nick returned the bow, but not as deeply, and he didn't smile.

"I was just telling Magwe that I'm taking you on a plantation tour," his father said. "We'll be gone a few days."

It didn't sound like that was all he was telling Magwe.

Three hours later, Nick sat behind his father, hanging on to the elephant saddle for dear life.

Their elephant's name was Choo Chin Chow (Chow for short), and no matter how Nick shifted positions, each step the bull took jarred every bone in his body. His father didn't seem bothered in the least by the elephant's awkward gait. Nor did Mya and Indaw, who were about fifty feet in front of them on Miss Pretty.

Every once in a while, Nick's father turned around to point out a tree, shrub, animal, or landmark.

"Cobra. Bad dispositions. Stay clear of them. Make sure to check for snakes before you sit down or hang your hammock. If you get a full load of venom you won't last the night. . . . Pangolin. Harmless insectivore. The young have the same armor plating, but in miniature. Their mothers carry them on their backs. . . ."

But for the most part they ambled along in silence, which was fine with Nick. It saved him the bother of disguising his discomfort, which was getting worse with each step Chow took. If it didn't improve, he was going to have to confess what had happened with Hannibal and risk becoming the laughingstock of the plantation.

They rode throughout the morning without stopping, cutting through dense bamboo stands, over blistering hot clearings, across cool streams—which Nick would have gladly jumped into, given half a chance. At times it seemed like they were going in large circles, but it was hard for Nick to tell, because everything looked remarkably the same.

"Wild pigs," his father said, pointing to their right. It took Nick a while to pick them out in the dense brush. There were at least a dozen in the group standing stock-still not twenty feet away.

"They're good eating and plentiful in the jungle," his father continued. "But the boars can be dangerous. Especially when wounded."

Food and survival seemed to be the theme of the tour, without any mention of teak, elephants, or plantation management, which is what Nick thought they would be discussing.

"Do you shoot?" his father asked.

"I beg your pardon?"

"Do you know how to use a rifle?"

Nick's mother hadn't liked guns, and there wasn't much opportunity for target practice in London, although he had always wanted to learn. "Not really," he said.

"We'll try to take care of that."

A little after noon they came to a wide, shallow river and stopped. His father started untying various bundles and tossing them down to Indaw and Mya, who had arrived well ahead of them. When he finished, he nimbly jumped to the ground.

Nick dismounted too, but not nearly as gracefully. He hit the hard ground on his butt and nearly passed out from the pain it caused him. Fortunately, his father was busy and didn't see it. But Indaw did. He rushed over.

"Are you all right?"

"Fine," Nick said, which wasn't even close to the truth.

Indaw grinned and helped him up. "I remember the first time I spent the day clinging to an elephant saddle," he said. "I could barely walk when I got off. It takes a while to get used to it."

Nick had been fully prepared to dislike Indaw because of his father's obvious affection for him, but upon meeting him that morning, he found it impossible not to like him. The way he smiled, his mannerisms, and his good humor were infectious.

"Is it more comfortable on the neck?" Nick asked.

Indaw nodded. "But that also takes some getting used to."

Nick wiped some of the dust from the seat of his pants and winced in pain.

"Are you sure you're all right?" Indaw asked. "Mya tells me you had an accident on the trail yesterday."

"Yes, I uh . . . I slipped."

"Did you tell your father?"

"No."

"I wouldn't have told my father either," Indaw said. "You didn't break anything?"

"I don't think so. I'm just a little sore."

Indaw stared at him in silence, clearly waiting for Nick to elaborate.

"Well," Nick admitted, "very sore." He wanted to tell him what had really happened. He felt Indaw would understand, but there was nothing to be gained by admitting how stupid he'd been.

"When we start again," Indaw said, "would you like to ride up with me on Miss Pretty?"

"I'd like that," Nick answered. "Where are we, exactly?"

"The river is called *Tawkaw*." Indaw pointed across to the other bank. "And that's not the shore you're looking at. It's a huge island with just as much river on the other side as on this side."

Nick looked across at the dense forest. "Is it part of the plantation?"

"Yes," his father said, joining them. "Freestone Island. It's what all the land looked like when the Sergeant Major arrived. Wild. Untouched. He wanted to keep the island that way so we would remember how the plantation started. It's like a maze in there and very easy to get lost. No one's allowed across unless I give them permission. We'll go over when it cools down. I wanted you to see it before . . ." He hesitated and looked at Indaw. "Where's Mya?"

"She took Miss Pretty downriver to give her a bath," he answered.

His father nodded and looked back at Nick. "Indaw and I are going to see if we can find Hannibal."

"Hannibal's near here?" Nick tried to keep the panic out of his voice.

"We've been tracking him all day," Indaw said. "There's a stream not far from here where he likes to hide. I think he's there."

"We'll take Chow," his father said. "He and Hannibal are old friends. I'd ask you to come with us, but dealing with Hannibal can be a little dicey."

"I'll be fine here." Nick had absolutely no desire to go looking for Hannibal.

"Depending on how cooperative he is," his father continued, "we'll cross over to the island in an hour or so. If we encounter problems, we'll camp here and go over tomorrow morning after we catch him."

"We're taking Hannibal to the island with us?"

His father nodded. "We need to get him as far from the village as we can. If you get a chance, you might want to start a fire. We could use a cup of tea."

Nick watched them walk away, then found the tea kettle among the supplies and walked to the shore. Mya stood in the cool river up to her knees, scooping water up with a bucket and splashing it over the prone Miss Pretty.

"Can I help?"

Mya turned around. "If you like."

He rolled up his pants and waded out to join them. The cool water felt wonderful on his bare legs. "What can I do?"

"We use sand to scrub the elephant's skin." She demonstrated by scooping up a handful from the bottom and rubbing it into Miss Pretty's gray skin, then rinsing it off. The cow seemed to love the bath, making satisfied high-pitched squeaks. When they finished the first side, Mya used her choon to get Miss Pretty to her feet, then laid her back down on the other side. It took nearly an hour to scrub Miss Pretty down, and despite Nick's injured ribs, he enjoyed every minute of it.

They tied Miss Pretty to a tree, where she could browse, then Nick walked upriver to fill the kettle with water while Mya got the fire started. The elephant bath had not only cooled him down, it had helped him regain some of his self-confidence. The hit by Hannibal had done more than just crack his ribs. He decided to ask his father if he could spend a week or two in the elephant training camp. If he was going to run the plantation one day, he would have to learn a lot more about elephants. Mya knew a hundred times more than he did, and she wasn't even a mahout.

Nick looked up from where he was filling the kettle and noticed a snag in the middle of the river with a vulture perched on it. The bird was eating something. He put the kettle down and waded out for a closer look, happy for another excuse to get wet. The vulture flew off, leaving behind a monkey carcass. Other than its eyes being pecked out, the monkey looked relatively fresh.

"What do you see?" his father shouted from the shore.

Nick turned around. His father and Indaw were back, and they weren't alone. Hannibal had a loose rope around his neck, tied to Chow's saddle. Sitting on top of Hannibal with a cloth bag over his shoulder and carrying an old choon, was Hilltop.

"A dead monkey!" Nick shouted back.

Nick's father slipped off Chow's back, said something to Indaw and the monk, then walked over to the edge of the water. He took his boots off and waded out to the snag.

"I guess Hannibal was feeling cooperative," Nick said.

His father smiled. "Chow's small, but he can be very convincing. And it didn't hurt to have Hilltop there."

"Is Hilltop really one of the original mahouts?"

"He is."

"When did he come back?"

"Right after you and your mother left."

"Where was he all those years?"

"Traveling. Seeking enlightenment."

"How old is he?"

"Old, but as you can see, age doesn't seem to have slowed him down very much."

They looked over at Indaw and Hilltop. Indaw was tying Chow to a tree. Hilltop was standing beside Hannibal, talking to him.

"So, Hannibal's in a good mood," Nick said.

"Yes, much better than yesterday morning at the village when he knocked you down."

Nick looked up in shock. "How did you know?"

"I just found out. Hilltop saw the whole thing. He followed you down from Hawk's Nest. You should have told me."

Nick shook his head. "I was stupid."

"No, you were lucky."

"Did Hilltop tell anyone else?"

"Just Indaw and me. Hilltop's about the only person on the plantation who keeps his own counsel. We'll keep it quiet to protect Hannibal."

"Protect him how?"

"If certain villagers found out about the attack, by the end of the day the story would be that Hannibal had gone on a rampage and tried to impale you with his broken tusk. There are those in the village who don't like me and will do anything in their power to undermine my authority. It's well-known that I'm rather fond of Hannibal in spite of his sour disposition. They can get at me by getting at him."

"Magwe," Nick said.

His father nodded. "He's one of them."

"Why don't you just kick him off the plantation?"

"He's a conniving little weasel, but the truth is, I like him when he isn't trying to take over the plantation. And I have to think of his family, which is rather large. If I booted him out, they would feel obligated to leave as well. It would be difficult for them to find work. I'm responsible for them."

Nick looked toward shore. Indaw and Hilltop were hand-feeding Hannibal tamarind branches.

Mr. Freestone followed his gaze. "Hannibal is not the rogue everyone thinks he is. He's dangerous, to be sure, but yesterday morning he was just showing you who's boss. He could have killed you, but he chose not to."

"It was terrifying," Nick admitted.

"There's no shame in getting knocked down by an elephant. I've lost count of how many times it's happened to me. Did he break anything?"

"I'm not sure. My ribs are bothering me."

"I'll wrap them up good and tight before we cross over to the island. Now, let's take a look at this monkey." He broke a stick off the snag and started probing the swollen corpse.

"Did it drown?"

Father shook his head. "It was shot."

"Shot?"

"Twice." He used the stick to point out the wounds.

"Why would anyone shoot a monkey?"

"To stop someone from eating it."

"You're kidding."

"The hill tribes eat monkeys during lean times. And I'm afraid there are lean times coming to Burma."

"What are you talking about?"

"Let's get out of the water," he suggested.

They waded to shore. As they were pulling on their boots, his father said, "The Japanese are here."

"Near the plantation?"

"Yes, but not in any great number yet." He nodded toward the snag. "I suspect the Japanese shot that monkey upriver. The soldiers are killing the hill tribes' food. If the tribes get hungry enough, they'll join the Japanese."

Nick shook his head in bewilderment. Two years of bombings, their apartment destroyed. He'd had his fill of war. "Why do the Japanese want Burma?"

"They need it to move supplies in and out of China, and they're going to fight hard to take it." His father paused. "I think they're going to win."

"But surely our soldiers—"

His father shook his head. "We don't have the manpower to beat them. And most of the Burmese want the Japanese to win, which is our fault. The Japanese slogan is 'Asia for Asians.' We should have given the Burmese their independence long ago, or at least promised it to them after the war."

"But we built this country up," Nick protested. "Any prosperity the Burmese have is because of people like you and grandfather and the Sergeant Major."

"We've worked hard, but so have the Burmese," he said. "And this is their country, not ours." He tied his bootlaces and got to his feet. "The situation is bad. We spotted a scouting patrol not five miles from the plantation yesterday." He took a deep breath, then locked his brown eyes on Nick. "I made a serious mistake in bringing you over here. We thought you would be safer with me. Away from the bombings."

"I wanted to come here," Nick said.

His father looked away. "I'm afraid your stay will be shorter than either of us expected. I'm sending you to Australia. I have a good friend in Alice Springs, and he's offered to look after you until this is all over. Mya is going with you."

Nick was too shocked to speak.

"It's not safe here anymore," his father continued in a rush. "Before you arrived in Rangoon, I had Nang try to find a way to get you to the States, or back to London, but everything was booked. People were leaving the country in droves; there wasn't a ship berth or airplane seat to be had. I only wish I'd figured this out before you left to come here. The only way out now is overland to India. Indaw will take you and Mya on Miss Pretty. From there you'll board a ship for Darwin."

"What about the plantation?"

"It's lost," his father answered. "At least for the time being. Perhaps after the war we'll be able to come back. In the meantime, I'm leaving Nang in charge of things there."

"What about you?"

He glanced away. "I'll be staying here."

"To do what?"

"To fight the Japanese."

"But you just said it was hopeless. The Burmese want the Japanese here."

"I said that *most* of the Burmese want the Japanese here, not all of them. And those who do will change their minds after they find out what the Japanese are all about. Indaw and I will be leading a small group of men to make things difficult for the Japanese during their stay. We'll also be gathering intelligence and sending it to the Allies, so when they decide to take Burma back, they'll be better prepared. I was born and raised here. I know a lot more about this jungle than the Japanese. I'll be fine."

"So will I," Nick said. "I'm not going to Australia."

"I'm not giving you a choice, Nicholas."

"It's Nick, and there are people younger than me fighting in this war. Indaw isn't much older than I am."

"True, but you weren't raised here. It takes a long time to get acclimated. Some people never adjust to this country." He pointed to Nick's ribs. "And you're in no shape to be running around the jungle."

"I'll be fine in a few weeks."

His father shook his head. "With luck, you'll be in India in a few weeks, and Alice Springs a week or two after that. You're not going back to Hawk's Nest. You're leaving for India tomorrow."

"Tomorrow?"

"This Christmas tour was just a ruse to get you and Mya away without panicking the villagers," he said. "If they knew I was pulling up stakes this early in the game, it's hard to say what they would do."

Nick glanced over at Mya and Indaw sitting near the fire. "Does Mya know?"

"She was told this morning. I asked her not to say anything until I had a chance to talk to you. She's as unhappy about the situation as you are, maybe more so. She's never been farther away than Rangoon, which is another reason you need to go. She'll need your help."

Nick doubted it. Mya didn't appear to need anyone's help. Especially his.

"So, you're not taking us to India?"

His father shook his head. "I can't. They could be here in force any day. By the time Indaw returns, Burma will have fallen." He looked across the river. "But before you leave, we'll go over to the island to let Hannibal go."

"Why are you letting him go?"

"Because that's where he was captured, and if we don't let him go he'll be killed. The Japanese or someone from the village will make sure of that. We also need to determine how many elephants the island can hold. The military wants us to kill our elephants so they can't be used by the Japanese. I won't do that. Killing an elephant is like killing a person, as far as I'm concerned. Over the next few weeks, Nang and some of the other mahouts are going to take our best elephants, secretly, over to the island and set them free." His father stood. "Let's get your ribs wrapped up."

"Wait a second," Nick protested. "That's it? No more discussion?"

His father shook his head. "There's nothing more to say, Nick."

Freestone Island 9

Nick rode up front with Indaw on Miss Pretty. Just behind them, Mya, unhappy about giving up her spot on her beloved elephant, was with Nick's father on Chow. And taking up the rear was Hilltop on Hannibal.

The iron bell's clang made Nick a little nervous, but the mysterious monk seemed to have the testy bull firmly in hand. Perhaps he really did know the secret language of elephants.

Nick wanted to ask Indaw about his father's plans, but the tangled jungle put a stop to any conversation. The island was dark, damp, and filled with swarms of biting insects. Most of the time they had to ride bent over with their faces flat against Miss Pretty's back so they didn't get scraped by the low-hanging branches. Within minutes, Nick was covered with bites and scratches, and he wasn't the only one suffering. Indaw had several gashes on his head. Nick caught a few backward glimpses of his father. He was totally disheveled, his clothes sopping wet, his hair disarrayed with clinging sticks, leaves, and dirt. Mya was not faring much better. Nick wasn't able to see Hilltop, who had dropped farther behind, but he suspected that the monk was even worse off than they were, as Hannibal was a good three feet taller than the other elephants. After what seemed like an eternity, they broke into a more open area deep in the island's interior.

"What's going to stop the Japanese from finding the elephants here?" Nick asked Indaw.

"The monsoon," he answered. "When the annual rains come, the river will swell and become a rushing torrent. Nothing will be able to cross from the mainland, and the elephants will not be able to leave the island. When the rains stop, the elephants will be used to it here and will not want to leave."

"Where exactly are we going to release him?"

"That depends on where the wild elephants are. Your father will ride into the herd on Chow, and Hilltop will ride Hannibal. When they are ready, Hilltop will climb onto Chow, and they will leave Hannibal behind."

"The opposite of an elephant capture," Nick said.

"Exactly."

Nick had read all about elephant captures and had always wanted to participate in one. If his father had his way about Australia, this was about as close as Nick was going to get to seeing one.

"I hear you're taking Mya and me to India," Nick said.

"True," Indaw said.

"Why are we going on elephant back instead of driving?"

Indaw smiled. "Elephants are slower than trucks, but they don't need petrol, they don't need roads, and they don't break down. We will have to stay off the main roads to avoid the Japanese patrols."

"I don't want to go," Nick said.

Indaw was silent for a few moments, then said, "Burma will soon be a very unpleasant place to be. My family is very grateful your father has offered to send Mya with you. She will be safe in Australia."

"Mya is Burmese," Nick pointed out. "The Japanese are at war with the British and Americans."

"Mya is also very pretty," Indaw said. "It would be better for her to be a long way from here."

Nick hadn't considered Mya in that way. She *is* pretty, he thought. Beautiful, really. It hadn't occurred to him that she might be in danger from the Japanese because of her good looks. But this still didn't explain why he had to go to Australia, and he was about to pursue the subject when Indaw brought Miss Pretty to a sudden stop.

"Elephant dung," Indaw said, jumping to the ground. He put his hand into the scat. "Fresh."

Nick got down, too, happy to stretch his legs.

"The herd's close," Indaw whispered. "We'll have to be quiet from here on."

Nick's father and Mya ambled up behind and joined them. His father looked at the dung and the direction of the tracks. A moment later, Hilltop arrived on Hannibal.

"Here's how we're going to work this," his father said to Indaw. "Hilltop and I will take the lead on Hannibal and Chow. Mya will ride with you and Nick. When we get to the herd, hold Miss Pretty back. We'll ride in. If we have a problem, drop Mya and Nick off and come pick us up."

Indaw nodded. "Mya and I will go ahead a little on foot and see if we can spot them."

"Quietly," his father said.

It didn't take Mya and Indaw long to spot the wild elephants. The small herd was foraging on the edge of a large clearing. Mya had seen wild elephants, but never this many, and never this close.

"We should head back and get the others," Indaw whispered.

Reluctantly, she followed her brother but stopped several times to glance back at the wild herd.

About halfway to where Mr. Freestone was waiting for them, Indaw stopped and put his shoulder bag on the ground.

"What are you doing?" Mya asked.

"This is about as good a time as any."

"For what?"

He reached into his bag and pulled out something wrapped in a burlap rice sack.

"What is it?"

"Open it."

Mya untied the string. Under the crude wrapping was the most beautiful choon she had ever seen. The teak handle was beautifully carved with elephants, their tusks inlaid with ivory.

"I made it for you," Indaw said. "And would have given it to you sooner, but I knew Father would be unhappy because it would just encourage your desire to become a mahout. I guess that doesn't matter now. . . ."

Tears filled Mya's eyes. Indaw held her close.

"I wish you didn't have to go," he said. "But the choon will remind you of home. Someday you'll be back, and perhaps you'll be able to use this choon. If I have anything to say about it, I'll make you the first female mahout on the Freestone plantation. You are already better with elephants than half the mahouts here."

Mya wiped her eyes. "Whether I get to use the choon or not, it's the most wonderful present I've ever received." She gave her brother a kiss.

"Of course you're going to be able to use it, little sister. We have a very long ride to India, and as far as I'm concerned, you are Miss Pretty's mahout. I'm just going along for the ride."

He took Mya's hand and led her back to the others.

"Can I borrow your knife?" Nick's father asked.

Nick fished it out of his pocket and gave it to him. His father walked over to Hannibal, cut the rope holding the iron bell, then walked back and handed both the bell and the knife to Nick. "A memento," he said.

Nick stood awkwardly in front of his father with the bell in one hand and the knife in the other. "Perhaps you should keep the knife," he offered again.

His father smiled. "No, it's yours now. I just wish I could have given you more than a knife and a rusty bell."

"I want to stay here with you," Nick said.

"You can't, son. I'm sorry."

"What about after the war?"

"If we can't come back here, we'll do something in Australia or somewhere else, but wherever we end up, it won't be like this." He looked up through the thick trees. "I told you that the Sergeant Major set this island aside so we would know what the land looked like."

Nick nodded.

"Well," he continued, "I'm not sure if that was his real purpose. Every time I come here I'm reminded just how tough the Sergeant Major was. I think he left it this way so you and I would know what he was like.

This island is your great-grandfather's heart, and it beats in both of us."

Nick would find himself thinking about this many times over the next several months.

"Ah, here come Indaw and Mya," his father said.

Indaw told them where the elephants were, then Mya showed off her new choon, to everyone's delight.

Nick was impressed with the carvings. They were even better than the Sergeant Major's.

"If you want," Indaw offered, "I can teach you how to carve on our way to India."

"I'd like that," Nick said, but he still had no intention of going.

"We'd better get moving," his father said.

Indaw held Miss Pretty back as they watched Nick's father and Hilltop ride Hannibal and Chow across the clearing toward the herd.

Nick balanced on his knees, holding a pair of binoculars with one hand and the saddle with the other. He counted nine elephants, but there may have been more hidden in the tall grass.

His father and Hilltop kept their heads down so their silhouettes would not frighten the herd as they approached. As they drew closer, a couple of the elephants flared their ears and trumpeted, but other than this, there was little commotion over the two new elephants.

Chow stuck to Hannibal's side as if he were glued to him. They worked their way closer and closer until they were right in the middle of the foraging herd, blending in so well it was difficult for Nick to keep track of them.

Hilltop stretched forward toward Hannibal's left ear and appeared to be talking to him. When he finished he clambered onto Chow. Nick's father backed Chow out of the herd, turned him, then started back across the field at a fast walk.

Nick kept the binoculars on Hannibal, wondering if some of the elephants in the herd were related to him. Brothers, sisters, uncles, aunts? Perhaps his mother or father was with the herd. It had only been nine years since his capture, and elephants are long-lived. Hannibal got into a pushing match with a smaller elephant, shoving it a good fifty feet away before returning to the herd.

His father rode up. Nick handed him the binoculars. He watched the herd a while then said, "He's making himself right at home. I just hope he stays here until the monsoon." He looked at Hilltop. "How many elephants can we bring here?"

Hilltop thought about it for a few moments. "I'll be able to tell you precisely how many in a few days."

"So you're staying on the island," his father said, not sounding surprised.

Hilltop climbed down from Chow. "I'll get word to

you as soon as I know. In the meantime, you can bring over two or three elephants. The island can certainly take that many more."

Indaw put some food into Hilltop's bag and handed it down to him.

The old monk slung it over his narrow shoulder, then looked up at Mya and Nick. "I won't be seeing you for some time. Travel safely. Australia has some interesting animals. Many of them have pouches on their bellies and only come out at night."

"You've been there?" Nick asked.

He nodded.

Even his father seemed surprised to hear this, but he didn't allow them to discuss it any further. "We had better go. I want to get back across the river before dark. Nick, you ride with me."

Nick climbed onto Chow behind his father. Mya climbed onto Miss Pretty in front of her brother.

"She's all yours," Indaw said.

Mya tucked her feet behind Miss Pretty's warm ears and tapped her with her choon, and they headed back toward the river.

Nick wanted to talk to his father about Australia again but felt it would be better to ease into the subject. "What's Hilltop looking for on the island?"

"Elephants, for one thing," his father answered. "There may be another herd—maybe more than one. If too many elephants get stranded on the island during the monsoon, all the elephants could starve. He'll look at food sources and try to determine how many elephants the island can sustain."

"What happens after the monsoon? Won't the elephants leave the island?"

"Some of them will, but by then they'll be firmly established in herds. In order to be useful to the Japanese they would have to be captured and retrained, which could take months to accomplish. I doubt the Japanese would bother with them."

Nick looked at him in the waning light. The exertion of the long day and many nights of sleepless worry were obvious on his father's weary face. He didn't have the heart or the energy to bring up Australia right then. He decided to save his final argument for the following morning, after they both had had some rest.

The Enemy 10

It was dark by the time they got across the river and set up camp. After they ate, Nick's father went to sleep. Indaw, Mya, and Nick stayed up a little while longer talking.

Indaw predicted it would take at least a month to get to India on Miss Pretty, and much longer if they ran into trouble along the way. He was taking them to a friend of Nick's father named Mr. Singh. From there Nick and Mya would be put on a train to Calcutta, where they would board a ship to Darwin, Australia. A man named Mr. Shute was to meet them there and take them to his home in a town called Alice Springs. Nick's father had chosen Alice Springs because it was of no strategic importance should the Japanese decide to attack Australia.

Mya appeared to Nick to be as unhappy about the situation as he was. She wanted to stay in Burma but seemed to have accepted that going to Australia was the best thing for them to do.

Nick had been looking at her a little differently since Indaw pointed out how pretty she was. She had a beautiful olive-colored complexion; her long black hair shone in the light of the campfire, and she had a wonderful smile.

Indaw told them that Miss Pretty had once belonged to Mr. Singh and he would be happy to have her back. He had thought he'd never see her again, what with the war and all. Transporting her to India would be his father's payment to Mr. Singh for getting them to the ship.

After they fed the elephants, they bedded down, but Nick couldn't fall asleep. And it wasn't the insects, hard ground, or sore ribs that kept him awake. It was the fact that this was probably the last night he was going to spend with his father in Burma, unless he came up with a better argument than "I don't want to go." His father was taking a stand. Why wouldn't he allow Nick to stand with him? He had just as much to lose as his father did. He thought about this through most of the night, dozing from time to time, until the sky started to lighten.

Quietly, Nick got up and walked upriver, then decided to go for a swim, thinking it might do his ribs some good. When he pulled off his pants he noticed they were a little looser around the waist.

I might just turn into one of the Freestones in the portraits yet, he thought. That is, if I get to stay in Burma.

He eased himself into the warm water and waded

out to the middle of the river, then began to float in the gentle current, mindful of his sore ribs.

As he floated, a fine mist drifted past the monkey snag fifty feet away.

As he swam, he went over the argument he was going to use on his father, but didn't get very far with it. The elephants began to trumpet. He turned his head toward the sound and saw a dozen men run out of the forest, shouting, brandishing rifles with bayonets. Japanese soldiers! Nick sank deeper into the water with just the top of his head showing, and looked toward the camp.

His father jumped up, grabbed his rifle, and looked as if he were about to defend the camp. But instead, he dropped his rifle and put his hands up in the air as soldiers swarmed out of the forest. Indaw and Mya got to their feet and followed his lead by raising their hands.

The soldiers were focused on the campsite and hadn't seemed to notice that Nick was in the river.

Nick looked at the tree line. It was too far away. He glanced across to the island. He would never make it across without being seen. But he might be able to reach the snag. If he hid behind it, the soldiers might miss him entirely. He started swimming toward it, with just his head above water, letting the slow current do most of the work. He wasn't certain what he hoped to accomplish if he managed to hide behind the snag, but he did not want to be captured by the Japanese.

The snag was twenty feet away.

An officer shouted something in Japanese, then said in English, "Down! Down!" His voice carried well across the water.

Mya, Indaw, and Nick's father dropped to their knees.

Fifteen feet.

The soldiers rushed in.

Ten feet.

His father looked directly at Nick and gave him a slight nod and smile. Nick grabbed the snag. Slowly, he worked his way around to the back side and watched through the gnarled branches and swarming flies feeding on the rotting monkey.

With the captives under control, the soldiers appeared to relax. Some lit cigarettes, others started going through their gear.

The officer started interrogating Nick's father in Japanese. His father had his head down and appeared to be answering his questions, but Nick was too far away to hear what he was saying. Apparently, the officer didn't like the answers. He raised his fist as if he were going to hit Nick's father, but the blow didn't come, because at that moment Miss Pretty and Chow came out of the forest with mahouts on their necks. One of the mahouts was Magwe.

Indaw jumped up and shouted at him. A soldier

hit Indaw in the stomach with his rifle butt, doubling him over. Mya was on the soldier in a second, jumping on his back. He threw her off and pointed his bayonet at her.

"Stop!" Nick's father got to his feet.

The officer fired his pistol into the air, then said something to the soldier with the bayonet. The soldier gave Mya a vicious kick and walked away.

The officer shouted out more orders. Soldiers rushed in and tied their hands. Nick let out a long breath, unaware that he had been holding it. He couldn't believe what he had just seen.

The soldiers handed the padding and saddles up to Magwe and the other mahout. When the saddles were secure, the gear was tossed up to them.

Nick stared at his father, hoping for some indication of what he should do, but his father didn't even glance at the snag. They were jerked to their feet and pushed into line, with soldiers on either side of them. Indaw was having difficulty staying on his feet.

The officer took one final look around camp, then shouted out another order.

Nick watched in despair as they all marched away, with the elephants in the lead. He wished he hadn't hidden. What was he supposed to do now? Where would he go? He didn't even know the way back to Hawk's Nest.

Nick stayed concealed behind the snag for several

minutes. Except for the river and the rattle of dry leaves blowing along the shore, it was quiet. It was almost as if the Japanese had never been there. He looked at his watch. It was 5:35 a.m. The whole incident had taken less than twenty minutes. Was he a coward to have hidden? he wondered.

He waded to shore feeling ashamed, wondering what else he could have done. He pulled on his pants and put on his shirt. Gray smoke rose from the campfire. The only thing the soldiers had left behind was Hannibal's iron bell. Another reminder of Nick's lack of courage. He'd hidden behind the snag because he was afraid, just as he had stood frozen before Hannibal the day before.

Did Magwe lead the soldiers to them, or had the soldiers forced him to come along in order to retrieve the elephants? It was clear that Indaw thought Magwe had betrayed them, but Nick wasn't so sure. He saw Magwe's expression when the soldier hit Indaw in the stomach. He seemed almost as upset as Mya, and for a brief moment, Nick thought he was going to jump off Miss Pretty and join in the fight. But the officer firing his pistol put an end to that.

Nick looked up at the sun. It would soon be unbearably hot. I'll be fine as long as I stay near the river, he thought. At least I won't die of thirst. But food will be a problem.

His father had pointed out a number of edible

animals along the way, but he couldn't very well get close enough to kill them with the Sergeant Major's knife.

The only thing Nick could think to do was to find Hawk's Nest. The Japanese might have already taken it over, but as his father had pointed out, not all of the Burmese were on the Japanese side. Nang would certainly help him.

Nick started in the direction the Japanese had taken his father, but didn't get far. He discovered that some words had been scratched in the dirt near the fire. It was hard to make out, but it looked like:

FOLLOW ELEPHANT TRACKS TO HILLTOP

Nick looked across the river at the island. He had completely forgotten about Hilltop. But finding him might not be easy. He was certain he could follow the elephant tracks, but he wasn't sure they would lead him to the monk. By now he could be anywhere on the island.

It's worth a try, he thought. If I can't find him, I can always retrace my steps and find Hawk's Nest. He started across the river.

Halfway across he heard a shout behind him.

"Hand up!"

Nick froze, then slowly turned his head.

"Hand up!"

A Japanese soldier stood on the shore pointing a rifle at him. Nick looked back at the island. Eighty or ninety feet at the most . . .

Bang! The bullet hit the water not a foot from where Nick was standing.

"Hand up!"

Nick put his hands up. He could not believe he had just been shot at.

"You come back now! I shoot!"

All thoughts of reaching the island vanished. Nick turned around and started back. Where had the soldier come from? Did they send him back to look for him? As Nick drew closer he could see that the man was different from the other soldiers—older, short gray hair, glasses.

Nick stepped out of the water.

"Hold hands out!"

The soldier tied his wrists, then pointed at Nick's feet. "How far you think you go without shoe?"

Nick looked down at his feet and nearly laughed. In his confusion he had completely forgotten that he was barefoot. He wouldn't have gotten very far on the island without his boots, which he saw now were lying on the ground next to the soldier. They must have taken them when they left, then realized there was an extra pair of boots without feet in them.

"You come with me."

In a way, Nick was relieved. At least he'd be with

his father now. The soldier pushed him over to the fire.

"Captain send me back to find you. Put on shoe."

"Kind of hard to do with my hands tied," Nick said.

"You manage."

Nick sat down and awkwardly pulled them on, but was unable to tie them. The soldier gave him an exasperated grunt, then squatted down and tied them for him.

When he finished he stood up and pointed to himself. "Sergeant Sonji."

"Nick Freestone," Nick said, although he had a feeling the sergeant already knew that.

"On feet!"

Nick got up.

"Must bow when speak to soldier." The sergeant demonstrated. "Keep head down or soldier hit. Whack. Whack."

Nick wasn't exactly sure what he meant by this, but he bowed. When he brought his head back up the sergeant was smiling.

"My English good?"

"Pretty good." It was a lot better than Nick's Japanese, which was nonexistent.

"Who Hilltop?"

It seemed that the sergeant read English as well. The sergeant pointed to the writing near the fire. "It say here follow elephant to Hilltop."

"You mean *what* hilltop," Nick said. "Not who."

The sergeant gave him a suspicious look. He couldn't possibly know who Hilltop was.

"It's a place," Nick added. "Not a person."

"What place?"

"The plantation house," Nick answered. "Hawk's Nest." The house sat above the river on a plateau, which could be interpreted as a hill. Sergeant Sonji nodded, then rubbed the note out with his boot, which is what Nick should have done before he started across the river.

The sergeant picked up Hannibal's iron bell. "You want?"

"I guess so."

The sergeant smiled again, then tied the bell around Nick's waist. "This way I find you if you run. Like timber elephant. We go."

"Where?"

"Hilltop," he answered, still smiling. "Hawk's Nest. Your father going there."

Sergeant Sonji 11

The sergeant seemed to be in no hurry to get to Hawk's Nest. He dawdled along the way, stopping to look at animals and plants as if he were on a nature walk.

Nick felt ridiculous with the iron bell clanging around his waist, but he didn't want to ask the sergeant to take it off because he was afraid that he might oblige him and throw it away. Nick wanted the bell. It was the last thing his father had given him.

"Do you see how the sunlight come through leaf here?" Sergeant Sonji asked.

Nick saw the leaf and the sunlight, but he didn't see the point. Now that he had been captured, all he wanted was to see his father. He was worried about him. The soldiers who had taken him were nothing like the soldier who had taken Nick.

"You thirsty?"

Nick shook his head. He had already drunk most of the water in the sergeant's canteen.

"You see cricket?"

Now what was he talking about? Nick was

beginning to think the sergeant was crazy.

"Look." He exposed the leaf's underside. "Cricket. You know haiku?"

"Is that the Japanese word for cricket?"

The sergeant laughed. "No. Haiku is Japan poetry. As we walk by I hear cricket chirp."

The sergeant *was* crazy.

"I think of haiku." He picked up a sharp stick. "Better in Japan language, but I write haiku in English for you."

> cricket
> beneath dew-covered leaf
> one final chirp

"See?" The sergeant beamed at him. "Japan poetry. Haiku."

Nick saw, but he didn't understand why the strange soldier was making up poetry, or why he thought Nick would be interested, which he wasn't.

As they continued on, Nick searched the dusty trail for his father's boot prints. They were difficult to pick out from all the others, but when he saw one, he breathed a sigh of relief. If his father was on his feet, he was still alive.

"What's going to happen to us?" Nick asked.

The sergeant gave him a sympathetic look. "For Colonel to decide."

"The officer who came into camp this morning?"

"No. That man captain. Colonel Nagayoshi in command. He wait for us at Hawk's Nest."

So the Japanese *had* taken over Hawk's Nest, Nick thought.

"What's he like?"

The sergeant thought about it for a moment before answering. "Bushido," he finally said.

"What's that?"

"Warrior," he answered. "Samurai. Must show great respect or . . ." He held his hands above his head, then brought them down, making a *whooshing* sound.

"He chops off people's heads?"

"Sometime. With my own eyes I have seen this. Deserter. Coward. We catch, and the Colonel . . ." He made the motion again.

Nick's anxiety must have shown, because the sergeant gave him a gentle pat on the shoulder. "I think you be okay."

"And my father?"

A worried looked flickered across the sergeant's face. "He be okay maybe. Must hurry now. Getting late." He cut the rope holding the bell and put it in his rucksack. "I keep. Give to you later."

They reached the elephant village late that afternoon. It had changed dramatically since Nick's last visit. A dead dog lay in the middle of the road with its head crushed. Not far from the dog was a butchered pig. Many of the bamboo houses had been ransacked. Two had been burned to the ground. There were no villagers to be seen, but there were plenty of Japanese soldiers, squatting in the shade beneath the houses, staring as the sergeant marched Nick through the dusty street.

Several of them called out to Sonji as they passed, but he didn't respond. His face was expressionless, his posture ramrod straight, looking nothing like the poet of an hour before.

Hawk's Nest had changed too. Hanging above the porch was a huge Japanese flag, its red sun fluttering in the warm breeze. Beneath it were two dead bodies. Nang and Captain Josephs. Nang had been horribly beaten and was barely recognizable. Captain Josephs had been decapitated.

Nick threw up.

The entire elephant village was seated on the ground in front of Hawk's Nest. They were separated into groups, with the women and children on the left side of the house and the men on the right. Both groups were surrounded by soldiers. His father was kneeling between the two groups, his hands still tied, and he didn't appear to know that Nick was there.

Nick looked at Sonji. The sergeant gave him a nearly imperceptible head shake, which Nick took to mean that he didn't know what was going on either. Nick wiped his mouth, then looked for Mya among the women and children, but he couldn't see her from where he was.

Two soldiers came through the front door of Hawk's Nest. Slumped between them was Indaw. He had been beaten. There was a scream of anguish from someone in the women's group, which was quickly muffled. The soldiers dragged Indaw around the side of the house out of sight, and for a horrible moment, Nick thought they were going to shoot him. He held his breath waiting for the shot, but it didn't come.

The soldiers came back around the house without Indaw and took up positions in front of the men. One of them pulled out a sheet of paper from his tunic pocket and looked like he was going to call out a name from it, when the other soldier noticed the sergeant and Nick standing in the back. He waved them forward.

"Time now to show respect," Sonji whispered.

"Is one of them the Colonel?"

He shook his head and pushed Nick forward.

Colonel Nagayoshi 12

Nick kept his head bowed the entire time the soldiers talked to Sergeant Sonji. When they finished, Sonji pushed Nick over to where his father was and made him kneel beside him.

"You all right?" his father asked.

"I'm fine," Nick answered. "I'm sorry, I didn't—"

"No talking!" Sergeant Sonji slapped Nick on the head, but not hard. "I come back."

He marched up the steps of Hawk's Nest and disappeared through the front door.

As they kneeled, Nick noticed the terrible stench in the air. It was the same smell that had come from the monkey on the snag. Nang and Captain Josephs had been dead for some time. They may have been killed as early as the day before, when Nick was on the island.

The sergeant came back outside fifteen minutes later, followed by an officer. Every soldier snapped to attention.

He was tall. His uniform was immaculate. A sword and pistol hung from his lean waist.

He shouted out some orders, and a handful of

soldiers ran forward. They picked up Nang's and Captain Josephs's bodies and carried them around the side of the house.

When the corpses were gone, the officer stepped off the porch and walked over to where Nick and his father were kneeling.

"My name is Colonel Nagayoshi," he said in perfect English with an American accent. "Hold your arms out."

Nick looked at his father. He nodded, and they did as he asked. Nick had read newspaper accounts of the Japanese maiming and torturing prisoners. They usually did it publicly as a warning to others.

The Colonel pulled his sword from the scabbard. Nick flinched and lowered his arms. Sergeant Sonji rushed forward and jerked his arms up.

"Be brave," he whispered in Nick's ear, then stepped away.

Nick managed to keep his arms out, but he couldn't stop them from shaking.

The Colonel brought his sword up, pausing with the blade above his head, then brought it straight down, stopping within an inch of the ground. Nick stared at him in defiance with his arms still out, determined not to flinch again.

The Colonel gave him a slight bow, then positioned himself in front of his father, whose arms were as solid as a teak plank.

Again the blade hissed, narrowly missing his father's forehead in its downward arc. Without another word, the Colonel returned the sword to its scabbard, then headed back up the steps into Hawk's Nest.

"Impressive scoundrel," Nick's father muttered under his breath.

More like a common bully, Nick thought. What was he trying to prove with the swordplay? It wasn't until he lowered his arms that Nick understood what his father was saying. The rope around his wrists had been cut clean through. Nick stared at his numb hands in astonishment. He hadn't even felt the blade cut through the ropes. The Colonel *was* impressive.

"Are you hurt?" his father asked under his breath.

"No. I can't believe—"

"No talking!" Sergeant Sonji said.

The soldiers with the list got back to business by calling out two names. The mahouts stood and were escorted into the house. Ten minutes later they came back out. One was taken to the side of the house. The other was sent back to sit with the men in front of the house.

More names were called. Some were sent back to the men's group, others were sent around the side of the house. Just before sunset, the last three men were sent into Hawk's Nest. Nick recognized them. They had all been with Magwe at the training camp. When they came back out they were told to sit with the other men still in front of the house. Were the Japanese segregating the men into those who were sympathetic and those who weren't?

The answer came a moment later when Magwe stepped out onto the porch without an escort. He had been inside the whole time, no doubt telling Colonel Nagayoshi who was on his side and who wasn't.

He began speaking to the assembly in Burmese. Nick looked at his father, expecting to see anger, or at least irritation, but instead he just looked sad.

When Magwe finished, the villagers all got up and started walking quietly down to the village.

His father watched his people leave, nodding at the few who acknowledged him. But most of them walked by without so much as a glance in his direction.

As darkness fell, the generator started up, and the lights came on inside Hawk's Nest. The last person to leave was Magwe. Unlike the others, he stopped in front of them and said something in Burmese. His father said something back. Magwe nodded and walked away.

"He apologized," his father explained.

"What did you say?"

"I told him that the people were his responsibility now."

The hours passed slowly. Dozens of trucks came and went, dumping supplies and soldiers. The

Japanese had arrived in force, and it looked like Hawk's Nest was their new headquarters.

Nick was thirsty, hungry, and his ribs were killing him. His father asked Sonji if they could stand and stretch, but he said they were to remain where they were by the Colonel's orders.

"Softening us up," his father said.

"For what?"

Sonji slapped them on the back of their heads. "No talking! Very serious."

Nick barely felt the slap above his other aches and pains, but he remained quiet, and so did his father.

More time passed. An hour? Two? Nick was getting weak and dizzy. It was all he could do to stop himself from pitching forward onto his face.

Finally, the captain who had captured his father came out onto the porch and barked out an order.

Sergeant Sonji snapped to attention. "We go inside now. You stand!"

Standing was much easier said than done. Nick had to get up in stages, waiting for the shooting pains to subside, before making his next move. When he finally got to his feet, his knees buckled. He grabbed on to his father and nearly pulled him down. Sonji put an arm around his waist and put his hand under Nick's arm to help support him. This is how they walked through the front door of Hawk's Nest.

As they stepped into the entry hall, Nick glanced

into the dining room. Half a dozen soldiers were sitting around the table eating dinner under the watchful eye of Bukong. He gave Nick a slight nod as they were escorted into the library.

Colonel Nagayoshi was sitting behind the Helm, sorting through a stack of papers. He didn't look up when Nick and his father were brought in. Hanging behind him was a Japanese flag and a photo of Emperor Hirohito. The Colonel's sword was displayed beneath the flag on a black enameled rack. Nick's cigar box was sitting on the desk with his lead soldiers carefully arranged on top. His father's rucksack was sitting next to it.

The Colonel finally looked up and said something to Sergeant Sonji in Japanese. Sonji retrieved a chair and gestured for Nick to take a seat.

"I'm fine," Nick said, although if his father let go of him, he wasn't sure he could stay on his feet.

"Sit down," his father said.

Reluctantly, Nick eased himself into the chair.

The Colonel regarded both of them for a moment, then said, "The combination to the safe."

Nick's father cleared his parched throat. "Right eight, left thirty-one, right twenty-seven."

Nick glanced up at him in surprise. He hadn't hesitated to give the Colonel the combination. And August 31st was Nick's birthday.

Sergeant Sonji turned the spindle, then pulled

open the heavy door. The Colonel got up and disappeared inside. After a few moments he came back out and resumed his seat behind the Helm. He pointed to the ashes in the fireplace. "It appears, Mr. Freestone, that you were expecting us."

His father ignored the comment. "What happened to Captain Josephs?"

"I executed him," the Colonel answered.

"Why?"

"He was my enemy."

His father gave him an angry glare. "And Nang?"

"An unfortunate accident. My men were told not to harm the Burmese, but in the heat of battle . . ." The Colonel shrugged his shoulders.

"Battle?" his father raised his voice. "What battle? There aren't any weapons here. Nang did not resist. Why was he beaten to death?"

The Colonel looked at him for a few moments before answering. "The man responsible will be punished," he said.

His father started to say something, then took a deep breath—no doubt trying to cool his Freestone blood. "And the men you took around back?" he asked.

"They will be sent to a work camp."

"Why?" Nick's father asked. "They're Burmese. They aren't your enemies. Their families are here on the plantation."

"I think you know why, Mr. Freestone."

The two men stared at each other. After a few seconds the Colonel said, "Their families' presence here will assure the men's cooperation while they are in the labor camp."

"Hostages," his father said.

"Do you think their wives and children would be better off in the labor camp?"

"No."

The Colonel shrugged.

"Sounds like you plan on staying."

"It's very comfortable," the Colonel said, looking around the library.

"Our soldiers may have something to say about that when they find out you're here."

"Unlikely, Mr. Freestone. The bombing of Rangoon started yesterday. It will not be long before it falls. In the meantime, your army is going to be too preoccupied to worry about a teak plantation in the jungle."

"Where is this labor camp?" his father asked.

"Some distance from here, I'm afraid. It will be a difficult journey."

A death march, Nick thought. He had read about them in the newspaper. It was rumored that the Japanese didn't actually have camps. To take care of the prisoner situation, they marched them for weeks or months until they died of starvation or disease. This way they didn't have to feed or take care of their prisoners.

The Colonel stood. "You will be going with them, Mr. Freestone. It is only fitting that you stay with the men who are loyal to you."

Nick's father gave him a stoic nod. The Colonel looked at Nick, then back at his father. "I know the British consider the Japanese barbarians, but the truth is that our culture has existed much longer than your own. We are anything but barbarians." He walked over to the window and looked outside, then turned back to them. "We have something in common, Mr. Freestone." He pointed to Nick. "I, too, have a son. Unfortunately, he and his mother are in America. I was there myself until a year ago."

"That's where you learned English."

The Colonel nodded. "San Francisco. The emperor called me home. My wife and son remained behind. I felt they would be safer there. Now I am not so certain. I have not heard from them since the bombing of Pearl Harbor."

The Colonel walked back to the Helm and picked up one of Nick's lead soldiers. "I understand that you were trying to get your son out of Burma."

"Yes."

"Where?"

"Australia, via India."

"I am sorry you did not succeed." The Colonel

started to put the soldiers back into the box one at a time. "I have a proposition for you." He put the last soldier into the box and closed the lid. "Leave the boy here on the plantation. When I get the opportunity, I will send him to India."

"No!" Nick protested, getting out of the chair.

The Colonel didn't take his eyes off Nick's father. "That is exactly how my son reacted when I told him I was returning to Japan without him. He will be much safer here than where you are going."

"I'll take my chances," Nick said.

The Colonel continued staring at Nick's father. "Decide."

"Now?" his father asked.

"Yes. You and the other men are leaving here in a few minutes."

Nick knew what his father's decision was before he opened his mouth. "Don't do this," he pleaded. "Please."

"Sergeant Sonji will take personal responsibility for the boy's safety," the Colonel said. "I just hope the Americans show my son and wife the same consideration."

Nick's father looked at him. "You're in no condition to travel, son. You can barely stand."

"I was fine on the plantation today," Nick protested.

"On elephantback." His father put his hand on Nick's shoulder. "This is the only way." He looked at the Colonel. "May I speak to my son alone?"

The Colonel thought about it for a moment, then nodded and walked out of the library with Sergeant Sonji.

"I'll run away," Nick said.

"There's nowhere to run. You can't make it to India alone on foot."

"This isn't right," Nick said.

"It's not the way I wanted it either, but it's your best chance."

"You don't really think Colonel Nagayoshi is going to send me to India?"

"Why else would he make the offer?" his father said. "Regardless, you will be much safer here than with me." He lowered his voice. "Listen . . . I have no intention of spending the war in a bloody labor camp. It will be a long march, and we are better suited to this climate than the Japanese. If I don't manage to escape on the way, I'll escape from the camp. The point is, I am coming back to Hawk's Nest. If the Colonel hasn't sent you off by then, I'll get you out myself."

"How?"

"I'm not sure. But I'll figure it out. In the meantime, you need to let those ribs heal. Keep your head down while you're here. And I mean that literally. Bow to them, even when you don't want to, no matter how humiliating it is. You need to keep yourself safe and healthy."

Nick didn't like it, but he knew his father was right. He was in no shape to travel. If he insisted on tagging along, his father would never escape.

"We don't have much time," his father continued urgently. "Not everyone the Colonel is leaving here is loyal to the Japanese. This means Magwe, or whoever was feeding him information, doesn't know everything that's going on. We still have friends on the plantation."

"Who?"

"Your best source of information for that will be Hilltop."

"What if the Japanese find him and send him away?"

"They wouldn't dare. He's an untouchable. They would have a riot on their hands, and not just here. Every Burman in the country would be up in arms."

His father opened his rucksack and took out the diary Nick had given to him. He scribbled something down on one of the pages and tore it out.

"This is the contact information for Mr. Singh in India. If you get there, all you have to do is tell him who you are. He'll take care of the rest."

"What about Mya?"

His father paused for a moment. "When you see Hilltop, tell him that I want her to go with you to Australia. He should be able to arrange it with the Colonel. In the meantime, keep an eye on her."

"I will," Nick said.

"One more thing." His father lowered his voice. "I need to tell you something about the house. There are secret—"

The Colonel and Sergeant Sonji walked back into the library, followed by Bukong leaning on his bamboo cane. The Colonel looked suspiciously at the piece of blue paper Nick was holding in his hand.

"I gave Nick the contact information in India," his father explained.

"Good." The Colonel took the paper.

His father picked up his rucksack and slipped the strap over his shoulder. He bowed to the Colonel and thanked him for his consideration, which Nick thought was more for his benefit than the Colonel's. He was showing Nick how to act while he was there.

"You will not have many guards on your journey," the Colonel said. "It's only fair that I warn you as I have the others. If something happens during your trip—an escape attempt, for instance—the family members that remain here will be punished." He looked at Nick. "Severely punished."

"I understand," his father said.

The Colonel gave him a crisp bow and said, "It is time to leave."

"I guess I'll see you after this is all over," his father said, giving Nick a hug.

It hurt his ribs, but Nick didn't care. He squeezed

his father back with all his strength. His father broke away, gave him a smile, then walked out of the library with Sergeant Sonji.

"Bukong will show you to your room," the Colonel said.

Nick couldn't find his voice, but he managed to give him a bow, which made his ribs scream. He followed Bukong out of the library, hoping to catch a final look at his father, but he had already gone. He started toward the stairs, thinking that he might be able to see him from his balcony.

"No," Bukong said. "This way."

"But my—"

"This way," he repeated.

They walked through the dining room. The soldiers had finished eating, and the table had been cleared. Bukong opened the door to the kitchen. Nick thought he might be taking him out back to see his father. Certainly Bukong was on his side. The kitchen staff was busy washing dishes. Nick looked at each of them, trying to determine which of them might be sympathetic. None of them made eye contact with him.

Bukong led him into the servants' hallway. At the end was a back door leading to the garden. Nick was certain now he was taking him to see his father. But halfway down the hall, Bukong stopped in front of the door to his old nursery.

"What's this?" Nick asked.

Bukong pushed the door open. Nick's trunk was on the bed. Bukong smiled, then hit him on the shoulder with his cane and pushed him into the room. Nick fell against the bed table. His cowboy lamp shattered into a hundred pieces.

"You are no longer the little master of this house," Bukong said, then slammed the door. A lock snapped into place.

Shocked by the hit—and in pain from the fall—Nick lay still for a moment. The room was pitch black except for the dim moonlight coming through the barred window. Slowly, he pulled himself up and looked outside, hoping for one final look at his father.

A guard walked by the barred window. Beyond him, all Nick could see was the jungle. It would be ten months before he heard from his father again.

Part Two

Hawk's Nest

After his father was taken away, Nick was locked in his room for thirteen days. The only person he saw during that time was Bukong. He showed up once a day with a bucket of kitchen scraps and a jar of water, which he pushed through the door without a word.

At first Nick would not touch the slop, but after a couple days he lost his squeamishness and attacked the sour pickings like a village dog. The thirteenth bucket had a mop in it. Bukong made him clean the room and beat him with his cane when he wasn't going fast enough or doing a thorough enough job. When Nick finished, Bukong had him strip out of his clothes and put on a longyi. Nick thought he was going to lock him back in the nursery, but instead he pushed him down the hall to the kitchen and made him scrub the floor.

After several weeks of this, Nick was saved by Sergeant Sonji. He put him to work in the garden. It was harder than scrubbing floors, but Sonji was much better company than Bukong.

The sergeant was the most unlikely soldier Nick had ever seen. He wasn't violent, although he did slap Nick occasionally for the benefit of Bukong and the Colonel, but never hard. The slaps were accompanied by loud shouting to prove to the staff and soldiers that the American boy was being kept in his place by the brutal sergeant. Nick would help the charade by over-reacting and sometimes faking injuries.

The first two months of his captivity, he expected the British to march onto the plantation and rout the Japanese. He expected his father to escape and take him away. He expected the Colonel to send him to India. He expected his ribs to mend. With the help of the Colonel's physician, his ribs did heal, but none of his other expectations had come to pass.

As the Colonel predicted, the Allied army had been too busy defending Rangoon to worry about a small teak plantation in the middle of the jungle. The city fell in early March, and the army went on a nine-hundred-mile forced retreat out of the country. According to Sonji, Burma now belonged to Emperor Hirohito, along with nearly every other country in Southeast Asia.

If his father had managed to escape, it would have been nearly impossible for him to get back to the plantation. Sonji told Nick he had been sent to an internment camp for British prisoners of war in Singapore. He would have to walk a thousand miles through Japanese-occupied territory to get back to Hawk's Nest.

At first, Nick thought Colonel Nagayoshi had every intention of sending him to India, but in April things changed. The Colonel got word that his wife and son had been put into a Japanese internment camp in the United States. After this, there was no more talk of Nick going anywhere.

Nick had asked Sonji what he thought the Colonel

would do to him if something bad were to happen to his family in the American camp.

"Let's just hope that nothing bad happens," was his grim reply.

The plantation became the site of a secret air base. Construction began the day after Nick's father was taken away and had continued steadily, although the monsoon had slowed things down. The rains had started in May and were just starting to ease up.

The airfield was on the plateau in the back of Hawk's Nest. All the trees had been cut down, the ground leveled, and the streams dammed to stop the water from washing the field into the river.

The entire village was put to work on it, including the children. They hadn't been liberated by the Japanese; they had been captured just like Nick. And yet, there were still some who were sympathetic to the Japanese.

The most ardent sympathizer was Bukong. It turned out that he was Magwe's older brother and a former mahout. Eight years before, Hannibal had attacked him and crushed his leg. Nick's father had sent Bukong to a hospital in Rangoon and called a specialist in from India. The doctor saved the leg, but Bukong's days on elephant back were over. When he got out of the hospital, Nick's father had given him the position of head houseman—a coveted and powerful position on the plantation—but Bukong never forgave

Hannibal or Nick's father. He and Magwe started secretly meeting with Japanese agents a year before the Colonel came to Hawk's Nest.

With the exception of Nick, those working inside the house were not forced to work on the airfield. If it was raining too hard to work in the garden, or if Sergeant Sonji had other duties, Bukong sent Nick up to the plateau to work with the villagers. It was backbreaking work, and Bukong thought of it as punishment, but it wasn't. It gave Nick a chance to get away from the house and talk to people, something he wasn't allowed to do at Hawk's Nest. Bukong made sure of that, hitting Nick with his cane if he so much as opened his mouth to speak to one of the servants.

The garden was the Colonel's private domain. No one was allowed into the garden without his express permission. Every morning at dawn, rain or shine, Nagayoshi would spend an hour in the garden, practicing with his sword.

Sonji had given Nick his father's Japanese books, along with a notebook to write down haikus and practice his Japanese characters. He tutored him as they worked, and Nick was getting pretty good at the language. But his fluency got him into trouble one morning six months after his capture.

The Colonel had finished his exercise and was speaking to Sonji about the garden. Nick was near them, trying to translate what they were saying, and something inside him snapped. He didn't know what caused it—his Freestone blood, no doubt. He saw red, then shouted in Japanese: "When are you going to send me to India? You are a liar! You have no honor!"

The Colonel's sword came out of his scabbard like a lightning bolt. And he might have killed Nick right there had it not been for Bukong, who had overheard Nick's outburst through the kitchen window. He rushed out into the garden, wielding his cane. He nearly beat Nick to death, but Sonji pulled him off.

It took Nick three full days to recover from the beating. When he was well enough, he had to apologize to the Colonel by kowtowing to him in front of the entire house staff and several soldiers. Everyone gathered in the entryway to witness the humiliating spectacle.

Nick had prostrated himself outside the library door. When the Colonel stepped out, Nick begged him for mercy and forgiveness for several minutes until the Colonel turned on his heels and walked back into the library. When Nick looked up, Bukong was staring down at him with a cruel, satisfied smile. Standing just behind him was Mya. All the other servants were staring at Nick with undisguised shame. But not Mya. She smiled, then put her palms together and gave Nick a bow of respect.

He had heard that Mya was living in the village with her aunt and working as a servant in Hawk's Nest during the day, but this was the first time he had seen her. He rarely saw anyone during his short walks down the servants' hallway in the morning and back to the nursery in the evening.

Hilltop had told him that Mya was doing well, under the circumstances. The Colonel had put out the word to his soldiers that they were to keep their hands off her. Nick was certain the order would be obeyed.

The second day he was locked in the nursery, he saw the soldier responsible for Nang's death executed through his barred window. The man had been killed in front of Hawk's Nest with the entire village looking on. The soldier had proclaimed his innocence and begged for mercy to the very end. Colonel Nagayoshi had not listened. He'd beheaded him with one swift stroke from his sword and wiped the blood dripping from the blade on the soldier's tunic.

The Garden 13

As Hilltop walked past Nick in the Colonel's garden he whispered, "Check the natshin."

Nick raked his way toward the small spirit house. Hilltop drew Sergeant Sonji away by asking him a question about the footbridge they had just built on the far side of the garden.

In the natshin, sitting among the offerings of incense, bits of food, and shiny stones, was a folded square of powder-blue paper. Barely able to contain his excitement, Nick glanced at Sergeant Sonji to make sure he wasn't looking, then snatched the note from the house.

He hadn't heard from his father since the night he'd left Hawk's Nest. The powder-blue note meant he was alive.

As much as Nick wanted to, he couldn't open the note in the garden. Not in front of Sonji. If the sergeant saw the note, he would be honor-bound to confiscate it and give it to the Colonel. Notes were not expressly forbidden, but Nick knew he would pay a price if he were caught with it. The Colonel would make him stand in the hot afternoon sun holding a heavy boulder above his head, beat him—or worse—turn him over to Bukong for punishment.

He slipped the note into the waistband of his longyi and went back to work, raking wave patterns into the white sand surrounding the central pond, called the *ginshanada*, or *open sands, open seas*. Over the past nine months, Sonji and Nick had transformed his mother's garden into a beautiful Japanese garden.

Before the war, Sonji had been a gardener in Tokyo. He was also a famous haiku master, according to Hilltop, who had met Sonji in Japan, which was just one of the places the monk had traveled to after he'd left Burma.

When Sonji saw Hilltop's name scratched into the dirt next to the river, he'd known it was a person, not a place. Both he and the Colonel were well aware the monk had returned to Burma. In fact, they were surprised he wasn't on the plantation when they took it over.

The old monk and Sonji wandered back over to where Nick was raking. Hilltop peered into the natshin. "No fresh offerings for the nats?"

Sonji smiled. "I have many superstitions, but giving presents to little devils is not one of them."

"Unwise," Hilltop said mildly. "The nats are always worse after the monsoon. They sit inside during the long rains and plan mischief for when the weather breaks." He looked at Nick. "How about you? Have you been paying your respects?"

"When I find something I think they'll like," Nick answered as he continued raking wave patterns. The Colonel liked his ginshanada perfect.

Bukong opened the back door and jingled his keys. This was the signal Nick was to be locked back in his room. He looked up and was surprised to see Mya standing next to Bukong. This was only the second time he had seen her in ten months.

Sonji inspected the ginshanada. "Is good enough," he said.

"May I speak to Mya a moment?" Hilltop asked Bukong.

Bukong looked as if he were going to say no, but nodded his assent. "I'll put the boy in his room."

Nick followed Bukong and Sonji into the house.

Mya 14

Hilltop waited until Bukong and the sergeant were well out of hearing before speaking.

"How is everything?" he asked her.

Mya shook her head. "I'm afraid. Three times this week someone has tried to get into my room."

"Bukong?"

"I think so."

Hilltop nodded. "I guess we will have to move things forward."

"What do you mean?"

"There's no time to explain now. Bukong will be back in a moment. Can you get a message to Nick?"

Mya shook her head. "Bukong doesn't allow anyone to talk to him."

Hilltop reached into his cloth bag, pulled out a piece of paper and a pencil, and scribbled something on it. "Can you slip this under his door?"

Mya nodded and took the note, not at all certain she would succeed. Nick's doorway was only a few down from hers, but the servants' quarters were busy night and day. And then there was Bukong showing up at odd hours when least expected.

"Before midnight," Hilltop said. "It's important."

"I'll try."

Bukong reappeared at the back door. Mya gave Hilltop a bow and followed Bukong into Hawk's Nest.

Mya had not forgiven the Japanese for what they had done to her father and brother, but she had learned to disguise her hatred of them. She had also learned that the Japanese were not her biggest threat. The past ten months had been the most difficult of her life.

Her great-grandfather, Hilltop, had returned to the plantation a week after the Japanese came. The day after he arrived, Mya was summoned to Hawk's Nest along with Kin-Kin. Bukong told her that the Colonel wanted her to work in the house. Mya's first impulse was to tell him no, but Kin-Kin said yes before Mya had a chance to reply.

Since Nang died, Kin-Kin had not been well. She was not sleeping at night and had a deep cough that would not go away. Mya didn't want to add to her burden by arguing with her in front of Bukong, but when they got to the village trail she could not contain herself any longer.

"I don't want to work at Hawk's Nest," Mya said. "Why did you say I would?"

"Because the Japanese are making everyone work," Kin-Kin answered wearily. "You saw the notice."

The notice had been posted on every house in the village, and it had not been well received. Everyone in the elephant village had always worked—life on a teak plantation was hard—slackers were not tolerated. What the Japanese meant by "work" was that everyone was to have an assigned task or job above the day-to-day business of surviving in the middle of a hostile jungle.

All able-bodied men and boys were put to work on the airfield. This left the woman and children to fill the other jobs. They weren't allowed to choose the job; they were assigned or "given" the job, as Captain Katayama, the Japanese officer in charge of the village, put it. In fact, just that morning, Katayama had walked into their house and *given* Kin-Kin a job in the officer's laundry.

"I won't work at Hawk's Nest!" Mya said as they reached the village. "I don't want to be anywhere near the Colonel."

"Better than washing soldiers' underwear," Kin-Kin said. "And Colonel Nagayoshi isn't the one who killed your father."

"He allowed it to happen."

"He chopped off the head of the man responsible."

Mya shuddered at the memory. She and Kin-Kin had watched the execution, but there was no satisfaction at seeing the soldier beheaded; only horror and regret. His death had not brought her father back.

"Besides, you must remember," Kin-Kin continued, "Colonel Nagayoshi is the only person who can tell us where Indaw is and how he is doing. Perhaps you'll be able to learn something inside Hawk's Nest."

This last point had convinced Mya to take the job. The next morning she arrived at Hawk's Nest at the appointed time. She knew very little about Bukong. She was just a little girl when he had been injured by Hannibal. After he took over the duties of running Hawk's Nest, no one in the village saw very much of him. His whole life revolved around running the house, and it was rumored that he was a cruel taskmaster.

During her time at Hawk's Nest, Mya had seen Bukong use his cane liberally on the other servants, but he had never used it on her. From her first day in the house he had been polite and patient with her. If she did something wrong, he would gently scold her, then show her how he wanted it done. Even so, Mya was leery of Bukong, uncomfortable, as if there were something on his mind he wasn't saying. At the end of her first month, he suggested that she move into one of the servants' rooms. She told him that she couldn't. She needed to be near her aunt. He said that that was fine but insisted that one of the other servants escort her to the village in the evenings for her safety.

Despite her uneasy feelings about Bukong, Mya continued to work at Hawk's Nest. Kin-Kin had been right, the house was a good place to get information. But so far, she had learned little about Indaw except that he was alive and working in a labor camp somewhere north of the plantation.

The best place to eavesdrop, Mya discovered, was the entryway outside the library. She volunteered to scrub the black-and-white tiles at every opportunity. Her Japanese was not very good, but she had picked up enough to understand some of what the soldiers talked about as they waited to meet with Colonel Nagayoshi.

Kin-Kin's health deteriorated with each passing week. In late August she came down with malaria, which had raged through the plantation during the long monsoon. The Colonel sent his personal physician to treat her. Hilltop chanted prayers. But in the end there was nothing anyone could do. Kin-Kin died the first week of September.

When Mya returned home after the funeral, she found Bukong sitting on Kin-Kin's steps, waiting for her.

"You can't stay here alone," he said. "I've had your things moved up to Hawk's Nest."

Mya was so distraught over Kin-Kin she didn't even argue. She simply followed him up the hill to the house. The small room Bukong had prepared for her was in the servants' quarters, but unlike the other household staff, she didn't have to share it.

A few days after she moved into Hawk's Nest, Bukong came to her room after all the other servants had retired for the night. He tapped lightly, then opened the door without being asked. Mya was lying on her sleeping mat.

"I just came by to make sure everything is all right," he said quietly.

"Everything is fine," Mya said, disturbed that he had come in without being invited.

"I was wondering if we might have a talk," Bukong said, taking a seat. "We need to talk about your future."

"What do you mean?" Bukong was acting oddly, even for him. He seemed nervous.

"You're all alone now," he said. "No one to take care of you."

Mya had been pretty much on her own from the time she could walk. Her father was off in the forest with the elephants for a good part of the year, and Kin-Kin let her and Indaw have the run of the village.

"I'll be fine," she said.

Bukong shook his head. "That's where you are wrong. You are very pretty. Certainly you've noticed the soldiers watching you?"

She had, but there had been no problems.

"You need protection," Bukong said. "Someone to watch over you." He paused. "You need a husband, Mya."

Mya stared at him. This was why he had given her the easy jobs, why he had never used his cane, why he had given her a room by herself. Bukong had to be at least thirty years older than she was, maybe more. Did he really think . . . ?

"One day the Japanese will leave here," he continued. "The war cannot go on forever. Magwe and I will own the plantation. We have Colonel Nagayoshi's word on this. Instead of being a servant, Mya, you will *have* servants. I will make you the queen of Hawk's Nest."

Mya was too shocked to speak. The silence grew uncomfortably long. Bukong finally got to his feet and picked up his cane.

"I know it's been a difficult month with Kin-Kin sick, then losing her. I would not have brought it up so soon, but I felt I should make my intentions known." He limped over to her and gently ran his finger down her cheek. "You'll see that it's the best course for you. The only course. I'll give you some time to adjust to the idea." He smiled. "We will be very happy together, Mya." He walked out of the room and quietly shut the door behind him.

Mya stared at the door for several minutes. The place on her cheek where he had touched her burned.

Bukong must have planned this from the very beginning. Queen of Hawk's Nest? If Bukong weren't so dangerous, the notion would be laughable.

She wasn't going to marry anyone, and if she were, Bukong would be the last person on earth she would consider. In fact, she wouldn't marry him if he were the last person on earth.

Bukong must be insane, she thought. That's the only explanation for him to think I would become his wife. And what did he mean, the Colonel was giving him and Magwe the plantation? Was this their plan all along? Use the Japanese to get rid of Mr. Freestone, then take the plantation over when the Japanese left? If Father were alive this would never have happened.

She opened the door and looked up and down the hallway. Bukong had gone into his room near the kitchen. No one else was about. Her first impulse was to flee, but she knew she couldn't, not right then. Hawk's Nest was heavily guarded at night. She would have to wait until daytime. But if she left, where would she go? Bukong would come after her, and with the Japanese helping him, she wouldn't get very far.

She closed the door and sat down on her sleeping mat. She had to think. Bukong said that he was going to give her some time to adjust. But how much time?

The next day, Bukong acted as if nothing had happened the night before. He told her to help clean the kitchen. When she finished, he sent her out to scrub the entryway. If anything, he was making her work harder than usual. Perhaps he was giving her a taste of what it would be like if she didn't consent to be his wife. Mya would rather scrub floors every day for the rest of her life than be married to Bukong for one minute.

Hilltop came through the front door. Mya nearly burst into tears when she saw him. Aside from Bukong and Magwe, he was the only one who had free access to the Colonel. Perhaps he could talk to Nagayoshi and get him to stop Bukong, she thought. Or maybe Hilltop could talk to Bukong himself. Hilltop was her closest blood relative. If he didn't consent to the marriage, Bukong wouldn't dare go through with it.

When Hilltop came out of the library after meeting with the Colonel, Mya approached him and asked if she could talk to him. Bukong overheard the request and hurried over.

He bowed to Hilltop, then said, "Mya, I need you upstairs."

"Surely you can give us a few minutes alone, Bukong," Hilltop said. "I haven't seen my great-granddaughter since the funeral. And by the way, thank you for moving her into Hawk's Nest. She'll be much safer here."

Bukong gave him a smile. "It was the least I could do. Mya's safety is always on my mind." He looked at Mya. "Don't be too long."

Hilltop took her out onto the front porch, where she told him everything that had happened the night before. He listened carefully with a frown on his face.

When Mya finished, he said, "We will have to get you off the plantation."

"How?"

"It will be difficult, but you leave that to me. In the meantime, secure your door at night. Spend as little time alone with Bukong as possible."

"Can't you talk to the Colonel?" Mya asked. "He would listen to you."

Hilltop shook his head. "We'll keep the Colonel out of this for now. Just be ready to leave at a moment's notice."

The Letter 15

Nick knew better than to read the note right away.

Within a few minutes someone would open the door and slide in a bowl of rice and a pot of green tea. Usually a kitchen servant brought his food, but sometimes Bukong brought it himself. If he caught Nick reading a secret note, he would take it away and beat him with the cane.

Reluctantly, Nick hid the note under a loose brick in the fireplace next to the Sergeant Major's pocket-knife and the carvings he'd been working on to pass the long nights. He wished Indaw had been able to teach him how to carve before he was taken away. He was getting better, but his elephants still looked more like pigs with trunks than elephants.

He sat down on his bed to wait.

It didn't take long. There was a light tapping on the door, which meant it wasn't Bukong—he never knocked. The door opened, the food was slid in, the door closed, and the lock was turned. It had been the same every night for ten months.

Before retrieving the note, he ate his rice and drank

his tea. As always, he was famished. He set the bowl near the door, then listened for a moment. Bukong was sneaky. Two or three times a month he raided Nick's room, looking for contraband, which was anything Bukong hadn't authorized Nick to have. The raids came without warning.

During one of the early raids, Bukong had discovered the Japanese books Sonji had given him. He accused Nick of stealing them. A ridiculous accusation, as Nick was only allowed to walk up and down the hall twice a day, always under guard. How could he steal books? After beating him, Bukong took the books away. Sonji returned the books a few days later, telling Nick that he should have told Bukong about them before he discovered them.

Nick was lucky to get them back. Aside from carving, the books were his only entertainment. He had learned a lot about the Japanese by reading them.

By seven o'clock, Nick could no longer contain himself. Bukong would be serving the nightly dinner to the Colonel and his guests. He wouldn't burst into his room during that time. At least, Nick hoped he wouldn't.

Like he did every night, he put an old longyi along the crack at the bottom of the door so Bukong wouldn't see the light from his candle. Bukong was drawn to it like a moth. Nick had forgotten a couple of times, and Bukong had rushed into his room shouting that Nick wasn't working hard enough during the day if he had the energy to read at night. He had taken his matches and candles, and it took Sonji days to get him to give them back.

He got the note and took it back to his bed.

Dear Nick,

If you are reading this, it means you are still at Hawk's Nest, and Colonel Nagayoshi has broken his word. I trust you are healthy and taking care of yourself.

Escape is never far from my thoughts, but the Japanese are much better jailers than any of us expected. When I left Hawk's Nest, we were marched to the coast, where I was separated from the mahouts and put aboard a boat with fifty or so captured Brits and Aussies (soldiers and civilians). We were taken to Singapore and put into an internment camp. It was a rough voyage, and we lost several good men on the way. Indaw and the other mahouts were sent to a labor camp north of the plantation.

Escape from Singapore was not practical. Even if I'd been lucky enough to get outside the compound, there was no place to go.

I am glad you didn't come with me. Aside from the sanitary conditions (which were abysmal) and disease, our biggest problem was lack of food. A good part of my day (everyone's day, actually) was spent trying to procure enough food to stay alive.

The Japanese did not anticipate so many prisoners. They

assumed we would fight to the death like good samurai. Perhaps we should have. Hundreds of men have died from disease here. I've had a few health problems myself, but I'm fine now and working hard to stay that way so I can see you again when this is all over.

The Japanese have forbidden us paper and pen, but the diary you gave me is easy enough to hide. (You would be surprised at what we've been able to hide from them, but I'll leave those details until I see you, on the off chance that this document falls into the wrong hands.)

There is a lot of time to think here, at night mostly. My deepest regret is having you come to Burma. It was selfish of me, really. My desire to have you with me fogged my thinking. When your mother left with you all those years ago, I should have followed. Things would be much different now if I had. I stayed because I thought it was the only way to keep the plantation and everything the Sergeant Major and my father had worked for. In the end I lost the plantation anyway, along with your mother, and ten years with you.

Knowing that the Japanese were coming, my original plan was to have Nang turn the plantation over to them peacefully. I didn't want anyone hurt. I drew up a document giving title of the plantation to the villagers in the event the Japanese retained possession of Burma after the war. I doubt the Japanese would have honored the document, but at least it would have given the villagers some legal standing. I didn't anticipate Nang's senseless death. Nor did I realize that Magwe was so deeply sympathetic to the Japanese. I *thought that Bukong had more control over him, but I guess none of that matters at this point.*

Nick read the last two sentences over again. The situation was worse than his father thought. From what villagers had told him at the airfield, Bukong was the ringleader, not Magwe.

On the bright side, I did get to see you for a few days, and we were able to get Hannibal over to the island, where he'll be safe.

You might be wondering how I managed to get this letter to you. A few weeks ago we were moved back to Burma to work on a railway.

Nick read the last paragraph over several times. His father was in Burma! He had heard about the railroad and wondered how far it was from the plantation.

A few days ago I overheard a guard talking. He said that Colonel Nagayoshi had a young American boy working for him at Hawk's Nest. I assumed you had been sent to India months ago! I hope the rumor isn't true, but just in case, I've made some arrangements.

A monk I've known for years has been staying at the mahout camp. He's leaving today. I'm hoping to slip him this note as he passes through my work area on his way up

151

north. If I'm successful, he'll get this letter to Hilltop, who will pass it on to you.

You're probably thinking I'll be able to escape from here. Get it out of your mind. I'm in terrible shape. I wouldn't make it ten miles in the condition I'm in right now. The Japanese control every country around here except for India, and that's over six hundred miles away.

I've also written a letter to Hilltop. I want you to do exactly as he says. He's a wise old bird and knows what he's doing. If it doesn't work out, continue to keep your head down—bow to them. The war will be over soon, and we'll be able to hold our heads high for the rest of our lives.

When I was at the Singapore camp I wrote to your mother telling her about our situation. I'm sure she has been in touch with Mr. Singh and Mr. Shute. If they have not seen you, then she will know that you are most likely at Hawk's Nest. With her and Bernard's connections in the American government, they might be able to do something to get you out of there. Don't give up hope. That's your most important asset.

I never told you this because I didn't understand it until now.

The last thing the Sergeant Major said to my father before he died was this: "In the end, the only thing that really matters is family. These are the ones who will be at your bedside when you die. Or you at theirs."

You're the only family I have, Nick. You're the only thing that matters.

The Visitor 16

A cold hand clamped over Nick's mouth.

At first he thought Bukong had caught him over-sleeping. He struggled to get up, but the hand held him firmly to the thin pillow.

"It's me," Hilltop whispered.

Hilltop had never been to his room, and, as far as Nick knew, Bukong had the only key. The servants had to borrow it to give him his food. Not even Sergeant Sonji had a key.

Hilltop took his hand away.

"How—"

"Shh . . . What time does Bukong come for you?" Hilltop whispered.

"Five. Sometimes a bit later."

"The time now?"

Nick squinted at his watch. "Two, I think."

"Enough time."

Nick sat up. "For what?"

"Follow me, but you must be very quiet."

Nick got up and started toward the door, hoping that Hilltop knew what he was doing. Servants wandered the hallway all night long. If Bukong caught Nick out of his room . . .

"This way," Hilltop whispered. He was standing next to the fireplace, pointing toward the opening.

Nick walked over and looked. The bricks in the back of the fireplace were gone! "What—"

"Quiet."

Hilltop got down and squeezed through the opening on his hands and knees. Nick followed him. It was so dark he couldn't see his hand in front of his face. Hilltop fumbled around a moment, lit a candle, then slid the secret door closed.

They were in a narrow passageway that seemed to stretch forever beyond the dim candlelight. Hilltop put his index finger to his lips and motioned for Nick to follow. They walked past ladders built into the walls and past the backs of other fireplaces. Every fifteen or twenty feet, a rubber hose with an odd funnel-shaped attachment dangled from the wall. The walls were insulated with the same type of bark the mahouts used to pad their elephants' backs.

They climbed and descended steps (nine steps up, a level area three or four feet wide, then nine steps down). Doorways. Nick tried to keep track of where they were, but it was impossible in the dark labyrinth. After ten minutes or so, they came to a stop in a small room. Hilltop lit another candle sitting on a wooden table next to his cloth bag. "A house within a house."

"I had no idea," Nick whispered in wonder.

"A carefully guarded secret," Hilltop said.

The room was furnished with a bed and a small cooking stove. A huge iron box protruded from one of the walls.

"The back side of the vault," Nick whispered.

"Yes," Hilltop confirmed in a normal voice. "The library is through there." He pointed at the bricks next to the vault. "And there is no need to whisper in here." He sat down at the table.

"Why was the house built this way?"

"The Sergeant Major was"—Hilltop paused, searching for the right word—"cautious. As a foreigner, he wanted a place to hide if things took a turn for the worse."

Nick walked over to one of the rubber hoses hanging from the wall. "What are these things?"

"Listening posts." Hilltop got up and put one of the funnels to his ear. "The guard outside the library. He had better wake up before Colonel Nagayoshi comes down the stairs."

Nick took the tube from him and listened. The guard was snoring.

"Are these in every room?"

"Every room."

"Why?"

"The Sergeant Major wanted to know what was going on in the house," Hilltop answered, hanging the tube back on its hook. "He eavesdropped on his guests."

"You're kidding!"

Hilltop walked back over to the table. "People seldom say what they mean in public, but in private? Let's just say the Sergeant Major learned a great deal about his competition by keeping his ear to the wall."

"Did my father—"

Hilltop shook his head. "He was uncomfortable with the idea."

Perhaps he should have reconsidered, Nick thought. He might have learned of Bukong's treachery.

"Did my mother know about this?"

"No, but she knew there was something about Hawk's Nest that wasn't quite right."

"She thought the house was haunted," Nick said.

Hilltop sighed. "I'm afraid that was my fault. When I returned from my travels, I hid in the walls of Hawk's Nest and told no one I was back. I hadn't yet decided if I would stay.

"I'm an old man and not as agile as I used to be. The narrow passageways are difficult to negotiate. I fell a time or two, scaring the wits out of your mother, I'm ashamed to say."

"Wasn't Father suspicious?"

"Yes. In fact, after your mother took you away, he found me sitting at this very table one night and demanded to know who I was and how I had gotten inside. At first he didn't believe I was Taung Baw. Like everyone else, he assumed I had died years before, but eventually I convinced him that I actually was who I claimed to be."

Nick looked around the room. "So you live down here?"

Hilltop laughed. "No, that would be too confining for me. But I have spent a good deal of time here since the soldiers came."

"Listening," Nick said.

He nodded. "And watching." He got up again and motioned Nick over to a spot between the vault and the fireplace. There was a small hole drilled into the wall with a hinged piece of teak over it. Nick saw the Helm; the library door, which was closed; and most of the bookcases on the far wall. The lamp on the desk was on, and the window shutters were closed.

"Do all the fireplaces have secret doors?"

"Why else would the Sergeant Major build fireplaces in Burma?" Hilltop asked.

Nick was shocked to hear about the secret passages, but the letter Hilltop had given him that afternoon was of greater concern. "What about my father?"

"He's back in Burma now."

"I know. But where?"

Hilltop looked back through the peephole, then listened through the tube. "I'll show you, but you must not speak. The guard will hear. And do not touch anything. The Colonel has a precise memory. He knows exactly where everything is. He is always the last to leave the library in the evening and the first to arrive in the morning. He has the only key. Not even Bukong has a key to the library. If something is out of place, the Colonel will know."

He pulled a small lever, and the back of the fireplace slid open with barely a sound.

The library had changed since Nick's last visit. A large map of Burma hung above the fireplace where the Freestone portraits used to hang. It was covered with little colored flags. There was a stepladder below it, no doubt used by the Colonel to move the flags around. In the center of the room was a snarling tiger-skin rug. On the wall opposite the shuttered windows was a long table with an array of radio and Teletype equipment.

Hilltop pointed to the plantation on the map, then moved his gnarled finger a few inches southwest and stopped. Nick stared at the spot on the map. His father wasn't more than a hundred miles away from Hawk's Nest!

A commotion erupted outside the library door. Someone shouted in Japanese. Apparently the guard had been caught sleeping. A key was inserted into the door.

Hilltop pushed Nick toward the fireplace. Nick

stumbled through the opening, scraping his head on the bricks. Hilltop came through right behind and yanked the lever down.

Hilltop put his finger to his lips and peered through the peephole for a long time. Nick had a horrifying image of the Colonel shouting the house awake: servants stumbling out of their rooms half-dressed, scrambling around for sledgehammers and crowbars to smash the fireplace apart.

Finally, Hilltop stepped away from the peephole.

"What did you see?" Nick whispered.

Instead of answering, Hilltop walked over to the other side of the room and rolled up a small rug. Beneath it was a trapdoor. He pulled the door open, and they were hit by a blast of cool air.

"Be careful," he whispered. "It's slippery."

The Colonel must have seen us, Nick thought, looking down into the dark hole. There was a ladder attached to the wall. He could not see bottom.

"Go," Hilltop whispered, grabbing his bag off the table.

Nick started down, with Hilltop following.

The deeper they went, the cooler it got. Nick began to wonder if the ladder would ever come to an end. Finally, his bare feet touched cold, damp rock. Hilltop lit another candle. They were in a tunnel. The walls were dripping wet. A rivulet of water trickled down the middle of the floor, disappearing into the darkness.

"That was very close," Hilltop said, smiling with relief.

"Close?" Nick said. "You mean the Colonel didn't see us?"

Hilltop shook his head. "He walked over to the radio and didn't even glance at the fireplace."

"Then why did we climb down here?"

"So we can talk without being heard."

"But you said we could speak freely in the room."

"As long as no one is in the library. I didn't expect the Colonel to come in. The radio call he was making must have been important. What time is it now?"

Nick was surprised to see how much time had passed. "Three thirty."

"I'll tell you as much as I can in the time we have. We don't want Bukong coming into your room and finding it empty."

"What is this place?" Nick asked, looking around.

"An underground stream bed," Hilltop explained. "It's been here for thousands of years. The view was not the only reason your great-grandfather built Hawk's Nest where it is. He wanted a private entrance, and more important, a private exit if he needed it." He reached into his bag and pulled out a folded sheet of powder-blue paper.

Old Friend,
If Nick and Mya are still there, please get them out of

162

Hawk's Nest. I know India is probably too far, but please find somewhere safe for them to wait out the war. I wouldn't ask, but there is no one else I can trust with the task.

    Jackson

"You look tired. Maybe doctor should look. You want me get?"

Nick told Sonji that he was fine and continued weeding. But the truth was that he was tired. Exhausted, really. He had spent the last three nights exploring the secret passageways, barely making it back to his room each morning before Bukong arrived to escort him to the garden.

Nick had not seen Hilltop since the night he'd appeared in his room. He hadn't seen him in the garden either, which was odd because Hilltop usually dropped by the garden entrance to the kitchen to collect offerings for his alms bowl every day.

"Have you seen Hilltop lately?" Nick asked Sonji.

Sonji shook his head. "Taung Baw, he come go as he please. Maybe today he come here. Airfield finished."

Nick looked up from his weeding. Sonji rarely volunteered information about the airfield.

"Very big day for Colonel. He happy man today."

Nick glanced over at the Colonel, who was

practicing with his samurai sword. This hiss of the blade cut through the morning air like a deadly whisper. He did not look happy. If anything, he looked grimmer than usual.

One of the things Hilltop had told him in the tunnel was that the Colonel's son had fallen seriously ill in the internment camp. "If his son dies," Hilltop had said, "I'm not sure what Colonel Nagayoshi's reaction will be." This was another reason for Nick to get away from the plantation as soon as possible.

Nick hitched up his longyi and stepped into the koi pond to skim algae from the surface. The Colonel didn't like the view of his precious fish obscured.

"What happen to knee?" Sonji asked.

Nick was hoping he wouldn't notice. He had slipped and cut it the night before. "I fell," Nick said. "It's nothing."

"Look like something to me. I get doctor to take look. Might be infected."

"Really, it's fine.

"How cut? I not see."

"I slipped getting a shovel out of the toolshed." Sonji gave him a suspicious look. Nick had to get him off the subject. "I thought of a haiku," he said.

"Good . . . good," Sonji said. "Say it for me."

"In Japanese," Nick said, which gave him time to think of the translation *and* the poem. He looked down at the koi swimming between his legs.

Golden fish
tickle feet
in morning sun

Sonji gave him a broad smile. "Not too bad. You be haiku master soon."

Nick bowed, relieved, promising himself to come up with a few more haikus for occasions like this.

The sound of the Colonel's sword sliding into its scabbard echoed across the garden, which was Sonji's cue to go over and talk with him. It was the same every morning. The Colonel was a man of rigid habits. Sergeant Sonji marched over, gave him a deep bow, and they started walking through the garden.

The water stung the gash on Nick's knee. Maybe I should have the doctor look at it, he thought. The night before he had walked all the way to the end of the tunnel. It was slippery and took a lot longer than he'd anticipated, but it was worth it. He discovered that his father had been using one of the side tunnels to store supplies for his private war. There were crates of rifles, pistols, ammunition, grenades, dynamite, and tinned food, which he helped himself to, stashing some extra tins inside the wall of his room.

At the end of the main tunnel was another ladder leading up to a trapdoor cleverly concealed in an old stump near the ancient pagoda where the villagers held their meetings.

Even though Nick spent his days outside in the garden, it felt different standing outside the pagoda by himself without a guard. He imagined himself simply walking away, but he knew he couldn't. Not yet, anyway. Hilltop hadn't told him how he was going to get Nick and Mya off the plantation. The Colonel was sure to come after him. He would lose face if his American boy got away. And after what Hilltop had told him about Bukong wanting to marry Mya, Nick knew that he would be after them as well. In fact, Mya needed to get away from the plantation more than Nick did. Indaw may have thought the Japanese would accost his sister, but it turned out that the threat was much closer to home.

It was thoughts like these that kept Nick outside longer than he intended. Before he knew it, the sun was coming up. He had run back down the tunnel, falling near one of the pools and cutting his knee. He got back to his room ten minutes before Bukong unlocked the door.

At Sonji's insistence, the Colonel's physician treated Nick's wound with an ointment that felt like bottled hornets. While he was at it, the doctor gave Nick a complete physical. When it was finally over he said that Nick was suffering from exhaustion, which Nick could have told him without all the probing and poking.

"He needs the rest of the day off," he told Sonji in

Japanese. "I will arrange it with Colonel Nagayoshi."

Bukong told Nick that he didn't believe the doctor's diagnosis, but that he had no choice. He locked Nick in his room.

Nick fell asleep as soon as he hit the bed and probably would have slept through the entire night had someone not shaken him awake. He rolled over expecting to see Hilltop, but it was Mya.

They both realized at the same moment that Nick didn't have a stitch of clothing on. Mya turned away as Nick hurriedly knotted his longyi around his waist and pulled on a shirt.

"What are you doing here?" Nick whispered.

Instead of answering, Mya ducked into the fireplace. Apparently, Nick was not the only one Hilltop had shared the secret with.

She lit a candle, then stuck her head back out with an impatient look. "Are you coming?"

Mya moved through the complicated passageways as if she had been through them a hundred times before. When they got to the room, she looked through the peephole to make sure the Colonel wasn't there.

She turned to Nick. "It's safe to talk," she said.

"What's going on?"

"Hilltop sent me," Mya answered.

"Is he okay?"

She nodded, then studied Nick until he started to feel uncomfortable.

"What?" he asked.

"It's just . . ." She looked away, embarrassed. "You don't look anything like you did the day we picked you up at the airport in Rangoon."

"You mean the longyi?"

"More than that," she said. "You almost look Burmese."

Nick hadn't seen a mirror since his capture. He knew he had lost weight and that he was brown from the sun, but it hadn't occurred to him that he might look like a Burman. Mya had changed too. She was pretty before, but now she was . . .

Beautiful, he thought. He cleared his throat, which seemed to have constricted on him. "I haven't had a chance to tell you how sorry I am about your father and your aunt."

"Thank you," Mya said, giving him a slight bow.

An awkward moment followed, where neither one of them seemed to know what to say. Nick finally broke the silence. "Why didn't Hilltop come himself?"

"He had something to take care of. He said he'll be gone a few days."

"Where?"

"He didn't say. I saw him this afternoon, but he didn't have much time to talk. He told me about the fireplaces." She walked over to a shelf by the wall.

"And he gave me this." She held up a wrench. "When we are ready to leave he wants you to remove the grate over your window."

"Why?" Nick pulled up the rug. "There's a tunnel that leads outside. If I climb out the window, the guard will know. He walks by my window all night long."

"You are not using the window," Mya said. "It's a . . ." She searched for the right word. "Ruse. An illusion. When Hilltop tells us to leave, we will hide right here. The soldiers will think that you escaped by the window. Just as they will think I left by the front or back door. But we will be right here until the search is called off. This way no one will come after us when we finally go."

"Brilliant," Nick said. "We can stay down here for weeks . . . months, if we have to. There's plenty of food stored in the tunnel. When?"

"Soon, I hope." Mya's face flushed.

"Yeah," Nick said quietly. "I heard about Bukong. Are you okay? I mean—"

"Yes. At night I wedge a chair under the door handle."

Nick didn't think that would stop Bukong if he really wanted to get in.

"How will we know when to make our move?"

She held out one of Nick's crudely carved elephants. He had given it to Hilltop several months earlier. "Hilltop will put this carving into the natshin."

Nick wondered if Hilltop had told her that he had carved it. He hoped not. He had gotten much better since then.

"You seem pretty familiar with the passageways," he said.

"Not really. Hilltop gave me a map, but I still got lost on the way to your room."

"Luckily you didn't stumble into Bukong's or the Colonel's room," Nick said.

Mya laughed. "That would have been very bad."

Nick took the wrench. "I'll hide this behind my fireplace until I need it. Bukong searches my room."

"He searches everyone's room," Mya said bitterly. Then she proceeded to tell him what had happened on the plantation since the Japanese came.

The Airfield 18

The next morning, Nick was up at dawn waiting for Bukong, but he didn't come. Nor did his breakfast. His first thought was that they had somehow found out about the secret passageways. Then he remembered his knee, and hoped the reason Bukong hadn't come was that the doctor had given him another day off to rest. But what if Hilltop had left the carving in the nat-shin?

To distract himself from worrying, he thought about what Mya had told him the night before. According to her, the Japanese had worn out their welcome. And not just on the plantation but throughout Burma. The Burmese weren't unhappy the British had left, but they were finding the Japanese far worse taskmasters. It was clear that the Burmese were not going to be given their independence. Apparently, the Japanese slogan *Asia for Asians* meant, Asia for Asians of Japanese descent. Tens of thousands of Burmese had been put into forced-labor camps to build roads, airfields, and a railroad through the jungle to Thailand. Thousands had died from disease, starvation, and exhaustion. There was talk among the mahouts of joining the British and American armies to help overthrow the Japanese, should the allies launch a counteroffensive.

The mahouts had thought that if they helped the Japanese build the airfield, they would be able to get back to logging when it was finished. But Colonel Nagayoshi had other plans for them. He was sending half the mahouts and elephants to work on the railway. Magwe and Bukong were to decide who would go and who would stay.

Mya hadn't heard from Indaw, nor had anyone else in the village. But it was rumored that he and Miss Pretty were working on the railway, perhaps in the same camp as Nick's father.

The other rumor Mya had heard was that now that the airfield was complete, the Colonel would be supervising the railway construction. He would do it from Hawk's Nest, visiting the site once or twice a month. There was an existing rail line that ran from Moulmein south to the town of Ye. The spur they were building over the mountains into Thailand was about halfway down the line—a twenty-hour trip at the most by rail.

Nick had seen Colonel Nagayoshi in the library late at night talking on the radio. He'd tried to eavesdrop, but the listening tube was too far away from the radio to hear anything clearly.

By midafternoon Nick was getting frantic, pacing

his room, wondering what was going on. Then he heard the jangle of Bukong's keys. The door opened. Bukong was not alone. Sergeant Sonji and Colonel Nagayoshi followed him in. Nick bowed and kept his head down. The Colonel had never been to his room before. He was certain now they had discovered the passageways. Out of the corner of his eye he saw the Colonel cross the room and pick up one of the books next to the bed.

"Are you studying to be a samurai?" he asked in Japanese.

Nick didn't answer.

"You may lift your head," the Colonel said in English.

Nick straightened up, trying to hide his anxiety.

"Do you find the samurai interesting?"

"Yes, sir."

Colonel Nagayoshi was wearing a dress uniform—pure white, including gloves—accented with glimmering gold braid. His sword was belted around his waist. Nick glanced at Sonji. He was in dress whites as well, all soldier today, standing at rigid attention, his eyes straight ahead, stone-faced. Bukong was staring at Nick with his normal arrogant sneer, holding his ever-present bamboo cane. What was going on?

The Colonel put the book down and walked over to the fireplace. Nick held his breath.

"How is your knee?" the Colonel asked.

"It's fine."

"Sergeant Sonji tells me you fell."

"Yes. It's just a scratch."

"The doctor said you are suffering from exhaustion."

"I told the sergeant that I would prefer working in the garden."

The Colonel smiled—a rare expression for him. "You would make a good samurai."

"Thank you." This was the first compliment the Colonel had ever given him. Nick began to think that maybe he wasn't here because of the passageways.

"Do you like airplanes?" the Colonel asked.

"Yes, sir." This wasn't exactly true. Nick used to love airplanes until the Luftwaffe attacks in London.

"My son loves airplanes too," the Colonel said. "Our airfield opens today. I thought you might want to see the first of our airplanes land."

"I'd like that," Nick said, wondering what had brought all this on.

"Good. Sergeant Sonji will escort you to the airfield for the ceremony."

"Thank you," Nick said, glancing at Bukong, who could not have looked more irritated. Nick tried not to smile.

The Colonel left the room, and Bukong followed. As soon as they were gone, Sonji relaxed.

"Big honor," Sonji said. "Colonel does not give personal invite to everyone."

"Why did he invite me?"

"Son better. Colonel got letter from him. Very happy. All Japanese boys love things that fly. I guess you substitute son today. How is knee?"

"Really," Nick answered. "It's better."

Sonji looked at him for a moment. "You look more rested today. Doctor be happy when I tell him. How come you not answer Colonel's question in Japanese? I tell him your Japanese good."

"I . . ." Nick hesitated. "It took me by surprise. The Colonel has never come to my room before." The truth was, he didn't want to remind the Colonel how well he spoke Japanese. It was easier to eavesdrop if they didn't know he understood the language.

Nick bowed. "I'm sorry if I embarrassed you in front of him."

Sonji accepted the apology by returning his bow.

"What should I wear?" Nick asked, changing the subject.

Sonji thought about it for a moment. "You still have American clothes?"

He did, but he had barely looked at them since his first day in the garden. They weren't practical in the heat. He opened his old suitcase and pulled out a pair of pants and a shirt. The white shirt hung on his shoulders like a tent. The pants were four inches too big around the waist and two inches short in the cuff.

Sonji started laughing. "Pants fall down. Better put on longyi."

Sonji and Nick walked along the well-worn path to the airfield. It had been two months since Nick had been up there, and he was surprised at the progress they had made. The hard-packed landing strip was a hundred yards across and several hundred yards long. Sandbagged antiaircraft gun emplacements were scattered along the edge. On the south end was a control tower made out of bamboo and teak. On the north end, tucked into the jungle, was a huge metal hangar for the airplanes. Off to the side of the hangar were barracks for the soldiers, pilots, and mechanics. All the buildings were painted jungle green and covered with camouflage netting.

While Nick toiled in the Colonel's garden, the plantation had been transformed into a major Japanese stronghold.

Sonji led him over to a raised platform with a podium and rows of chairs. Officers were shouting at the soldiers to form ranks in front of the platform. Nick was surprised by how many men there were now. Two hundred—maybe more.

The villagers were being lined up behind the troops. And they didn't look happy about it. They stood stone-faced, staring at the platform as officers in their dress uniforms filled the seats on either side of the podium.

Next came the mahouts, mounted on their elephants, led by Magwe. Nick hadn't seen him since the Japanese took over at Hawk's Nest. He wondered if Magwe had decided who would go and who would stay. The last to arrive was the household staff. Mya stood next to Bukong. Neither of them looked in Nick's direction.

A black car pulled out of the hangar and slowly drove down the runway, stopping close to where Sonji and Nick were standing. The Colonel got out first, followed by an older officer in a white uniform decorated with a forest of ribbons and medals.

"General Hoshi," Sonji whispered. "Hero of Japan. Must bow deep."

Nick bowed along with everyone else as the Colonel and General Hoshi stepped onto the platform. The Colonel addressed the gathering in Japanese for about five minutes, complimenting the soldiers for their hard work on the airfield, although they had done little of the physical labor themselves. Their job was to make certain the Burmese did the work. When he finished, he switched to English and gave roughly the same speech to the Burmese.

The General stepped up next and gave a long speech about the war. If what he said was true, the Japanese had conquered all of Southeast Asia. And the

Germans had conquered most of Europe. He ended by saying that he thought the war would be over soon.

The soldiers cheered. The Burmese did not.

The Colonel quieted the soldiers down. Nick thought he was going to make another speech, but instead he nodded to an aide. The aide spoke into a radio, and a moment later, Nick heard a sound he hadn't heard since he was in London. Airplanes. He shaded his eyes and looked up at the sky. A formation of Japanese Zeros flew in low over the tops of the trees, followed by another formation, then another. The airplanes circled the airfield twice, then started to land, one by one.

The pilots slid back the windscreens and jumped out of the cockpits wearing tight-fitting leather helmets and flowing white scarves. They stood at attention outside their aircraft. The Colonel and the General walked down the runway to inspect them. When they finished, the General boarded a transport airplane and took off into the gathering darkness, ending the ceremony.

The villagers started to make their way back down to the village, the soldiers dispersed and headed toward the barracks, and the Colonel got back into the black car and drove away.

Bukong dismissed the household staff, including Mya, and walked over to Nick. He looked at him with distaste and said to Sonji, "I'll take him back to the house."

"I take him back," Sonji said. "He work in garden tomorrow, and we talk about what to do."

Bukong was clearly displeased.

Nick was certain Bukong would find a way to punish him, but he would have to wait until later. As they passed through the garden, he glanced at the nat-shin. His little carved elephant stood among the offerings.

Escape 19

Loosening the bolts holding the iron grate was more difficult than Nick thought it would be. On top of this, the guard circled Hawk's Nest every five minutes, giving Nick very little time to work.

He made slits in the screen with the Sergeant Major's knife so that he could reach the eight bolts along the bottom and sides. He decided to leave the bolts along the top so the grate would stay in place. Better to have Bukong discover his escape than the guard. This way the Colonel would think he and Mya had had several hours' head start.

The first bolt took him an hour to get out. The second bolt took nearly as long. At this rate it would be midmorning before he got the grate loose enough. He thought about postponing the escape, but he had already slit the screen. Bukong or the guard would see it when it got light out.

Mya had been waiting in the room behind the library for more than three hours. Had Nick overslept? Did he miss the carving in the natshin? Had he been caught removing the grate? If he didn't come soon she might have to return to her room and wait for another day. That afternoon when Hilltop told her that this was the night, he had emphasized that it must look like they had left Hawk's Nest together. Why, she didn't know. But her great-grandfather had a reason for everything, even if he didn't explain what the reason was.

She decided to check on Nick. Like all the rooms in Hawk's Nest, there was a peephole into Nick's. It was difficult to see in the dark, but she could make out his silhouette in front of the window. She pulled the lever, crawled through the fireplace, and touched his shoulder.

Nick jumped and nearly dropped the wrench. He thought it was Bukong. Mya stifled a giggle.

"It's not funny," Nick whispered. "You nearly scared me to death."

"Sorry. What's taking so long? It will be light soon."

"I know. The bolts are rusted."

"Let me try."

"Be my guest." He gave her the wrench.

She tried, but didn't have any better luck.

"I'll be back," Mya said, disappearing through the fireplace before Nick could ask her where she was going.

He started in on the bolts again, but was interrupted when the guard decided to stop outside Nick's window for a smoke. He crept over to the fireplace to intercept Mya. From where the guard was standing, he'd be able to hear them, even if they whispered. When she came back through, Nick grabbed her arm and put his fingers to his lips. The guard stood smoking outside the window for ten more minutes, before resuming his duty.

When they returned to the window Nick saw that Mya was carrying a lead pipe and an oilcan.

"You can't pound the bolts out," he whispered, pointing at the pipe. "You'll wake the entire house."

"That's not the way I'm going to use it," she said. "How long before the guard returns?"

Nick looked at his watch and was shocked to see that it was already four o'clock. Bukong would be opening the door in an hour, maybe less.

"We'll wait until a guard comes by again," he said. "Then you'll have four or five minutes."

After what seemed like an eternity, the guard walked by. As soon as he passed, Mya went to work.

"Time me," she said.

She stuck the oilcan spout through the slits and dribbled oil on the bolts.

"Four minutes," he said as she finished oiling the last bolt.

Instead of using the lead pipe as a hammer, she slipped it over the wrench handle, extending it by at least a foot. Lubrication and leverage. Nick shook his head. Mya was not only pretty, she was smart.

"Three minutes."

She slipped the extended wrench through the opening, fitted it on the bolt, and gave the handle a hard yank. The bolt turned with a loud screech, making both of them wince.

"Two minutes."

She repeated the procedure on each bolt.

"One minute."

She pulled the wrench back inside. Thirty seconds later the guard came by. Nick was sure he must have heard the noise, but he didn't even look in their direction.

Mya got all the bolts out before the guard's next pass. After he passed, Nick slit the screen the rest of the way and pushed on the grate, making sure it was loose enough for someone to slip through.

"We'd better go," Mya whispered.

Nick arranged his bedding to make it look like he was still there, grabbed his bag, and followed her through the fireplace. He closed the door, and she lit a candle.

"You go ahead," he told her. "I'm going to wait here for a while."

"Why?"

"I want to hear what they say," he answered, but his real reason for staying behind was to see Bukong's expression when he discovered he was gone.

Mya gave him a doubtful nod, then turned and

made her way down the narrow passage.

Nick picked up the listening tube and looked through the peephole. He didn't have long to wait. Bukong had wanted to catch him sleeping, so he showed up early. He came into the room very quietly and stood next to Nick's bed with his cane raised, as if he were relishing the beating he was about to give. The cane came down once . . . twice . . . a third time—hard. It wasn't until the fourth blow that Bukong stopped. He lit a candle and tore the bedding off, then glared around the room. He walked over to the fireplace and looked inside.

Nick nearly bolted down the passageway. Did he know the secret? He knew everything else that was going on in the house, and Nick wouldn't put it past him to keep it to himself so he could spy on the Japanese and the servants.

But after checking the fireplace, Bukong backed away and walked over to the window, discovering the slit screen and the loose grate.

He shouted for the guards. A whistle blew from somewhere in the house, and a stampede of boots echoed through the halls. The room quickly filled with soldiers, some in their uniforms, some in their underwear, most of them carrying pistols or rifles. It was mass confusion. People shouting, bumping into each other, until Colonel Nagayoshi came in, fully dressed in a crisp, green uniform.

Everyone bowed. He ignored them, walked over to the window, and looked at the grate. He turned around and gave three orders.

"Assemble the patrols in front of Hawk's Nest. Get Sergeant Sonji. Bring me the guard on duty."

Nick couldn't help but grin. Bukong was in for another surprise when he discovered that his "fiancée" had fled as well.

Everyone left the room, leaving the Colonel and Bukong alone. Bukong kept his head down.

"Give me your stick," the Colonel said.

Reluctantly, Bukong handed it over. The Colonel looked at the cane for a moment, then swung it over Bukong's head, missing him by a fraction of an inch.

"I blame you for this," the Colonel said, hitting him on top of the shoulder. Bukong fell to his knees.

Nick shuddered. He knew how that cane felt.

The Colonel lifted Bukong's chin with the end of the cane. "Perhaps if you had used this cane less frequently, the boy would not have been compelled to leave." He let Bukong's chin drop and hit him again. This time across the back. Bukong stifled a scream.

Nick thought he was going to hit him again, but instead he snapped the cane in two over his knee and dropped it on the floor.

"If we fail to find him," the Colonel said, "or if something happens to him while he's in the jungle, it will be you who answers for it." He jerked Bukong to his feet. His legs were shaking.

Nick didn't have much sympathy for him. If he'd been lying in bed, it would have been *his* legs that were shaking.

Sergeant Sonji came into the room, out of breath, as if he had sprinted over from the barracks. He bowed to the Colonel without so much as a glance at the ailing Bukong.

The Colonel asked him if Nick had given him any indication he was planning to escape.

"None," Sonji answered. "As you know, we gave him a day and a half off to rest, but other than that . . ." He glanced at the window. "Is that how he escaped?"

The Colonel nodded, and Sonji walked over for a closer look. He turned back, holding one of the bolts. "How did he get these out?"

The Colonel took the bolt from him and looked at it. "Oil," he said. "Could he have smuggled oil into the room?"

"Yes," Sonji admitted. "We use lubricating oil on the tools. A small amount would be easy to hide." He got down on his knees and looked under the bed. "But these would be very difficult to conceal." He came up with the wrench and the lead pipe.

The Colonel looked at Bukong. "You have the only key to this room. In fact, you insisted on this."

"He must have had help," Bukong said. "Perhaps one of the villagers slipped them through the screen . . ." He paused, an expression of horror cross-ing his face. "Mya!" He rushed out of the room.

Nick moved to another peephole farther down the wall. Bukong stood in the middle of Mya's room. Sonji and the Colonel stood in the doorway.

"She's gone," Bukong said, stating the obvious. "She must have slipped outside and given him the wrench through the bars."

Runaway bride, Nick thought with a grin and made his way down to the secret room.

The Walls Have Ears 20

The search went on longer than any of them expected. Colonel Nagayoshi sent out patrols in every direction. When the soldiers came back empty-handed, he sent them out again. A week passed, then another, and he still continued searching.

Everyone in the village was interrogated, some two or three times. Even Hilltop, normally considered above suspicion, was questioned.

Nick and Mya spent long days inside the walls of Hawk's Nest, watching and listening:

"It's been two weeks, Colonel," Hilltop tells the Colonel. "You are not going to find them. People have underestimated Mya her entire life. She is intelligent and resourceful. There is no one I would rather be with in the forest than my great-granddaughter. And the Freestone boy? You toughened his body by putting him to work in your garden. By subjecting him to Bukong's cruelty, you toughened him inside. It's no wonder he chose to leave here. Who would stay under those circumstances? The children have made their way to safety by now, or else they have perished in the forest. Searching for them is a waste of time."

Bukong and Magwe sit at a table in the kitchen, a list of names in front of them.

"This was not part of our agreement with Colonel Nagayoshi!" Magwe glares at Bukong across the table.

"Keep your voice down," Bukong hisses. "Someone will overhear."

"We told the mahouts they would be able to stay on the plantation," Magwe says, a little less loudly. "How am I to pick who goes and who stays?"

"It's not like they'll be prisoners," Bukong says. "Colonel Nagayoshi has even promised them a wage, which is more than they received for building the airfield."

Magwe looks at his brother for a moment. "I can't understand how you can still support Nagayoshi after the beating he gave you."

"I see the long picture," Bukong responds. "When this is all over, Hawk's Nest will be ours. The teak on the plantation is like money growing out of the ground. You and I will be rich. I think that's worth a beating."

"Any word about the Freestone boy and Mya?" Magwe asks.

Bukong's expression turns dark. "No. And I still can't believe that they escaped without help." He snatches the list off the table, runs a finger down it, then stops. "What's this?" he asks.

"It seemed only right," Magwe answers.

Bukong shakes his head. "You're not going to the labor camp, Magwe. I need you here. You're my eyes and ears in the village. I can't run the house and be the singoung at the same time. Besides, I don't think that Indaw and the other mahouts would be very happy to see you." He takes a pencil from his shirt pocket and crosses out Magwe's name. "I'll give this to the Colonel. Tell the mahouts to be ready to leave in three days."

An officer strides into the library and stands at attention before the Helm.

"The bunkers are filled to capacity with armaments," he reports. "We're using the hangar for the overflow, but it's a dangerous situation. If one of the pilots or mechanics drops a cigarette, the whole place could explode."

Colonel Nagayoshi looks up from his paperwork. "Well, Captain, I suggest you make certain no one smokes in, or anywhere near, the hangar. Our airplanes will make room soon enough by dropping bombs on our enemies. Is there anything else?"

"Yes, sir." The captain hesitates. "One of our soldiers was injured this morning."

Injuries on the plantation were not unusual. The Colonel waits for the captain to explain.

"He was gored by an elephant."

"An accident?"

"So the mahouts claim. But witnesses say the mahout caused the elephant to attack."

"Who was this mahout?"

"Magwe."

The Colonel takes a deep breath. "Where is he?"

"I have him under guard outside."

"Bring him in."

Magwe enters and stands before the Helm with his head bowed.

"What happened?" the Colonel asks.

"We were working on the dam in back of the airfield, and the soldier got too close. We've warned them before. It's not safe to be wandering among the elephants while they are working. It's lucky he wasn't killed."

The Colonel raises his voice. "You are lucky he wasn't killed!"

Magwe appears unfazed by the outburst.

"If it were another mahout, I would have them punished . . . severely punished."

"I should not be treated differently than the other mahouts," Magwe says.

The Colonel glares at him. "Get back to work."

Magwe bows and leaves. After he's gone, the Colonel calls the captain back in.

"I want you to keep an extra eye on Magwe and all

of the mahouts. I don't like what's going on here."

Sergeant Sonji walks into the library, looking tired, disheveled, his uniform sweat-stained and spattered with mud.

"Well?" the Colonel asks.

Sonji shakes his head. "No sign of them. We've searched everywhere. It's as if they've disappeared off the face of the earth."

"They have to be somewhere! Someone must be hiding them, or at least helping them. Keep looking!"

The Colonel resumes reading the reports scattered on the Helm. Sergeant Sonji continues standing at attention. Finally, the Colonel looks up.

"Is there something else, Sergeant?"

"Yes, sir. I passed through the garden on the way in."

"And?"

"It's in terrible condition."

"A casualty of war, Sergeant. We no longer have time for such luxuries. You have forty-eight hours to find those children. If you don't, I'm transferring you to the railway. You'll escort the mahouts there and stay on to assume guard duties."

Sonji looks as if the Colonel has just slapped him.

"Dismissed." The Colonel waves his old friend out of the library.

* * *

That night Nick watched as the officers gathered in the dining room, eating dinner with the Colonel at the head of the table. Major Riku, the commandant of the railway camp, was spending the night.

"This is really a fine meal, Bukong," Major Riku said. "I wish I had you up at the camp."

Bukong gave him a slight bow from his post in the corner.

"How is the schedule?" the Colonel asked the major.

"We have fallen a little behind," Major Riku answered. "But not too far behind. Most of the delays have been caused by rough terrain and prisoner disease . . . malaria, beriberi, malnutrition, tropical ulcers . . . but more prisoners are arriving every day to replace those who have died. They're newly captured and in better physical condition than the last few batches we've had. Jackson Freestone is down with something. He was in the infirmary for a few days last week, but he's out now. We've put him on light duty, but I'm not sure he's going to recover. Most of the prisoners with him from Singapore have already died."

"What kind of light duty?" the Colonel asked.

"Burial detail," Major Riku answered. "Do you want me to give him special consideration?"

The Colonel shook his head. "Mr. Freestone is a prisoner of war and is to be treated like any other prisoner."

Nick's knees buckled. He put his hands out to catch himself and banged the listening tube against the wall. He held his breath, putting the tube back to his ear. The conversation continued as if nothing had happened. The officers had moved on to another subject.

How ill was his father? What did Major Riku mean by "burial detail"? When Nick had escaped, he'd worried the Colonel might retaliate by punishing his father. Perhaps having his father treated like any other prisoner was the Colonel's way of punishing him. If Nick had stayed put, would the Colonel have handled the situation differently?

As he thought about this, he glanced at Bukong standing in the corner. Usually Bukong was focused on the diners, ready to swoop in to fill a saki glass or remove an empty plate. But not now. Instead, Bukong was staring at the wall Nick was standing behind as if he were trying to see through it.

This was not the first time Nick had seen Bukong staring at the walls. The day after he and Mya slipped away, he'd caught Bukong in the nursery searching the room for clues. He examined every seam, crack, and brick. Nick thought for sure he would figure out the secret, but a few days later a servant moved into his old room, and as far as Nick knew, Bukong had given up on the idea.

By the way Bukong was staring at the wall now,

though, it looked like his interest had been renewed. Hawk's Nest was old, filled with creaks, groans, and other unsettling noises. There were also animals— mice, rats, lizards, bats—skittering throughout the walls. Mya had even found a snake one day, which she crushed with the choon Indaw had made for her. Nick hoped Bukong would dismiss the bump as coming from one of the resident creatures.

The dinner ended, and the officers wandered off to their rooms for the night. Bukong did not move. Sweat trickled into Nick's eyes and down his neck. Even though the walls were insulated, to be safe, he and Mya tried to arrive before people entered a room and leave after the room emptied. His legs began to cramp, but he stayed perfectly still. If he retreated now and happened to stumble, which was easy to do, the secret would be out.

He was saved by someone else stumbling. As the servants cleared the table, one of them dropped a plate. Bukong lashed out with his cane, which he had replaced the same day the Colonel snapped the old one over his knee. Nick didn't stick around for the second swing. He made his way to the little room behind the library.

Letters from Home

Mya wasn't in the room behind the library when Nick arrived. He wasn't surprised. She liked to listen to the kitchen gossip as the servants cleaned up after dinner. Later, when everyone was asleep, they would share what they had overheard that day.

He paced back and forth across the small room, more agitated than he had ever been in his entire life. He had to figure out a way to help his father.

His first thought was to turn himself in and beg the Colonel to send his doctor to the camp. But how would he explain where he had been for the past three weeks? If he told the truth, Mya would get caught. He could lie and say that he had been wandering in the jungle all that time. But if the Colonel believed him, which wasn't likely, how would he bring up the subject of his father's illness? There was only one place he could have gotten that information, and it wasn't in the Burmese jungle. The other problem with turning himself in was that there was no guarantee he wouldn't be executed. His escape had caused the Colonel to lose face. He wasn't going to welcome Nick home like the prodigal son. *All is forgiven. I'm just glad you're safe.* Right, Nick thought.

Mya returned from her kitchen eavesdropping. Before saying anything, she checked the library to make sure it was empty. Nick continued his agitated pacing.

"What's the matter?" she asked.

He told her about his father.

"What can you do?" she asked.

"I have no idea!" he snapped. He saw the surprise on Mya's face and felt embarrassed. She didn't deserve to be yelled at, with her father and aunt already dead.

"I'm sorry," he said. "I'm just upset."

Mya nodded. "Did they say anything else?"

"No, but when I heard about my father I slipped and banged the wall."

"Did they hear you?"

"Bukong might have. He kept staring at the wall. We'll have to keep an eye on him the next few days."

Nick began pacing again, then stopped. "How far is the railway camp from here?"

"What do you mean?"

"How long would it take to get there?"

Mya shook her head. "I don't know exactly where it is."

Nick walked over and looked through the peephole into the library, then picked up the listening tube. He turned to Mya. "I'll show you on a map," he said.

Nick hadn't been in the library since that first night with Hilltop

"It's not safe," Mya said.

"We'll have to be quiet," Nick admitted.

"What if the Colonel comes in?"

"I'll go up and make sure that he's in bed. He never leaves his room without dressing. If he's sleeping, at best, it would take him ten minutes to get into the library. It won't take us more than five minutes to look at the map."

Mya gave him a reluctant nod.

Nick returned fifteen minutes later and announced that the Colonel was sound asleep.

Mya followed him through the fireplace. This was the first time she had actually been inside the library, and it made her nervous. The room had always been a place of power, a place where fates were decided under the British and now under the Japanese.

Nick climbed a stepladder and pointed to a tiny red flag on a large map above the fireplace. Indaw and her father had talked about the area where the camp was, but Mya had never been there herself. If the weather was good, it was probably a two-or three-day trip on elephantback. She nodded to Nick, then started toward the fireplace, eager to get out of the library. But Nick did not follow. Instead, he walked over to the Helm and started looking at the papers on the Colonel's desk. What was he doing? Maya thought. She got his attention and pointed to the fireplace. He shook his head and pointed to the library door, motioning her to go over and listen for the guard.

Mya wanted to argue, but if she said something, the guard might hear. If she had known he wanted to search the library, she wouldn't have agreed to go. Annoyed, she crossed over to the door and put her ear to it.

Nick hadn't had any intention of searching the library when they'd entered, but he was desperate to find out more about his father and the railroad camp.

Finding nothing useful on the Helm, he walked over to the radio area. Again, there was nothing there about the camp. He glanced at Mya. She was watching him, clearly irritated. He held up his hand to indicate five more minutes, then walked over to the vault. Right 8. Left 31. Right 27. His birthday, which he had entirely missed this year. He pulled the handle down, and there was a loud click. He looked over at Mya. She listened for a few seconds, then gave him a shrug as if the guard hadn't heard.

Nick pulled the heavy door open and took a surprised step backward. His father was staring at him. The Freestone portraits were leaning against the back wall with his father's portrait on top. He wondered why the Colonel had saved them. Did he get some kind of pleasure seeing Jackson Freestone every time he opened the vault?

The file cabinets were stuffed with papers. It would take Nick weeks to go through them all, and tonight was probably not the night to begin. He had heard that the Colonel was leaving in a few days on an inspection tour. If he and Mya were still at Hawk's Nest, that would be a perfect time to start rifling through the files. He took a final look at his father's portrait and was about to leave when something on the shelf across from the file cabinets caught his eye. The old cigar box with his toy soldiers.

If something is out of place, the Colonel will know. Nick remembered Hilltop's warning, but he couldn't help himself. As long as he didn't move anything, it wouldn't hurt to open the box and look inside. He lifted the lid and was surprised to find a packet of letters lying on top of his lead soldiers. He immediately recognized the beautiful cursive on the outside of the envelopes. The letters were from his mother. There were at least a dozen of them, all carefully sliced along the top with the Colonel's razor-sharp letter opener.

He grabbed the letters and returned with Mya to the secret room.

Safely back behind the wall, Nick sat and read all of

the letters in the order they were sent.

Dear Nick,

I hope things are well on the plantation with you and your father. I'm sure he was as happy to see you as you were to see him. It's a comfort to know you are away from the bombing, which has been terrible here this past week.

I have found a new apartment, not as nice as our old one, but it will do. In my spare time I'm fixing it up to keep my mind off of missing you!

You'll be happy to know that a few days after you left I heard from Bernard. A letter. He couldn't disclose where he was, but he said that he was fine and that he hoped to be home for Christmas or the New Year. I was so relieved!

I'll keep this short so I can make the post. It won't arrive until after Christmas, so . . . Merry Christmas to you and your father! I know it won't seem like Christmas where you are, but I'm sure you'll enjoy the Christmas ride, if your father is still doing that.

All my love,
Mother

The next two letters were much like the first. She missed him and spent the loneliest Christmas she ever had. Bernard made it back a few days after New Year's. He had been wounded in the leg and was recuperating at the apartment, but eager to get back into the fight.

The remaining letters were written after she had discovered what had happened to him.

I just received word from your father that he is a prisoner at a camp in Singapore and that you are still at Hawk's Nest under the protection of the Japanese army. I am doing everything in my power to get you back home through the embassy here. Bernard, too, is working on getting you out with his military connections. One of us will succeed.

I'm desperate to hear from you. . . .

⌒

Perhaps you are not getting my letters. If a Japanese officer is reading this, please let me know how my son is doing. Give Nicholas a pencil and paper so he can write to his heartbroken mother.

⌒

I've managed to get transferred to the American embassy in Calcutta. I'm close, sweetheart! Perhaps I'll be able to do something for you from here.

Bernard is with me. He's working hard to get you out of there, too. . . .

Nick closed his eyes and recalled the map hanging on the Colonel's wall. Calcutta, India, was on the Bay of Bengal. His mother was right. She was only six hundred miles away. He wondered how Bernard had managed to get transferred. Nick didn't know exactly what he did for the army, but according to his mother, it was extremely important to the European war effort. One day Nick had asked Bernard if he was spy. Bernard laughed and said, "Nothing so romantic. I'm more of an organizer. A go-between."

Dearest Nick,

This damn war! There are hundreds of foreign nationals being held throughout Southeast Asia. The Japanese are steadfast in their refusal to let these innocent noncombatants go home to their families. Nonetheless, we continue to write letters and talk to everyone we know who might have some influence over the situation.

Please don't give up, Nick. Know that we love you and are trying everything in our power to win your release.

You have inherited your father's will and spirit. I saw it in your eyes the day you were born. God knew you would face these difficult circumstances and gave you the heart to conquer them. . . .

Nick was crying by the time he'd finished the last letter, and he didn't care that Mya was there to see it. They had allowed him to write his mother four letters in the ten months he had been there. But they either hadn't sent them, or the letters had gotten lost.

Why hadn't the Colonel let him read these letters? There were no military secrets in them. Just a worried mother writing to her son. Was it punishment for the way his wife and son were being treated?

Nick wiped the tears away and looked up at Mya. "I guess I'd better get these back."

"I'll go up and see if the Colonel is still in bed," Mya offered.

"It's not necessary." Nick carefully slipped the letters back in their envelopes, then sorted them into the order he had found them. "I'll just make sure the library is clear and put them back in the vault."

The library was empty. He ducked back through the fireplace. As he left the vault he took one last look at the portrait, and he remembered what his father had said on Freestone Island about the Sergeant Major's heart beating in their chests.

Nick could feel it.

In the end, the only thing that really matters is family. These are the ones who will be at your bedside when you die. Or you at theirs.

Part Three

Hannibal's Mahouts

Hilltop waded across the Tawkaw river.

The cool water was up to his waist. The week before, it had been up to his chest. This was his third journey to Freestone Island since the monsoon ended.

When he reached the island he slipped out of his robe, wrung it out, then placed it on the hot sand to dry next to his cloth shoulder bag.

The sun felt good on his skin, and he found himself getting drowsy, which had been happening to him more and more lately. It seemed as if his old body could not get enough rest these days.

But there was no time for a nap today. An old friend awaited him. He got to his feet, put on his robe, and headed into the dark forest.

The Japanese soldiers had not been on the island yet, but now that the river was down, they would come. He didn't think they would find it to their liking. Most people did not. Hilltop, on the other hand, found the ancient tangle soothing and full of memories.

Of all the places he had been, the plantation was where he felt most at home. This was his land. The mahouts and villagers were his people . . . and Hilltop had let them down. Colonel Nagayoshi and Sonji's appearance on the plantation was not an accident. Hilltop had brought them here—unintentionally, but still the fault was his.

When he was in Japan, he and Sonji had become fast friends. Sonji had invited him to see a garden he was building for a man named Tanaka Nagayoshi. Tanaka was a successful engineer from an influential and wealthy family. He invited Hilltop to stay in his guesthouse behind the garden. They, too, became friends. Hilltop, Tanaka, and Sonji would sit in the garden discussing philosophy, religion, politics, literature, and poetry late into the night. It was during one of these conversations that Hilltop told them about the plantation. Little did he know that there would be a war, or that Tanaka would become a colonel and be assigned to build a secret air base in Burma.

Hilltop blamed himself for what had happened on his beloved plantation. His grandson, Nang, and granddaughter, Kin-kin, had both been killed. His great-grandson, Indaw, was in a labor camp along with Jackson Freestone. The least he could do was to make certain that Mya and Nick reached safety.

Shafts of sunlight began to pierce the thick canopy. A few moments later Hilltop stepped out into the open.

The old monk heard the elephants long before he saw them. They were browsing along the edge of a vast stand of timber bamboo. The snapping stalks sounded like firecrackers going off. It was easy to pick out Hannibal among the herd. He had thrived during the monsoon and was already a couple of feet taller than the next biggest elephant in the herd.

As Hilltop approached, a young bull flared his ears and charged.

"Terrifying," Hilltop said, stopping. "You are magnificent! Truly!"

The bull skidded to a stop twenty feet away and began thrashing the ground with his trunk. Hannibal watched the scene as he chewed on a bamboo stalk.

"Now you've done it," Hilltop said.

Hannibal started walking toward the young bull as the other elephants looked on.

"You had better run." Hilltop waved his hands, but it was too late.

Hannibal rushed in, knocking the young bull to his knees, and he was about to hit him again, but Hilltop stopped him.

"Enough!" he shouted.

Hannibal froze, ears flared, his trunk rolled under, ready to strike. The young bull struggled to his feet and ran away, crashing through the dense bamboo.

"Hmit!" Hilltop commanded.

Hannibal looked longingly toward the broken swath the young bull had cut through the bamboo.

"Hmit!" Hilltop repeated. "We have no time for family squabbles."

Reluctantly, Hannibal dropped to his knees and stretched out until his belly touched the ground. Hilltop clambered up onto his neck, then leaned over and whispered in the bull's ear.

"Your holiday is over, old man. We have much work to do."

The Novices 22

"You've been with elephants," Mya said, taking a deep breath of the musky odor coming from Hilltop's robe.

He had been waiting for them in the secret room when they returned from their respective listening posts.

Mya was relieved Hilltop was there. Nick had hardly said a word to her since he'd learned two days before that his father was sick. He had also been spending a lot of time in the library, which Mya was furious about. She begged him to stay out of there, but he insisted that he had to find out what was going on. He was putting them both at great risk. Mya's only choice was to listen at the library door while he went through the files inside the vault, writing things down in the little notebook he carried. Perhaps Hilltop could talk some sense into him.

Hilltop looked tired, but happy to see them. "Everything is fine here?" he asked.

Mya glanced at Nick. Everything was not fine, but she didn't think it was her place to say so, at least not yet.

"Yes," Nick said.

Hilltop nodded. "I have good news. Colonel Nagayoshi has called off the search for you. We will leave tomorrow night after everyone at Hawk's Nest has gone to sleep."

Mya nearly jumped for joy. It was wonderful to finally be on their way. She looked at Nick, expecting him to have the same reaction, but, surprisingly, he was frowning.

"I'm not going," he said.

"What are you talking about?" Mya asked. He hadn't said a word to her about this.

Nick looked at Hilltop. "I can't leave," he said. "My father's sick."

"How do you know that?" Hilltop asked.

Nick told him about the conversation he had overheard.

"I'm very sorry to hear this," Hilltop said after he finished. "But how will you staying here help your father?"

"I'm going to turn myself in," Nick answered. "I'll wait a few days to make sure you and Mya are safely away."

"I still don't understand."

"I'm going to tell the Colonel about the passageways in exchange for helping my father."

This explains why Nick has been acting so strangely the last few days, Mya thought.

"What if the Colonel doesn't care about the passageways?" she asked.

"Oh, he'll care," Nick said. "I'm going to be waiting for him up in his bedroom, and I'm not going to say a word about how I got there until he promises to help my father. When he does, I'll tell him that you left weeks ago."

"And what will you tell him when he asks why you didn't leave with Mya?" Hilltop asked.

"I'll say that Father promised to come back to Hawk's Nest and get me, if the Colonel didn't send me to India like he promised. When I heard Father was back in Burma I was confident he would find a way to escape."

"You've certainly thought it through," Hilltop said.

Nick looked at Mya. "Sorry I've been such an ass the past few days. I didn't want to tell you about it until I'd figured out all the details." He pulled out the notebook tucked into his longyi and handed it to her. "This is what I've been doing in the library. When you get to India you need to give this to my stepfather, Bernard Culpepper. He's an officer in the American army. You can reach him through my mother at the American embassy in Calcutta. There's good information in here about what the Japanese are doing in Burma."

Nick had spent a lot of time thinking about his

stepfather the past couple days. Bernard had not come all the way to India just to help his mother. He was still in the fight in some capacity and would know what to do with the information Nick had gathered.

Mya flipped through the notebook. There were maps and notes about the airfield and other Japanese emplacements. Hilltop asked to see it. She handed it to him, and he looked at a few pages.

"You've been busy," he said. "But we're not going to India. It's too far overland. We're going to Umphang."

"But that's in Thailand," Mya said. "The Japanese are in Thailand."

"There's a monastery in Umphang," Hilltop explained. "I have many friends there. They will make sure we are safe from the Japanese."

Nick all but ignored the exchange since he wasn't going to India or Thailand with them. "There's a lot more information in the vault," he said. "But what I've written down should be of some use. Maybe you can give the notebook to one of the monks at the monastery, and they can get it into the right hands."

Hilltop sighed and put the notebook on the table. "Nick," he said. "There are some flaws with your plan."

"Like what?" Nick asked.

"Colonel Nagayoshi might execute you, for one," Hilltop answered.

Nick had already thought of this. The Colonel would be furious, but Nick didn't think he would kill him. "I'll take my chances," he said.

"Then there's Bukong," Hilltop continued, "who is much worse than the Colonel. He will certainly beat you."

"He's done it before," Nick said.

"He might beat you to death."

"I don't think so," Nick said, though he wasn't so sure.

"Things are about to go very wrong here. The Japanese have not handled things well. People are upset. It's not safe."

"I'm staying," Nick said quietly.

Hilltop let out another sigh, then sat down at the table. He closed his eyes and rested his head in his hands. He sat this way for such a long time that Nick and Mya thought he had fallen asleep. Finally, he took a deep breath, opened his eyes, and looked at Nick.

"I guess we'll just have to try to get your father out of that camp," he said.

"What?" Nick thought that maybe he had misunderstood.

Hilltop ignored the question and looked at Mya. "And while we're at it, we might as well try to free Indaw too."

"Is that possible?" Mya asked, stunned.

"I don't know," Hilltop answered wearily. "The

very least we'll do is go to the camp and see how they're doing. You and Nick will of course have to stay out of sight. But I should be able to get inside."

"I wrote down a lot of information about how the camps operate," Nick said eagerly. "I'm sure some of that info—"

Hilltop held up his hand. "First we have to get you to the camps without alerting the Japanese."

"We can travel at night," Mya said.

"We will have to," Hilltop agreed. "But we might still run into Japanese patrols. What I have in mind is a disguise. It won't be perfect, but it should work at a distance."

"What kind of disguise?" Mya asked.

"You are not going to like it." Hilltop looked at Nick. "Nor will you, but it's necessary."

He pulled two orange robes out of his bag, along with a pair of scissors and a straight-edge razor. Mya gasped, knowing exactly what Hilltop had in mind. Nick had no idea what the robes and the instruments meant.

"Both of us?" Mya asked.

"Yes," Hilltop answered. "It's the only way. It would be difficult to explain why I was traveling with a young woman and an American boy."

"What are you talking about?" Nick asked.

"We're to become novice monks," Mya answered.

"We have to shave off our hair?"

"And our eyebrows," Mya added.

Nick stared at Mya's hair. She had washed it just that morning in one of the pools in the tunnel. Even in the room's dim light it shimmered like black silk.

"There must be another way," Nick said, more for Mya's benefit than his own.

Hilltop shook his head. "And there is more to it than cutting hair. If we happen to encounter soldiers, they will be Buddhist themselves, or very familiar with Buddhist practices. To be convincing you must not only look like novices, you must act like novices. After I cut your hair, I will give you the ten precepts of the novice, which you must try to follow. Who will go first?"

"I will," Mya said bravely, sitting down in the chair.

Hilltop picked up the scissors. Mya's expression changed from courage to worry at the sight of the scissors trembling in the monk's old hands.

"Perhaps you should let Nick do the cutting," she suggested.

Hilltop nodded and gave the scissors to him. Nick's hands trembled too, but not because they were old. He had thought about touching Mya's hair dozens of times, but not like this.

Hilltop picked up a bucket and walked over to the trapdoor. "I'll get water."

Nick was grateful to be standing behind Mya so

she couldn't see how nervous he was. "Are you sure you're okay with this?"

"Yes," Mya answered. But she sounded a little nervous too. "I would do anything to help get Indaw out of that camp. My hair will grow back."

Nick took a handful of her hair and opened the scissors.

"Just cut it," Mya said.

He snipped and nearly cried out when the heavy lock of hair fell to the floor.

"Hurry," Mya encouraged him.

By the time Hilltop returned with the water, Nick had finished most of the scissoring. Mya's hair was piled around her feet like raven feathers. He soaped her head and very carefully started shaving the rest. It took a long time. When he finished he stood in front of her. The transformation was shocking, but she was still pretty. He wasn't sure she would be mistaken for a boy.

She gave him a shy smile. "My head is cold."

Nick laughed. "Are you ready for your eyebrows?"

She closed her eyes, and he shaved them off.

Nick took the chair next. As Mya cut his hair, Hilltop read through the information Nick had gathered in the library. "Some of this might be useful in getting your father out of the camp," he said. "Where did you get the information?"

"What?" It was a little difficult to focus with his hair falling in his lap and Mya touching his head.

"The information," Hilltop repeated, pointing at the notebook.

"Oh . . ." Nick said. "I found it in the vault. There's a file on how the camps are operated. Rules, organization, punishment, work quotas . . . things like that."

Nick had been horrified when he'd read through it. Even with his limited Japanese it was clear that the soldiers didn't care whether the prisoners lived or died. Their only interest was in how much labor could be accomplished. If someone got sick or injured, the only medical attention came from fellow prisoners. There was even a list of approved punishments for various infractions. If a cigarette butt was thrown on the ground, the prisoner would be made to stand in the sun for hours holding a boulder above his head. Theft, escape, and assault were all punishable by beheading or hanging. If the prisoners didn't fulfill their daily work quota, they didn't get to eat.

The railway was being built in a leapfrog fashion from both ends. An advance group of laborers, made up mostly of Burmese, hacked an opening in the jungle and constructed a prison camp. When the camp was finished, the railway laborers—British, American, Australian, and other nationalities—were moved in, and the Burmese laborers went farther up the line to build the next prison camp.

Mya soaped Nick's head.

"Your father is on the burial detail?" Hilltop asked.

"He was as of a couple days ago," Nick answered, really having a hard time concentrating now. "Light duty, Major Riku called it."

"Hold still," Mya scolded.

She started shaving the stubble from his skull. When she finished, Hilltop showed them how to put on their robes, then asked them to sit on the ground in front of him.

"You must request to become a novice," he said. "Repeat after me: *Venerable sir, I respectfully ask you to ordain me as a novice in order that I may be free from the cycle of existence and attain Nirvana.*"

Nick and Mya repeated the words.

Hilltop gave them a toothless smile.

The Tunnel 23

The next night, Nick and Mya followed Hilltop down into the tunnel, closing the trapdoor on Hawk's Nest for the last time.

Nick lit a candle. Hilltop looked even frailer than he had the night before. Nick wondered how he was going to make it to the camp and out of the country in his weak condition.

"Perhaps we should stop on the way out and get some of Mr. Freestone's food to take with us," Mya suggested. She and Nick had talked about this earlier in the day. They assumed they would have to avoid people whenever possible. For monks this meant no food. Nick wanted to take his rucksack with him, but Mya had pointed out that a novice would not have a rucksack. She spent most of the day sewing two traditional monk bags for them out of an old longyi.

"We'll need food," Hilltop agreed.

Nick led the way with the candle, although he had been down the tunnel so many times to get food he hardly needed it. The side tunnel was steep and slippery. He suggested Hilltop wait for them, afraid the monk might fall and hurt himself.

"I am fine," Hilltop said.

Nick started down the long grade, moving slowly, with the candle slightly behind him to light Hilltop and Mya's way. If he had been paying closer attention to what was in front of him instead of his two companions, he might have seen the hidden man before he grabbed him.

"So this is where you've been hiding," Magwe said.

"Run!" Nick shouted.

But it was too late. There were three other mahouts with Magwe, and they had already grabbed Mya and Hilltop. Mya struggled to get away, but Hilltop stood calmly with a bemused look on his face.

"So you followed me," Hilltop said.

Magwe nodded. "And we found the arms and ammunition. I knew Jackson had them stored somewhere on the plantation. We've been searching for weeks."

We were so close! Nick thought, feeling sick to his stomach. Mya had stopped struggling and looked as sick as he felt. Now what? Magwe would tell Bukong, and Bukong would tell the Colonel. Nick no longer had anything to bargain with. It would have been better if he had stayed in the nursery, working in the garden all this time.

Magwe lit his own candle and held it toward Mya.

"All that beautiful hair gone." He laughed. "My brother would be very disappointed."

Nick stared at Magwe. Did he say *would*, not *will*?

"Where are you taking them?" Magwe asked Hilltop.

Nick didn't dare believe what he was hearing. Was Magwe going to let them go?

"Someplace safe," Hilltop answered.

"A dangerous time to be traveling." Magwe released Nick's arm.

"We have some help," Hilltop said.

This was news to Mya and Nick. They looked at each other, wondering what was going on.

"You'll need food," Magwe said, and started down the tunnel toward the supplies.

Nick, Mya, Hilltop, and the other mahouts stared after him, not moving.

Magwe paused and looked back. "Hurry," he said. "You need to get as far from Hawk's Nest as you can tonight."

Mya started crying in relief, and Nick was on the verge of tears as well. They followed Magwe into the storage tunnel and saw that several of the crates had been pried open.

Magwe looked at Nick and Mya. "You're wondering why I'm not turning you in," he said.

"Yes," Nick said.

"Six month ago I would have, but things have

changed. It turns out the Japanese are no better than the British."

"What about Bukong?" Mya asked.

"My brother hasn't quite figured out the problem with the Japanese yet," he said bitterly. "But that might have changed. Colonel Nagayoshi dismissed him this morning." He pointed at Nick. "Punishment for your escape. Right now he's in Moulmein, boarding a train with my mahouts and elephants. The Colonel has given him to Major Riku. Like he was a slave. That should change his mind about our new taskmasters."

Mya and Nick had heard the mahouts had left that morning, led by Sergeant Sonji, but they hadn't heard that Bukong was with them.

Hilltop pointed to an open crate of grenades. "What are you going to do with these?"

"I'm going to get my mahouts back," Magwe answered.

"How?" Hilltop asked.

"The nats are restless," Magwe said with a slight smile. "The Japanese should have paid closer attention to them. There's going to be an accident up at the airfield tonight. The soldiers have been very careless with their bombs and ammunition. The Colonel has been warned they could go off at any time. After the accident he will have no choice but to bring the mahouts back to rebuild what's been destroyed."

"What about the soldiers in the hangar?" Hilltop asked.

"Casualties of war, as the Colonel is fond of saying."

"And like all wars," Hilltop said, "when it's over, people will wonder why it was even fought. Senseless."

"You had best be on your way." Magwe took Mya's bag and started to fill it with tins of food. "So tell me, what other secrets do these tunnels hold?"

Mya looked at Nick.

"These are the only weapons," Nick answered. He figured Magwe could find out about Hawk's Nest on his own.

He held his bag out, and Magwe filled it up. It was heavy. Hilltop stepped forward with his bag.

"I think we have enough," Nick said. They didn't, but there was no way Hilltop could carry the weight. Not for long, anyway.

"Without an offering I can't give Magwe a blessing." Hilltop held his bag out. "And he deserves a blessing for the help he has given us."

Magwe put a few tins in the old monk's bag and bowed. Hilltop gave him a long blessing, then motioned his two novices to follow him out of the tunnel into the night.

Nick had not been outside since the night he had cut

his knee, and Mya had not been out since she'd taken up residence in the walls of Hawk's Nest. They hadn't realized how stuffy and stale the air in Hawk's Nest had been until they emerged from the stump near the pagoda.

The food tins in their bags clattered together like tambourines. Hilltop waved them into the pagoda, where they reorganized their supplies, wrapping the containers in their clothes.

It was a perfect night for walking. The sky was clear, the moon half full. Nick and Mya wanted to stretch their legs, but when they set out again, Hilltop set a frustratingly slow pace. At the rate they were going, they wouldn't make three miles before sunrise. Nick offered to take Hilltop's bag, hoping that would speed him up, but it didn't. If anything, Hilltop seemed to move even slower without the extra load. They crossed the river near the village and climbed the far bank. It had been an hour since they'd left the pagoda and they could still see the lights of Hawk's Nest behind them.

"Where are we going?" Mya finally whispered.

Instead of answering, Hilltop stopped and looked back toward Hawk's Nest. A moment later a huge explosion erupted on the plateau behind the house, turning the dark horizon red. The initial blast was followed by the loud popping of shells and ammunition igniting.

"We don't have far to go," Hilltop said, turning away.

Nick and Mya followed along in silence. Hilltop was walking much faster now. They realized he had slowed their departure so he could see the airfield explode.

Another hour passed, and Nick began to feel the weight of the two bags he was carrying. Hilltop finally stopped at a stream. Nick gratefully dropped the bags and gulped down several handfuls of water. He was doing better than he had during his first trip into the jungle with Mya all those months ago, but it was still difficult, and the sun wasn't up yet.

"Wait here," Hilltop said.

They watched him walk away, happy for the rest.

"I can't believe Magwe let us go," Mya said.

Nick slapped a rather large insect that had landed on his neck. "I can't believe he blew up the airfield," he added.

By the size of the explosion, Nick was certain soldiers had been injured or killed. He was relieved that Sonji had left that morning with the mahouts.

"Do you have any idea where we are?" he asked.

Mya looked around. "It's a little confusing in the dark, but I think we're close to where the training camp used to be."

The training camp had been abandoned the day the Japanese arrived. The Colonel needed every mahout to build the airfield.

Nick shook his head in disgust. Hilltop was right; the whole thing was senseless. The mahouts spent months breaking their backs building an airfield, then blew it up after it was finished. Magwe had saved British and American lives, but that's not why he destroyed the airfield. He did it to get half a dozen mahouts back to the plantation and *rebuild* the airfield.

The Sergeant Major was right, family is the only thing that really matters. Nick looked at Mya . . . and friends, he thought guiltily. His desire to help his father was putting Mya and Hilltop in jeopardy. And they were more than friends. In the past ten months they'd been the only family he'd had.

"Maybe you and Hilltop should just head out to Thailand without me," he said.

"Now what are you talking about?" Mya asked, exasperated.

"I just don't want to see you or Hilltop get hurt because I want to help my father."

"I don't see how you could get him out of the camp on your own," Mya said. "And don't forget, we're going to try to free Indaw too. That alone is worth whatever risk and hardship I have to go through."

"What about Hilltop?" Nick asked. "He's not in the best shape."

"I've noticed," Mya said, looking worried. "But Indaw is his great-grandson, and your father is like a son to him as well. He wants to get them out of the labor camp as much as we do. I think we need to see how it goes the next day or two."

Despite his concern, Nick was relieved Mya was still willing to go. And she was right; he had no chance of getting his father out of the camp on his own. He was about to thank her but was interrupted by a crashing sound. At first he thought it was a Japanese tank plowing through the woods. He grabbed Mya's arm and was about to pull her behind a tree when he saw the gleam of a tusk in the moonlight.

"Hannibal," Mya said.

"Yeah," Nick said. Incredibly, Hannibal looked even bigger than he had before. Nick touched the spot on his chest where Hannibal had hit him. Maybe it was the fact that Hilltop was perched on Hannibal's neck, or maybe Nick had changed over the past few months, but he wasn't as terrified as he had been before. Afraid, yes—he felt his heart thumping a little faster—but he wasn't frozen in place, nor did he have the urge to run for his life at the sight of the former koongyi.

Hilltop tapped Hannibal on his broad head, and the bull stretched out so he could get down.

"You didn't expect us to walk all the way to the labor camp and to Thailand?" the monk said.

"We did," Mya said.

Hilltop laughed. "Not on my old legs." He looked

at Nick. "And if your father is as ill as the major said, he'll be in no condition to walk."

"How long have you been working with Hannibal?" Mya asked, still keeping her distance, just as Nick was.

"Since the night you disappeared into the walls of Hawk's Nest." He scratched the bull behind the ear. "He'll be fine as long as we don't run into a tiger along the way."

Not much chance of that, Nick thought. The Japanese officers' favorite pastime was hunting tigers. He had listened to them bragging about their kills around the dining room table. Nick doubted there were many tigers left in the area.

Hilltop started searching through the brush as Hannibal remained prone, picking at the plants and leaves within reach of his huge trunk.

"What are you looking for?" Nick asked.

"Hannibal's ohndone. I hid it somewhere around here a few nights ago."

Nick was surprised. Hilltop was obviously stronger than he looked. Elephant saddles were heavy.

Mya and Nick helped him look, careful to stay out of Hannibal's reach.

"Here it is," Mya said.

They pulled it out, along with the bark padding, and threw them onto Hannibal's back. It wasn't easy. Stretched out, the bull was still taller than any of them.

"Lutt! Lutt!"

Hilltop told Hannibal to get to this feet, then cinched the saddle on tight.

"Hmit!"

Hannibal stretched back out without hesitation. Nick and Mya were both amazed. He seemed like a completely different elephant.

Hilltop climbed up onto his neck. Nick and Mya climbed up behind him.

"Lutt!"

Hannibal got back to his feet.

"Tet!"

Hannibal started forward.

The Three Monks 24

The first two days on elephant back were uneventful. They traveled at night and slept during the day.

Nick had no idea where they were or how far they had come. Mya didn't either. Hilltop carefully avoided all trails and roads. As a result, Mya was getting a different view of the forest that she had lived in her entire life. She and Nick were also getting a different view of her great-grandfather.

At the plantation, Hilltop rarely spoke, and almost never about himself or his past. But on elephant back in the deep forest, he couldn't seem to stop talking. He sounded so much like Nang, there were times when Mya thought she was listening to her father, as she had so many times before.

He told them about his travels. It seemed that the only places Hilltop had not visited were North and South America. He admitted that Colonel Nagayoshi coming to the plantation was his fault.

Nick was of the opinion that the Colonel would have found the plantation on his own without Hilltop's help. When he was in London, Bernard had explained that the best way to find an enemy installation was to simply look at a map and ask yourself where you would put the installation, then send an operative in to see if it was there. Bernard and his mother were tight-lipped about what Bernard did for the army, but Nick was pretty sure he was an operative.

The most interesting things Hilltop shared with them were the details of the night Hannibal was attacked by the tiger.

"The attack was your father's fault," he told Nick. "And Bukong's."

Back then, Hilltop explained, Bukong was one of the best mahouts on the plantation. The only mahout better was Nang, who had just been promoted to singoung, which Bukong was very upset about. When Hilltop left the plantation, the Sergeant Major had appointed Bukong and Magwe's grandfather singoung. The position had stayed in their family through two generations, and it was assumed when Bukong and Magwe's father died, Bukong, the older son, would become the head mahout. But Nick's father broke the tradition and made Nang singoung.

"Nang was a better mahout," Hilltop said. "But more important, a better leader than Bukong or Magwe—who wanted to become singoung even more than Bukong."

"Magwe got his wish," Nick commented.

"Yes," Hilltop agreed. "But back to our friend here." He scratched Hannibal's ear. "Nang assigned Hannibal to Bukong and sent them up to Swe Hill—a difficult and very dangerous place to log—but what made it worse was Hannibal's tendency to wander during the night. Even with his front feet hobbled, he could cover miles before sunrise. In order to fulfill his logging quota, Bukong had to wake up hours before the other mahouts to search for Hannibal. He went to Nang and asked to be assigned to a different elephant. Nang said he didn't have an elephant to spare. Bukong then went to your father and asked if he could tie Hannibal at night. Your father said yes.

"That night the tiger came. Hannibal could not get away."

"Why would a tiger attack something as big as an elephant?" Nick asked. His father had never explained this in his letters.

"Tiger cubs," Hilltop answered. "No one was there, but this is what I think happened. A mother and two cubs were drawn in by the sound of Hannibal pulling on his ropes. One of the cubs got too close. We found the cub in the brush some distance away, his ribs crushed."

Nick knew how that felt.

"To protect her remaining cub, the mother attacked. Hannibal killed her as well."

"What about the second cub?" Mya asked.

"We never found it, so it must have gotten away. I assume that was the last time that tiger ever got close to an elephant."

Nick wondered if the tiger lying on the library floor was the one that got away.

"When Bukong found Hannibal the next morning he thought the elephant was dead," Hilltop continued. "We all did. The blood around Hannibal's body had turned the ground into mud.

"When Jackson arrived he sent the mahouts back to work so they would not see him cry. Nang and I stood with him, looking at the fallen koongyi for quite some time, when we were startled out of our mourning by a deep heave of Hannibal's chest. At first we did not believe our eyes, but he took another breath and his trunk moved.

"We spent the rest of that day and part of the night treating his wounds. We had to use other elephants to turn him over. It took three days to get him to his feet. No one thought he would live. Nang and your father built a crush around him and put slings under his chest and belly to help him stand. We did not leave his side for six weeks, treating his festering wounds several times a day." He laughed. "Tending the wounds became more difficult as Hannibal regained his strength.

"Eventually we were able to let him out of the crush, but he was never the same. If anyone attempted to fetter or hobble his feet—this included your father, Nang, or myself—Hannibal would try to kill them. And as far as I know, after the tiger attack, he never slept at night again. Without proper rest at night, an elephant cannot move logs during the day."

So avoiding Japanese patrols wasn't the only reason they were traveling at night, Nick thought. "What happened to Bukong's leg?" he asked.

"Your father blamed himself for Hannibal's injuries," Hilltop answered. "But Hannibal blamed Bukong. One year after the attack, almost to the day, he came into the village while everyone slept.

"Bukong had kept the female tiger's skin as a souvenir. It's difficult to know whether Hannibal scented the skin or Bukong, who had tied him, but he went on a rampage, tearing Bukong's house apart. He would have killed Bukong had it not been for Nang.

"Several mahouts tried to pull Hannibal off Bukong with choons and spears, and were injured in the process. Nang used the tiger skin. He pulled it out of the rubble and waved it in front of Hannibal like a matador's cape. Hannibal chased after him. When they were safely out of the village, Nang threw the skin into the air and dove behind a tree. Hannibal picked up the skin and ran off into the forest, slapping it against tree trunks.

"After this, Bukong lost his desire for being a mahout, and his leg injury made it impossible. Your father appointed him as head houseman. Little did he know that Bukong's ambitions went far beyond supervising the staff at Hawk's Nest."

Nick was still nervous around Hannibal. It wasn't easy to forget his first encounter with him in the village. Mya, on the other hand, was feeding Hannibal by hand at the end of their first day together. His favorite treat seemed to be the large seedpods of the tamarind tree. Before she slept, Mya climbed high into trees and collected pods that were out of Hannibal's reach and fed them to him throughout the night.

Hilltop's only rule was to stay away from Hannibal's feet. "If he thinks you are trying to restrain him," he told them, "he will kill you. It doesn't matter how many tamarind pods you have fed him."

Nick hadn't been anywhere near Hannibal's feet the day he got hit, but after watching Mya he decided he should give Hannibal another chance. He took a pod out of her bag and tentatively held it out to him. Hannibal stepped forward, sniffed the pod with the tip of his trunk, then picked it from his hand as if it were a delicate flower. After this, Nick started filling his own bag with tamarind pods before going to sleep.

Sleeping during the day was difficult because of the heat and swarms of biting insects, but it was made up for by the cool nights on elephant back listening to Hilltop. In fact, it was so pleasant, Nick and Mya sometimes forgot the danger they were in.

It all came back to them on the third morning. They were out of food, and although Mya and Nick were able to gather fruit here and there, it wasn't nearly enough to fill their stomachs. A year earlier, Nick couldn't imagine eating a monkey. Now he eyed the chattering primates playing in the canopy hungrily, wishing he'd thought to bring a rifle from the tunnel.

"There's a village not far from here," Hilltop said as they shared the last bites from the last tin. "I'll go down with my bowl and see if any of the villagers are in need of a blessing."

"We'll go with you," Mya said.

"I don't think that—"

"If you visit the village," Mya interrupted, "every village within fifty miles will know that Taung Baw is in the area. If you go there alone, and someone sees you with us later, they will wonder where the two novices with you came from."

"Besides," Nick added, "we need to practice being novices. What better place than a friendly village? We'll also have three bowls of food to share instead of one."

Hilltop thought about it a few moments, then reluctantly agreed, but he insisted they all bathe and wash their robes before they left.

"If a villager smells elephant on us they will know we are not on foot. We are close to the railway. The soldiers may not care about three monks, but they would certainly be interested in confiscating a trained timber elephant."

They walked into the village single file, with Hilltop first, followed by Mya, then Nick. The village was small, with only a dozen or so ramshackle houses that looked as if they would blow over in the next breeze. There wasn't a person, dog, or chicken to be seen.

"Abandoned," Nick said, his stomach growling with disappointment.

"Silence," Hilltop said.

A man stepped out from behind one of houses. He walked up to them cautiously and bowed.

"It's an honor to have Taung Baw in our humble village."

"The honor is ours." Hilltop returned the bow. Nick and Mya followed suit.

The man glanced at the two novices curiously, then turned his attention back to Hilltop. "They call me Kya Lei."

"I have heard the name," Hilltop said.

In Burmese, Kya Lei meant Tiger's Breath. An odd name, even for a Burman, Nick thought.

A few more people began to show themselves. They came out of the towering jungle surrounding the houses. Women, children, old men. Oddly, Kya Lei appeared to be the only young man in the village.

"What brings you here?" he asked.

The people drew nearer. Perhaps twenty of them in all.

"A pilgrimage," Hilltop answered.

"A dangerous time and place to be traveling."

Hilltop did not comment.

Kya Lei whispered something to a girl standing near him. She smiled and ran off. A few moments later she came back carrying a pot of rice and a large bag filled with dried fish and meat, which she could barely lift.

"It's not much," Kya Lei apologized, handing the food to Hilltop. "They have to hide what they have, or the soldiers come along and take it from them."

Hilltop handed the heavy bag to Nick and the pot of rice to Mya. It was enough food to fill their bowls twenty times. He was about to give Kya Lei his blessing, when somebody shouted a warning. People scattered as two jeeps roared into the village, sending up plumes of choking dust. Two rifle shots into the air stopped everyone in their tracks. Half a dozen soldiers jumped out of the jeeps and began pushing and prodding everyone into a tight group. There were two Burmans with the soldiers, carrying rifles slung over their shoulders. They stood to the side and did not participate in rounding up the villagers. The seats of the first jeep were covered in tiger skins. Sitting in the back was a young captain holding a teak baton inlaid with ivory.

"Heads down," Hilltop whispered.

Nick took furtive glances at the frightened villagers. To his surprise, Kya Lei was not among them. Where had he gone?

The captain got out of the jeep slowly. He ordered three of the soldiers to search the houses, wiped the dust from his tunic with distaste, then swaggered over to the group.

"Who are you?" he asked Hilltop in Burmese.

"Taung Baw."

"Of course," the captain said, but he didn't seem impressed. He looked at Nick and Mya. "And these two?"

"My novices."

The captain took the bag out of Nick's hand and looked inside, then lifted Nick's chin with the end of his baton. "Where did you get this?"

Nick knew enough Burmese to understand the question, but not enough to answer.

"My novices have taken vows of silence," Hilltop intervened. "The food is from Colonel Nagayoshi at Hawk's Nest. We brought it to the village because the people here are hungry."

"He has light eyes," the captain said, staring at Nick.

My mother's eyes, Nick thought with rising panic.

"An unfortunate flaw," Hilltop said. "They are orphans."

There were many orphans and abandoned children in Burma now, their parents dead or sent off to work in labor camps. One of the ways they survived was to become novices. This way they were at least able to get food.

The captain lost interest in Nick and turned his attention to Mya, lifting her chin with his baton. Hilltop had had them shave their heads and eyebrows again, but Nick wasn't sure it would be enough to disguise the fact that Mya was a girl. He scrutinized her for a long time, then let her head drop back down, to Nick and Hilltop's relief.

The three soldiers came back from searching the houses and reported they hadn't found anything.

The captain nodded, then without warning, slapped one of the old men across the face with his baton, leaving an angry-looking welt on his cheek.

"We heard that Kya Lei was here," he said.

All the villagers vigorously shook their heads.

"He is a thief and a traitor. Anyone caught hiding him or helping him will be executed." He looked at Hilltop. "What about you, monk? Do you know this Kya Lei."

"I have heard the name," Hilltop said, meeting the captain's gaze without a glimmer of fear.

"Have you seen him?" the captain shouted.

"I have never seen a tiger's breath," Hilltop answered. "Have you?"

The captain raised his baton as if he were going to hit him. Hilltop's expression did not change. The captain's face turned red with rage, but he lowered the baton.

"Burn a house!"

A soldier trotted over and set one afire. It went up in flames like it was made of rice paper, but it was an empty gesture. A bamboo house could be rebuilt in a day, and a new house in this village would be better than any of the others still standing. The villagers knew better than to keep anything of value in their houses.

"Your Colonel may not be able to protect you much longer, monk," the captain said. "You've heard about the airfield?"

"Of course," Hilltop answered. By now everyone within two hundred miles would have heard about the explosion.

"Were you there?"

"How could we be here now if we were there then?"

The captain looked confused. Nick was confused too.

"We are on foot," Hilltop said. "Several days from Hawk's Nest. I understand the accident happened three days ago."

Nick understood now. The captain was trying to trip Hilltop up. If Hilltop admitted he was at Hawk's

Nest when the airfield blew, the captain would know that they weren't on foot.

"Nagayoshi is in serious trouble because of the accident. Dozens of soldiers dead. The airfield was all but destroyed. All because he didn't have the sense to store the armaments properly."

So Magwe had gotten away with it, Nick thought. The Japanese thought it was an accident.

"I suspect he'll survive the setback," Hilltop said, although he did not believe this.

"We will see." The captain handed the bag of meat to him. "If he doesn't, perhaps I will have the pleasure of running across you again. By the way, my name is Captain Moto. Perhaps you have heard of me?"

Hilltop shook his head.

Captain Moto motioned his men back to the jeeps. The two Burmans with rifles scowled at Hilltop before they climbed into the captain's jeep.

Hilltop gave them a bow, then watched them drive away.

The Second Camp 25

"Who were those two Burmans with the captain?" Nick asked.

"Hill tribesmen," Mya answered. "Trackers."

"Kya Lei is really a thief?"

"Notorious."

"Did you notice the tiger skins?"

"They would have been hard to miss," Mya said. "Hannibal noticed too. We must have picked up some of the tiger scent. That's why he flared his ears and threw his trunk back when we got here. We are lucky he didn't charge us."

"He seems all right now," Nick said.

He and Mya were thirty feet up a tamarind tree, picking pods for Hannibal.

After they had eaten, Hilltop had fallen asleep beneath the tamarind tree, and was still asleep despite the racket his novices were making above him.

"Tell me more about Kya Lei," Nick said.

"Before the war, the British tried to put him in prison," Mya said. "But they were never able to catch him. And the villagers continue to protect him because he gives them money and food."

"Like Robin Hood," Nick said.

"Who?"

Nick explained who Robin Hood was.

"Yes," Mya said. "He's like that. I thought he had been killed or sent to a labor camp. I've heard stories about him my whole life, but that's the first time I have ever seen him."

"Why do they call him Tiger's Breath?"

"People say he is as elusive and dangerous as a tiger's breath."

"Well, he sure vanished from the village. I looked up, and he was gone!"

"I thought I would faint when the captain pointed out the color of your eyes," Mya said.

"Yeah, me too. There's nothing I can do about their color, but I should have thought about it beforehand."

When they got down from the tree they were still too excited by their close call to sleep. They walked down to the stream so they wouldn't disturb Hilltop. Hannibal followed, but it wasn't long before the previous night caught up with them, and they, too, fell asleep.

And this is where Hilltop found his novices just before sunset, lying next to each other, both fast asleep.

Hannibal was lying on his side across the stream.

Unlike the children, he had heard Hilltop's approach. He lifted his trunk and sniffed the air, but didn't bother to get up when he determined it was just his mahout.

Hilltop returned to where he had been sleeping, scribbled a fast note for Nick and Mya, put it near the food, then picked up his bag and walked off into the forest.

Although he had enjoyed being on elephantback with Mya and Nick, it felt good to be alone again, walking through the forest with only his thoughts to keep him company. And he had much thinking to do.

Their encounter with the captain in the village was disturbing. Hilltop knew he could no longer rely on Colonel Nagayoshi's protection. The Japanese did not tolerate mistakes. Those who made them were punished. The power was shifting, as it always did. The captain had sensed it. If they had gone to the village a day or two later, the outcome might have been very different.

The safest thing would be to get Nick and Mya out of the country right now. They could be in Umphang in two days. But of course they would never consent to it. Not now. Not with Indaw and Jackson still in the labor camp. Mya and Nick were just like their fathers and their fathers' fathers—stubborn, brave, and at times foolish.

Hilltop shook his head and felt a shiver go down his spine. They had no idea how close they had come to being killed that afternoon. The captain had wanted to do it. Make an example of the three of them to the villagers. If Taung Baw and his novices were not safe, no one was safe. He saw it in the captain's eyes as he raised his baton. The only thing that stopped him was that he didn't yet know where the power would go. And it was all about power. Big and little power. Who had it, how much, and how long it would last.

Hilltop sighed. He would just have to find a way to get Jackson and Indaw out of the camp. That was the only way to get Nick and Mya out of the country to safety. But how? In the short time he'd had, Nick had gathered a lot of information about how the camps operated. But none of it would do Hilltop any good if he couldn't figure out a way to use it. There were two problems to solve: freeing Jackson and Indaw, and then getting them out of the country. There were no secret passageways at the labor camp where they could bide their time until the Japanese gave up the search.

He needed to get inside the camp and look around, perhaps even talk to Jackson and Indaw, which was why he had left Nick and Mya behind. He had to move quickly.

He came upon an area of forest that had recently been logged. He could see where they had cut the trees into ties for the iron rails. It wouldn't be far now.

Mya heard Hannibal stripping tree bark with his tusks and opened her eyes. She was surprised to find it was dark out. Hilltop usually roused them before sunset so they could pack and saddle Hannibal while there was still light. She shook Nick awake.

He sat up and looked around in confusion. "What's going on? Where's Hilltop?"

Mya was already on her way to the spot where Hilltop had been sleeping that afternoon. When Nick caught up to her she had found the note and was trying to read it. He lit a candle.

I've gone ahead to the labor camp on my own to find out what's going on there. Please stay here with Hannibal and await my return. I should be back in a day or two. No fires. If you see someone, hide yourselves.

H.

"Why didn't he tell us?" Nick asked.

"He probably didn't want us to try to argue him out of it."

"We might be able to catch up to him," Nick suggested.

Mya thought about it for a moment, then shook her head. "He could have left hours ago, and it would be difficult to follow him in the dark. I think we should stay. Hilltop knows what he's doing."

"Yes, he does," a man said in Burmese.

Nick and Mya jumped.

"Who's there?" Nick asked.

"No need to be afraid," the man answered in English. "It's Kya Lei." He struck a match, lit a cheroot, then walked over to them.

"You followed us," Mya said accusingly.

Kya Lei shrugged. "Apparently your vow of silence has ended." He looked at Nick. "You are Nicholas Freestone."

Nick didn't respond.

"And you," Kya Lei said, looking at Mya, "are Indaw's sister and Taung Baw's great-granddaughter, Mya, if I'm not mistaken." He smiled. "Don't worry. Your secret is safe. Taung Baw did not tell Captain Moto about me, and I will not tell anyone about you." He pointed to the note. "You were right about Hilltop. He left some time ago. He wasn't here when I arrived, and I've been here for two hours."

"Why did you follow us?" Mya asked.

"Curiosity. At the village I wasn't certain you were the two youngsters from Hawk's Nest. The rumor was that you'd both died in the forest. Now I know you didn't."

"But you're not going to tell anybody," Nick said.

"Not a living soul."

Mya and Nick weren't sure they believed him.

Hannibal came up from the stream and started sniffing around a stand of tamarinds to see if any pods had fallen while he slept.

"Magnificent elephant. Where did he come from?"

"He belongs to my father," Nick answered.

"If the Japanese find out you have a trained timber elephant, they will follow you to the ends of the earth. They are short of elephants."

"They're not going to find out," Nick said.

"They might. If I found you, they can find you."

"Only if they're looking," Mya said.

"True," Kya Lei said with another smile. "Now tell me, why has the old monk gone to the labor camp?"

Nick and Mya were not about to tell him anything about their plans.

Kya Lei laughed. "Another vow of silence? All right, let me tell you why I think he's gone there. You're wondering if you can get Jackson Freestone, or Indaw, or perhaps both of them out of the camp. Yes?"

Nick hesitated, then nodded. Mya shot Nick a sour look, which he ignored. Maybe Kya Lei could help them. "Have you been to the camp?"

"Many times. And there are actually three camps." Kya Lei squatted down and motioned for them to join him. He put Nick's candle on the ground and smoothed a patch of dirt near it. "The first camp is here." He drew an *X* with a stick. "It's abandoned now. They moved to the second camp, here, a few weeks ago. This is where Jackson and Indaw are. The third camp is up here, and it's just about completed, so I think they'll be leaving for the third camp soon."

"Have you seen my brother or Mr. Freestone?"

"Indaw, yes. Jackson Freestone, no. I don't even know what he looks like. There are hundreds of British laborers."

"How is Indaw?"

"He was fine when I talked to him a few weeks ago."

"How could you talk to him?" Nick asked.

"The mahouts are in an adjoining camp," Kya Lei explained. "It's guarded, but much less so than the compound where the foreign prisoners are being held. If you are on good terms with the guards at the mahout camp, you can come and go as you please."

"I don't understand," Mya said. "If it is so easy, why hasn't Indaw escaped?"

"Because of you," Kya Lei answered. "Colonel Nagayoshi promised to punish you if Indaw tried to escape. It's their family members that keep the mahouts there, not the guards. Indaw doesn't know you left Hawk's Nest. I would have told him myself, but as I said, I haven't been to the camp in several weeks. It's not safe for me to go there now."

"Why?" Nick asked.

"Captain Moto. He has gotten it into his head that I am working with the Kachin guerrillas."

There was a lot of information about the Kachins among the Colonel's papers. They were a fierce mountain tribe from northern Burma, fanatically dedicated to destroying the Japanese. Small bands of guerrillas had successfully attacked supply convoys and depots, gun emplacements, and patrols. The Colonel was afraid they would try to destroy the airfield, but Magwe beat them to it. This was one reason Nick wanted to get the notebook to his stepfather. He thought Bernard would be very interested in the Kachins' activities.

"Are you working with the Kachins?" Nick asked.

Kya Lei smiled. "Let's just say that Captain Moto is a smart and ambitious officer. He has made it very difficult for me to move around freely." He stood up. "In fact, I should be going. I have some people to meet. I just wanted to thank you for not mentioning my name to Moto. Please tell Taung Baw that I'm very grateful."

"We will," Mya said.

"If I were you, I would forget the labor camp," Kya Lei said. "I'll get word to Indaw that you are no longer at Hawk's Nest. He won't need your help to get out of the mahout camp."

"What about my father?" Nick asked. "He's sick. He needs to get out of there too."

Kya Lei gave him a sympathetic look. "I wish I could help you," he said, then walked off into the darkness.

Hilltop reached the outskirts of the first camp a little after midnight. The barbwire had been taken down, but the fence posts and bamboo guard towers were still standing.

A great sadness filled him as he walked through the abandoned camp. It was much bigger than he thought it would be. Lined up in the center were the bamboo prisoner barracks—the roof thatching caved in now, the woven walls in tatters. In a year, or less, the jungle would reclaim the camp, hiding all traces of the suffering and death that had taken place there.

On the far end of the camp, outside where the fence had been, were the graves. Row after row of bamboo crosses with dog tags hanging from them.

A few hundred yards outside the camp, Hilltop found the tracks. He followed them.

Hilltop reached the second camp at sunrise. A sleepy sentry stepped out in front of him and asked where he thought he was going.

"To see my great-grandson, Indaw," Hilltop

answered in Japanese, which clearly startled the sentry. Not many Burmese spoke Japanese, and fewer still with a perfect accent.

"By whose authority?" the sentry asked, a bit more respectfully.

"Colonel Nagayoshi."

The sentry stood up a little straighter when he heard the name. Hilltop was relieved. It meant that the Colonel still held the power, or else his loss of it hadn't filtered down to the sentry level yet. The soldier gave him directions and bowed when he left.

There was no barbwire around the mahout camp, and only a handful of soldiers, who barely looked at him as he walked by.

The camp reminded Hilltop of the elephant village below Hawk's Nest, although it was somewhat bigger. A neat row of bamboo houses near a shallow river, goats tied beneath them, chickens pecking in the dirt. The elephants were tied to a rope picket line in front of the houses—twenty-one elephants all together. Hilltop recognized Choo Chin Chow, Miss Pretty, and several others.

Normally, mahouts preferred their elephants to be free at night so they could feed themselves. The Japanese, no doubt, thought catching the elephants in the morning was a waste of time and had ordered the mahouts to tie them. This meant the mahouts had to go out and gather food in the evening. A hungry elephant will not work. The Japanese would need dozens of soldiers to guard the mahouts as they gathered food, unless they trusted them. Which they obviously did in this camp.

The mahouts were just waking up, checking their elephants, putting their tea water on the fires. Hilltop heard Indaw before he saw him. His warm laugh pealed through the dark morning. He found his great-grandson sitting next to the fire nearest the elephants. He was telling a story to a group of mahouts. When Indaw spoke, all eyes were on him, and they didn't notice Hilltop walk up. He waited for the story to end and the laughter to die down before speaking.

"Indaw," he said.

Indaw jumped up. "Taung Baw?" He ran over and threw his arms around Hilltop in a hug that hurt the monk's old bones.

The other mahouts were on their feet as well, heads bowed, honored to have the great Taung Baw pay the camp a visit.

Indaw guided him over to the fire, sat him down, and gave him a cup of green tea.

"Are you hungry?"

"The tea is fine for now."

"Where did you come from?"

"The forest."

"I know that, but—"

"I suppose you have to go to work soon," Hilltop

said, feigning regret. A few of the mahouts were already saddling their elephants.

"Ahh," Indaw said with a conspiratorial smile, "unfortunately, Miss Pretty pulled a leg muscle just this morning." He looked at the other mahouts. "Remember?"

They all nodded and smiled back at him.

"I've told the Japanese that the elephants should be free at night so this wouldn't happen. She'll have to rest today. If she doesn't, the injury will certainly become worse. And we would hate to lose a great timber elephant like Miss Pretty, as she can outwork any three elephants in the camp."

The other mahouts laughed at this.

Indaw stood. "I'd better go tell the officer in charge."

While Indaw was gone, Hilltop chatted with the other mahouts, two of whom were from the plantation, and watched as they saddled and put the dragging gear on their elephants.

Indaw returned in time to see the elephants saunter off into the forest, leaving Miss Pretty behind.

"The officer thought it was quite a coincidence that Miss Pretty was injured the day my great-grandfather showed up in camp," he said. "But he gave us the day off anyway. He's not a bad sort, as far as Japanese go. Now tell me, how is Mya?"

"Is there someplace we can talk without anyone overhearing?"

"Of course." Indaw fed Miss Pretty, then led Hilltop into his house.

Roll Call 26

Indaw was astounded to hear that Mya had not only left Hawk's Nest, but that she was ten miles away with Nick Freestone.

When Hilltop told him about their disguise, Indaw laughed.

"That's a high price to pay for leaving Hawk's Nest. She's always been vain about her hair."

Hilltop did not tell him about Bukong's interest in his sister. He felt it would be a distraction, and he needed his great-grandson's full attention right now.

Indaw had already heard about the explosion at the airfield, but he had no idea that Magwe was responsible. He told Hilltop that the mahouts from the plantation had been sent back to Hawk's Nest as soon as they arrived at the camp.

"They didn't even unload the elephants from the train—just put the engine into reverse and backed up all the way to Moulmein. We needed the help here, but we were happy that they got to go back home to their families."

"Bukong was on that train," Hilltop said.

Indaw frowned. "I hadn't heard. There are many mahouts that would like to get their hands on him, including me. Why is he here?"

Hilltop told him.

"Bukong's punishment may be short-lived," Indaw said in disgust.

"Why?"

"The rumor is that Colonel Nagayoshi is getting the boot and Major Riku is taking his place. I wouldn't be surprised if Bukong is over there right now, packing Riku's belongings for the move to Hawk's Nest."

Big and little power, Hilltop thought again. Who had it, and how much, and how long would it last. He looked at his great-grandson. Indaw had lost some weight but looked as fit as ever.

"How are you treated here?" he asked.

"It was bad at first, but they've eased up. The Japanese need mahouts. But it's not the same over there." He nodded toward the prisoner-of-war camp.

From where they sat, they could see two of the guard towers and the top of the barbwire fence.

"Have you had a chance to talk with Jackson?"

"A few times, but it's difficult. They keep the mahouts and POWs separate. Whenever I get a chance, I volunteer Miss Pretty for rail duty. Jackson is usually assigned to that crew. It's terrible work because you're exposed to the sun all day. But the last two times I volunteered, he wasn't there."

"He's been sick," Hilltop said.

"I didn't know," Indaw said. "It's been bad lately. We've lost two mahouts to malaria in the past two months. Do you know what is wrong with him?"

Hilltop shook his head.

"If we could find out, I might be able to get medicine to him. There isn't a lot of it around here, but I'm friendly with a couple of orderlies. They can get it from the infirmary if the price is right."

"I have something a little more permanent in mind than medicine," Hilltop said.

"Such as?"

"Escape," Hilltop answered. "For both of you."

"Now that Mya is safe, I can leave whenever I want," Indaw said. "It's a simple matter of walking away from Miss Pretty while we're working in the forest. If I leave first thing in the morning, I'll have an eight or nine-hour start before they know I'm gone. The soldiers will search, but if I leave Miss Pretty behind, they won't care if they find me or not. They are more interested in the elephant than the mahout."

Indaw looked out the window, staring at the guard towers for a few moments, then said, "Getting Jackson out is a different situation. Come. I'll show you."

Indaw and Hilltop stood outside the POW camp, watching through the barbwire as the sun began to scorch the day.

The prisoners were lined up in the main yard, surrounded by dozens of soldiers. A Japanese officer stood on a small platform in front of them, flanked by four other soldiers holding clipboards and pencils.

Hilltop scanned the faces of the prisoners but did not see Jackson, and he wasn't certain if he would recognize him if he had. The men were gaunt, worn down by work, heat, lack of food, and disease. It was hard to believe that any of them would survive the day.

"They're taking roll call," Indaw explained. "It takes at least an hour. We've caught the end of it. No one is allowed outside the camp until everyone is accounted for. When they finish work, they are marched back into the yard, and no one is allowed into the barracks until the evening roll call is complete."

He pointed to the soldiers around them. "Most of the guards are Korean. Each man knows the faces of his group of prisoners. No chance of fooling them with a substitution or some other trick. If someone escapes, the guard responsible is executed. It happened at Camp One. An Australian slipped away. They caught him the next day and executed him and the guard together."

Hilltop watched the proceeding carefully as he listened to Indaw's explanation.

"Prisoner six-five-nine!" the officer shouted from the platform.

A man stepped forward and bowed.

"Prisoner six-eight-three!"

"Deceased!" a British officer replied.

The man on the platform looked to the soldier to his right. He consulted his clipboard and verified that prisoner six-eight-three had died during the night.

The roll call continued. Five more present, two more dead, three in the hospital . . .

Standing on the porch of the headquarters building next to Major Riku was the man Hilltop hoped he would never see again. Captain Moto.

Indaw noticed Hilltop staring at him.

"Moto," Indaw said. "Major Riku's lapdog. Dangerous."

"I've seen enough," Hilltop said, turning away and walking back to the mahouts' camp.

When they got to the house, Indaw poured him another cup of tea and offered him a bowl of cold rice.

"Even if we managed to get Jackson out of the camp, we wouldn't get far on foot," Indaw said.

"We have Hannibal," Hilltop said.

"Really?" Indaw said in surprise. "And how is the old rogue?"

"Fine, if you stay away from his feet. He's been no trouble at all."

"Captain Moto has very good trackers," Indaw said. "Two hill tribesmen."

"I saw them yesterday," Hilltop said. "But they

won't be looking for us on elephantback. No one knows that I have Hannibal, and he's big enough to carry all of us. There will be no tracks but his. The trackers will mistake him for a wild elephant."

Indaw thought about it for a moment but still didn't like their chances. "The best thing we can do for Jackson is to get him medicine and get his son out of Burma safely."

"Nick Freestone would not agree," Hilltop said. "He's not the boy you met a few months ago. He's not going to take your word, or mine, about his father's situation here. He'll want to see for himself. He's a Freestone. I can't force him to go with me."

"You mean us," Indaw said.

"You're coming?"

"Now that Mya's away from Hawk's Nest, I'm not staying here. Where are you taking them?"

"A monastery in Umphang. I'll try to get them to India from there, but if I can't, the monks will keep them safe until the war is over."

"Then bring them here," Indaw said. "Tomorrow will be perfect. We're having an open market. We have them once a month. People come from all over, selling food and supplies. No one's going to notice an old monk and his novices. And the soldiers won't cause any problems. They look forward to the market as much, if not more, than we do. It's the only place they can get cigarettes, sweets, and other luxuries.

"We're ten miles closer to Umphang from here. I know the perfect spot for Hannibal. A lot of tamarind for him to eat. You can leave him there and bring Mya and Nick into camp tomorrow evening."

"I'm worried about Captain Moto." Hilltop explained their encounter with him at the village.

"You're right to be worried about him," Indaw said. "But he rarely comes to the mahout camp, and I've never seen him at the market. I hear he's nervous around elephants."

"You're certain it's safe?"

"Nothing is safe with the Japanese, but it will be safe enough." He drew a map on a scrap of paper of where Hilltop was to take Hannibal.

Hilltop put it in his bag. "Then I'll leave now."

"Perhaps you should rest first."

"It's better if I get back to the children. I'll rest when I get there."

Indaw gave his great-grandfather a deep bow. "I'll try to find out more about how Jackson's doing, so I can tell Nick." He smiled. "Just tell Mya when she sees me, she has to act like a humble novice, not my little sister."

The Graveyard 27

Nick and Mya were relieved to see Hilltop, and a little alarmed at his condition when he arrived late in the afternoon. He had obviously walked a long way and was exhausted. They sat him down in the shade and gave him water and some food from the bag Kya Lei had given them.

They had spent the entire day worrying, and had so many questions they could hardly contain themselves, but they let him eat before they started in.

"Did you see Indaw?"

"Yes. He's lost some weight, but he's the same old Indaw. You'll see him yourself tomorrow."

"He's escaped?"

"No. We're going to the mahout camp."

"What about my father?" Nick asked.

"I didn't see him," Hilltop answered. "But Indaw is going to try to find out how he's doing today. I'm sure he'll be able to tell us something tomorrow."

"But he's alive," Nick said.

Hilltop thought about the officer calling names from the platform and the grim reply, *Deceased!*

"As far as we know," he said.

Nick didn't like the sound of this.

Before they could ask any more questions, Hilltop lay down on his mat.

"We'll have plenty of time to talk tonight," he said wearily. "Don't worry if I sleep past sunset. The camp's not far on elephant back, and we can't go there until tomorrow evening."

He closed his eyes and sensed the children staring at him for a long time before they gave up and quietly walked away.

Nick and Mya thought Hilltop would never wake up.

It was an uneasy day for them. Mya was ecstatic at the prospect of being reunited with Indaw, and overjoyed that he was well, but she could hardly share her happiness with Nick. His father's fate was far from clear.

She tried to cheer him up by telling him about how clever Hilltop and Indaw were and how strong his father was, but it did little to lighten his worry. Nor did the conversation they had with Hilltop when they were finally underway.

"I think it's going to be difficult, if not impossible, to get your father out of the camp," he said.

"But we'll try," Nick said.

"We'll see. There is more at stake here than your father. We have to consider what failure might mean.

If we try, and get caught, it's likely that all of us will be executed, or at the very least, imprisoned. I don't think your father would want that to happen. Do you?"

"No, sir," Nick answered quietly.

"Here's another question to think about," Hilltop continued. "If it had been possible for your father to escape, don't you think he would have by now?"

This was not as easy to answer as the first question. "I'm not sure," Nick said. "He doesn't really know that I'm still in Burma. If he thought I was in danger at Hawk's Nest, I think he would try to save me no matter what the consequences."

Hilltop gave him a smile. "I think you are right."

They reached the first camp an hour before dawn. It was darker than the previous night but light enough to see the skeleton shapes of the buildings and towers. No one spoke.

The camp was laid out like the plans Nick had studied in the vault, but the precise drawings had missed the oppressive hopelessness of the place. As bad as it had been at times, he realized he was lucky to have been in Hawk's Nest all these months.

From the drawings, Nick knew they were heading toward the graveyard long before they reached it.

"So many," Mya whispered when they saw the crosses.

And one of them could be my father, Nick thought,

listening to the dog tags rattling in the breeze.

They were relieved when they reached the tracks. Even Hannibal seemed to relax as they left the camp behind.

They arrived at the spot Indaw had chosen for Hannibal just after sunrise. He was right about the tamarinds. There were so many pods lying on the ground that there was no need for Nick and Mya to pick any, which was just as well. They were too tired to climb trees. They ate a few handfuls of rice with a bit of meat, then found some shade to sleep in.

Two hours later, Nick awoke with a start and sat up. He wasn't sure if he had heard something or had had a bad dream. He scanned the jungle and listened. Nothing seemed amiss. Hannibal was sleeping under a stand of trees about thirty yards away, his belly swollen with pods. If something was wrong, he'd be on his feet. This is why Hilltop didn't worry about somebody coming upon them while they slept. "An elephant is the best sentinel on earth," he had told them.

It must have been a dream, then, Nick thought, trying to remember what it had been about.

Mya was lying ten feet away, and Hilltop another ten feet beyond her, both of them sleeping soundly.

Nick realized that he was incredibly thirsty. Maybe that's what woke me up, he thought. He walked over to the water jug and nearly emptied it. When he stooped to put it back down, he saw the scrap of paper Indaw had used to draw the map for Hilltop. He picked it up. There was a stream about midway between where they were and the camp. Two miles at the most, he estimated. It wouldn't hurt to refill the jug. He could be back before Hilltop and Mya woke up. He started off.

This was the first time he had walked alone outside in nearly a year, and it felt a little strange not to have someone with him. The forest was relatively open, but with no road or trails, he wasn't really worried about running into any soldiers this far from the camp. He *was* worried about getting lost, though. Every once in a while he marked a tree with the Sergeant Major's pocketknife, so he would be able to find his way back.

Wouldn't do to get lost in the jungle this close to seeing Father, he thought. It was then that he remembered his dream, which stopped him in his tracks. His heart beat quicker, and his mouth went dry again. He had been dreaming about the camp graveyard, but this one was different from the one they had gone through the night before. The bamboo crosses seemed to stretch for miles. There were grave diggers wielding shovels and picks, scooping out holes for the dead, which were piled at the edge of the yard. They picked up a body from the pile and tossed it into a hole like a sack of oats. And this is what made Nick's heart pound in his chest and his mouth go dry. The man in the grave was his father.

Nick continued down to the stream, but when he got there, he didn't stop to get water; he crossed it. He knew he was being stupid, but he couldn't seem to make his legs stop until he reached the edge of the clearing, where the POW camp had been hacked out of the jungle.

He stood in the shadow of the trees, out of breath, covered in sweat, staring at the barbwire thirty feet away. He could see the guards in the towers clearly. They were more worried about people breaking out of the camp than into it, so their attention was not directed at the jungle.

The camp was virtually empty. The prisoners were out working in the jungle, but not all of them. The long bamboo barracks on the right side had a red cross painted on the thatched roof. This was to stop enemy fighters from strafing the camp, killing their own sick and wounded.

He saw movement through the open windows and wondered if one of the shadows was his father. But it couldn't be. This wasn't why he had risked everything by coming down here. His father was in the graveyard.

He slowly worked his way through the jungle fringe, stopping often to glance at the camp to make certain he wasn't being observed. But every time he looked, the soldiers on the other side of the barbwire were completely at ease, talking with each other, laughing, smoking, as if they didn't have a care in the world. The relaxed atmosphere was no doubt very different when the prisoners were back in camp.

The cemetery was smaller than the graveyard at Camp One—sixty or seventy bamboo crosses—some with dog tags hanging from them, others with a name scrawled on a wood plank tacked beneath the cross. He would have to get closer if he wanted to read the names, but that would mean stepping out into the open. If a guard happened to look his way . . .

He heard the rattle of a teak gate swinging open, and scooted farther back into the forest. Voices. The squeak of wheels. He climbed a tree for a better view. Three prisoners pulling a heavy oxen cart with a corpse in the back. A single Japanese guard followed behind. Burial duty.

Nick watched their slow approach and nearly fell out of the tree with relief and joy when he saw that one of the men pulling the cart was his father!

His father was thin and had let his beard grow out, but there was no mistaking the Freestone eyes—alert, darting around like a bird of prey. Of the three prisoners, he was clearly the healthiest. One of the men had a bandage around his leg and a severe limp. The other had a terrible oozing sore on his face. They stopped the cart and pulled out picks and shovels. His father started swinging the pick as soon as it was in his hands. The other two prisoners watched him work.

"Bury deep! Animals might dig up. Not respectful to dead."

Nick had been so fixated on his father, he hadn't paid any attention to the guard. It was Sergeant Sonji.

"Speedo! Make quick work here. Hot sun not good for health."

Sonji appeared to find the burial duty even more distasteful than the prisoners did. He sat down on a log and wiped the sweat off his face with a handkerchief. He, too, had lost weight in the few days he had been in camp.

His father rested while the other two shoveled out the dirt he had broken up. He was breathing hard, with his hands on his knees, obviously not in as good shape as it first appeared.

When they finally finished the hole, Sonji leaned his rifle against the cart and helped them lift the body. Nick doubted any other guard would assist like this. Unlike in his dream, they carried the man gently, tenderly laying him in the grave. Sonji removed his hat and bowed his head while Nick's father said a prayer. When he finished, they shoveled the dirt over the top of him.

"Don't tell," Sonji said. He picked up a shovel and helped them.

Nick stayed up in the tree for several minutes after they left. A warm breeze blew across the graveyard. He thought of a haiku.

On the way back, Nick got lost. He found the place where he had first seen the camp, but after this, nothing looked familiar. In his hurry he hadn't stopped to use the Sergeant Major's pocketknife on this side of the stream. It was getting late. Hilltop and Mya would soon be awake—if they weren't already—wondering where he was. He began to think that he should just stay put, wait for dark, and make his way to the mahout camp. To find it, all he had to do was follow the perimeter of his father's camp. Hilltop and Mya were sure to show up there, even if they couldn't find him. He turned around to head back to the camp.

"Are you lost?"

Nick jumped and swore.

Kya Lei stepped out from behind a tree, a gleeful smile on his face.

"You scared me half to death!"

Kya Lei bowed. "My apologies."

"What are you doing here? I thought you said it wasn't safe for you to come to the camp anymore."

"It isn't," he answered. "But I've been instructed to keep an eye on you."

"Why? By who?"

"Was that your father in the graveyard?"

"Yes, but you still haven't answered my questions."

"Follow me. I'll put you in the right direction to Hilltop and Mya."

Kya Lei started off in the opposite direction Nick thought he should go.

He caught up to him. "Who told you to keep an eye on us?"

"I can't tell you that," Kya Lei answered. "But when I told them you were alive, they became very excited and asked that I make certain you stay out of trouble."

"You promised that you wouldn't tell anyone about us," Nick said.

Kya Lei shrugged. "I meant Japanese. The people I told are happy you are free."

"Who are they?" Nick asked again.

Kya Lei answered the question with his own question. "You didn't heed my warning about the camp. Why are you here?"

"I can't tell you that," Nick answered, parroting Kya Lei's answer.

Kya Lei laughed. "Then tell me this. It's been rumored that your father has a large cache of arms hidden on the plantation. Do you happen to know where they are?"

So that's what this is about, Nick thought. Kya Lei wants my father's weapons. To sell them, no doubt.

"I don't know what you're talking about," he answered. "My father is a plantation owner."

"*Was* a plantation owner," Kya Lei corrected. "Now he is a prisoner of war."

Not for long, Nick thought hopefully. They reached the stream and waded across. Kya Lei led him to the last tree Nick had marked.

"You should be able to find your way from here," he said.

"You're not coming?"

Kya Lei shook his head. "I have to go. I have some people to meet."

"That's exactly what you said the last time I saw you," Nick pointed out.

"Different people," Kya Lei said. He started back the way they had come, then stopped and turned. "I don't suppose there is any way I can convince you to leave this area?"

Nick shook his head. "Not a chance."

"Where have you been?" Mya asked angrily.

Nick held up the water jug. "I went down to the stream to get water."

"What stream?"

Nick pointed vaguely behind him. He wanted to shout *My father is alive!* But he wasn't ready to admit how foolish he had been. It would just make her more angry. Hilltop, on the other hand, didn't appear to be upset by Nick's absence in the least. He was sitting against a tree, watching with a bemused expression.

"I saw Kya Lei."

"He's still following us?" Mya asked. "I thought he said it was too dangerous for him to go near the camp."

"What's that scoundrel up to?" Hilltop asked.

"I'm not sure." Nick told them about their conversation. Most of it, anyway.

"Who told him to keep an eye on you?" Mya asked.

"He wouldn't tell me."

"I don't trust him," Mya said.

"Neither do I," Nick said.

"Where did he go?" Mya asked.

"He said he had some people to meet."

"Again?"

Nick shrugged and handed the water jug to Hilltop.

The Market 28

The mahout camp was crowded. Torches lit the dusty path running between the river and the houses. There was music and dancing. Dice games were being played around nearly every campfire. Food sizzled in giant woks. Everything imaginable was being sold—chickens, goats, pigs, rubies, tobacco, betel nut. Japanese soldiers seemed to be the biggest customers, crowding around some venders so thickly that Nick and Mya couldn't see what was being sold.

It was difficult for the novices to keep their heads down in such a festive atmosphere, as Hilltop had instructed—especially for Mya, who could barely contain her excitement at seeing Indaw. The only way she managed it was to concentrate on the frayed hem of Hilltop's robe.

They weren't more than twenty feet into camp before their alms bowls were overflowing with food. It seemed everyone they passed recognized Taung Baw. Each time they were stopped, Nick bumped into Mya's back. He obviously wasn't concentrating on the hem of *her* robe. He had been different since he'd returned from the stream. On the way to the mahout camp he had even smiled a couple of times, which she hadn't seen him do since he'd heard his father was ill.

"Taung Baw!"

Mya and Nick recognized Sergeant Sonji's exuberant voice. Nick kept his chin glued to his neck, hoping the sergeant wouldn't make him lift his face. Mya was frightened too, but not nearly as badly as Nick. She'd had very little contact with the sergeant at Hawk's Nest.

"What brings you here?" Sonji asked in Japanese.

"My great-grandson, Indaw," Hilltop answered easily.

"I see you have company."

Nick squeezed his eyes closed.

"Yes. It's good for an old monk to have help on a long journey. I heard that you had been transferred here."

"A terrible place," Sonji said. "I hoped that Colonel Nagayoshi would bring me back to Hawk's Nest, but with his dismissal . . ."

He didn't need to finish the sentence. Both men knew what this meant.

"Major Riku has always been fond of the garden," Hilltop said. "And there is no one in Burma who can maintain it like you. Perhaps you'll be going back to Hawk's Nest sooner than you think."

Sonji shook his head sadly. "Perhaps, but that is not likely. And even if I were so lucky, it would be difficult to find someone as good as Nick Freestone to help me. Have you been to the garden lately? It's an embarrassment."

Nick's face flushed. He appreciated the compliment, but why was Hilltop spending so much time with Sonji? Every second they lingered increased the chances of Sonji discovering who the monk's novices really were.

"I hear that Bukong has shared the same fate as yourself."

"Bukong!" Sonji said, spitting the word out like a piece of spoiled fish. "He will be back at Hawk's Nest long before I am. I don't believe the house staff will be pleased to see him return. Some of the bruises he's left on them with his cane have not had time to heal."

"I imagine not," Hilltop said. "When will he be returning?"

"Two days. Maybe three. Major Riku's replacement arrives early tomorrow by train. Perhaps his replacement will be better for this place. I have seen things here that . . ." He took a deep breath and once again let the sentence go.

"Will Captain Moto be going with the major?"

"I assume so," Sonji answered. "And that will be a blessing for both the prisoners and soldiers at the camp. He's worse than Major Riku and Bukong put together. If Colonel Nagayoshi had known what was going on here, he would have put a stop—"

"This Captain Moto," Hilltop interrupted, trying

to keep Sonji on track. "Exactly what is his position here?"

"No one really knows. He spends most of his time out in the forest hunting tigers and harassing villagers. He has killed seventeen tigers so far and boasts that he will kill one hundred before the war is over."

"Let's hope the war doesn't last that long, for our sake and the tigers,'" Hilltop said. "Will you be staying at the mahout camp long this evening?"

"Yes. I just arrived. It's pleasant here compared to the prisoners' camp."

"I had better find Indaw," Hilltop said. "Perhaps I will see you later, then."

"I hope so." Sonji bowed.

Hilltop returned the bow, then continued deeper into the camp. It was all Nick could do not to turn around and look. He felt Sonji staring at his back. Those eyes had watched him for ten months, and Nick knew they were watching him now.

After two more delays they finally made it to Indaw's house, but were disappointed once again. When they got inside they saw that Indaw had guests. Two men from a local village. Indaw waved the two novices over into a corner and introduced his great-grandfather. The villagers of course knew who he was. They paid their respects, then quickly excused themselves, to everyone's relief.

Before the door closed, Indaw rushed over to Mya

and raised her head, before she had a chance to do it on her own. She threw her arms around him and cried.

"Not too loud," he whispered. "Not too loud." He held her at arm's length to get a better look. "Even without hair you are the prettiest girl in Burma." He turned to Nick and took a step backward in surprise. "You are not Nicholas Gillis Freestone."

"I go by Nick."

Indaw smiled. "Seriously. I wouldn't have recognized you if Taung Baw hadn't told me. You look like a Burman." He put his hand out and Nick shook it.

"Is it safe to talk here?" Hilltop asked.

"I have people watching outside. If someone comes . . ." He lifted a mat from the floor. Underneath was a trapdoor. "A trick I picked up from the Sergeant Major. It's not nearly as comfortable as Hawk's Nest, but your novices should fit." He grinned at Mya and Nick. "Just don't sneeze. My walls are paper thin."

They sat down on the floor. Mya continued to hold her brother's hand and would not let go.

"Did you find out anything about Jackson?" Hilltop asked.

"He's been sick, but he's better. He's still on the burial crew. I think the major would have put him back on regular duty if he wasn't busy getting ready for his new assignment." He looked at Nick. "This is good news for your father. The longer they wait, the stronger he'll be when they put him back to work in the forest. If he's lucky he'll—"

"Wait a second," Nick said. "I thought we were here to talk about how to get my father out of the camp."

Indaw looked at Hilltop, who was resting his chin on his old hands. He met Indaw's gaze and said, "That's what I thought, too."

Indaw turned his attention back to Nick. "I know the camp routine backward and forward. I know most of the guards. Getting someone out of that camp is impossible."

"He could just walk away from the graveyard," Nick said.

"What about the guard?" Indaw asked. "Your father would be shot in the back before he got ten feet."

"The guard is Sergeant Sonji," Nick said.

Indaw and Mya looked confused.

"Of course," Hilltop said with a smile. "And how did your father look this morning?"

"He's weak," Nick answered. "And he's lost a lot of weight, but he seemed okay."

"You were at the camp?" Mya said.

"No one saw me . . . well . . . except for Kya Lei."

"Kya Lei is here?" Indaw said. "The Japanese would like to get their hands on him. He's working with the Kachins. Who's this Sergeant Sonji?"

Nick told him about Sonji and ended by saying,

"Sonji wouldn't shoot anyone."

Hilltop nodded in agreement.

"If this sergeant got back to camp short one man, he'd be shot himself," Indaw said. "We'd have a ten-minute start. The soldiers would be on us before we got a mile from the camp."

"There has to be a way," Nick insisted.

"Maybe there is," Hilltop said, standing up.

"Where are you going?" Indaw asked.

"To talk to an old friend."

"I'll go with you," Nick said, knowing exactly who Hilltop was going to talk to.

"No. This is something I have to do alone."

Nick rummaged through his bag and pulled out his notebook. He wrote something down, tore out the page, and handed it to Hilltop.

"Will you give this to him?"

Hilltop found Sonji sitting on a teak log near the river. He had a small fire going and was cooking a fish he had bought from one of the vendors. Hilltop sat down next to him, and they watched the current for a while without speaking.

"I was relieved to see that Nick was still alive," Sonji said quietly. "That was Mya with him?"

The two old friends spoke in Japanese.

"Yes," Hilltop answered.

"Novices. Very clever disguise."

"I'm sorry for the deception and the problems it has caused you."

"He's a good boy, caught in a war."

"Like all of us," Hilltop said. "He asked me to give you this."

Sonji took the piece of paper, opened it up, and held it in the light of the fire.

> dog tags
> hung on bamboo crosses
> sounding like wind chimes

Sonji smiled, then put the note in his tunic pocket.

"So he saw his father today."

Hilltop nodded.

"His father is a good man, too. In the hospital he helps others even though he himself is sicker than they."

"So, he is staying in the hospital?"

"Yes. The burial detail is always made up of the sick and injured. Major Riku believes the men will get better if they bury the dead. He says it teaches them to fight for life, but I'm told that no one on the burial detail lives for very long. You need to leave this place, Taung Baw. Get Nick and the girl someplace safe."

"I'm trying," Hilltop said. "But Nick will not leave without his father."

"The only way his father will leave the camp is to

die, and I'm afraid we will be putting him on the oxen cart soon. Before I arrived he was very close to death. Twice, the British doctor was ready to sign his death certificate, but somehow he recovered. The doctor said he had never seen anyone cling to life harder than Jackson Freestone."

"The doctor is British?"

"Yes, Major Riku does not waste Japanese doctors on the prisoners. Why?"

Hilltop stared across the river for several moments before answering.

When he finished, Sonji looked at his old friend sadly and shook his head. "I don't know, Taung Baw. I may not be a good soldier, but I am a good Japanese. What you're asking is treasonous."

"The soul does not have a nationality," Hilltop said.

Sonji gave him a smile, then picked up a piece of wood and tossed it into the river. They watched it until it drifted out of sight.

"Before you walked up, I was thinking about Colonel Nagayoshi's garden," Sonji said. "Even if Major Riku asked me to return to Hawk's Nest, I do not think I would go. I do not want to make a garden for him. It is he and Captain Moto and others like them who have brought all this upon us. I think I will stay at the railway. Maybe here I can prove that Japanese people are good. I have to try."

Hilltop smiled and put his hand on his friend's shoulder.

Sonji gave him a sad look. "I wonder if we will ever be forgiven."

"In time," Hilltop said.

"I hope I live to see this." Sonji stood. "I will go and check on Jackson Freestone's health. Sadly, he may not live through the night."

A jeep was parked outside Indaw's house when Hilltop returned. A driver sat at the wheel, with two trackers sitting in the back. The seats were covered in tiger skins. The two trackers gave Hilltop a snide smile as he walked past them.

Captain Moto was not alone in the house. Bukong bowed when Hilltop entered. Hilltop returned the bow and looked over at Captain Moto. He was smiling, tapping his teak-and-ivory baton on his free hand. Indaw was sitting on his mat in the corner, a dark look on his face.

"We heard you were here, monk," Captain Moto said. "We could not have the great Taung Baw so close and not pay our respects."

"Thank you," Hilltop said.

"Where are your novices?"

"They come and they go," Hilltop answered. "Orphans are driven by food."

"We heard they were in the camp tonight."

"They may still be," Hilltop said. "Have you looked?"

"We have. The mahouts say they have left, but it seems odd that they would leave without their master."

"As I said, they come and they go. And I am not their master. I am just an old monk."

"Where did these novices come from?"

"Near Moulmein, I believe."

Captain Moto looked around Indaw's house as he spoke. "The last time I saw you, you were under the protection of Colonel Nagayoshi." He turned to face Hilltop. "Now who will protect you, monk?"

It had suddenly grown very quiet outside. The music had stopped, the laughter, the loud talk. Bukong walked over to the window and looked out.

"Captain?"

Captain Moto joined him. It appeared that the entire camp had gathered outside Indaw's house, including people visiting from other villages. They were staring up at the house solemnly. In their hands were torches, choons, and dahs. The Japanese soldiers stood to the side, uncertain about what they should do.

"Colonel Nagayoshi has never protected Taung Baw," Indaw said. "The people protect him. Colonel Nagayoshi knew this."

Captain Moto turned around, his knuckles nearly

as white as the inlaid ivory on his baton.

"If there is a riot tonight, mahouts will be injured," Indaw continued. "This will stop work on the railway. Major Riku will not like this. You will be blamed. He may even send you to a place where there are no tigers to hunt."

Captain Moto regained some of his composure. "Once again, monk, you have sidestepped my gun sight. But I am a very patient hunter." He smiled. "I come and I go. I am driven by my prey."

Bukong followed him out of the house.

Indaw got up and watched them push their way through the crowd to their jeep. The driver started it, and they roared away.

When the jeep was out of sight, Indaw waved to the crowd and gave them a grin. The crowd started to break up and return to the night's business. The Japanese soldiers dispersed as well, still not clear about what had just happened, but happy to get back to their trading.

"It will be safe for you to leave in a few minutes," Indaw said.

He closed the covers over his windows and pulled back the mat. Mya and Nick came through the trapdoor, covered in sweat and bamboo dust. They were both unnerved by the cramped quarters and the conversation they'd overheard through the thin floor.

When they had recovered, Hilltop sat them down

and said, "We leave tomorrow morning." He looked at Indaw. "You will meet Mya at the tamarind stand. When you get there, ride Hannibal down to the stream. No closer to the camp than that."

Indaw nodded.

"Nick and I will go to the cemetery. If we are able, we will bring Jackson up to you."

"If?" Nick asked.

Hilltop nodded. "Your father is very ill. Even if Sonji decides to help, and it's not clear that he will, your father may decide that it's too dangerous to come with us. Regardless, we have to leave tomorrow with or without your father. Captain Moto and Bukong know, or at least suspect, that you and Mya are alive."

"Kya Lei," Nick said bitterly.

"Perhaps, but it doesn't matter why they suspect, or how they found out. We have all risked a great deal to get your father out of the camp, and we will take one final risk tomorrow morning. After that we will have done everything we can possibly do. I need your word that you will come with us, even if it doesn't work out the way you want."

Nick looked at his three friends. Hilltop was right; they had taken huge risks. If it hadn't been for him and his father, they would all be safe at the monastery in Umphang by now.

"You have my word," he said.

The Bamboo Cross 29

Early the next morning, Nick and Hilltop headed toward the cemetery, leaving Mya and Hannibal behind to wait for Indaw.

Nick felt a strange calm as they walked through the unusually cool morning. A thick mist blanketed the forest floor, making Hilltop, in his orange robe, appear to be floating instead of walking.

The old monk had not told him anything about his conversation with Sonji, and Nick had not asked. It was out of his hands now. His father would either leave the camp today or he would not, but Nick hoped and prayed it would be the former.

When they reached the stream, Hilltop stopped to get a drink and rest for a few minutes. Nick was eager to get to the camp, but knew there was still plenty of time. There were two burial details a day, three if necessary—decomposition set in quickly in the tropics. The first detail was right after roll call, for the men who had died during the night.

"Did you give Sonji my haiku?" Nick asked.

Hilltop nodded.

"Did he say anything about it?"

Hilltop shook his head.

While she waited for Indaw, Mya reorganized their gear. Hannibal was a huge elephant, but with five people on his back, they would need the extra room.

She had not slept well the night before, worrying about everything that could go wrong. Hilltop and Nick could be caught at the POW camp; Indaw might not be able to get away from the soldiers as easily as he let on; Captain Moto could very well track them down. . . .

Her consternation must have been obvious, because before Hilltop and Nick left for the camp, Hilltop took her aside and said, "Just remember this, Mya. We are what we think. All that we are arises with our thoughts. With our thoughts, we make our world."

"I don't understand," she said.

Hilltop smiled. "It means, don't worry."

That was an hour ago, and Mya was still worried. Indaw should have been there by now. What was going on at the camp?

She was startled from her packing by a crashing noise behind her. She stood and turned, expecting the worst. It was Indaw! And unexpectedly he was straddling the neck of Miss Pretty.

"Hello, little sister," he said.

The night before, she had gotten a glimpse of Miss Pretty tethered to the picket line, and it was all she could do to stop herself from rushing over to her. She could see now in the morning light that Miss Pretty had lost a tremendous amount of weight.

"The Japanese work them too hard," Indaw said by way of explanation. "We can't get the food they need to them when they are tied to that picket line."

Mya nodded. "Didn't you say you had to leave Miss Pretty behind, or the soldiers would—"

"I thought you might want to drive her one more time before I let her go," Indaw interrupted. "Do you have your choon?"

"Yes!"

Mya quickly rummaged through her bag and found it. Indaw pulled her up onto Miss Pretty, then scooted back, giving Mya the cow's neck. She put her feet behind Miss Pretty's warm ears, then looked back at Indaw. "Where are we taking her?"

Indaw pointed to the right. "About a mile from here. We'll fetter her there, and one of the mahouts will bring her back to the Japanese this evening."

Mya applied pressure behind Miss Pretty's ear with the big toe of her left foot.

"*Tet!*"

Miss Pretty started forward, and Mya left all her worries behind.

* * *

Nick and Hilltop reached the camp just as the prisoners were filing out the front gate to go to work on the railway. Nick climbed the same tree as the day before. Hilltop squatted on his haunches directly below, using the trunk as a backrest.

The cemetery had a mournful look to it with the ground fog floating beneath the crosses like thin clouds.

The back gate rattled open, followed by the squeak of the oxen cart bumping along the rutted road. Nick strained to see. Sergeant Sonji led the way, his rifle slung casually over his shoulder. Behind him were the two men that had been with his father the previous morning. His father was not with them.

Had the major put him back to work in the forest? Had Sonji decided not to help? Nick looked down at Hilltop, who didn't seem at all disturbed. He wanted to climb down and confront the sergeant. But he couldn't. He had given his word.

There were two bodies in the cart, but all Nick could see of them were their feet. One had boots, the other was barefoot.

"Him first!" Sonji said, pointing at a corpse. He took two bamboo crosses out of the cart and walked over to the yard. "Bury here." He dropped a cross on the ground. "Speedo! Quick! Major Riku say we taking too long to bury dead." He dropped the second cross fifty feet away from the first.

The men started digging, but without his father to

help, they were very slow, even with Sonji berating them.

Nick expected Hilltop to signal him to climb down any second. They were far enough away to slip into the forest undetected. But the monk remained sitting, looking toward the graves, as still as the tree he was leaning against.

"Deep enough!" Sergeant Sonji said.

The men wearily climbed out of the shallow hole and followed him back to the oxen cart. Sonji unslung his rifle and helped lift the first man out. His head drooped back, and Nick stifled a distraught moan. The man with the boots was his father.

He looked down at Hilltop again, tears blurring his vision. The old monk was looking up at him now, his index finger in front of his lips for Nick to be silent.

Hilltop had known all along. Sonji must have told him the night before. He hadn't been brought here to save his father; he had been brought to pay his last respects. Nick could not be at his father's bedside when he died, so Hilltop had risked everything to make sure Nick could witness the burial.

They carried his father over to the hole and lowered him into it. Nick tried to climb higher, so he could get one last look at him, but the next branch up was out of reach.

"You dig next hole," Sonji told the two men. "I cover this one. Go!"

The men moved off, and Sonji started shoveling dirt into the hole. After a minute or two he paused to check on the prisoners, then got down on his knees and picked up the cross. His lips moved as if he were praying or giving a Buddhist blessing. Gently, he placed the cross at the head of the grave, then got back to his feet and continued shoveling. When he finished, he walked over to the two prisoners and helped them with the other man.

Nick wanted to climb down the tree and run all the way back up to the stream. But Hilltop remained beneath the tree, watching, in no hurry to leave. The other prisoners finished the next hole, placed the second man in, and filled it up.

Unlike the day before, there were no words spoken over the mounds. The prisoners threw their shovels into the cart, turned it around, then started back toward the camp. Nick waited until they were out of sight before climbing down and joining Hilltop

"You knew," he whispered.

Hilltop gave him a perplexed look, then said, "Let's go see your father."

"No, thanks," Nick said. "I've seen enough. We should go. There's nothing we can do for him now."

"Come," Hilltop said, starting toward the cemetery.

It seemed insane to expose themselves like this, but Nick followed. When they reached the grave, Nick closed his eyes. He didn't want to even look at the mound.

"Dig," Hilltop said.

"What?" Nick opened his eyes.

Hilltop was holding a shovel. "Hurry," he insisted, glancing at the camp. "But be gentle."

"No," Nick said.

Hilltop started using the shovel himself.

"What do you think you're doing?" Nick demanded.

"Your father is alive."

Nick stared at him.

"Dig," Hilltop repeated. "He is breathing through the hollow bamboo cross."

Nick grabbed the shovel from him. When he got about a foot deep, he and Hilltop got down on their knees and started to dig by hand, concentrating on the area where his father's head would be.

The base of the bamboo cross was in his father's mouth. Nick brushed the dirt away from his face and gently pulled the cross out of his mouth.

His father opened his eyes and smiled. "Hello, Nick," he said hoarsely.

They quickly finished the rest of the digging and helped his father out of the grave.

"We have to go," Hilltop said. "But first we must fill the hole back in."

Nick started shoveling.

"Wait," Hilltop said, pointing to the ground. "Sonji left you a message."

Nick looked down.

your haiku not too bad

Nick shoveled the rest of the dirt with tears streaming down his face.

Tiger's Breath 30

They had to half drag, half carry Nick's father the last mile up to the stream. As soon as Indaw saw them, he ran over, picked him up, and carried him the rest of way.

Jackson broke into a broad grin when he saw Hannibal.

"*Hmit,*" Hilltop said.

Hannibal stretched out. They got Nick's father onto the saddle first, then clambered up after him.

Finally underway, Jackson thanked them for coming after him.

"And Sonji," Hilltop added.

"Yes," Jackson said. "When he came into the hospital last night, the doctor and I didn't quite know what to make of him. At first we thought he was drunk, but when he mentioned that he had just talked to you at the mahout camp, and that Nick and Mya were there as well, we began to take him a bit more seriously."

He closed his eyes for a moment and took a deep breath.

"I have to say, I had some bad moments after he buried me. I began to think that maybe the whole thing was a hoax. That Sonji was mad and that I had fallen into his trap. If it had taken you any longer to unearth me, I think I might have gone mad myself. You can't imagine my relief when I felt the spade cut into the dirt."

His father talked for twenty minutes straight, and Nick couldn't get the grin off his face. It was the most animated he had ever seen him. He was obviously weak, but he was going to live.

"Where are we going?" he asked.

"The monastery in Umphang," Hilltop answered. "You can try to get to India from there after you are better."

His father nodded, then looked at Nick and Mya. "I'm sure there's a story behind the way you two look. Tell me about it."

It took them some time to fill him in on what had happened at Hawk's Nest in his absence. Indaw was interested as well. He and Jackson asked questions here and there, but they mostly listened, their faces darkening in anger at times, especially when they heard about Bukong.

Mya thought for a moment that her brother was going to jump off Hannibal right there and run back to the camp to avenge her honor. Indaw had a temper, but she had never seen a look like that cross his face.

301

Bukong was lucky that Indaw was on his way out of the country.

Soon after they finished their story, Nick's father fell asleep—a difficult feat on elephant back—and they continued on throughout the morning, their confidence growing with each step closer to the Thai border.

By early afternoon, Hannibal started to get agitated. He hadn't been allowed to forage that day, or sleep, and with five people on his back, he'd had about enough. He began tearing off overhead branches, tossing dirt on his mahouts, and trying to shake his saddle off.

"We will rest here for a few hours," Hilltop announced, bringing the bull to a stop. "Hannibal needs to eat and sleep."

Hilltop looked as if he could use some food and sleep as well. He had been driving Hannibal for nearly five hours. Indaw had offered to take over the neck several times, but Hilltop insisted that he was fine.

Now he was nearly as exhausted as Jackson Freestone. As soon as they dismounted, they both staggered over to the nearest tree and fell asleep.

Indaw was tempted to try his luck at hobbling Hannibal's front legs, so he wouldn't wander too far, but the maniacal look in the bull's eyes, when he drew too close, dissuaded him.

"Okay, old man, have it your way," he said with a grin. "Just don't wander too far."

He watched Hannibal amble off into the forest,

then joined Mya and Nick for a bowl of rice before the three of them fell asleep.

They did not hear Captain Moto's jeep until it was too late.

The trackers were out of the jeep with their rifles pointed before the fugitives had a chance to sit up. Captain Moto and Bukong climbed out of the backseat, looking smug, but the captain's expression turned to a frown when he saw Jackson Freestone sitting next to his son.

"Risen from the dead," he said. "You will tell me exactly how you managed this!"

Jackson met his gaze but said nothing.

"You will tell me," Moto said, lowering his voice. He pulled a coil of rope out of the back of the jeep and tossed it to Bukong. "Tie them."

The trackers waved everyone into a tight group with their rifles. Bukong limped over and proceeded to bind their wrists behind them.

"I'll kill you," Indaw said to Bukong when it was his turn.

Bukong merely smiled and made certain Indaw's manacles were painfully tight.

Mya was the last to be bound. Bukong tied her wrists, then brushed his hand over her scalp. "It will grow back," he whispered in her ear. "Don't be afraid. You will be safe with me at Hawk's Nest."

Mya spit in his face.

Bukong raised his cane and hit her across the shoulders. Indaw and Nick lunged at him, but both were thrown to the ground by the trackers.

Captain Moto ignored the altercation and walked over to the elephant saddle.

"An escaped prisoner, a runaway mahout, and a timber elephant," he said. "I will be a major before the end of the day. Perhaps even a colonel." He turned toward them. "Where are the others?"

"What others?" Nick asked.

"Kya Lei and the two men with him," Moto answered impatiently. "We have been tracking them since noon, which is how we came upon the elephant tracks. Bukong recognized them as belonging to . . ." He looked at Bukong.

"Hannibal," Bukong said. "The toenail missing on the right front foot."

Kya Lei again, Nick thought. He may not have told them about Mya and him, but by following them he had led Moto and Bukong right to them! Nick looked at the others. The expression on their faces reflected his own broiling emotions—disbelief, fear, confusion, anger, defiance. The only one of them who appeared unperturbed was Hilltop. He sat on his haunches, utterly calm, as if he were back in the Colonel's garden meditating beneath a shady tree.

Captain Moto paced back and forth in front of

them, slapping his baton in his palm.

"Before we leave here, there are two things I will know," he said. "The first is the location of Kya Lei." He looked at Nick's father. "The second is how you managed to escape from the camp. You obviously had help. The doctor in your hospital, the two other men on the burial detail. But I suspect there were others who assisted."

He walked over to Jackson and struck him across the face with his baton, then turned and hit Indaw. "You two are safe for the moment. We will take you back to camp to be executed in front of the others."

He smiled at Mya. "You are also safe. I promised Bukong that I would give you to him." He pointed his baton at Nick and Hilltop. "That leaves you two. Bring them out into the open."

The trackers dragged Nick away from the others. Hilltop got to his feet before the trackers returned and joined Nick on his own accord.

"We know nothing of Kya Lei," Hilltop said.

"That's a shame," Captain Moto said. "Because if someone doesn't tell me where he is, you are going to lose your head, monk, and so is the boy."

The trackers pushed Nick and Hilltop to their knees, about ten feet apart. The captain strode over to the jeep and pulled out a samurai scabbard covered in tiger skin. He brought it over to them and unsheathed the shiny blade.

"I'll spare this old monk if one of you tells me about Kya Lei." He brought the sword high above his head.

Hilltop's expression hadn't changed. He looked as if he didn't have a care in the world.

"We don't know about Kya Lei!" Nick shouted. He tried to get up, but one of the trackers hit him in the back with the butt of his rifle.

A terrible crashing sound arose from the trees. Nick turned his head just in time to see the charging Hannibal, ears flared, trunk curled, with fury in his bulging eyes.

"Run!" Bukong yelled, and ran to the jeep with Captain Moto right on his heels.

This was exactly the wrong thing to do. Hannibal was not angry that his mahout was about to lose his head. It was the scent of the tiger-skin seats that had enraged him.

Bukong and Moto realized their mistake too late. Before they could scramble out of the jeep, Hannibal hit it like a locomotive engine. The jeep flipped over, landing right on top of Captain Moto. Bukong, who was thrown free, tried to crawl away, but Hannibal was on him instantly, running a tusk into his back. Gunshots erupted, and Hannibal trumpeted in pain and fury.

It took Nick a second to realize that the trackers had stood their ground and were shooting at the bull. He lashed out with his feet and managed to trip one of them. The tracker rolled away and came back up on his knees, pointing the rifle at Nick's chest.

Mya screamed.

"No!" his father shouted.

But the tracker never got a chance to pull the trigger. He fell forward onto his face. Then the other tracker went down, too, blood spilling onto the ground from a bullet wound through his head.

What's happening? Nick thought. Who shot them? He started to get up.

"Don't!" Hilltop said, pulling him back down. "Hannibal is in a rage. He'll kill anything that moves."

Nick looked over at the bull in time to see him tear a wheel off the upturned jeep and toss it away. Blood trickled from a bullet hole in his back leg, but Hannibal didn't seemed bothered by it. He got down on his knees, slipped his tusks beneath the jeep, flipped it over, and triumphantly tore the tiger skin off the backseat.

They watched as he ran off into the forest, waving the tiger skin over his head.

Nick helped Hilltop to his feet, still confused about what had just happened. "Who shot—"

Kya Lei and two men with rifles came out from behind the trees.

"Hello, Nick," one of the men said.

It was Nick's stepfather, Bernard Culpepper.

Bernard 31

Bernard had dropped in by parachute near Hawk's Nest five days before. His mission was to organize a group of Kachin guerrillas and to destroy the airfield if possible.

"And to bring Nick out if he was still at Hawk's Nest," he added. "Although I didn't share this part with my superiors."

They all laughed.

"But someone got to the airfield before I arrived," he told them. "My Kachin guide said you had escaped weeks before and were presumed dead." He looked at Nick. "I wasn't looking forward to going back and telling your mom that.

"I was on my way to the coast when a runner caught up to me and said you were still here. It took a while to make my way back and hook up with Kya Lei. I just got in late last night. We found your tracks this morning and started following you. Where were you heading?"

"Thailand," Nick answered.

Bernard shook his head. "Wrong direction. I have

a sub waiting for me just south of Moulmein. It will take us right into the Bay of Bengal. You'll see your mom in a few days." He looked at the others. "I'll take all of you. The army has set up a new outfit called the OSS—Office of Strategic Services. Kya Lei and some others are coming with me to India to be trained." He looked at Nick's father. "We're definitely going to need some old Burma hands like you, Jackson."

"I'm in," his father replied, although at the moment he didn't look in good enough shape to help anyone.

Hilltop shook his head. "You can't, Jackson."

Nick's father looked at him, confused. "Why not?"

"Jackson Freestone is dead," Hilltop explained. "If you are caught in Burma, or even rumored to be alive, they'll dig up your grave and find you aren't there. Sonji will be blamed. They'll execute him. Your fight is over."

Jackson stared at Hilltop for a moment, then nodded. "Of course," he said.

"I don't know what you two are talking about," Bernard said. "But we need to get moving. The sub's not going to wait forever, and it's a two-day hike to the coast."

He stood up, and everyone started gathering their gear. Except for Hilltop. He went over to one of the trees and sat down, with the trunk behind his back.

"You're not coming?" Nick asked.

Hilltop shook his head. "I've been to India."

Everyone stopped what they were doing to listen.

"I know," Nick said. "The mahouts found you on a hill. You were born there."

"But Burma is where I will die," Hilltop said. "And there's Hannibal. He's wounded, confused . . . What kind of mahout would I be if I left him in such a state?"

He got back to his feet.

"I have lived my life," he said, bowing. "Now you go off and live yours."

Alice Springs 32

August 15, 1945

Nick sat on the front steps of their station house carving a kangaroo out of eucalyptus wood with the Sergeant Major's pocketknife. His carvings had improved over the past three years.

Beyond the steps lay a vast red-and-brown desert that at first glance looked barren and dead, but as Nick had learned, the arid land was actually teeming with life, if you knew where to look.

A cool breeze came in off the MacDonnell mountain range, scattering the wood shavings around his boots. Nick took a deep breath, savoring the pungent scent of eucalyptus from the grove near the house and the incense burning in the natshin. His father had built the natshin just after they'd bought the cattle station from Mr. Shute. In fact, it was the first improvement they'd made to the property—before they even fixed a fence or an outbuilding. They nailed the shrine to a post outside their gate for everyone to see.

The locals had scoffed at the idea of nats and

"dollhouses" to confine them, but the aborigine ranch hands had great respect for the nats and stopped by daily to make offerings of their own.

The locals had also scoffed at his father when he bought the station. "What does a Burmese tree farmer know about raising beef in the desert? He's as much of a jackaroo as I am a lumberjack." The truth was that Nick's father knew nothing about running a cattle station in the outback—none of them did—but they had learned, and the cattle station was quickly becoming one of the most successful in the region.

There were days when Nick was out fixing fences, rounding up cattle, or exploring, that he forgot all about war. But every time he returned home and saw the natshin, it all came back.

1945 had brought good news and bad.

On May 1, Adolph Hitler was found dead in his bunker in Berlin.

On May 2, the British and American armies, with the help of the Burmese, liberated Rangoon.

On May 7, Germany surrendered.

The war in Europe was over but not in the Pacific. The Japanese fought on. A week after Rangoon fell, the airfield at the plantation was bombed by Allied forces. Nick's mother sent them a letter with the news. "The airfield was utterly destroyed without a single loss of a villager, thanks to Indaw and Magwe. Unfortunately, Hawk's Nest—the house and everything in it—was destroyed in the attack as well . . ."

His father took the news calmly, as if he knew all along that it was only a matter of time before Hawk's Nest was hit. Nick asked if he would rebuild after the war.

"I don't think so," his father answered. "It's time we give Burma back to the Burmese."

Nick finished the carving and looked at it critically, not quite satisfied with the outcome. He stood, stretched, and put the Sergeant Major's knife back in his pocket. That was when he saw the red dust rising in the distance.

His father had left the night before to go to town and pick up Nick's birthday present. Nick had a good idea of what the present was. His mother would not miss his eighteenth birthday for anything in the world. It had been nearly a year since she'd visited the station. She was still attached to the embassy in Calcutta, in order to be near Bernard, who was still fighting in Burma. Nick was looking forward to seeing her.

He thought about going inside and changing his clothes, but decided not to. He figured he looked presentable enough for his eighteenth birthday.

It was another ten minutes before the car pulled up in front of the house. There were three birthday presents inside.

His mother was the first to get out. Nick met her

halfway to the gate, gave her a hug, picked her up off her feet, and swung her around."My God, Nick," she said. "You look like a cowboy."

"We're called jackaroos around these parts, ma'am," he said.

His mother laughed. Nick put her down and looked back at the car. Bernard was standing next to his father, along with a smaller man Nick didn't recognize at first.

Nick hadn't seen Bernard in more than three years. He looked good, considering everything he'd been through. Nick hurried over to him and gave him a hug.

"I didn't expect you to be here."

"Thought I would check out your spread before we head back to the States."

"You're going back to the States?"

Bernard nodded.

Nick looked at the third man, and his jaw dropped in shock. The man was dressed in western clothes—slacks, suit coat, shirt—all a little rumpled from travel. Nick had never seen him in anything but a longyi, but there was no mistaking the face and the grin. It was Indaw!

"This is turning into quite a birthday," Nick said, embracing him. "I guess I don't understand how you and Bernard could—"

"Haven't you been listening to the radio?" his father said.

Nick shook his head.

"Then you haven't heard," his mother said.

"Heard what?"

"The war is over," she said.

"With Japan?" Nick could not believe the Japanese had surrendered. It wasn't in their nature. It wasn't the way of the samurai.

"The United States dropped a new type of bomb," his father said.

"Actually, two of them," Bernard added, shaking his head sadly. "One on Hiroshima, and one on Nagasaki. A lot of people died, but at least the war is over."

Indaw was glancing left and right at the house and the yard, clearly not interested in talking about bombs. "Where is she?" he asked.

"Of course," Nick said, still in shock. "She's out back. I'll show you."

They all followed him around the side of the house, hands on each other's shoulders, grins on their faces.

Mya was in the paddocks training a horse, her long black hair pulled back into a ponytail, a bush hat on her head. She had broken and trained every horse at the station, but preferred to ride her camel, Miss Pretty, who was tied to the fence, bellowing for Mya to give her a treat. She and Nick had caught the wild camel a year earlier on one of their many trips into the outback.

They watched Mya work the horse for a few minutes, her concentration so acute she hadn't realized they were there. She finally finished the session, unsnapped the lunge line, then turned to give Miss Pretty a treat.

"Hello, little sister," Indaw said.

Mya nearly fainted.

Indaw and Bernard sat on the porch and told war stories late into the night. One by one, the adults went inside to sleep. First Nick's mother, then Bernard, then his father.

"It gets cold here at night," Indaw said, turning the collar up on his suit coat. "I don't think I've ever seen so many stars or anyplace with so few trees."

"You get used to it," Mya said. She was sitting between Indaw and Nick on the front steps. "So, no word from Hilltop at all?"

Indaw shook his head. "The last time I saw him was the day Hannibal killed Captain Moto and Bukong. I've heard wild rumors, though. Some say that on moonlit nights, an ancient mahout riding a giant koongyi can be seen along the shore of Freestone Island."

"I wouldn't be surprised if it were true," Nick said.

"And what about Miss Pretty?" Mya asked. "You haven't said a word about her."

"She's fine," Indaw assured her. "After the POW

camp was liberated, Tin took her back to the plantation. She had a calf last year—a little bull, and he looks a lot like Hannibal—which reminds me!" Indaw clapped Nick on the shoulder and stood up. "I brought something for you from a friend."

"What friend?" Nick asked.

"You'll see." Indaw disappeared into the house.

Nick and Mya looked out at the desert.

"I am so happy, Nick," Mya said, taking his hand. "The war is finally over."

"It's hard to believe. I wonder what we'll do now?"

Mya gently turned his face toward hers. "Whatever we do," she whispered, "we will do it together."

Nick kissed her.

"I'm not interrupting anything, am I?" Indaw asked from behind them.

They broke apart, but continued holding hands.

"Not anything that is any of your business," Mya said.

Indaw laughed and handed Nick something tied up in a longyi.

"What is it?"

"Unwrap it and find out."

Nick slowly untied it.

Inside was Hannibal's iron bell. The last time Nick had seen the bell was outside the elephant village on the day he was captured. Sergeant Sonji had put it into his rucksack and told him that he would give it to him later. The sergeant could not have kept it all these years.

"Where did you get this?" Nick asked.

"From Sergeant Sonji," Indaw answered, "who is a prisoner of war himself now. When we liberated the camp, Sonji was the only Japanese the POWs stood up for."

"We?" Nick asked. "You were there?"

Indaw nodded. "So was Bernard. The guards did not put up much of a fight."

"How is he?"

"He is in better shape than the men they made him guard. But the soldiers said that he had saved countless lives. When I told him you were in Australia, he asked if I could get this to you."

"What are you going to do with it?" Mya asked.

Nick looked out into the darkness.

"It has to go someplace special," he said after a while. "A place where we'll remember Sonji, Hilltop, and Hannibal every time we see it." He stood up and walked toward the gate, with Mya and Indaw following.

Underneath the natshin was a nail, which Nick had snagged his sleeve on a dozen times. He had been meaning to get a claw hammer and yank it out ever since they'd put the natshin on the post. This is where he hung it.

Metal on metal, faint, but growing louder as the desert wind caught Hannibal's iron bell.

Acknowledgments

This novel was many years in the making. Along the way I had a lot of help and I have many people to thank. Among them are: Michael J. Schmidt, veterinarian, and great friend, who accompanied me to Myanmar (formerly Burma). Without his help I would never have gotten into the forest with the elephants. Donna Brooks who called me out of the blue and asked if I wanted to write a novel about elephants. The result of that conversation is the novel you just read. I owe a huge thanks to Alessandra Balzer at Hyperion Books for Children for seeing the merits of this novel and giving it life. My agent, Barbara Kouts, who has been with me for over a decade, encouraging and representing me with unwavering faith and grace. Jennifer Besser, my editor at Hyperion, who made many thoughtful changes to the manuscript. My steadfast friends and readers, Pam Muñoz Ryan, Bob Jonas, Susan Stronach, Jerry Pallotta: your comments and corrections were fabulous! I can't thank you enough for poring over this manuscript. A very special thanks goes to the astounding Judy Gitenstein for her brilliant comments and suggestions. And finally, my wife, Marie, who has read and commented on this novel so many times over the years she should rightfully be the co-author.

Roland Smith is the author of *Jack's Run*; *Zach's Lie*, an ALA Quick Pick for Reluctant Readers; *Cryptid Hunters*; *Thunder Cave*; *Jaguar*; *The Last Lobo*; and *Sasquatch*. He lives outside Portland, Oregon, with his wife, Marie, who also writes children's books.

Literature Circle Questions

Use these questions and the activities that follow to get more out of the experience of reading *Elephant Run* by Roland Smith.

1. Why did Jackson Freestone miss his son's birth?

2. Who is Taung Baw (aka Hilltop), and why is he such a legendary figure?

3. Why does Nang encourage his son, Indaw, to become a mahout but forbid his daughter, Mya, to do the same?

4. Describe the conflict between Nang and Magwe when the story begins. What do we learn about the political situation in Burma from their conversation?

5. After Nick is knocked down by Hannibal, he refuses to let anyone know that he is injured. What does this decision reveal about him?

6. In chapters 11 and 12, Nick finds that Hawk's Nest has been transformed after the Japanese invasion. What changes indicate that the Japanese Army has taken over Hawk's Nest?

7. Nick's mother has warned him that the Freestone men often get in trouble because of their bad tempers, and she advises him to learn to control his anger. Find an example from the story of a time when Nick follows his mother's advice and controls his temper, and also find an example of a time when Nick fails to control his anger. What is the result of each?

8. Indaw gives Mya a *choon* that he has made. What does this gift represent?

9. What kind of a leader is Colonel Nagayoshi? What methods does he use to retain his control? Why do you think his plans for Nick change after learning that his own family is in an internment camp in the United States?

10. Nick's mother writes in a letter to him: "You have inherited your father's will and spirit. I saw it in your eyes the day you were born." In what ways is Nick similar to his father?

11. When Nick first arrives in Burma, he is a slightly overweight, fearful boy used to life in a big city. How does Nick change as a result of his adventures in wartime Burma?

12. At the end of the novel, Nick learns that Sonji's life has been spared and that Sonji has sent him Hannibal's iron bell. Imagine that Nick could communicate with Sonji one last time. What do you think Nick would like to say to him?

13. In the final chapter of the story, Nick and his father have settled in Alice Springs, Australia, to run a cattle farm. Why do you think Nick chose to stay with his father and live in Australia? Does their new life have any similarities to their old life in Burma?

14. Were you surprised by Hilltop's decision to remain in Burma rather than escape to India? Why did he make this choice? Use evidence from the story to explain your response.

15. After experiencing World War II on two fronts — in London and in Burma — what do you think Nick Freestone has learned about war, its victims, and its violence?

Note: These questions are keyed to Bloom's Taxonomy *as follows: Knowledge: 1–3; Comprehension: 4–5; Application: 6–7; Analysis: 8–10; Synthesis: 11–13; Evaluation: 14–15.*

Activities

1. In chapter 6, Nick visits the elephant-training camp and learns how the timber elephants are taught to do their work. Create a storyboard illustrating the major events in the training of a timber elephant, using the information that Nick learns in this chapter.

2. Sergeant Sonji is a master poet, and through him Nick learns about the Japanese form of poetry called haiku — a short, unrhymed poem often about nature. Experiment with writing your own haiku, following this format:
   First line: 5 syllables
   Second line: 7 syllables
   Third line: 5 syllables

3. Hawk's Nest, the plantation home built by Nick's great-grandfather, is full of surprises. Draw a diagram of Hawk's Nest, based on the descriptions of it in chapters 3 and 16, including the secret passages.